WIZARD'S HAT

A PROPHECY FORETOLD NOVEL

Self-Published by
Sarah M. Wasson

Copyright © 2024 Sarah M. Wasson
ISBN: 979-8-9907928-6-9

DEDICATION

This book is dedicated to Paul, my loving husband, critique partner, and scene enhancer, and to my father, without him consistently placing fantasy books in my hands, my love for fantasy and sci-fi would never have grown.

EPIGRAPH

Forgotten Kingdoms lost to tyranny, the realm of beasts, and the realm of magic fade away.

The birth of twins in the darkness of night, upon uniting, the fates of the Royal Lines shall intertwine.

In winter's tight embrace, an eclipse will paint the sky red before their sixteenth year. The two sets of twins will be bathed in red light, their lives entwined by fate's design, their futures revealed in this divine.

Infinity embraced; royal birth rights restored.

Gods & Goddesses
in Ombrasia

Grielan - the God of the Afterlife
Oshan - the Goddess of Life
Ahara - the Goddess of Healing
Iton - the God of Wisdom

Spirit Helpers of the Gods

Isoa - the Herald of Death
Mortal form is a hyena
with unblinking black eyes that walks upright like a man.
Chihara - the Essence of Life
Mortal form is a pure white stag
with silver antlers and emerald eyes.
Rei - the Blessing of Wellness
The mortal form is a silver fox
with an enormously bushy, blue-tipped tail and blue eyes.
Minori - The Seeker of Truth
Mortal form is a phoenix with gold eyes.

OSHANA
The Wyvers Fortress
Sanctuary of Iton
Ombrasia's Gate
Griffin's Keep
The Wizard's Hat
Brisbin Ocean
Wyvern Empire
Firebone Mountains
Monastery of Iton
Black Mountains
The Crags
The Waste
Thrinity
Brightbane Forest
Kingdom of Evansshire
Lire Shack
Creekside
Verdale
Firemist River
Esther's Cottage
Firemist Rock
Esset Creek
Lower City
Kingston

PART 1

KINGDOM OF EVANSSHIRE

PERCIVAL Theodoric sat at his desk in his study, skimming through various scrolls. A mysterious sickness had spread through the kingdom, afflicting only a few. A small smile turned the corner of his lips. He flinched slightly when a knock on his door broke his concentration. Without looking up, he grumbled, "Don't just stand there. Come in."

His clerk peeked his head through the door. "The next batch is ready to release, sire," the clerk said in his high-pitched, squeaky voice.

A shudder rippled through the king; the clerk's voice was like nails on a chalkboard. "It's about time." Swiftly getting to his feet, he marched out of his study and followed his clerk through the throne room and up a narrow, winding staircase to one of the castle's many towers. The king's shoulders almost brushed the sides of the stone walls, and his boots thudded on the thick wooden planks that seemed to jut out from the stone. The clerk sneezed behind Percival and muttered his apologies for the dust. The stairway was dim and stifling. Percival glanced out the dirty stained-glass windows spaced every five steps.

At the top of the tower, sitting in the middle of a large circular room, he found his alchemist. The strange, bald little man, with far too much facial hair and tiny spectacles, was seated at his cluttered worktable, muttering to himself. Percival looked around the room, taking in the multitude of dusty bookshelves crammed with books, scrolls, and jars filled with innumerable items floating in cloudy liquid. Removing his gaze from the various objects, he bore it into the alchemist's back and cleared his throat.

"Ah, sire, I was just on my way down to see you. The third batch is ready for release." The alchemist spun around, nearly knocking his glasses off his face.

"Excellent," Percival rubbed his hands together. "Are you sure this batch will be even stronger?"

"Oh yes, sire. I made sure this set of birds will be even more potent. My two assistants have been most helpful," the alchemist snickered.

"And pray tell, how did you get more cooperation out of the pair?"

"I promised them leniency, sire."

The King glared down at the little man. "You have no authority to grant them leniency," he boomed.

The alchemist quickly raised his hands and bowed. "I know, sire, I know—but they don't," he added, laughing hysterically.

A small smile cracked the King's lips. "Where are your two assistants right now?"

"Oh, they're back in their cage. I can only tolerate the sight of them for so long—such disgusting creatures."

"Yes, quite. But I suppose I should stop by and show them my appreciation. And what of our other little project?"

"I have been working on a few ideas, but I need more test subjects to be sure."

"Tell everybody to keep proceeding as planned. The Twin's Prophecy will end in my reign."

"Yes, sire, of course, sire. My midwives assure me they have witnessed every birth, even those born during the day. None will escape their watch."

A knock at the door startled the alchemist. He clutched his chest, breathing rapidly, then rushed to open it. A young girl of about twelve, dressed in little more than rags, stood in the doorway with her head bowed and her hands trembling.

"What is it, girl? Can't you see I'm with the King?"

"I'm sorry, sir," she whispered, "but two more were brought in."

"Where from this time?"

"Creekside, sir."

The alchemist looked at the King and said, "Twins were brought in, Your Majesty. If you excuse me, I need to go see them."

"I think I will join you."

The alchemist's face blanched. "Of course, Your Majesty," he hesitated briefly, "it is a rather tedious procedure and one not all that pleasant to watch."

"I will join you," Percival said sternly.

"Of course, of course, this way, sire." The alchemist bowed deeply and then scurried down the hallway. The young maid was already gone and out of sight.

Further and further they walked through the castle, descending to its lowest depths and into the dungeons. The deeper they went, the more nervous the alchemist seemed to grow. The king chuckled internally. *I love making people squirm,* he thought. As they moved through the dungeon, the king held his breath, trying to avoid gagging from the stench. For a moment, he considered improving the air quality but quickly dismissed the thought. *If you've earned a place down here, you don't deserve any dignity.* At last, they reached the very bottom, where the smell was slightly more tolerable than the three levels above.

"Right this way, sire. Welcome to my workshop," the alchemist said with a flourish of his hands.

The king surveyed the room, one he'd never seen before. Numerous cells lined one side, while cages occupied the other. In the center of the vast chamber were about a dozen tables, with nearly as many servants busily working at various tasks. The king raised an eyebrow; he hadn't known his alchemist had such an elaborate facility. He made a mental note to ask his clerk about the alchemist's arrangements. *But then again,* he thought, *as long as the results are worthy, he can keep his little solitude down here.*

Two of his royal knights stood in the center of the room, accompanied by a young woman with a smug expression. She bowed deeply to the alchemist as he rushed forward, shook her hand, and eagerly examined what she had brought. "Heather, my dear, so glad to see you're back. What do you have for me today?"

"Twin boys from Creekside, Goosted," she replied.

"Did anyone suspect there were twins?" Goosted asked, still peering at the sleeping newborns.

"I think so. The head midwife for Creekside, Alma, called in the town's healer for assistance," Heather replied.

"And why did that raise suspicion?" Goosted asked, narrowing his eyes at the babies.

"The labor was progressing normally; there was nothing unusual to warrant a healer's involvement. But the moment the healer arrived; Alma whispered something to her. Thankfully, I was already suspicious. Alma hadn't called the knights to witness the birth. When she sent the baker to fetch the healer, I made an excuse and sent word to the knights. They were there when Healer Maya arrived."

"I bet she was surprised to see a witness for the birth," Goosted, the alchemist, chuckled.

"Oh, most definitely, sir. Everyone was confused by their presence."

"And why would they be confused by the presence of my knights? That was my decree, was it not?" the King interrupted.

Heather's face paled as she finally noticed the king. She immediately dropped into a deep curtsy, keeping her head low. "My apologies, Your Majesty, I didn't see you enter the room."

He waved his hand dismissively at her. "And why was my decree not being followed?"

"Alma claimed she had just received the missive and that the babies were coming early. She said there wasn't enough time to notify the knights. She even pretended not to know they were stationed just outside the village." Heather's legs began to tremble from holding the curtsy, and a small moan of discomfort escaped her lips.

"Stand and continue with your story," King Percival said impatiently.

Gripping the table beside her for support, Heather rose and nodded. "Thank you, my King. After the babies were born, everything proceeded as decreed. I confiscated the children, and the mother was eliminated."

"And how did the father handle all of this?" the king asked.

"As expected. He wept and cried but made no attempt to stop us," Heather said, pausing as she glanced up at the king's face. "What shall become of Alma and Maya?"

Goosted raised an eyebrow and looked toward the king. King Percival scratched his chin briefly before answering, "I want them under constant watch. Heather, you will not be returning to Creekside; send someone else." He then turned his full attention to the alchemist. "Send a bird to Creekside. Let's see if anyone falls ill."

"Excellent, Your Majesty. It shall be done immediately." Goosted opened a small notebook and thumbed through the pages. "Ah,

Your Majesty," he said, tapping his notebook with a slightly crooked finger. "Maya and her son Keelan are already on the watch list from the Summer Festival."

"Are they the ones who visited Healer Bertlesen when the gates... malfunctioned?"

The alchemist bobbed his head, "Yes, sire. I will have the watch amplified on them at once." The king gave a curt nod. "Now, tell me, what procedure are you using to determine if these are the twins from the prophecy?"

Goosted hastily shoved his notebook into his pocket and began bouncing on the balls of his feet, clearly excited. "As you know, I've dedicated my life to researching the prophecy and learning everything possible about twins. What you may not know is... my mother was a twin."

Percival's eyes blazed. This was something he did not know.

The alchemist quickly raised his hands in surrender, his shoulders rounding. "Fear not, my lord. In the time of your grandfather, it was common practice to separate twins at birth and either eliminate one or relocate it to the other side of the kingdom. My mother's twin was killed at birth. Your father implemented the policy of automatically executing both. But what your father didn't know is that twins can sometimes skip a generation. That's why I advised you to eliminate the mother who gave birth to these twins. However, I still recommend eliminating any other children she bore, as they may one day give birth to twins themselves. My mother was lucky—she only had me. And rest assured, it has been made certain that I will never father children."

The King regarded Goosted thoughtfully for a moment, his gaze scrutinizing the alchemist. "Proceed," he said, exasperated, clasping his hands behind his back and beginning to pace.

"In my years of research, I've discovered that the prophecy requires not one set of twins but two for it to unfold." Goosted rubbed his hands together nervously.

"What are you talking about?" Percival stopped mid-stride and spun to face Goosted.

With a cautious tone, Goosted whispered, "The prophecy, Your Majesty, mentions that the Royal Lines must unite and entwine." His voice cracked, and beads of sweat formed on his brow.

"I am fully aware of what the prophecy states," the King growled.

"Yes, sire." Goosted bowed his head, his gaze falling to the floor. "I understand that, but like most prophecies, the true meaning has been obscured by its words. Twins from both bloodlines are needed—and those bloodlines must intertwine. How that will happen, I cannot yet say, but I am certain both lineages must produce a twin, and those twins must meet." Goosted paused, watching the King intently. When Percival gave no indication of stopping him, he continued.

"In my research on twins, I've discovered that not all of them share a magical bond. For such a bond to exist, magic must run in the bloodline. Your grandfather understood that, with magic outlawed, it became harder to find those who carried it. People learned to suppress their magic, to hide it deep within. Allowing twins to stay together increased the likelihood that their bond would ignite, but even then, they could keep their abilities concealed, biding their time to fulfill the prophecy.

"As with all magical beings, their magic doesn't manifest at birth; it develops as they mature, often requiring a stressful event for it to surface. I've devised a series of tests to force their magic to reveal itself prematurely. Once we confirm the twins possess magic, we can eliminate them and prevent the prophecy from ever being fulfilled. By eliminating the mother and any other siblings, we also eradicate the bloodline."

"But what if the mother had siblings?" the king asked, raising an eyebrow.

"An excellent point, Your Majesty. Honestly, I hadn't considered the possibility of her siblings continuing the bloodline," Goosted admitted, looking down with a sheepish expression.

The king narrowed his eyes, silently studying the alchemist. *He's trying to manipulate me,* Percival thought. *He's too shrewd to have simply overlooked that. I'll need to keep a closer watch on him.* With a sigh, the king said, "I'll issue a new decree. Now, tell me about these tests."

"I've devised a series of experiments with the gracious assistance of the fairies given to me as helpers," Goosted paused to chuckle. "The magic flowing through their veins allows them to perform all manner of unnatural feats, but it also acts as a shield, protecting them from harm. When brought to the brink of death, their magic flares up in an attempt to save them. While this protection doesn't always succeed—fairies die quite frequently—on occasion, it saves them. And every time, their magic becomes visible, even if briefly. My tests are designed to push the twins to that brink, and if they are magical or of the prophesied bloodline, their magic will flare to save them."

"And how can you be certain your tests will work?" the king asked. "You've experimented on fairies, yes? What were the results?"

"I have had numerous adolescent fairies at my disposal, and I have developed a couple of experiments that will make their magic surface without fail."

"And if they are not magical?"

"Well then…" Goosted spread his hands, "Two less mouths to feed, sire, either way."

"Is there a possibility the twins could be magical and not be the prophesized ones?"

"Oh yes, of course, Your Majesty."

He sighed deeply, "Then… if they died and were magical, we will never know if they were the prophesized ones. Your testing will never end."

"That is true, but the alternative takes far too long."

"And what is the alternative?" The king said, growing impatient.

"Letting them grow up and develop their magic naturally, sire."

"And how will that show us they are the prophesied twins?"

"I found an obscure reference in the restricted section of your library. It mentions a deleted section of the prophecy."

Percival's eyes widened, "Truly? What is this deleted section?"

"In winter's tight embrace, an eclipse will paint the sky red before their sixteenth year. The two sets of twins will be bathed in red light, their lives entwined by fate's design, their futures revealed in this divine."

"And what does that mean?"

"I can only guess, during the winter before the twin's 16th name-day, there will be a solar eclipse, and the sky will turn red. At that point, the twins will know their destiny."

The King scowled at the two sleeping infants in the basket on the table, "So, we have to wait sixteen years to find out if these are the prophesized children or not?"

"Unfortunately, yes, sire. If that's to be believed."

"Where did you say you found this deleted prophecy?"

Goosted went to one of the shelves, grabbed a book, and handed it to the king. "This book was supposedly written by Eldjren, the same man who wrote the prophecy."

"Have you found any other mention anywhere else about this deleted prophecy?"

"No, sire. According to this book's author, he kept it out of the original prophecy, hoping to ensure the prophesized twins would only reveal themselves when they were ready. He feared for their lives, Your Majesty."

"Rightly so. Have you told anyone else about this prophecy?"

"No, sire, only those attending this meeting are privy to that knowledge."

The King glanced at the two knights and the midwife. "You will not harm these infants; we must know if they are the foretold ones. Until then, we proceed as planned—every set of twins shall be brought to the castle. We'll find caretakers to raise them. If they prove non-magical, they'll be released into society. If they are magical, and the sky does not turn red on their sixteenth name-day, they will either serve the kingdom under my watchful eye or face death for being an outlawed magical being."

He paused, his gaze hardening. "My last decree—to kill those who give birth to twins—is hereby rescinded. However, the mother, her children, and any siblings will remain under watch. This prophecy must end, but I need to see it through to its conclusion. Killing every twin that's born without understanding the prophecy will haunt me—and my son—forever. We need someone to oversee this orphanage," the King said, turning his eyes toward the midwife.

She bowed and curtsied, "It would be my honor, Your Majesty."

"Good, make it so," the King turned on his heels and marched out of the alchemist's workshop with a smug smile. Soon, the prophecy would end, he thought to himself. "Oh, and Goosted, my dear alchemist," he called over his shoulder, "let us not forget your precious little bluebirds. Magic must be eliminated."

CHAPTER
-2-

WYVERN EMPIRE

AN elderly woman hurried down the hallway, her head bowed, shoulders hunched, and eyes fixed on the floor. It was best not to draw attention, especially for someone who looked human in a fortress teeming with wyverns. Theresa paused at a corner, cautiously peeking around to ensure she wouldn't cross paths with anyone. Her destination was just a short distance down the next corridor. As handmaid to the Queen Mother, she enjoyed slightly more freedom than most—and certainly more than the Queen Mother herself.

The Queen Mother's chamber was set off by itself, far from any residing wyvern and the rest of her family. She reached the Queen's door but paused, her hand hovering above the doorknob. Footsteps echoed down the hall toward her; she looked up briefly to identify who was coming. She turned to face the pair, falling swiftly to her knees and pressing her forehead to the floor.

"Rise, Theresa," Zarret said.

"Thank you, sir. Greetings, Princess Drakaina," she said as sweetly as she could.

"You know this human's name?" Ashrozo asked her brother.

"Of course, she is mother's handmaid. I have spoken with her numerous times."

"You… speak… to… humans?" she said each word slowly, pausing in between each.

"She's not human. Really, Ash, you need to curb your hatred a bit. Like all our servants, Theresa is a dragon trapped in human form. Do you see that bracelet?" He pointed to Theresa's wrist. "That bracelet is what keeps her in that form."

Ashrozo frowned at the prostrated woman, then shifted her gaze to the bracelet on Theresa's wrist. It bore a striking resemblance to one her father had given her when she was very young, with strict instructions never to remove it. Shaking off the unsettling feeling as mere coincidence, she impatiently waited for Theresa to stand and hold the door open. Ashrozo briefly glanced at the massive door; like all the fortress doors, it was two-fold—a gigantic one for the wyverns, with a smaller, human-sized door nestled within.

"In what form did Father leave her?" Zarret asked.

"She is in human form, Your Highness, Prince Drake Zarret," Theresa said formally, her eyes widening as she took in Zarret's human appearance for the first time.

Ashrozo marched in without acknowledging the servant.

As Theresa stated, their mother was in human form, sitting in front of a roaring fire with a book in her hand, her blonde hair draped over one shoulder, unbraided. She glanced up when the door opened, her silvery blue eyes sparkling in the candlelight; a smile bloomed as soon as she saw Ashrozo. *Why is she always so happy to see me?* She scowled. *It's not like I give her any reason to like me.*

Zarret entered right behind her, crossing the room swiftly to stand before their mother. Her eyes widened in astonishment. "Zarret?" He nodded his head. "How is this possible? How long have you been able to do this?" she asked in a hurry. She placed her hands on his cheeks, moving his head from side to side.

Zarret took her hands in his. "I have been able to change for about a month now," he replied.

"And you're now just showing it to me?"

He nodded his head and looked down. "Father's decree."

She nodded, letting the subject drop. "Please sit, sit." She pointed to the chair beside her. "Ash, would you care to join us?"

Zarret looked back at his sister and motioned for her to come forward.

Sighing, she decided she might as well get this over with. She walked over, taking the chair furthest from the one her mother was sitting on. She sat with her back straight at the edge of the chair, her hands lightly folded in her lap.

The Queen Mother looked at her handmaid. "Theresa, can you please give us some privacy?"

"Yes, of course, ma'am." Theresa exited the room.

"Thank you, my son, for keeping your promise to visit me again," the Queen Mother said, her voice warm.

How can he genuinely look happy to see her? Ashrozo thought to herself.

"And an absolutely wonderful surprise to see you, my dear daughter. How have you been?"

"We didn't come here for pleasantries," Ashrozo snapped.

"Mother," Zarret interjected, his tone becoming serious. "Father has given me a critical mission, and I need your help. My mission is to…"

"Oh, don't bore Mother with the details," Ashrozo interrupted, her voice dripping with feigned warmth. "I'm sure Father will tell her everything in due time. We're pressed for time, after all." She forced a sweet smile at Zarret, though her thoughts simmered—*the less she knows, the better.*

The Queen Mother glanced between them. "What can I help you with then?"

"As you can see," Ashrozo continued smoothly, "Zar has finally found his human form, Arlayna. Father wants him to learn how to be human—and quickly, before spring."

"That is... an unusual request," the Queen Mother replied, her brow furrowed. "Why does he need you to learn how to act like a human? You are a wyvern-dragon cross, after all."

Before Zarret could respond, Ashrozo cut in again. "In order for him to become a proper ruler, he must master every form he can take. Since he can now shift into human form, like you and me"—she shot a glance at her brother, her frown deepening—"Father wants him to be comfortable and, shall we say, *proficient* in acting human."

Arlayna's expression flickered—her smile was back, though it had been replaced with a brief flash of displeasure so fast that Ashrozo almost missed it.

"Of course, my child, I will help you. I see merit in that request."

"Excellent," she said, "you can teach us both."

"It fills my heart with joy that you've asked for my help. I'll truly enjoy spending more time with you—my Ash and my Zar," Arlayna said, her smile softening.

"I would prefer if you called me by my full name, Arlayna."

Arlayna sighed, "Of course, Asher..ah," she held a hand up to her mouth and coughed, "Ashrozo, whatever makes you happy."

Ashrozo clamped her mouth shut. *What would make me happy would be never to see you again,* she thought.

Arlayna awoke with a scream, her chest heaving as she gasped for air. Her hair clung to her damp face, and her nightgown was soaked with sweat. Shivering, she pulled the covers up to her chin, trying to calm her racing heart.

Suddenly, a gust of wind blasted through the window, slamming it open with a deafening crash. The force snuffed out the fire in the hearth, plunging the room into suffocating darkness.

Her pulse quickened, and she bolted upright, her eyes darting wildly around the room. Shadows seemed to shift in the corners. With trembling hands, she fumbled for the fire starter, her breath coming in shaky bursts. After what felt like an eternity, she managed to ignite the lamp beside her bed, casting a flickering, fragile light over the room.

"Are you all right, my lady?" a booming voice asked from the hallway.

"You may enter, Samuel," she called out.

"I heard a crash. Is everything okay?" Samuel asked.

"The wind blew the window open again, that's all."

Samuel nodded and hurried over to the window. "I wish we could get this repaired," he muttered under his breath.

Arlayna smiled as she watched Samuel struggle to close and bar the window shut. Once a knight in her father's royal guard, Samuel was now her personal protector and dear friend. Though his back was slightly hunched with age, he still moved with the grace and practiced skill of his younger years. Satisfied that the window latch would hold, he turned his attention to the hearth, building the fire back up. As the warmth began to spread through the room, Arlayna let out a shaky breath and laid back down.

Samuel stood and stretched his back. "I don't recommend getting old, my lady. Especially on nights like tonight."

She smiled and nodded. "No one plans on getting old, my friend," she replied.

After warming his hands by the fire, he turned toward her, a frown creasing his forehead. "Did you have it again?"

She nodded.

"When did these nightmares start up again?"

"Right after, Ash and Zar came to see me. I hadn't seen Ash in a couple of years—well, not alone like that. The dreams started again that night, just as vivid as the first time."

"You need to stop torturing yourself. Ash being taken from you wasn't your fault. It was mine." Samuel lowered his head, guilt weighing heavy in his voice.

Arlayna sat up and reached for Samuel's hand. "You are not to blame." He opened his mouth to speak, but she continued before he could. "And it wasn't my fault either. Neither of us could have stopped her kidnapping."

Samuel sat heavily in the chair next to her bed.

"I still remember that night like it was yesterday," Arlayna said.

They both fell silent, replaying that night from over forty years ago.

It had been a cold, stormy winter evening. Arlayna and her husband were sitting by the fire in their small cabin, both weary from the war briefing they had just attended. An untouched platter of food and two glasses of wine sat forgotten on the table beside them. The peaceful silence was shattered as the door was flung open.

"Spruce Encampment is under attack!" the resistance commander shouted. Her husband turned to her, his expression tense.

"Any other camps reporting attacks?" Arlayna asked.

"No, my lady, just Spruce."

An image of a map sprang into Arlayna's mind. Spruce Encampment—their furthest outpost. It would take several hours to reach it, even by flight.

"I'll handle this. You stay with the children," he said softly. "Until we meet again, my love goes with you." He kissed her gently on the cheek.

Once outside, he shifted into his dragon form, taking the resistance commander with him as they soared into battle.

Arlayna hugged herself, staring into the fire.

She couldn't remember how long she sat there, but then a muffled crash came from their shared bedroom, startling her. She stood and quickly crossed the room. "Drake, if you woke up the children, Ombrasia, help you; I'll be dining on Firedrake tomorrow."

She hesitated at the door, her hand hovering just above the knob. Pressing her ear against the coarse, knotty wood, she listened closely. A sigh escaped her lips; her children were still asleep. Just as she turned to return to the couch, a loud crash echoed from inside the room, followed by a tiny roar.

"Mama, Ash!!" a child screamed.

She rushed to the door and threw it open; the room was on fire. Drake was crumpled in a ball at the foot of her son's bed. Her son, in dragon form, was spraying a thin stream of fire everywhere. Her daughter was nowhere to be seen. Arlayna looked around the room frantically. There—the window was open; she ran to the window and peered into the night.

Their tiny home sat at the edge of a cliff. The bedroom window gazed at a vast ravine; the bottom shrouded in darkness.

"Noooo!!!" she screamed, a roar ripping from her throat. She heard a commotion behind her but kept her eyes glued on the wyvern flying from her home.

"My Lady, what's happened in here? Where's Ash?" Samuel said, laying a hand on her shoulder. "What are you looking at?"

With a shaky hand, she pointed to the wyvern. "She stole my Ashera. *She will regret that!*" she fumed, leaping onto the windowsill.

"My queen, what are you doing?" Samuel grabbed her arm.

"I'm going to get my daughter back."

Shaking his hand off, she looked at him. He took a step back at the ferocity he saw in her eyes. "What about your son? And the kingdom?"

Her gaze softened as she looked over at her son, back in human form, crying on the shoulder of his nanny, Theresa. Jumping off the windowsill, she rushed to him and swept him up.

"It's okay, my love, it's going to be okay."

"Where's Ash?" he asked, sniffling.

"She's just gone for a little while; I'm going to get her. Theresa will stay with you, and Dadda will be back soon." She kissed him on the forehead and wiped tears off his cheeks. She tried to smile but knew she failed by the look on her son's face. "Tell my husband I will return before sunset tomorrow," she said, choking back tears.

"Yes, ma'am."

The firedrake crawled to his feet and shook out his wings with a roar and spray of fire.

"Wait, I'm going with you," Samuel said.

"No, we need you here."

Samuel shook his head. "Obviously, I am not fit to guard the Encampment," he said, sweeping his arm to show the burnt room, "but I can protect my queen."

Tears glistened in her eyes as she nodded her head. Without looking back, she ran for the window and leaped through it, taking dragon form as soon as she started to fall—Samuel and Drake were right behind her. "Forgive me, my husband; I will see you soon," she whispered. "Forgive me, my son, my dearest Lancet. I will see you again."

Arlayna opened her eyes. Samuel was still sitting beside her.

"Terrible night that was," he said with a huff.

She sighed. "I found her, though, that I did."

"Yes, we found her, but a lot of good that has brought us. Couldn't free her, so you surrender yourself to him," he sneered.

"I had to; I had to be close to her."

"And she hates you now because of him," he spat.

"Someday, I will be able to tell her the truth. Tell her about her real father and her brother, her twin," she whispered.

Samuel hissed, "Do not say that out loud. You did not have twins; Lance is older. We have to keep the story going. It is the only thing keeping you alive."

"I know," she buried her face in her hands. "If he thinks he can have twins with me, Lancet and Ashera will be safe."

"Ashrozo," he corrected.

"I hate that name."

"We will escape; if Theresa can make it in, we can make it out."

Arlayna looked at Samuel. "She's been here a decade already."

"What? Are you not a dragon? Are you not over a hundred years old? A decade to us is a drop in a bucket. Pfff, we will get out of here; I know we will."

CHAPTER
-3-

THE CRAIGS

GENERAL Lucas smiled as his men advanced on the two rich boys. *They may have gotten lucky the last time I encountered them,* he thought, *but now I have the advantage of numbers.* Something caught his eye—a phoenix appeared out of nowhere, torching one of his men as it flew impossibly fast around the unfortunate soul. Then, a flash of blue light drew his attention. *Curses, a sorcerer,* his mind screamed.

Slowly, Lucas edged closer to the trees, and with his men sufficiently occupied, he dove under a bush. His eyes popped wide when the other boy transformed into a dragon right before his eyes. *These forests are cursed, and now I know by what.* He watched in horror as all his men were roasted alive. With the two boys engrossed in their conversation, Lucas silently backed away and slipped out of The Craig's, unseen.

He waited for nightfall before approaching a small hut, set apart from the main rock house and stable. Without knocking, he crept in through the back door. A woman sat at a table in the middle of the room, gems of various sizes and types scattered across every surface.

"I told you to wait for me down below," the dark-haired woman said without turning her head.

"We have a problem."

"And what could that be, dear General?" she asked sweetly.

"All my men are dead!"

She turned her eyes to him now. "How?"

"Two richlings, that's how. A dragon and a sorcerer."

"Come now, General. Don't tell me you believe in fairytales and ghosts in the forest. A dragon and a sorcerer, you say. I thought a General of your standing in the Evansshire Royal Command, even disgraced as you now are, wouldn't believe in children's tales."

"Believe what you may, I witnessed it myself. I ran into that pair almost a year ago outside of Creekside. I thought they just got lucky, beating my boys. But now I know the truth behind their deceit."

"Describe them," she said dryly.

"The sorcerer is a brunette, and the dragon in his human form has red hair; both appear to be mid-teens."

The woman glanced up, "And in his dragon form?"

"Sapphire blue with blue and black wings."

She looked back down. "Interesting. So, how many did you lose?"

"All you can say is, interesting? How many did I lose?" He roared, "I lost all that I had with me."

"Interesting," she said again.

"You better start explaining yourself, woman, before I pull out of our deal."

The oil lamps in the cabin dimmed, and the fireplace snuffed out. Lucas cast a nervous eye at the front door, but it remained closed. He spun around, dagger in hand, looking for danger.

"Watch your tone with me, General."

He turned to look at the woman again. Her long, black hair stood up, framing her head like a cape, and her eyes shone blood red.

"You may be powerful in your own circle, but you are out of your depth here." Her voice dropped two octaves as she spoke.

Even though she was over a foot shorter than him, he took several steps back. "Our deal is still on, puny human. I will ensure you are protected from here on out— you and all your men. I will not fail… You will not fail me."

"Yes, my lady." He fell to his knees, placing his head on the ground. "Forgive me, my lady."

"Rise, you fool. The time for bowing is not upon us. You have work to do and two halves of a prophecy to steal." Her voice was still deep and gravelly.

A soft knock on the door broke the trance Sephra was in. The fireplace relit, and the oil lamps brightened.

"Hide in the back room and do not make a sound. Cedric must not know you are here," she hissed to Lucas. He nodded his head quickly and scurried from the room.

Another knock at the door.

"Come," she said, regaining her composure.

A man with sandy blonde hair entered her home.

"Good evening, Sephra. I come bearing gifts." He held up the two sacks full of gems.

"I didn't know anyone was harvesting this week." She gestured for him to place the sacks down.

"Lance and a village boy named Keelan found them."

"Oh, I've heard a little about Keelan."

"Well, I just learned a lot more about him."

Lucas listened closely to the story the newcomer told his mistress. He shuddered at the memory of her frightful eyes and demonic appearance. A dragon lad befriended an ordinary boy, only to discover that the boy was a sorcerer and hadn't known it. He cursed his luck for encountering that pair not once but twice. *I hope my mistress is right that she can protect me from such misfortunes.*

"Lucas," she said sweetly after Cedric departed.

"Yes, my mistress." He cowered before her.

She smiled at the strong, powerful man in front of her—putty in her hands. "I need you to follow the dragon." Her smile widened when she saw his face blanch. "No need to engage; I just need him tracked. I must know where he is at all times. Is that understood?"

"Yes, my mistress."

"If he moves, you must get word to me immediately."

"How, my lady?"

She sighed. "Must I think of everything myself? And stop with the *my lady* title. That doesn't do my greatness service. Mistress Warlock will suffice."

"Yes, Mistress Warlock." He bowed his head.

Sephra smiled again. "I will be sending my precious pet with you. She will be able to get word back to me, and I can communicate through her to give you instructions. Your original mission of recruiting an army for me still needs to be completed as well. I trust you can handle all of this. The rewards will be great." She tossed him a heavy bag from her table. He caught it easily and fingered it slightly before stuffing it into his cloak pocket.

"Where do I find your precious pet?" he asked quietly.

A small, blue, sparkling light zipped into the room and hovered beside Sephra's ear. "This is my pixie, Meta. Don't let her size and cute looks fool you…"

Meta fluttered close to Lucas, looking like a perfectly formed human woman with long copper hair that sparkled. Her large emerald-green eyes contrasted with her light blue skin. She smiled sweetly at him for a moment before her face contorted into a vicious snarl, the pupils of her eyes growing until they were solid black.

"…Pixies can be quite evil."

"I don't want that vile thing with me!" Lucas backed away quickly, shielding his face.

"Don't worry, my dear General. Meta will only be seen when I need a report. You won't see her unless necessary. And to ensure that your mission succeeds, I will be using something that just fell into my lap." She opened one of the bags Cedric left with her and poured several sapphires into her hand. "Perfect," she purred. She selected one and held it up to the light. "This star sapphire will be imbued with a spell that allows Meta to track it. Follow her, and you will be able to follow the boys."

Meta zipped around the room, her eyes returning to their soft emerald green, and landed gracefully on Sephra's shoulder.

"Then why do you need me? Just have her track them and send word back." Lucas glared at the pixie.

"Ah, that would be simple, wouldn't it? Alas, while pixies are marvelous messengers, they do not stay on task for long periods of time. She will follow you, and since you'll be sending regular messages, she won't have a chance to stray. Now, Lucas, do you understand your tasks?"

"Yes, Mistress Warlock," he replied, trying to keep his voice steady. The thought of having Meta near him, even if unseen, made his skin crawl, but he knew better than to defy Sephra. He took a deep breath, steeling himself for what lay ahead.

"Good," Sephra said, her voice returning to its sweet, almost soothing tone. "I trust you will not disappoint me."

Lucas bowed deeply before turning and leaving the cabin, the weight of the bag in his cloak pocket a constant reminder of his daunting tasks. As he stepped into the night, he glanced back at the cabin one last time, shuddering as Meta's eyes gleamed from the darkness.

PART 2

CHAPTER

-4-

THE sky was bright, but no sun shone through the dense cloud cover. The wind howled, rattling the window shutters. The snow continued to fall, three straight days now.

Shaylee sat at her desk in the small classroom, staring into the dancing fire as it crackled and popped in the hearth. The warmth from the flames carried her mind away, soaring through the clouds on the back of a pegasus, far from where it was supposed to be—paying attention to the teacher's lecture on elven history. A gust of wind swooped down the stone chimney, almost blowing out their fire, snapping Shaylee's mind to the present.

"Welcome back, Shaylee," Fawn whispered.

Shaylee smiled and leaned over. "What did I miss?"

"Don't worry," Fawn said, pointing to a small rock on the table before her.

Now, why didn't I think of that? Shaylee shook her head. She'd discovered how to enchant rocks to absorb everything they heard, and then she could make the stone play back the audio at another time. Fawn instantly loved the idea and had Shaylee make up several of them. Shaylee hadn't used them since they first joined The Chosen, what felt like years ago, but in reality, only a few months had passed.

"I'm sure I've bored all the elves with history they've heard time and again. We'll have our final test on this section tomorrow, and I truly hope all the fairies and humans were paying attention," the teacher said, clapping her hands. "To recap, we've covered the history of fairies and elves. Our next section will be on the history of humans and dragons. Yes, Elas?" she asked, pointing to the young elf.

Elas sat near the front of the class. His brother Jurren snickered at him from the rear of the classroom. Elas was always attentive and always early, so different from his brother. Shaylee's mind took her back to the last time she was near either of them, in the middle of the night, as they raided her garden and almost killed her. She shook her head to remove the image and feelings.

"Why are we learning about humans and dragons at the same time? Are their histories that closely aligned?"

"Excellent question, Elas. While humans and dragons may have had separate origins, the history we'll focus on begins when humans learned to harness magic—with the dragons' help. Without their interaction, there would be no sorcerers or witches," the teacher explained.

"Now, since this eternal snow refuses to stop, there will once again be no weapons training. You are all excused for the rest of the day, but don't forget to study."

Everyone quickly stood, gathered their belongings, and left the classroom. Shaylee and Fawn walked down the central corridor of the Monastery together. Shaylee hated the walk from the classroom to the courtyard; the Monastery was always too quiet.

Shaylee thought about what their teacher had said about humans learning magic from dragons. She shook her head slightly at the idea. Leo'venath, a sorcerer and one of the leaders of The Blade and the Academy she was enrolled in, told her that he believed humans mixed with elves and fairies centuries ago, and that was where they got their magic. Shaylee was a unique blend of magic, with her elf and fairy heritage and ability to detect and replicate human magic.

Soon, they stopped at a small room near the entrance to gather their heavy cloaks and boots before braving the elements.

"So, when do you think they'll be back?" Shaylee asked. Her mind swirled from one thought to the next.

"Who are you talking about?" Fawn looked at her, confused.

"Our supposed allies, the pegasi and griffins. Tarrid introduced us to them, and then they just left."

"Well, you know he said they were going to gather others of their kind. I'm sure they've decided to wait until spring. Would you want to fly in this weather? And don't forget about the unicorns and great stags."

"Oh, I haven't forgotten. And I suppose I wouldn't want to fly in this weather either. Come on, we'd better get home."

They waited until everyone was ready to leave the building. No one was in much of a hurry to walk through the blizzard. A couple of boys pried the doors open, and the unrelenting storm howled, blowing bits of ice and snow into the faces of the waiting students. Bowing their heads against the wind, they trudged into the storm.

"Shaylee? Shaylee, where are you?" Rosepetal called as she flew between the houses and over the barren garden beds.

The sun blazed brightly overhead, finally breaking through after the long storms. The air was crisp, and a fresh layer of frost coated everything in sight, but spring was just around the corner. The days were growing longer and warmer. Everyone in the village had smiles on their faces and a little spring in their step. The change in attitudes was unmistakable.

Winter was brutal this year. The unnatural storms struck one after another, forcing everyone to stay indoors. Rumors circulated that Wyverns or humans had enslaved sorcerers to enchant the weather and disrupt the growing rebellions. Rosepetal shook off the thought. Now, where could Shaylee have gone?

In the distance, she finally spotted Shaylee outside the Monastery's walls. Lyra was flying above her.

"There you are, child."

"Sorry, were you looking for me?" Shaylee asked, looking at her mother.

"Obviously. Come on. Fawn says she has some news to share with us."

Shaylee jumped up and whistled for Lyra. The snowy white vaskakat flipped in the air before soaring toward her, gracefully landing on Shaylee's shoulders.

"I think you're getting too big to ride there," Rosepetal remarked.

Shaylee laughed as Lyra tried to find room on her shoulder. "Ow, watch the claws. Face it, Lyra. You're just too big now."

Lyra hissed and took flight once more. Her black-tipped wings slapped Shaylee in the face when she pushed off.

"Oh, good, you found her!" Fawn exclaimed, running toward them.

"Sorry, I didn't realize I would be missed so. What's going on?" Shaylee asked.

"Tar spoke with me this morning. He says you and I will be moved to the advanced weapons group. Here's your new pin." Fawn handed Shaylee the pin. She ran her finger across the raised metal, tracing the bow and arrow set inside a shield. When she was only ten years old, Shaylee had learned archery from her father, Talon. She was far more skilled than most of the students at the Academy and dreamed of the day when the leadership would recognize her abilities. With a sense of pride, she unclasped her current pin from her shirt, placing it in her pocket before pinning the advanced archery pin in its place. However, her expression fell as she brushed her fingers across the pin once more.

"Why are you sad?" Fawn asked, confused. "You and I were just saying our current class is beneath us. This is great news. Now we will be able to join scouting missions."

"Oh, it is great news. Don't get me wrong, this should have happened weeks ago. Weapons training might have been sporadic lately, but we are still far better than most of the students."

"What do you have to pout about then?" Rosepetal asked.

"I wish he would have given it to me himself," Shaylee said softly.

Fawn hugged her. "He tried; he couldn't find you, and I didn't know where you went," she whispered in her ear.

Shaylee nodded. "Makes sense. So, what next?"

"Leo is the instructor for the advanced archers; we will meet with him tomorrow."

"Good morning, everyone," Leo'venath roared, "Please welcome Shaylee and Fawn to the group. These two have shown remarkable skill with the bow. They'll be joining us from now on."

There were five already in the group, all men. Three elves and two humans, three humans if you counted Leo'venath. "This is Aiwin, Gaelin, Elmar, Wilfred, and Dale."

Hellos and nods went around.

"Okay, everyone here knows how to hold still, take aim, and let loose. You also know how to hit a moving target or a stationary one while moving yourself. Now, we will learn how to keep your head while shooting. And I mean that in the literal sense. Your targets will be shooting back."

Fawn's eyes widened in shock. "Shooting what at us?" she squeaked.

"Concentrated streams of water. I won't lie; it's going to hurt some, but it's not life-threatening," he said with a smile.

Leo'venath took them out, past the walls, and further into the forest.

"These are our enemies," he said, pointing to several trees with crude elf drawings etched into the bark. "These are the ones you will be targeting, and they will be firing back. However, more will appear once we begin; some you will never see but will be able to see you. Your objective is to hit your marks without being seen or hit. Stealth is crucial for an archer in The Blade. We expect you to hit your assigned targets cleanly and come back alive. I will demonstrate."

Leo'venath removed his bow from his back and walked toward the course. He lined up with the first target and aimed. Suddenly, a stream of water shot toward him, which he narrowly evaded. Another stream shot from the forest behind him, striking him on the shoulder. He ducked down behind a log and vanished from sight.

Shaylee saw a shimmer for a moment and then nothing. Suddenly, an arrow appeared out of thin air and thudded into the first target."

"Do you see him?" Fawn asked.

Shaylee shook her head.

"Us elves won't be able to see him while he's cloaking himself with magic," Aiwin said.

"Well, us humans can't see him either. I caught a glimpse of his signature when he first cloaked himself, but then he was just gone. I know his arrow was guided, but I couldn't see the tracer."

Shaylee nodded; she experienced the same thing.

Another arrow found its mark, and then a third and fourth.

"There he is!" Shaylee exclaimed, pointing close to the fifth and final target.

"I still don't see him," Wilfred stated, and Dale nodded in agreement.

"Don't look for him; feel for him. Try to remember what his shimmer felt like before he disappeared; search for that feeling."

"His shimmer?" Dale asked.

"She means his signature," Wilfred explained.

"Signature?" she asked.

"The shimmer you saw is called a magical signature. Everyone has a unique signature, which is how we can identify who casts a spell. Even if you can't see them, you'll see their signature or a tracer of their magic leading back to them," Dale explained.

Shaylee nodded, "That makes sense, thank you. Are you able to feel his signature?"

"I've never tried," Dale shrugged. Wilfred shook his head.

"Who wants to go next?" Leo'venath said, returning.

Shaylee's hand snapped up. "I will." She turned to the other humans, "Try to feel my signature."

She walked over to the same log where Leo'venath had disappeared. *I can do this; I am invisible, but not my signature. I am invisible to the eye,* she thought. She steadied her breath, aimed at the first target, and then moved to the next. After hitting the third target, one of the humans called out.

"I found you; this is amazing. I've never felt for a signature before."

"I found you too; how about you, Leo? Anything yet?"

"Hmm, no… oh wait, okay. Now I understand what I'm looking for. This is truly amazing, Shaylee."

A grin slid across her face. *OK, boys. Now try this,* she thought.

"Hey, wait. Where did you go?"

"What? What are you talking about?" Fawn asked, panic raising her voice an octave. "You said you could feel her."

"I could, and then nothing. She vanished."

"SHAYLEE!!" Fawn shouted.

An arrow appeared out of thin air, thwacking into the fourth target and then the fifth.

"Don't mess with my emotions!" Fawn yelled at her.

"Sorry," Shaylee said, causing everyone to jump and spin around at her sudden appearance.

"How did you do that?" Leo'venath asked. "First, we could feel your signature, and then you just disappeared."

She smiled broadly. "I thought about being completely hidden—hidden from sight, scent, and feel."

"Truly amazing," Leo'venath said.

"No one's ever done that before?" she asked.

Leo'venath shook his head. "The sorcerers in The Chosen used to belong to The Circle of Illumination—an ancient order of magic-users who assisted the dragons against the Wyverns. The Circle were the most advanced sorcerers and witches known to man, with several universities across the land to train those gifted with magic. They claimed neutrality but allowed Evansshire to defeat the Kingdom of Oshana. Afterward, Evansshire outlawed magic. Those not killed or captured went into hiding. I don't know if what you are doing was just lost to history or if you are doing something entirely new.

"But I want to learn how you do it if you will teach me. The Wyverns have several magical slaves whom we have come across on occasion. We haven't figured out how they are controlling them yet. But we do intend to find out. So, what do you say? Will you teach us?"

Shaylee's smile stretched from ear to ear. "Of course, although I'm not sure how I do the things I do. I see a problem, and the solution springs to mind, and I do it. Lyra once told me to stop thinking and just do."

"Who's Lyra?" Gaelin asked.

Lyra meowed loudly, swooping down from a tree as if on command.

"This is Lyra. She's my familiar."

Greetings, she projected to everyone.

"Lyra, I heard your voice! How is that possible? Elves can't hear familiars," Fawn said.

So much history has been lost to you bipeds, a new voice projected.

Everyone looked around in surprise, trying to find the source of the voice.

Look up, the voice said.

All eyes went to the sky; two pegasus and four griffins flew in lazy circles above them.

"You're back!" Shaylee shouted, waving her hands in the air.

We said we would return, the voice said.

One of the pegasus landed gracefully and folded her wings with a snap.

My name is Dreamcrest. She bowed her head slightly.

Dreamcrest's coat was silvery white, reflecting the bright sunlight. She pawed the ground with her slender legs, making the light feathering on her pasterns dance. The tips of her feathery wings shimmered with blue, purple, and gold and almost appeared to twinkle.

"What is this that you speak of? What has been lost to history?" Elmar asked.

All magical creatures can speak to those with magic if they wish to, telepathically.

"Why has it never happened to me before?" Wilfred asked.

We live in difficult times. Magic, as well as magical creatures, have been outlawed. But even so, there are those with magic who have allied themselves with the ones who outlawed them. Most magical creatures would never initiate a conversation with a random elf or fairy unless they knew they were not working for the Wyverns or Evansshire.

"But why didn't we know that we could do this? I would have done it if I knew I could speak to a pegasus or a vaskakat," Elmar stated firmly.

In the War of the Lost, some magical creatures aligned themselves willingly with the wyverns—the trolls and the ogres, to name a few. Elves and fairies barely trust each other, and you think they would readily teach their children to trust all magical creatures?

They pondered her words for a moment.

"What you're saying makes sense. What brought you to trust us?" Leo'venath asked.

Your leader, Tarrid, was persuasive in his actions, not words. He was just as surprised as you to learn that he could hear our projections. We are living in a new era. You will all be witnessing the birth of new kingdoms.

"You sound so certain of that," Fawn said. "Do pegasi possess the gift of foretelling?"

No, she shook her head, her mane flipping from side to side. *I wouldn't call it foretelling. We see glimpses of what may or may not come to pass. There are too many variables at play that can change the outcome. A seer can see the broad picture but only many, many years into the future. Some unicorns have seer abilities. Those like me can see possibilities that may happen closer to the present. We shall leave you to your work. Shaylee, I will find you this evening. We have much to discuss.* Dreamcrest bowed deeply before leaping into the air, her wings snapping open with a powerful gust of wind as she propelled herself into the sky. Everyone shielded their faces from the dust and debris that swirled around them. Fawn and Shaylee braced themselves, trying to stay on their feet.

"What does she want with you?" Leo'venath asked.

"I don't know, but I can't wait to find out." Shaylee smiled, watching the pegasus gain altitude.

CHAPTER

-5-

SHAYLEE couldn't focus. *What could a pegasus possibly have to say to me?* she wondered, her thoughts swirling in her head.

Fawn stayed close to her for the rest of the day, even skipping her usual afternoon visit to her mother. Shaylee didn't comment; she already understood why. She wouldn't have wanted to miss the conversation either if their positions were reversed.

Once the kitchen was cleaned up from the evening meal, Shaylee and Fawn decided to go for a walk. After completing a full loop around the Monastery and nearing their house, something finally caught their eye. A shadow moved across the sky. Shaylee and Fawn exchanged a quick look before breaking into a sprint toward the courtyard.

As they reached the front of the Monastery, they saw Tarrid, Leo'venath, and Prioress Leilatha Moryra descending the stone steps.

"Good evening, girls," Prioress Leilatha said.

"What brings you two about?" Leo'venath asked.

I asked Shaylee to meet with me, Dreamcrest projected.

Tarrid locked eyes with Shaylee before quickly looking away. His demeanor around her had shifted significantly since their first festival at the Monastery. Shaylee remembered that night well—he had smiled at her from a distance, but ever since then, he averted his gaze whenever their eyes met. Now, with the official start of classes, she had barely seen him.

Shaylee, walk with me, please, Dreamcrest's voice echoed in her mind.

Shaylee glanced at Fawn, unsure if she should allow her to come.

Alone, please, Dreamcrest added gently.

"Okay, I'll wait here," Fawn said. "It's okay; you can tell me later." Fawn grinned.

Dreamcrest turned and started walking toward the main gates with Shaylee beside her.

Fawn watched as her sister-friend strolled away with the winged horse. Sighing, she walked over to the steps and sat down to wait. Nearby, two griffins stood next to the three leaders of *The Blade.* A smile tugged at her lips as she recalled the day Tarrid announced he was leaving The Order of the Chosen to form his own resistance group, The Blade of Freedom. This later led to the establishment of the *Norell-Spencer Academy of the Blade.*

Her mind drifted back to when she and Shaylee had arrived at the Spring Equinox festival. Tarrid had stood at the top of the steps with Leo'venath. His eyes had locked on Shaylee, a small smile pulling at his lips before shifting toward her. Fawn had been wearing her best dress and had just washed and re-braided her hair. She remembered how his smile had faltered for a moment, his cheeks flushing, before a wide grin broke across his face. Fawn felt her own cheeks warm at the memory. But then, Aspen—another former warrior of *The Chosen,* wearing next to nothing—had walked between them, stealing Tarrid's attention. Thankfully, Aspen wasn't an instructor at the Academy and had left after the storms ended.

Lost in thought, she was startled when Tarrid tapped her on the shoulder. She jumped, holding her hand on her chest to still her beating heart.

"I didn't mean to startle you."

"That's okay; I guess my mind was just wandering," she said, looking at him and then back at Shaylee.

Tarrid followed her gaze. "Isn't it strange to find out something about yourself… to find an ability none of us knew we had? To think we have been able to hear the projections of magical creatures all this time." He shook his head.

She turned her eyes to Tarrid once again. "Why do you think they waited so long to approach us?"

He shrugged. "I'm glad I was in the right place at the right time."

"How did you meet them?"

Tarrid raked his hands through his hair, sighing deeply, clamping his hands behind his back. "We were on our way back, and five ogres ambushed us. They had us surrounded. Thankfully, they were a lone troop and didn't have any wyverns with them. We managed to kill three, but we were wearing down. I wasn't sure how much longer we'd be able to hold them off. Suddenly, there was a screech from the sky. My exhausted brain screamed danger. My first thought was it was a wyvern joining. Thankfully, it was a flock of griffins. They swooped down and took out the last two ogres for us. After the battle, I expected the griffins to take off or attack us. I've never personally encountered any, but I've met those who have. After seeing how easily they dispatched the ogres, I wasn't looking forward to a battle with them. I figured diplomacy was going to be my best bet. I approached the one who appeared to be the leader and bowed, thanking him for his assistance," Tarrid started to chuckle.

"The griffin stared at me with an almost dumbfounded expression, if you can believe that. It took me by surprise when he spoke to me. I always assumed telepathy was a human and dragon thing only."

"Have you ever met a dragon?" Fawn asked, looking up at him, her eyes wide.

He shook his head. "No, but I hope to someday. Having them help us battle the wyverns who have enslaved them would help tremendously."

"Are the griffins and others staying?"

"Sort of. That's why I came over here to speak with you. The griffins say they have encountered the birds with which we associate the wasting disease. They believe they know a cure."

Fawn jumped to her feet, reaching up to grab hold of Tarrid's shoulders. "Truly?"

He smiled down at her, placing one hand on her shoulder. "They think so, but until we find this cure of theirs, we won't know for sure. I don't want to get your hopes up, but I just wanted you to know we haven't given up the search."

"So, does that mean you'll be leaving again?" she asked, her voice falling to a whisper.

"Yes, soon."

Fawn sat back down, trying to hide her reaction. Tarrid slowly sat beside her. "It's okay. I'll be back soon," he said.

"Where will you have to go?"

"There's another griffin clan who guards a grove of firebush. Years ago, when human magic users were more prevalent, a wasting disease would afflict them. They say it sounds similar. However, the wasting disease has never attacked elves before. It was strictly a human thing."

"Why do they think it's similar or the same thing?"

"All the symptoms are the same."

"Was it caused by a bird years ago?"

"Maybe. Nobody knows exactly where it originated from."

"Somebody must be doing this intentionally."

"That's my thought, too."

"Will you come say goodbye before you leave?"

He looked over at her, staring into her turquoise eyes. *How did I not realize how brilliant her eyes were?* He thought.

"What?"

He shook his head. "Sorry, I just didn't realize how much your eyes reminded me of my mother's."

"I hope you two had a good relationship."

Tarrid tilted his head, giving her a puzzling look.

She laughed, "If it was a strained relationship, you might take it out on me."

Her laughter was infectious. After a moment, he nodded. "My mother and I got along very well. She passed several years ago."

"Oh, I'm so sorry." She placed a hand on his knee.

He looked down at her hand, then back into her eyes, and cleared his throat, "I'll make sure I find you before we leave."

"Thank you, Tar. Thank you for everything you're doing."

He squeezed her hand and lingered a moment longer before returning to Leo'venath and the griffins. Fawn watched his retreating form before glancing over to where Shaylee was finishing her conversation with the pegasus. She saw her nod with a giant grin on her face. The pegasus took flight with a gust of wind blowing Shaylee's hair from her face. As Shaylee watched Dreamcrest circle above the Monastery, Fawn approached.

"So, what was that all about?"

"She wants me to be her rider."

"Isn't that kind of degrading?"

"That's what I thought, and I asked her about it. She said many years ago, it was common for pegasus, griffins, and others to partner with a rider for battle."

"So, what did you tell her?"

"I told her I'd be honored, of course."

Fawn looked up at the pegasus flying above them. The setting sun glistened off her coat, making her shine like a thousand diamonds adorned her coat. "How does that work? Do you use a saddle?"

"No, that she was offended by," Shaylee giggled. "It appears I must learn to stay on with my magic."

"That sounds scary. Are there others who are going to be requesting riders?"

Shaylee nodded. "She said she plans on recruiting others for that purpose. She's going to be the commander of the Ariel Guard. She says she plans on having each flight a mix of griffin and pegasus."

"What's a flight?"

"That's what she will be calling each patrol group."

"It has a cool sound to it."

"She said there will also be a land force comprised of unicorns and stags. I saw Tar speaking to you; what was he saying?"

"He said the griffins may know a cure for the weakness disease."

"That's great news," she said brightly but then her face fell, "does that mean he'll be leaving again?"

Fawn nodded sadly, "He said soon, but he didn't know exactly when. He said he would speak to us before he leaves, though. I hate to see him go again, but a cure must be found. I want to figure out a way to make him let me come with him," Fawn said quickly.

Shaylee looked at her friend, "I don't think he'll let you."

"I want both of us to go. I know we can help. Will you come with me?"

Shaylee thought momentarily, "If we can figure out a way to go, of course, I'll go with you."

"Thank you, Shaylee."

CHAPTER

-6-

LEO'VENATH adjusted the pack on his shoulder and knocked on the door before him.

"Come in," a voice called.

He opened the door and quickly entered. "Are you about ready to go?"

Tarrid stood in the main room, packing his bag while checking items off a list. "Just about. I think I've got everything. Are the griffins ready?"

"They're waiting for us over by the Monastery."

"Good, how many are coming again?" Tarrid asked as he pulled everything out of one bag and repacked it.

"I saw six out there this morning. Are you sure you don't want to bring anybody else with us?"

Tarrid shook his head. "No, I think the two of us should be fine with the griffins' help. We don't want to look like an invading force to the other clan. This should be a relatively straightforward task. We must convince the griffins to give us some firebush. We're not riding into battle."

"Whatever you say, you're the boss."

Tarrid smiled and shook his head. "Okay, let's head to the griffins."

"Aren't you forgetting something?"

"No, I think I have everything we need." He glanced at his list again,

"All right, let me rephrase that. Aren't you forgetting to go say goodbye to someone?"

Tarrid glared. "I haven't forgotten. I planned on stopping by and saying goodbye to the girls. It's not a big deal."

"I think both of them would disagree with you."

"What's that supposed to mean?"

"You know you have both of them wrapped around your little finger."

Tarrid's eyes widened in shock. "I have no such thing."

Leo'venath laughed. "Well, if you saw them from my eyes, you would think differently. Just tread lightly, my friend." He slapped him on the back and left his house.

Tarrid grabbed his gear, exited his house, and started across the camp. The sun had yet to rise in the brightening sky, and a few stars still twinkled dimly overhead. The early mornings were cool, with summer still a month away. As he neared the girls' house, he considered writing a letter to say goodbye; it was pretty early, and he didn't want to disturb the household. He turned the corner and was going to keep going, but he saw a light on in their main room.

Through the window, he could see Fawn and Shaylee were already awake. *Well, there's no getting out of this now*, he thought to himself. He adjusted his pack to prevent it from sliding off his shoulder as he walked the rest of the distance to the house. Both girls saw him before he could knock on the door.

"How long do you think you'll be gone?" Fawn asked as she exited the house.

"We're not sure. It will take us a couple of days to reach the grove, and then we must convince the clan to allow us to take some of the plants."

"Do you think they'll deny you?" Shaylee asked.

He shrugged. "We don't know. Cloudfeather says he's never met any of the griffins from this clan. We will have to approach cautiously so we are not deemed a threat."

"Be careful," Fawn said quietly.

"I always am." Both girls lifted their glistening eyes and batted their eyelashes. *I see what Leo means now.* He swallowed loudly. "I'll see you both soon." Both girls looked like they wanted to throw their arms around him, but they hesitated. He backed away, gave them an awkward wave, and walked briskly to the waiting griffins.

"I see you made it back in one piece," Leo'venath said.

"Why wouldn't I have?"

He shrugged. "I don't know. Wasn't sure if they would fight over you or knock you over the head to keep you from leaving."

"Very funny. Are we all set?"

We are ready when you are, Cloudfeather projected.

Tarrid and Leo'venath tightened the straps of their packs one last time, exchanging a quick glance before squaring their shoulders. With renewed determination, they approached their 'transportation.'

"So, have any of you carried somebody before?" Leo'venath asked.

This will be a first for all of us, Cloudfeather responded calmly.

Leo'venath and Tarrid glanced at each other and shrugged.

"Hold up, don't leave yet!" a voice called out. Ben came sprinting toward them, breathless and clutching a large bundle to his chest. He bent slightly at the waist, struggling to catch his breath. "I think I have something that will help you return safely."

"I want nothing more than to come back in one piece. What do you have for us?" Leo'venath replied, curiosity glimmering in his eyes.

Ben revealed the contents of the bundle: two strange-looking saddles, each paired with harnesses and ropes. "I made these so you can secure yourselves to the griffins," he explained, his voice tinged with excitement. "It'll be much safer than just holding on.

"The other day, while studying in the monastery's library, I stumbled upon an ancient book—completely by accident, mind you. Inside, there was a diagram of a griffin warrior, an elf riding a sleek black griffin. At first glance, it didn't seem like he was using a saddle, but as I examined the illustration more closely, I realized they did use some form of saddle. I've done my best to replicate it for you."

Ben turned to the enormous griffin and bowed deeply, holding the saddle out with trembling hands. "Noble griffin, will you allow me to fit this saddle to you to keep our leaders safe?"

The griffin eyed the contraption; with a couple of tentative steps, he got closer, lowering his head and then raising it to sniff the leather. ***How do I know this is not a trick?*** Cloudfeather stretched his neck toward Ben. Ben's eyes widened in shock at the sudden movement. With the griffins' beak mere inches from his face, his breath stopped, and he found it difficult to swallow. Cloudfeather breathed in deeply and then snorted. Ben's eyes watered as he winced when the hot, humid breath wafted over him, ruffling his hair. He attempted to suppress the gag that rose in his throat from the carrion smell.

Ben stared at the griffin, surprised. "How am I hearing you? I thought only those with magic could hear you?"

You must have a spark; it is the only answer. Now, talk about this thing you hold.

"I mean, you no harm, and I meant no offense. My only concern is how Tarrid and Leo'venath will stay seated when you are in flight. I am also concerned about how their weight will affect your balance."

Do you have this book with you, and do you know the name of the black griffin portrayed in it? Cloudfeather slowly walked around Ben with his tail swaying silently.

Ben nodded, quickly reached into his pack, and pulled out a leather-wrapped book. The cover was worn and tattered and looked extremely fragile. He promptly opened the page and held it out so Cloudfeather could see the image of the griffin with his rider. As the griffin stared at the image his tail mindlessly started to swish faster and then thwacked Ben in the head.

"Many pages in this book are faded and hard to read, but I believe the griffin's name was Soulcatcher," Ben said, rubbing his head.

Cloudfeather stared intently at the image before gazing at the saddle contraption Ben had created. ***Soulcatcher is a distant relative of mine. You may fit the saddle to me. Tarrid, I would be honored to carry you on our quest.***

Tarrid bowed deeply, "No, you honor me. So, how does this work?" he asked Ben.

"Well, from what I can gather, there are two parts." He placed the saddle down and picked up one section that would go around Cloudfeather's neck. He hesitated for a moment; Cloudfeather nodded. Ben walked up, laid a modified sloping saddle on top of his neck above his shoulders, and buckled it securely around his neck and girth just behind his wings. Another strap connected the girth to the neck harness between the legs.

"And what about this strap?" Leo'venath asked.

"That is for the rider. Right now, it's just a few straps to go around your shoulders, chest, and waist. I have one for each of you. They should be snug, but I did make them adjustable. While you're gone, I'm going to improve the design."

He assisted both men into their harnesses. "So, the next step would be when you're mounted."

Tarrid gave his harness and belt another quick tug before walking to Cloudfeather and looking up at him. Griffins were much larger than horses.

"What do you suggest is the easiest way to get on your back?" he asked Cloudfeather. Cloudfeather looked at his soon-to-be rider and then knelt on the ground. "So, how do I sit in this thing?"

"Sit in the middle of the saddle." Tarrid did as instructed. "Now you will see two wings in front of your knees. Hook your legs over those. Great, now you will find a couple of slits in the saddle for your toes. I thought about a traditional style stirrup but then thought that might be too dangerous."

"Wouldn't a normal saddle work just fine?" Leo'venath asked.

"Not in flight. From what I have read, if you were to sit straight up like you would on top of a horse, you would get blown backward and throw off the flying characteristics of your companion."

"Well, I'm glad you thought of something," Leo'venath chuckled. "I've been worried sick about how we would stay on. Okay, so if we don't sit up while in flight, how will we do this?"

"Connect your chest strap to the saddle. Alright, now for the fun part," Tarrid looked at Ben sideways. Ben smiled, "It's going to be fine, but it might be uncomfortable until you get used to it. Grab the two handles up at the top of the saddle sled and lean forward."

"Saddle sled?"

"Yeah, I'm still working on the name."

Tarrid leaned forward so his chest rested on Cloudfeather's neck, and he grabbed hold of the handles tightly.

"Okay, while in flight, keep leaning forward. Your strap will help keep you in place."

Again, Tarrid did as instructed. Soon, he was sitting on the modified saddle in a crouch with his knees at his chest. He leaned forward and gripped the handles tightly.

Leo'venath started to laugh, "That looks pretty silly. Should we give it a test?" Cloudfeather took that as his cue and vaulted into the air. A startled cry escaped Tarrid, but he quickly muffled himself. Cloudfeather flapped his great wings, propelling himself up and forward. He made a couple of slow circles around the camp.

Are you ready for further testing? Do you feel secure?

"Well, so far, so good; I haven't moved."

Please hold tight.

That was Tarrid's only warning as Cloudfeather shot straight up in the air, gaining altitude quickly. He banked hard to the right and spiraled into a nosedive. Right before they plummeted to the ground, Cloudfeather snapped his wings open and glided gracefully to a stop. Tarrid's knuckles were white as he gripped the handles, his eyes squeezed tightly shut.

"I think it's safe to open your eyes now," Ben said.

Leo'venath was laughing so hard he almost fell over.

"I think your saddles are a success," Tarrid said finally, "but before we try that again, Cloudfeather, please give me some more warning."

Cloudfeather squawked, and a low rumble, almost like a purr, came from his throat. *Who will carry the human?*

All the griffins were silent, sharing looks between them.

"What's going on?" Leo'venath whispered.

Cloudfeather glanced at him. *They are deciding amongst themselves who is willing to carry you.*

A female griffin stepped forward; her lion body was a deep mahogany red, and her feathers were a mixture of red, orange, and yellow. She was only slightly smaller than Cloudfeather himself. *I will carry the human,* she said proudly.

Leo'venath bowed, "My name is Leo'venath Spencer. I am honored you have agreed to carry me."

The honor is mine, Leo'venath. I am called Starfire.

Ben quickly fitted her with her saddle sled, and Leo'venath mounted up.

"What's with the extra straps?" Tarrid asked.

"Well, these I made for the packs. You're going to have to carry the firebush back. I figured it might be easier to strap them to the back of a griffin," he said with a cringe. Six pairs of black eyes stared at him.

We shall not be used as pack animals, one of them projected.

Ben immediately bowed, "I did not mean any offense. Do you have any suggestions?"

Get us large bags to fill, and we shall carry them, one of the smaller females said, opening and closing a taloned foot.

"Excellent suggestion," Ben said quickly. He approached her and laid a pack before her, "There are four large bags inside of this one." Ben turned to his leaders and smiled. "Good luck out there. We'll be waiting for your safe return."

Tarrid took a deep breath, feeling a mix of excitement and nerves. He looked at Leo'venath, who gave him a reassuring nod.

"Ready?" Tarrid asked.

"Ready," Leo'venath confirmed.

With a powerful beat of their wings, the griffins took to the sky, carrying Tarrid and Leo'venath toward their uncertain mission. As they soared higher, the camp below grew smaller, and the vast expanse of the forest stretched out before them. Tarrid couldn't help but glance back at the camp one last time, hoping this journey would bring the answers they desperately needed.

CHAPTER

-7-

KEELAN, Lance, and Jonal made their way across the kingdom, carefully avoiding towns and settlements. Their one encounter with the King's guards had raised some eyebrows, but they'd managed to escape without too many questions. In a land where magic was outlawed, advertising their quest for a cure to a rare illness affecting only magic users would be reckless.

Keelan slumped in his saddle, allowing his horse, Rogue, to choose the path. His thoughts drifted to his mother, sick, vulnerable, and all alone. *No, she's not alone,* he thought. Lance's father must have taken her to his ranch by now. He tried to reassure himself.

The weight of his family's secret still hung heavily over him. When his father, Elliot, discovered Maya's magic, his reaction had been... catastrophic. The revelation that she was the last of the Kingdom of Oshana's royal line—and that mantle now passed to Keelan—had shaken the foundations of their lives.

Keelan's own magic had fully surfaced shortly before this conversation, though his mother insisted he didn't have magic. He was born a twin, but his sibling had died at birth, and she believed his magic would never fully manifest because of it. But she had been wrong. His magic had awakened, though he kept it hidden from her, not wanting to add to her worries in her weakened state. *I'll tell her once I find the cure,* he thought grimly. The bright sun overhead forced him to squint, but he couldn't shake the disbelief that he had once had a twin. Learning this secret had unsettled him in ways he couldn't yet fully grasp.

As they traveled farther from Kingston, the capital, and into the unknown, Jonal—an experienced wizard and the man who had raised

Maya—worked tirelessly with Keelan, helping him hone his magic. Control was the hardest part. Keelan could mimic Jonal's spells effortlessly, but the cost was steep. Each spell drained him, demanding every ounce of his strength until he was left exhausted.

"You need to calm down and focus, Keelan," Jonal instructed as they traveled. "Some spells require a gentle touch. You can't control the outcome if you let too much in at once."

Keelan nodded, but frustration tugged at his expression. "I'm trying, but it's hard. I can feel the magic flowing inside me, but it's like a raging river held back by a fallen tree. The moment I move the tree, it floods through me uncontrollably."

Jonal pursed his lips thoughtfully. "Sorcerers aren't usually dependent on artifacts to control their magic, but it almost sounds like you need a reverse artifact."

"A what?" Lance asked, bringing his horse up beside them.

Jonal turned to explain. "Let me put it this way: mages or witches have a spark of magic running through their veins. To channel that magic, they use an artifact," he said, pulling a long, slender wand from his cloak. "For me, It's this wand. Others might use a staff or a ring with a gem. The enchanted artifact acts as a bridge, allowing us to access and direct the magic. Without it—or the proper spell—I can't cast anything."

"Can you make an artifact?" Keelan asked.

"No, I'm afraid not. Only a natural-born can enchant items, like your star sapphires."

Lance squinted his eyes, looking at the sapphire in his bracer.

"What is it?" Jonal asked him.

"Well, Sephra is my family's gemist. She made Keelan's bracer and enchanted it for him. She's a witch."

"Impossible." He shook his head. "She must be a natural-born. It is the only way."

"She told me herself that she was a witch. Why would she lie to me? It's not like my family, a family of dragons, has anything against sorcerers."

"That's a question I will ask her if I ever meet her."

"First chance I get, I'll introduce you to her." Lance nodded.

"So, back to the artifact," Keelan said, redirecting the conversation. "Do you think I need to use a wand or something?"

"After we stop for the night, I'll let you try mine. I've never heard of a sorcerer using a wand, but then I never heard of one having a familiar."

Aurora screeched from above, banking and twisting in the air. The sun gleamed off her feathers, making her look like she was on fire. *We familiars choose who we bond with, old man,* she laughed in all their minds.

"Sassy bird you have there, boy."

Keelan laughed but said nothing.

That night, the sky was awash with millions of sparkling stars, and a crescent moon was nothing but a tiny sliver. The air was warm, with only a whisper of a breeze to rustle the leaves in the trees. Their small fire crackled merrily. After they ate, Jonal handed Keelan a slender stick.

Keelan turned it over in his hands; he could feel the magic locked inside. An image popped into his head, "Sally made this?" he asked.

"Good," Jonal nodded his head. "Tell me how you knew? Did you recognize her magical signature?"

Keelan looked at him, puzzled, "Magical signature? Not sure what that is, but when I touched the stick…"

"Wand."

"Um, ok, wand. Her image popped into my head."

"Interesting," Jonal started to rummage through his bag. "Where is it? Aha!" he announced. He pulled out another slender stick, which was about half the length. "How about this one?"

Keelan accepted the small wand. An image of an old grizzly man popped into his head. "I see an old man, fairly short, pure white hair and a beard reaching almost to his knees."

"Simply amazing. He was my mentor, Sorcerer Dedrick. I've never heard of someone being able to see the magic user's image."

Aurora paused her preening to look between the two before walking closer to the fire and laying down within the rock ring. She fluffed her feathers and clicked her beak contently.

"Not even my mother?"

He shook his head, "No, it must be because you were born a twin."

"What about my grandfather? He was born a twin, right?"

"Yes, that is true. I never heard about him manifesting any powers, though."

Keelan's eyes brightened, "Then that means my twin must still be alive, out there somewhere."

"I'm afraid not. It died at birth."

"But what if one of the midwives just hid it and raised it as their own?"

"I don't know. I guess it is possible. Finding your twin would be impossible, though. No, for our sake, it's perishing as an infant would be for the best."

Keelan's face twisted in rage, "How can you say that?"

"Think about it, my boy. If the baby perished, the prophecy still lives within you. If your twin lives and you never find it to complete the prophecy, it dies, and so do all our hopes and dreams."

Keelan pursed his lips, "I suppose."

"Now, come, let's see if you can connect with the wand." Jonal took the smaller wand back from him.

Keelan shook his head to clear it and focused on the task at hand. He concentrated on the wand in his hand; again, he saw Sally's face and felt the magic flowing inside it, "I feel the magic."

"Good, good. Now, try to make sparks come from the wand."

"But I already can do that one with just my hands. It's the more powerful one I'm having problems with."

"I know, but let's start small."

"Okay." He thought about what he wanted - *purple sparks, light only, no heat.* He looked at the top of the wand in his outstretched hand; nothing happened.

"Well, that didn't work," Lance said, sitting beside the fire.

Keelan looked at him and noticed his other hand was shooting purple sparks. Aurora squawked and took flight when the sparks shot toward her.

"Okay, like I suspected, a natural-born can make artifacts but can't use them."

Silly mage, Aurora projected, circling above their heads. ***Sorcerers can't use made artifacts; they need a natural artifact.***

"Whatever are you talking about, bird?" Jonal snapped.

Aurora landed and hopped close to the fire again before answering. ***Do you really think the first artifact was just thought up out of nowhere? The sorcerer who made the first one copied something already in use. Truly? You did not know this? The magical ban for these past hundred years has really destroyed your memories.***

"What's a natural artifact?" Keelan asked.

A unicorn horn or a griffin claw, to name a couple.

"Oh, is that all," Jonal scoffed.

"What about a feather from a Phoenix?" Lance asked.

From what I know, a sorcerer cannot use an artifact that comes from their own familiar. It has to be found or freely given from another. You all really should learn your history! Aurora chuckled in all of their minds.

"Well, then, I think we're at a loss. Magical creatures stay away from Evansshire," Jonal replied.

Well then. It's a good thing we will be leaving Evansshire soon. Maybe the elves and fairies who live in Threndy will know where you can find something.

"Will we be going through Threndy?" Keelan asked, looking up from the wand in his hand.

Jonal nodded, "We should reach it by mid-morning. Hopefully, the sentries let us through."

As it turned out, all the sentry trees they passed were empty. Jonal said nothing, but the boys could tell he was worried.

They rode their horses as quickly as they could through the heavy underbrush. Soon, the forest thinned, and they came upon the remains of a village. A few homes were still visible, with a charred wall or two still standing.

In the center square, the remnants of a small building—the only building that had not burned—were still present. Jonal and the boys approached the village cautiously.

"Stay mounted and stay alert," Jonal said while he dismounted. He walked closer to the collapsed building, wand held at the ready. He walked around the wreckage, pushing aside a few boards with his foot. Slowly, he bent over and picked something up.

"What did you find?" Keelan asked.

He held up a small black object. "Lance, is this what I think it is?"

Lance urged his horse forward and took the object from him. "Wyvern scale," he said.

"Are you sure? Not dragon?"

Lance shook his head, "A dragon scale, even a black one, would still shimmer and sparkle and be warm to the touch. Wyvern scales are dark, cold, and dead-looking."

"How long will a dragon scale live?" Jonal asked.

"My father still has one from his great, great-grandfather, and it's still vibrant."

"Wait, what? Dragon scales are living?"

"Not truly alive, my boy. But the magic within the dragon is also in their scales. Long ago, people would try to steal and use scales."

"Use them how?" Keelan asked.

"They thought that they could be used to heal or use them as an artifact, which they can't."

"Wyvern scales are different?"

Lance nodded, "Wyverns are still magical, but they have less magic. They can't transform into a human, for one."

"Do you think a dragon scale would work as a natural artifact for me?" Keelan asked.

Jonal opened his mouth but then closed it, "I don't know."

Keelan and Jonal both glanced over at Lance and raised their eyebrows.

"What are you two looking at me for? You're not taking one of my scales. It's painful."

Keelan laughed, "I'll just keep looking for a unicorn horn or griffin talon, then."

"When do you think this happened?" Lance asked, gesturing around them.

Jonal closed his eyes. A gray mist poured out of his wand. Suddenly, the building was intact, and a black wyvern was perched on top; everything was in shades of gray. The wyvern was moving his mouth like he was speaking, but no sound could be heard.

"What's he saying?" Keelan asked.

"Unfortunately, I don't know the spell for sound. I can only replay what visually happened."

Keelan closed his eyes and concentrated on Jonal's magic. Absentmindedly, he placed his hand in his pocket and ran his fingers across the strange pottery shard he found at Lance's line shack. Jonal's spell abruptly ended. Jonal shook his wand, frowning at it.

With a flash of light, the image reappeared in vibrant color. The wyvern roared, causing all three men to jump and look around.

"How did you do that?" Lance asked.

"I don't know," Keelan said.

"Do you think you can find the point in time when the wyvern first appeared?" Jonal asked him.

Keelan shrugged, closing his eyes, his hand still wrapped around the pottery shard. The image flashed; trolls and an ogre were rounding everyone up next to the central hut. The wyvern roared overhead. An ogre loomed over a small group of elves with his club raised high.

The wyvern crashed through the canopy with a roar, landing next to the villagers. The elves screamed and huddled closer together. The wyvern slowly stalked closer to his terrified captives.

He snaked his lethal neck from side to side, hissing. "Where is she? Where's the human?" The wyvern was challenging to understand as he hissed the *s's* and slurred his speech. His snake-like tongue flicked back and forth.

"What human? No humans live in this village," one of the elders said.

"Don't lie to me. I can smell her," he hissed.

"Honest, we don't know any humans. Their closest settlement is Verndale. It's that way," the elder pointed.

The wyvern growled, swinging his tail around, and stabbed the elder in the chest with his long tail spike. Everyone screamed as the elder slumped to the ground without a sound.

The trolls arrived, pushing a few more survivors into the huddled group.

The wyvern growled and barked at them.

"This everyone alive," one troll garbled out, "all fairies and elves, no humans."

The wyvern raised his head and roared, followed by sparks and a bolt of lightning. The lightning hit a tree with a deafening crack.

"Kill them all, no witnesses."

The trolls and the ogre grinned menacingly, readying their weapons.

Thunk, thunk, thunk, the rapid firing of three arrows felled the ogre where he stood. The trolls whirled around, looking for the attacker.

Two men strode into the village, one with a bow and an arrow notched, pointed at the closest troll, and the other held his hands in front of him. Both hands glowed bright blue.

"I don't think we will let you kill anyone else today," the one with the bow said.

"This doesn't concern you. Leave now, and you may live," the wyvern barked, a puff of smoke escaping his mouth.

"The Order of the Chosen begs to differ. We are making this our business, and you may not leave," the magic wielder said. He thrust both hands at one of the trolls, uttering a primal scream; blue lightning streaked from his hands, striking squarely into the troll's chest. The troll grunted at the impact and was thrust backward; it hit a tree with a sickening crunch. The man with the bow fired three arrows in quick succession into the other troll. Two in the chest, the third struck it in the eye. The troll crumbled to the ground with a startled grunt.

Both men turned to face the wyvern, bow and glowing hands ready. The wyvern looked at its three companions and then at the two warriors walking purposefully toward it. It hissed and growled one last time before springing into the air. Both men let their weapons fly. One arrow bounced ineffectively off the black scaly hide, and the wyvern dodged the lightning bolt that careened for its head.

"Damn it. It got away. I knew we should have attacked it first."

"That would have been too dangerous. Come on, we have work to do."

The two men helped the remaining villagers to their feet and then led them back to the village.

Keelan stared in awe at the image playing out in front of them. The villagers returned to their homes and lit numerous sentry fires around the village.

The phantom replay darkened as the village descended into evening. Keelan concentrated on the image and thought, *Speed up, find more action.* The image blurred for a moment and then slowed again. Soon, four people entered the village. He focused his attention on the foursome. It looked like three elves and a fairy. The taller female elf turned her face toward his vantage point. His breath caught, "Shaylee?" he asked out loud.

"Who? You know that elf?" Jonal asked.

"She's beautiful," Lance said, approaching her apparition.

"She's not an elf; she's an Elvenfae. I met her in Verndale on my first trip to Kingston."

"An elvenfae, you say? Half elf, half fairy?" Lance questioned.

Keelan nodded.

"Interesting, I've never heard of that cross surviving infancy."

"Really?"

"Something about the magics not aligning or something. She's definitely one of a kind."

Keelan closed his eyes again, and the image blurred as he sped through time. He slowed the image when he saw everyone fleeing into the woods. The wyvern had returned. It landed on top of the central hut. His back talons sank deeply into the sod roof with a loud crunch as the rafters were snapped in half.

The wyvern stretched his bat-like wings out wide and lifted his beak-like snout to the sky. When he opened his mouth to roar, lightning bolts shot into the heavens.

When the wyvern inhaled finally, he lowered his head and looked around at the deserted village.

"RUNNING AND HIDING LIKE THE MICE YOU ARE," he yelled in slurring speech. "WHERE ARE YOUR SAVIORS NOW?" He paused, waiting for an answer that never came; slowly, a sneer crossed his scaly face. He opened his mouth wide, so wide it looked like he unhinged his jaw like a gigantic python. An inferno came spewing from his mouth this time. He drenched every building on the ground with a thick green foam that quickly ignited in flames.

The fire burned bright green and made quick work of the elven houses and licked at the trees surrounding the village.

When the wyvern finally closed its maw, most of the houses were nothing but piles of ash. He looked around the village again and emitted a strange sound that sounded somewhere between a laugh and a struggling cough. When he was confident nothing moved, he jumped off the council hut, smashing his spiked tail into it three times until it collapsed in a heap. He made a slow circle through the village before leaping into the air and flying north. Shaylee was the first to emerge from their hiding place, with two elven men following quickly behind her.

"She's fearless to venture out first," Lance said, his gaze fixated on her.

Keelan let the image fade after the villagers regrouped and left the ruined village.

"Tell me, my boy, what did you do just before that image appeared."

"I just concentrated on what you were doing and thought about how much I wanted to know what was being said."

"What else were you doing?" Jonal asked.

"What do you mean?"

"Were you muttering anything? Were you running your hand across a sapphire?" Jonal pressed.

Keelan's eyes opened wide. "Not a sapphire, a bronze pottery shard I found."

"A pottery shard?" Lance questioned.

Keelan pulled it from his pocket and held it in the palm of his hand. Lance looked at it first.

"That's not a pottery shard. That's one of Cedric's scales."

"Your uncle?"

Lance nodded. "Looks like we found your artifact."

"Great, let's camp here. We will be out of Evansshire by the end of the day tomorrow," Jonal said.

Crossing the imaginary boundary of Evansshire didn't prove to be as exciting as Keelan had hoped. He didn't know exactly what he thought would happen, but fanciful images of phoenixes and dragons flying through the air raced through his mind.

A week later, they reached the Brisbin Ocean. Keelan stared in amazement, watching the waves crash against the rocks below. An enormous cliff separated the forest from the deep blue water.

"Let's make an early camp tonight. I need to look at my map again."

"Okay, Jonal. We're going to see if we can find something for dinner."

"Don't wander too far."

Keelan and Lance returned quickly with four rabbits.

"Have you ever seen the ocean before?" Keelan asked his companions. Jonal shook his head, but Lance nodded.

"Once, a long time ago. My mother brought Ashera and me here when we were really little."

"You've never spoken about your mother," Keelan said.

"I know."

"Who's Ashera?"

"My sister."

"Wow, you have a sister? Where is she?"

"I don't know. She was stolen one night. My mother went after the abductor. We never saw them again."

"Oh, I'm so sorry, Lance."

He nodded his head.

Jonal looked up from his map, having heard none of Lance's story. "We're close, boys. Three more days, and we should reach the valley of the Griffins."

"How are we supposed to get up that?" Keelan said, looking at the impossible-looking mountain in front of them. They found themselves at the base of a mountain that appeared to have been shaped by the wind. The ground rose sharply before them, sweeping in a massive wave formation.

"Can we go around?" Lance asked.

"No, afraid not. The map says you must enter from here or be denied entry."

"Well, there's no way the horses can make that climb. I'm sure Lance and I could make it on foot, but it will take a week, maybe more. Do you think you could make it, Jonal?"

"Twenty years ago," he replied.

"There's only one way to go from here," Lance said.

Jonal and Keelan looked at Lance, waiting for his suggestion.

"We will have to leave the horses here. Rogue and Trotter will handle what's coming, but I'm unsure how your horse will react."

"What are you planning on doing?" Jonal asked, raising one eyebrow.

"I'm going to fly us to the valley. I'm sure a species of flyers limiting access to their valley will only respect another flyer."

Oh, I'm sure you're right, Aurora projected.

Jonal's face went ashen. "I can stay with the horses," he offered.

"No, we stick together. And besides, I'm sure your knowledge will be needed."

"H-how," Jonal stuttered, then cleared his throat before continuing. "How do you plan on carrying us?"

"In my claws," Lance said with a mischievous smile, opening and closing his hands.

Jonal's face went even whiter.

"I'm kidding, Jonal. You should see the look on your face," Lance almost fell off his horse laughing.

Aurora swooped down, landing on Lance's horse's rump. *That would be a sight to see,* she projected.

"You will ride on my back, just like a horse. Come on, let's find a safe place for the horses."

"Have you seen a dragon transform before?" Keelan asked Jonal.

"No, never met one before Lance. I must admit I am looking forward to seeing it."

Lance stepped into the middle of the field. A mist of blue and black swirled around him until he was shrouded in the cloud. The misty cloud grew and grew and then slowly dispersed. In Lance's place was a large dragon, almost three times as large as their horses. He shook his great body and stretched out his wings.

"Now that was a sight to see," Jonal chuckled. "And to think you were a mere human just moments ago."

I was still a dragon, just in a compressed state. Our strength, speed, and stamina are still greater than any human.

"I can attest to that. I thought I was weak and slow until I discovered the truth," Keelan said.

Lance lay on his belly. "Okay, mount up, you two."

"Um, so, how do we do this?" Keelan asked.

I'm not really sure. I've never carried anyone before.

"Now he tells us," Jonal grumbled.

Keelan walked up and looked at Lance's back above his head. He placed his hands on Lance's side and a foot on his leg. "Is this going to be okay?"

"Go on," Lance urged.

Keelan pushed off the ground and scrambled up Lance's side using his scales and spines. Once standing on his back, Keelan looked around. Lance had long spikes that ran from his head down his neck but thankfully ended just before his shoulder blades.

Keelan sat down astride Lance's back in front of his wings. "Your turn, Jonal."

Jonal eyes opened wide as he looked up at Keelan. "I'm not as young as I once was. I don't think this is going to work."

Keelan closed his eyes briefly and then raised his hand out toward Jonal.

A surprised yelp came from Jonal as he was lifted off the ground and floated onto Lance's back behind Keelan. Jonal held his hands out wide, trying to steady himself. Once seated, he glared at Keelan.

"Next time, my boy, a little warning, please."

"You got it. Lance, let's go get my ma's cure."

CHAPTER

-8-

LANCE jumped straight up, pumping his wings to gain altitude. Jonal screamed, wrapping his arms around Keelan. Keelan frantically grabbed onto the spines before him to avoid being pulled off by Jonal's weight.

"A little less steep, please," Keelan yelled at Lance. "We don't have a saddle back here."

Sorry, Lance projected as he leveled off, beating his wings slowly. *I told you I never carried anyone before.*

"Well, if this becomes a habit, we must look into a saddle or something."

A laugh rumbled and vibrated through Lance's body.

The windswept mountain loomed up ahead. As Keelan looked at the terrain below, he was immediately relieved they decided not to walk.

You look good in the sky, Aurora projected, flying beside him. *We need to do this more.*

I must admit, I thought I would be terrified, but this is great.

How are you two holding up? Lance asked.

"Don't ask," Jonal yelled. "Just get us back on the ground."

"This is great, Lance. I wish I had wings," Keelan shouted. He removed his hands from Lance's spines. After a moment, he stretched his arms out wide. He smiled as the wind whipped through his hair and tugged on his cloak. He threw his head back and howled. His eyes blurred from the wind, causing a stream of tears to streak across his face. He wiped at his eyes to clear them, his smile plastered on his face. His shirt billowed and rippled in the fierce wind like a flag.

"Oh, good gods in Ombrasia, save me from reckless boys," Jonal tightened his hold, burying his face into the howling boy's back.

Lance continued his slow climb up and over the mountain. The top was barren of vegetation. The rock face was sharp and jagged, with deep cracks and scars from hundreds of years of snow, rain, and wind.

The air grew colder and thinner the higher they climbed. Soon, Keelan and Jonal were gasping for breath as they huddled down low on Lance's back, trying to keep the wind out of their faces and lungs. Keelan felt Jonal's grip loosen slightly and then felt him sliding off Lance's back. He grabbed one of Jonal's wrists and forearms to keep him seated.

"Jonal, are you okay?" he called back to him.

He didn't answer. "Lance! Is Jonal okay?"

He's still breathing, but it's thin and labored. I think he passed out. Hold on. I'll get us down as quickly as possible.

Lance banked his wings slightly as he crested the top of the mountain. A large valley spread out before them. Smaller but still imposing mountains and cliffs circled the valley, making it look almost like a large nest. A thick forest covered the valley floor with a large lake in the middle. A rock formation stood in the middle of the lake. From their vantage point, it almost looked like a castle.

They started to make a slow descent into the valley.

Incoming!! Aurora screeched.

Five enormous, terrifying-looking creatures flew straight for them. With the heads, wings, and front legs of a giant eagle and a lion's body and rear legs, the creatures were a sight Keelan had never even imagined he would see.

Leave Griffin's Keep NOW! one of the griffins screamed into their minds.

Please, I need to land. One of the humans passed out, Lance projected to the griffin in the front of the V-formation. This one appeared to be the leader, as it was the only one wearing chest armor.

Why is a dragon allowing humans to ride it like an animal of burden? The lead griffin asked.

These are my friends. We need to speak to your king. Please allow me to land, Lance replied.

The griffins circled Lance from all sides and from below. They were forcing him to crash into them or fly higher.

Aurora's wings and tail ignited as she flew in between the griffins, blinding them briefly. She turned her attention to the lead griffin and flared her flames. *We mean you no harm, Commander Eagle-cat!* She yelled at him.

The lead griffin pawed the air in front of him, *Your embers will not harm me, phoenix. And my name is not Eagle-cat. I am RockWing.* He squawked loudly.

Growing frustrated, Keelan's hands started to warm. *No,* he told himself, *violence will not get us the firebush.* He then focused his thoughts on the griffins. *Please, great griffins. I need to speak to your king; my mother needs his help,* Keelan projected.

The griffin wearing armor positioned himself in front of Lance, forcing Lance to hover in place. *How did you project to us, human?*

Keelan shrugged his shoulders. *I don't know. I project to Aurora all the time. I just thought about speaking to you, and it worked.*

Follow me. The griffin spun around and flew toward the rock castle in the middle of the lake.

How did you do that? Lance asked.

"I don't know, Lance. I didn't know that was something that couldn't be done."

Magical creatures can project to any being that has magic. But humans, elves, and fairies can only hear us. They can't talk to us.

That seems strange to me. Elves, fairies, and magical humans are magical creatures, aren't we? he projected to his friend.

I'm not a magical scholar. That question will have to wait.

As they neared the rock formation, the shape of it became evident. It was a castle carved out of a monolithic rock spire. The bottom twenty or thirty feet of the structure was left natural rock. Numerous windows lined the following four stories. The griffin led them to a large door on the bottom level with a large landing platform in front. Lance followed the griffin's lead and landed on the rock slab. As soon as all four of his feet were down, Keelan turned around to look at Jonal. He was still out cold. Using his magic, he lowered Jonal and then himself to the ground. Keelan took his waterskin out and splashed Jonal's face.

Jonal's eyes fluttered open, and he bolted upright. "Where are we? Are we alive?"

"We're fine. The griffins have brought us to their castle."

This is Griffin's Keep. Chief Stormwing will see you shortly. Stay here. The griffins left them standing alone on the rock ledge.

Jonal accepted the waterskin from Keelan, drinking deeply. It was a few minutes later before he trusted his feet to stand.

The sun started to set before the griffin returned. *Follow me. Dragon, you will not fit inside.*

Lance nodded his head seconds before he was covered in swirling mist. When three humans stood on the platform, the griffin turned and led them inside.

The entire Keep was carved out of a single rock. The walls were still rough to the touch, but the floors were polished and smooth. The windows were just openings cut in the walls with no glass or coverings.

"I bet it gets cold here during the winter," Keelan remarked.

The griffin swiveled his head. *Too cold for you, maybe.*

Keelan chuckled but didn't comment.

They were led down the large corridor, almost big enough for Lance to fit through in dragon form, but it would have been tight.

At the end of the corridor, two floor-to-ceiling doors were already open for them. When they entered, the sight was amazing. The colossal room might be better off being called a cavern. The room was circular and larger than the courtyard in Kingston. The ceiling couldn't be seen. Along the walls were platforms that circled the room, eight to ten separate platforms per level. Each platform held two or three griffins. Keelan stretched his neck, trying to count how many levels of platforms he could see; he stopped counting at eight because he couldn't see into the darkness. The lower four levels had floating orbs of light spaced out, providing the only light in the cavern.

A golden griffin was in front of them, on a high pedestal that was level with the first platform. His feathers almost seemed to sparkle. He glared down his hooked beak as he watched them enter his chamber. To the platform's right, another set of double doors stood open. A group of six griffins and two humans walked in. The five humans shared confused looks before their attention was returned to the griffins of Griffin's Keep. Chief Stormwing screeched and growled, rearing up on his lion haunches, pawing the air with his taloned front feet. The chamber erupted into roars as the rest of the Keep joined their leader. The six griffins on the ground bowed low, the two humans with them mirroring them. Keelan and Lance looked at Jonal.

"Better bow, boys," Jonal said.

When the noise stopped, a loud voice ripped through their minds. *RISE! Welcome to my Keep. Why are you here?* His gaze settled on the griffins before him.

One griffin stepped forward.

Aloud for all to hear, Chief Stormwing projected.

Yes, Chief Stormwing, the griffin projected. *We are here looking for a cure for an illness affecting our elf allies.*

Step forward, elf.

One of the humans took a few steps closer and bowed. Keelan looked at him again; upon closer inspection, he could see the difference that marked him as an elf. He was tall and slender, with pointed ears and long black hair tied in a ponytail.

"Thank you, Chief Stormwing. A new illness has started attacking elves. We are linking the start of the illness with the appearance of strange bright blue birds with yellow spots. After they land near an elf, they shed feathers and pollen; the elf immediately feels weak, with no other symptoms. Just too weak to get out of bed."

"The wasting?" Jonal spoke.

All eyes swiveled to him.

He bowed, "Forgive my outburst, but what you are describing used to only affect natural magic users, never an elf. We are also seeking a cure."

Affecting males? Chief Stormwing asked.

The elf and Jonal spoke at the same time, "No."

Stormwing turned his gaze to Jonal, *Do you know of these birds?*

Jonal pursed his lips, "I saw strange blue and yellow birds being released from Kingston two years ago. But I don't know if Maya, Keelan's mother, saw them or not." Jonal looked at Keelan.

"She never mentioned birds. But the last time I saw her, I saw large bright blue and smaller yellow feathers on her bedside table."

Stormwing fell silent. He turned his head as he looked at each griffin on the first-level platform.

The minutes stretched. Finally, he returned his gaze to Jonal and the elf. *We will help you if you can pass the trials.*

"What are these trials?" the elf asked.

The trials are a rite of passage all young Keep griffins complete before being allowed to sit in this chamber.

"How will we complete this without wings ourselves?" the elf asked.

The dragon will help his two companions; we will allow the two youngest griffins to assist you.

The elf and human glanced at Keelan and Lance with eager expressions on their faces.

Our friends will show you bipeds where you will roost for the night. Food will be brought to you as well. We will speak more with the rising sun.

Two elves appeared; one approached each group.

"Follow us, please," they said at the same time.

The seven bipeds left the chamber and all the griffins behind. The enormous corridor seemed even bigger without a griffin's presence. Halfway down the hall, one of the elves opened a hidden panel in the wall. A human-sized doorway appeared.

"We do not receive many human or elf visitors; I apologize now for the lack of accommodations."

"A dry roof over our heads will suffice," Jonal replied.

"We can do slightly better than that," the other elf said with a chuckle.

They led them down the much smaller hallway that seemed to spiral deep into the Keep.

The passage opened into a large circular room. The walls were lined with beds and curtain dividers.

"We don't have separate living spaces here. We hope you don't mind. We can give you these beds over here during your visit." He led them to the far side of the room. Eight beds were pushed relatively close to each other and appeared to have not been used in quite some time.

"Do you live here all the time?" the human asked.

"Our families have lived here for generations. Some leave, and sometimes they return later in life with their families. It's a harmonious life. We assist the griffins with tasks they cannot do on their own, and in turn, we have safety and plenty to eat."

"It is a life of choice, is it not?" the elf asked them.

"Yes, of course. We are not forced to stay here, fear not. Dinner will be ready soon. You may join us or dine here. Your choice." The elves bowed and departed.

"I think introductions are in order," Jonal said. He held out his hand, "My name is Wizard Jonal Bertelsen."

The human approached and accepted his hand, "I am Sorcerer Leo'venath Spencer; this is Tarrid Norrell."

"Greetings, Leo'venath and Tarrid."

"This is Sorcerer Keelan Keifman and Dragon Lancet Firestorm."

"Firestorm?" Tarrid asked. "You wouldn't be related to General Douglas Firestorm by any chance?"

"He's my father. How do you know him?"

"I only know of him. I've never had the honor of meeting him. I was once a warrior for The Chosen. Your father was a member once, long ago. One of the few dragons to grace our ranks."

"He didn't leave The Chosen when you think he did."

"What do you mean?"

"He changed his name long before I was born. Your members would probably remember a Douglas Firestrum."

"I'm not familiar with that name."

"Not surprising, he tried to lay low. After my mother's disappearance, we went into hiding and became humans."

"Tough life, I imagine."

Lance nodded.

"You're not a member of The Chosen anymore?" Jonal asked.

"It's a long story," Leo'venath said.

"Are the Circle of Illumination still fighting?"

"If you mean fighting amongst themselves, then yes."

"Oh," Jonal's face fell. "I've always dreamed of being inducted into their ranks."

"Aren't they all sorcerers?" Tarrid asked.

Leo'venath shook his head, "Most are, but a few wizards have been welcomed over the years. I can shed some light on their current situation, though. I grew up in Evansshire, hiding my magic. I grew angry and tired, so I left. I came across Tarrid…"

"Rescued by me, you mean."

"Yes, Tarrid saved me from being eaten. And he'll never let me forget it," he chuckled. "Anyway, I joined The Chosen. The Circle approached me and tried to recruit me. I quickly learned there are two factions now. The Circle of Illumination that you have heard of fighting against the Wyverns and helping the people. And The Shadow of Illumination…"

"The Shadow? That doesn't sound friendly," Lance said.

"For the most part, I guess they're okay. They are fighting against the Wyverns and helping those they want to."

"What's the difference?" Keelan asked.

"They don't want The Prophecy to be fulfilled," Leo'venath said.

"More like they found their own prophecy to follow," Tarrid interjected.

"There's another prophecy?" Keelan's eyes opened wide.

"Right after Seer Eldjren announced the Twins Prophecy, two sisters who were also seers—some say they were twins—were overtaken with sight. They both foresaw two paths that could happen. The Circle follows one, and the Shadow follows the other."

"Do you know what these prophecies say?" Jonal asked.

"Unfortunately, no," Leo'venath said.

They were interrupted when a small group of elflings brought them food and drinks. They ate in silence, all deep in thought. Keelan was the first to break the silence.

"Do we have any idea what these trials will be tomorrow?"

Everyone shook their heads.

"I guess we'll find out in the morning. Get some rest, boys; I think we'll need it," Jonal said.

CHAPTER

-9-

THE predawn light glowed pink and orange in the sky, but the sun had yet to crest the jagged mountaintops. Three humans, an elf, a dragon, and two griffins stood waiting beside a large boulder at the shore of the lake next to the Keep, just as the sun started to brighten the sky. A Keep elf instructed them to wait, and wait, they did, for almost three hours. The griffin's of the Keep joined them when the sun finally peaked over the mountains. Hundreds flew out of the Keep, filling the sky. It looked like every griffin was coming to watch the trials. Some of the griffins were old and had grey feathers; others were obviously warriors, complete with battle armor on their chests, flanks, and talons. Still, others looked to be the average griffin, with softer features and well-kept feathers. That group kept an eye on the young—miniature versions of the adults, cute but no less deadly. Stormwing was the last to arrive, circling above those gathered below before landing softly on the boulder.

Welcome to the Firebush Trials, he projected to everyone. *Today, you will be witnessing a rare event. Today, those you see below me will run our trials. If they succeed, they will be given some of our precious firebush to help their people. Tarrid and Leo'venath will have the assistance of the two youngest griffins who brought them here: Blackfeather and Suncloud.*

Roars erupted around the valley as the first group was introduced.

Jonal and Keelan will have the assistance of their dragon friend, Lancet.

Another round of roars shook the valley. Lance took that as his cue to change into his dragon form. Tarrid and Leo'venath approached their griffins and strapped themselves to what appeared to be a saddle. Lance watched with rapt attention.

We need to build something like that, he projected to Keelan.

I was thinking the same thing, Keelan projected back.

There are three tasks for you to complete. For the first test, you will fly two complete circles around the tops of our mountains. The thin air is the challenge to overcome. The second test will be a strength test. You will be expected to cling to the side of Beak Mount until we say drop. You will then perform a free-fall until we say soar; then, you will not collide with the ground—you will soar back into the sky. The final test is an endurance test. You will follow one of our warriors through our forest course. Dragon, you may find it the most challenging; some parts might be a tight fit.

Lance nodded. *Thank you, Chief Stormwing. I will do my best.*

Each group must have everyone complete the course in order for that group to pass. It's not a race but a test of skill, endurance, and desire. Jonal and Keelan, please take your positions, Chief Stormwing said, snapping his wings out wide.

From somewhere within the crowd, a griffin roared.

Speak if you must, Stormwing projected, sounding annoyed, ruffling his wings to lay them down again.

I shall speak. You are not treating our guests equally.

A young griffin with brown and gold feathers flew forward, landing next to Lance.

What do you mean I am not treating them equally, Stormbreaker? Asked Stormwing.

You have always mistrusted dragons, Father. Making him carry two humans through the trials is setting him up for failure, and you know it. The young griffin glared at his chief.

I am doing no such thing. They should have come prepared. Only bringing one flyer with two riders is their fault.

Truly, Father. That's how it's to be?

Watch yourself, Stormbreaker. The griffin chief glared at the smaller griffin.

I will not let you disrespect the first dragon to grace our valley in over forty years. I will carry one of the humans, and we will fit the dragon with a saddle.

You dare to tell me what will be done. I am your father and your Chief.

I only speak out when I see an injustice being done.

They glared at each other for a few moments until Stormbreaker turned to face Lance. He bowed deeply until his beak touched the ground. *Forgive my Father, my Chief. Will you allow me to carry one of your friends?*

It's up to them, Lance said, bowing his head.

Jonal looked at Keelan. "I'd prefer to stay with Lance if you don't mind."

"That's fine." Keelan walked toward Stormbreaker. *I am honored by your offer. Thank you.*

Stormbreaker's eyes almost bulged out of his head. *I heard that you could project, but didn't believe it.* He moved his eyes back to Lance. *A saddle is being brought for you.*

Several Keep elves ran toward them, hauling a hand cart behind them.

"We got here as quickly as we could. Sir Dragon, if you will allow us to, we will fit you with a griffin saddle. I think we can make it big enough."

Two elves pulled out two sloped saddles and placed them on the ground. Another elf grabbed thinner straps and approached Jonal and Keelan.

"These are for you, Sir Wizard, and for you, Sir Sorcerer."

Jonal and Keelan quickly placed the belts around their waists and tightened the chest straps.

When they were finished, Keelan glanced back to Lance; the straps would be too small.

One of the elves broke down in tears. "I'm sorry, but these are just too small, and strapping more together would not be safe," she sniffled.

I have an idea, Lance said. He closed his eyes. Blue and black mist obscured him from sight, causing the elves to jump back quickly. When the fog cleared, Lance in dragon form stood before them, but he was half the size. He was now only slightly bigger than an average griffin.

"How did you do that?" Keelan asked.

Lance shrugged, causing his wings to unfold slightly. *I used to be this size. I just thought about transforming to only this big. I wasn't sure if it would work.*

"Do you think you could go smaller?" Jonal asked him.

"I suppose, but why?"

Jonal shrugged. "Never know when a pint-sized dragon might become useful."

While they spoke, the two elves attached all the saddle parts and straps to Lance and Stormbreaker. Tarrid and Leo'venath mounted their rides and connected their straps to their griffin's saddle. Jonal and Keelan followed suit.

Now that everyone is ready, Stormwing projected loudly. *Let the trial begin.* Stormwing launched into the sky, followed closely by three griffins and the dragon.

Stormwing flew high in the sky, circling as he ascended. *From here, you will fly along the tops of our mountains, flying no lower than this altitude. Two complete trips around and then meet back here.*

"Sounds easy enough," Leo'venath said.

Don't speak too soon, human, Stormwing said. *We don't usually give warnings about this test because all those who fly it have seen it completed. As you are new to this, I think it is only fair. We are not alone in these mountains. After your first pass by their territory, they will be looking for you. Keep your wits about you.*

"What are we keeping a lookout for?" Tarrid asked.

Begin!! Stormwing shouted in their minds.

Keelan patted Stormbreaker on the neck as they sped through the sky. *Riding a griffin wasn't much different than riding a horse,* Keelan mused, well, except that he was flying above mountaintops, his knees were next to his chest, and he was leaning forward with his hands stretched toward the griffin's head.

Stormbreaker and Lance flew side by side. Tarrid and Leo'venath flew directly behind them. Aurora flew up above them all, scanning the mountaintops for danger.

So, what are we keeping an eye out for? Keelan asked Stormbreaker.

I wish I could tell you that, unfortunately, I have never watched the trials before.

How is that possible? Your father made it sound like every griffin watched the trials growing up.

Every one of them except me. I am the runt of the clutch. I don't know how much you know about griffins.

Absolutely nothing.

Griffinesses have a clutch of three to five eggs once or twice in their lifetime. My mother had three clutches, very rare. There were six eggs in the last, which is also rare. All six of us hatched. I was the sixth and half the size of my siblings. I was the only one that survived to leave the nest. As each of my siblings died, I grew stronger. My father thought I was a demon, but thankfully, my mother knew it was not my doing. But even now, I am still smaller than the average griffiness.

Well, you're still bigger than my horse. Keelan laughed aloud.

I'm not sure if that's a compliment or not. But because of my father's dislike for me from birth, I will never be allowed to run the Trials and earn a place of honor in the council chamber.

I'm sorry about that. I'm glad you were able to assist us and give you a chance to run the trials, even though it'll not lead to your goal.

We are starting our second run, Stormbreaker said.

Aurora, have you spotted anything yet? Keelan asked her.

Nothing out of the ordinary that could harm a griffin or dragon.

"We are starting our second lap. Keep your eyes peeled," Keelan yelled.

Tarrid, Leo'venath, and Jonal waved.

They flew past the starting point, where several griffins flew in lazy circles, watching them pass.

Are you sure there's anything dangerous on this mountain? Lance projected to everyone.

Keelan looked around, straining his neck to look above them to see if anything was hiding in the clouds. He then turned his gaze to the ground. A deep canyon sliced through one of the mountains they were passing. *What kind of birds are those?* he asked, patting Stormbreaker on the shoulder.

Stormbreaker banked his wings slightly to get a better look at the canyon. *I'm not sure,* he replied. *I don't think we have anything to worry about. They're just birds.*

But there's a lot of them, Keelan said, a little worried.

The birds continued flying straight for them. Stormbreaker continued watching the enormous flock of birds as they got closer and closer. Suddenly, Keelan was thrust forward. He wrapped his arms around Stormbreaker's neck as the griffin reared up and almost stopped in mid-flight.

Those aren't birds. Those are harpies. Everybody quickly, we must get out of here, Stormbreaker projected to everyone.

What's a harpy? Keelan asked.

A monstrosity. Stormbreaker pumped his wings, flying faster, but the distance between the harpies and themselves was diminishing.

Keelan pressed himself down, trying to keep out of the wind. He looked behind him as the first individual harpy came into view. They looked like enormous vultures but had the chest and head of a human female. *How is that creature even possible?*

The closest harpy let out an ear-shattering screech. "How dare you violate the truce! These are our sacred grounds; no griffin shall pass over our nests. Stormwing shall hear of this, you filthy vermin. Land and explain yourselves or face the consequences."

"We mean you no harm. Please just let us leave, and we will be on our way," Keelan pleaded with her.

"I said land or face the consequences," she screeched.

What do you think, Stormbreaker?

I think we better do what she says. There are just way too many of them for us to try to fight off.

Keelan, I can take them! Harpies are no problem for a phoenix, Aurora boasted.

Keelan glanced at his familiar keeping pace with Stormbreaker and shook his head. *No, I don't think that would be wise, but thank you, Aurora.* Without thinking of what he was about to do, Keelan projected to everyone in his group. *I feel we should land and try to resolve this peacefully.*

Tarrid and Leo'venath stared in shock but nodded and instructed their griffins to follow Stormbreaker to the ground.

They found a break in the trees large enough for them to land. Keelan started unbuckling himself from his saddle.

"Hold up there," Jonal said. "Everyone stay mounted until we figure out if we're going to make it out of this or not."

Everyone nodded grimly. Soon, the sky grew dark as all the harpies circled above their heads. Slowly, in groups of two or three, they landed in the trees surrounding the clearing. The harpy that had spoken earlier landed on the ground.

She stood before them, ruffling her feathers and glaring at them. Measuring about three feet tall from the top of her head, she had greasy blackish-brown feathers on her body with pure white feathers on her chest and long, razor-sharp talons but a pleasing human facial appearance, with black hair and striking green eyes.

"I am Queen Xyniphis. What gives you the right to fly over our territory outside the established trials?" she asked with her chin held high.

Stormbreaker bowed, which was difficult with a person sitting on his back. Keelan scrambled to stay mounted. ***Please forgive us, oh Queen of the harpies,*** Stormbreaker projected. ***I am Stormbreaker— the youngest of Stormwing's cubs.***

"Then you, of all griffins, should know the error of what you were doing." She stretched her wings out and fanned her tail.

If you will, please let us explain. I think everything will become quite clear.

"Proceed," she said, clearly annoyed.

The group traveling with me is on a quest to obtain firebush to heal a mysterious illness affecting their people. My father told them that if they could pass our trials, he would give them the item they sought.

The queen's eyes widened. "He would do such a thing and break our truce? And you did not know you'd be breaking the truce, young griffin?"

Even though I am a Storm cub, I have never been allowed to participate or watch the Trials. As a runt, I will never be given that honor, he bowed his head in shame.

Xyniphis scowled in thought. "Many years ago, after much bloodshed, a truce was struck, allowing harpies and griffins to live in this valley. We have sport, your Trials, and our Rights of Wing each year. We engage in competition to hone each other's skills without loss of life. But if we ever cross paths outside that time of year, the trespasser is free game." She paused and looked at the group before her. "I see two griffins not from this valley; you may go. You, Stormbreaker, are free to go. I see one elf; you are free to go. I see a dragon; you are free to go. But the three humans, you will stay."

"Wait! What?" the three humans said simultaneously.

"Look around you," she commanded sharply.

Everyone swiveled their heads. Every harpy smiled at them; some almost appeared to be leering.

"Do you see any men in our ranks? We are a cursed species; we're all female. You three will stay. We require you."

"Forgive me, Queen Xyniphis. But we will not do," Leo'venath said boldly.

"You are human, are you not?" Leo'venath nodded. "Then you are what we need. We haven't seen a human in many years, so have had no new clutches hatch."

"What? You need us so you can have babies?" Keelan asked, a horrified dread squeezing his lungs.

No strange bird-human creature is detaining my sorcerer! Aurora screeched, landing beside Stormbreaker.

The harpy queen ignored Aurora's statement, her eyes locked with Keelan's. "Yes, we need a human man to couple with, and then we can start raising the next generation. Don't worry, fifteen to twenty each should do nicely, and then you can be on your way."

"Unless they want to stay," a harpy screamed. All the harpies broke into laughter.

"Again, I'm sorry. But we will not do," Leo'venath repeated. "You see, we are all sorcerers."

"Sorcerers? I have seen no magic. When we first started to chase you, why didn't you attack and defend yourselves?"

"We mean you no harm. We wanted a peaceful outcome." Leo'venath produced a sun-orb in his hand and nodded to Jonal and Keelan to do the same. Keelan instantly materialized a sun-orb to match Leo'venath's. Jonal did so as well but kept his wand hidden from sight.

"Then you shall go with the others," Queen Xyniphis said sadly. "Magicborns will produce a tortured soul."

Over half of the gathered harpies started to weep.

Keelan dismounted and approached the queen. He pulled out four petite sapphires from his pocket and clutched his hands tightly around them. He knelt in front of Queen Xyniphis, staring intensely into her eyes. His hands glowed bright white, slowly changing to red and softening to pink.

When he uncurled his fingers, the blue sapphires had red veins sliced through them.

"What are these?" the queen asked, taking a couple of steps closer.

"I'm not sure what to call them or if they will work, but here," he held one out for her to take.

Aurora hopped along the ground until she was next to Keelan and studied the sapphires as intently as the harpy queen.

The queen reached a taloned foot forward, hesitating briefly before carefully picking up the tiny stone. Instantly, the gem flared bright red, engulfing her and shrouding her in light. Her flock panicked and started to advance as one.

"Hold!" the queen screeched. The light faded, and a harpy no longer stood before them. Instead, a beautiful, petite human woman stood clothed in a gown of pure white feathers where the harpy once stood.

"How did you do this?" she asked as she inspected her body and clothing.

"Our beautiful queen! What have you done to her? You shall pay for this," a harpy screamed. More cries rose, and angry harpies once again advanced.

"I said hold!" she glared at her flock. "I am unharmed. Is this real?" she asked Keelan.

"I'm not sure. May I touch your arm?"

She held her hand out toward him. He touched her fingers and arm gently. "It feels like flesh, not feathers. May I see the sapphire, please." He turned his palm upward.

She placed the stone in his hand. A flash of light caused everyone to close their eyes, and then the woman was gone, and a harpy stood before Keelan again.

"Amazing. With these stones, we can become human, but why?"

Keelan shrugged, and a small smile crept on his face. "I just thought if you could appear human, you might be able to attract a mate without kidnapping."

"But we would have let you go?" a harpy yelled.

"I will keep the gems if you don't want them." Keelan turned his shoulders, pretending to leave.

"No, wait!" the queen stretched her wings out wide. "We accept them and will gladly try them."

Keelan nodded. He placed the four stones in a small bag and handed them to her. "You should make them into necklaces," he said.

"Thank you. You may leave our territory. What's your name?"

"I am Keelan Keifman." He bowed at the waist.

"Well met Keelan Keifman. If you ever need assistance, harpies are now your friends." She tipped her head slightly and leaped into the air, clutching the bag of sapphires tightly in her taloned foot.

"How did you do that?" Leo'venath asked.

"Like I said, I'm not sure. Jonal used an illusion on Lance and me once. I just thought about making it a bit more real and tried it."

"Who are you? I've never seen anyone use conceptual magic before. I've only read about it."

"You're wrong, Leo. We've heard of another one. We've just never seen her do it."

Leo'venath froze and nodded, "You don't think?" he asked without finishing the question.

"I don't know what to think," Tarrid replied.

"I've heard of conceptual magic," Jonal said. "I thought it was a mere legend."

"Until now, I did as well," Tarrid agreed.

Shall we continue? Stormbreaker interrupted.

Back to the sky, boys. We are burning daylight! Aurora chuckled and took to the sky.

I agree. Task one is complete, I believe. What was task two again? Lance projected.

A strength test, Stormbreaker replied.

CHAPTER

-10-

OUR *son returns,* a griffiness projected.

Stormwing sighed with relief. Even though his son was a cursed sixth runt, he was still his son. He sucked in a surprised breath as he saw the entire group returning, including the humans. Surely, the harpies wouldn't have let the two young men go. *What happened?* he thought. **Welcome back,** he projected to the Trial group. **Explain your encounter with the harpies.**

Stormbreaker approached his father, stopping within a foot of touching beaks if Stormwing was as short as him.

Queen Xyniphis confronted us as you knew she would. You almost ruined the truce, Father.

Mind your tongue. Why are the humans still here?

According to Xyniphis, Magicborns will produce a tortured soul. But you knew that, didn't you?

That matters not. Why did she allow them to leave?

Keelan gave her a gem, allowing them to take a human form to find their desired mates.

Impossible, such a stone does not exist.

It does now, Keelan projected.

Stormwing looked up at the sorcerer on his son's back, **How did you break into a private cast?**

When I want to do something, I just do it. I wish everyone would stop asking how I do things. I am told it's conceptual magic. Now, let's complete these Trials. What's next? Keelan snapped.

Stormwing narrowed his eyes, **Follow me.** He vaulted into the sky and turned toward the south side of the valley.

This is Hanging Rock, Stormwing announced.

The Rock was a large boulder that jutted away from the cliff face on the side of a volcano. The volcano was active, with a small tendril of smoke drifting into the sky. Keelan watched the smoke as it curled and floated on the gentle breeze. Cracks in the cliff leaked lava, causing the whole area to be slightly warmer than anywhere else in the valley.

You shall hang on Hanging Rock until I say to fall. At that point, you will free fall until I say soar. You will soar back into the sky without touching a feather or talon to the ground. Begin!

Everyone shared a look before finding a decent place to grab a hold of the boulder. Lance punched holes into the rock to slide his talons into. *How long do we have to hang here?* He asked.

I'm sorry. I wish I knew, Stormbreaker told him.

This shouldn't be too hard. Just pretend you're a bat, Aurora said. Everyone groaned at her attempt to lighten the mood.

"I'm so thankful for these straps," Jonal said with a whine in his voice.

"Don't tell me you're scared," Keelan said with a chuckle.

"Only a fool wouldn't be scared about hanging off a boulder, jutting off a volcano while being strapped to the back of a flying lizard."

Hey, I'm not a lizard.

"Sorry, my boy. When I'm nervous, my mouth has a mind of its own."

Don't worry. I can hang like this for hours.

"Oh, I hope we aren't up here for hours."

Everyone laughed as Jonal's knuckles went white, and his face paled to match.

I don't know how much longer I can hang on, Leo'venath's griffin projected. *My legs are starting to go numb.*

"Hang on, Suncloud, you can do it," Leo'venath told her.

No, I agree with her. I can't hold on much longer either, Stormbreaker said.

FALL! A shout slammed into their minds.

Almost as if the voice commanded their talons, all four flyers let go of the rock and started their fall.

Jonal screamed as he was pulled from Lance's back, held on only by the straps.

Keelan glanced at their Trial companions. Tarrid's eyes were slammed shut, while Leo'venath was actually smiling and seemed to be enjoying himself as much as Keelan.

Aurora fell as well, keeping pace with Keelan and Stormbreaker.

Uh, the ground is approaching quickly. I hope your father realizes that I'm bigger than any of you, and I will reach the ground first, Lance projected as loudly as he could, trying to reach the griffins on the ground. He was falling quicker than the griffins and pulling away from them.

DRAGON SOAR, GRIFFINS KEEP FALLING! Stormwing yelled.

Lance snapped his wings open and stretched his head upward, trying to elevate his chest and front legs.

GRIFFINS SOAR!

The three griffins snapped open their wings and soared back into the sky using their falling momentum.

I never want to do that again, Lance said with a growl as he joined the griffins.

LAND! came the following command.

Well done, everyone, the griffiness praised as they landed next to her and Stormwing.

Thank you, mother.

The griffiness brushed the side of her cheek against Stormbreaker's. *The next task will begin at sunset. Return to the Keep, eat, and rest.*

Stormwing vaulted into the air without a word.

Is he displeased with me?

It matters not. I am proud of you, my son.

It does matter, mother. Come. I know where we can rest. Stormbreaker remained on the ground with his wings tucked at his sides.

I will have food brought to you, the griffiness said before departing.

The sight before them looked like a page out of a fairytale. Keelan marveled at the picturesque pool in front of them. A waterfall cascaded down the volcano's walls, splashing into the body of water. Steam rose from the water, and condensation beaded on the leaves of the ferns that surrounded the pool, making them sparkle in the afternoon sun.

Moments later, five griffins circled above them.

Watch out below! One of them projected.

An elk, three boars, and a bag were dropped.

Tarrid opened the bag, "Waterskins and food for us bipeds, I'll get a fire going."

Lance eyed the elk. *Does anyone mind if I stay a dragon and eat?*

"Why would we?" Keelan asked.

Because you've never seen a dragon eat. A throaty rumble escaped Lance as he chuckled.

"First time for everything," Keelan shrugged.

In the end, Lance was right — Keelan and the others did mind after all. Lance and the griffins tore into their food with sickening squishing, tearing, and bone-cracking sounds. Aurora seemed to be having the most fun, watching everyone's reactions.

The final task will start as soon as the sun is not visible, Stormwing projected. *This is an agility test. My general has picked the quickest among us. You will follow her through the forest. If she takes a path, so must you. I expect few scratches and no broken wings or legs. Good luck, especially you, dragon.*

Why me?

Even though you've shrunk yourself, you are still bigger than anyone who has tried before. A broken wing or leg disqualifies you, and your group will not receive any firebush.

Keelan, I may need some help, Lance said.

"What do you need?" Keelan jumped back when Lance surrounded himself with his cloudy mist.

Tighten my straps, please, Lance said after he was the same size as Stormbreaker.

When you are ready, Stormwing snapped, clearly annoyed.

Keelan tightened Lance's saddle straps quickly and then mounted Stormbreaker.

They stood in silence, watching the sun slowly sink behind the mountains. When the last sliver disappeared, a griffin roared and took flight.

At least she'll be easy to follow, Lance remarked as she sped away from them.

The griffiness's feathers were pale gray tipped with silver, which made her albino white hide seem even whiter.

Come, we must hurry, Stormbreaker projected. *Snowcap is fast.*

They took chase. Lance was able to get the closest to her. His diminished size seemed to increase his speed.

With Lance keeping pace with Snowcap, the others could follow relatively easily.

Snowcap wove her way through the trees, keeping under the canopy. There didn't seem to be a path she was following, but she knew exactly when to turn or bank her wings to avoid a tree or rock. She raced through the forest until she came to the lake. She slowed slightly, looked behind her, and dove into the water headfirst.

Take a deep breath, Stormbreaker projected moments before he dove in after her.

Keelan was surprised at how well griffins could swim, *Learn something new everyday,* he mused to himself.

Lance seemed to fare the worst until he figured out he could move his tail like a snake and push himself forward. Just when Keelan thought his lungs would burst and his short life would be over, Stormbreaker broke through the water's surface. Keelan sucked in a grateful breath looking around to make sure everyone was alright.

Snowcap roared in what Keelan could only guess was frustration, *Are they trying to make us fail?*

Snowcap flipped around to face them, bringing them all to a halt to hover in the air, dripping wet. Another griffin appeared.

You two will follow Greytail, and you two will follow me. Each group must do this next part alone.

Greytail nodded to Tarrid and Leo'venath and then took off.

We will wait a few moments, Snowcap told them.

Soon, it was their turn. Snowcap resumed her neck-breaking speed, twisting and turning around the trees. They flew closer to the mountains that encircled the valley until a canyon appeared in front of them. They entered the dark canyon with its jagged walls and rocky protrusions.

Keelan held on tighter, hoping Stormbreaker could keep up. Suddenly, a roar shook the canyon walls, causing rocks to shower down on them. A large rock struck Snowcap in the head, and she plummeted to the ground.

Stormbreaker roared as he dove after her.

The canyon floor offered no escape from the falling rocks. Lance grew to his full size, snapping his saddle straps and spreading his wings wide. *Take cover,* he projected. With Stormbreaker's help, Keelan and Jonal dragged Snowcap under Lance's wings. Lance snaked his head under his wings and closed his eyes tight as the cascading rocks continued.

The roaring grew louder and closer.

"What's making that noise?" Keelan asked.

Trolls, I believe, Stormbreaker told them. *But I didn't think trolls could get into the valley.*

"Aurora, wait!" Keelan shouted as she left the protection of Lance's wings with her feathers ignited and flew toward the incoming troll. If she heard him, she chose to ignore him.

"Dragon!" A shout echoed through the canyon, dislodging another volley of rocks.

"Seize it!" A slurred cry came from above.

Lance uncoiled his head and closed his wings. Five trolls sprinted toward them; clubs raised high above their heads.

Keelan had never seen a troll before. They were tall and almost as wide with black stringy fur and large flat faces with a boar snout. Their mouths were full of crooked, razor-sharp-looking teeth, and they had no ears that Keelan could see.

Keelan drew his sword, and Jonal lifted his wand.

The trolls roared again; Lance answered it with a roar of his own. Lance leaped over his biped companions and landed on the closest troll, snapping his great jaws at another.

Jonal screamed in a language Keelan didn't know. Black and Gold sparks flew out of his wand.

Keelan felt his hands start to tingle. He gripped his sword with both hands, trying to focus his mind and slow his breathing as Lance's father, Douglas, and his uncle, Cedric, had taught him.

The world around him slowed. Lance grabbed a troll by the head and flung it into the air while still sitting on the other troll. Jonal was casting magic with his wand but was only slowing his troll, not stopping it. Stormbreaker joined the fight, clawing and slashing at a troll.

Keelan advanced, his movements accelerated compared to everyone else's. He slashed the first troll across its chest as it brought its arms above its head. The troll's eyes widened with surprise, dropping his club on the head of another troll behind it.

Both trolls crumbled to the ground. Stormbreaker snapped the neck of the unconscious trolls as soon as they stilled.

With the five trolls dispatched, the foursome looked around, anticipating another attack. Keelan slipped back into normal time. He shook his head to clear it. He still didn't understand what happened. Was everything truly going slower, or was he moving faster?

"I think we got them all, boys," Jonal said.

Another chorus of roars shook the canyon. With no moon in the sky, it was impossible to see in the canyon. The small group gathered close to Snowcap, who was still unconscious. Trying to stay as still as possible, they hoped whatever was coming would move on without seeing them.

The roaring was coming from the pitch-black sky. Keelan looked up, fearful of what was unseen.

Several creatures entered their section of the ravine. With large wings, they buffeted the group below with great gusts of air.

"Come out and fight. We can smell you. It's no use hiding," a wyvern slurred.

You have no business in this valley. This valley belongs to the Griffins. Be gone or feel the full wrath of my entire flock, Stormbreaker projected.

All the wyverns started to laugh, a strangled, coughing-like sound.

"You are outnumbered, griffin. Surrender, and we will let you live. Fight, and you will all die," it sneered and slurred.

Lance roared, stepping away from the canyon wall. ***You will intimidate no one, and we will not surrender.***

Stormbreaker stood at his side with his head held high.

"What about you, Jonal?" Keelan asked.

Jonal squared his shoulders, "I'd rather go down fighting than surrender willingly."

Keelan nodded. He adjusted his grip on the hilt of his sword, starting his breathing routine. His hands began to glow; he was thinking how he wanted the wyverns to burn. Burn the way they burned that elf village and countless others. Burn for what they were doing to the world.

He stared at his sword when he saw a flame appear on the hilt and slowly travel up the length of the blade, engulfing it in a white-hot flame. All eyes went to him when the glow from his flaming sword bathed the canyon in light.

"Sorcerer!" One of the wyverns shouted.

Six wyverns circled the canyon from above; two clung to the rocky walls, and one was on the ground.

"Attack!" The grounded wyvern screamed. It unleashed a column of green flames from its unhinged jaw.

Jonal screamed, flinging his hand and wand in the wyverns' direction. An invisible force stopped the fire, causing it to fan out and up harmlessly.

The two wyverns perched on the rocks dropped to the ground, attacking Lance—three of the flyers dove into the small canyon to join the fray.

Keelan slashed at the first one that got too close but was still too far away for his sword to reach.

Frustrated, he screamed, pointing his weapon at the creature. The flames from his sword elongated, piercing the wyvern in the chest. The wyvern roared in pain before crashing in a heap. The remaining wyverns in the sky flew off. Keelan focused his attention on the ones left behind. So far, Keelan was the only one who managed to kill one.

The ground started to shake, and more roaring and growling came their way. Four enormous ogres rushed toward them. One ogre was swinging a bola above his head. He aimed, throwing it at Lance. The three heavy rocks at the ends of the weapon propelled it with great speed. The weapon hit and entangled around one of Lance's front legs. Lance looked at it and started to laugh, but then his eyes bulged as he was engulfed within his transformation mist. Lance looked around fearfully in human form and then down at his wrist.

Keelan sprinted to his side, "What happened?"

"I don't know. I can't transform back."

Keelan looked at the bracelet that was now on Lance's wrist. They both tried to remove it, but it was locked on. Jonal cried out, making Keelan and Lance spin in his direction. An ogre had Jonal by the wrist, shaking it until Jonal lost his grasp on his wand. Another ogre approached, stepping on the wand. It snapped like the twig it was. The ogre clasped a bracelet on Jonal's wrist. At the same time, Keelan felt a bola wrap around his arm; he cursed under his breath for letting himself be distracted. He tried to remove the bola, but the bracelet was already locked and closed. He felt his connection to his magic break like a shattered mirror.

"What are these things?" Keelan asked no one in particular.

Stormbreaker squawked before he slumped to the ground, clubbed from behind.

"Surrender, vermin," a wyvern hissed.

"They don't have a choice; they are powerless now."

Another wyvern prowled closer to them, opening its jaws wide. Slowly, a gray mist poured out of the wyvern's mouth.

Don't breathe in the mist, Stormbreaker screamed into their minds.

Panicked, Keelan sucked in a breath and then held it. Jonal was the first to collapse. Keelan rushed to his side, placing his fingers on his neck; he was still alive, thankfully. He sat beside him, struggling to hold his breath. *When will this mist stop,* he thought angrily to himself. ***Lance, I can't last much longer.***

You have to, don't breathe in.

Aurora, where are you? He hadn't seen her since the trolls first attacked. No reply came.

Keelan's lungs burned, and his eyes watered from the mist. Unable to stop himself, he opened his mouth, his lungs greedy for air. As he filled his lungs, his eyes rolled back, and he passed out.

CHAPTER

-11-

 slowly stepped through the forest, pausing only long enough to notch an arrow on her bow string. Holding the bow with a firm grip, her nerves rising, sweat beaded on her brow and slowly dripped down her nose and cheeks. She could feel her heart rate elevating; she proceeded so quietly that every step, every crunch of a leaf, or snap of a twig seemed almost deafening. The rest of her group was spread out, all heading in roughly the same direction. The sun was high overhead, but even with the canopy cover provided by the giant trees, the heat and humidity were causing Shaylee's shirt to stick to her uncomfortably. She wiped the sweat from her forehead with the back of her arm again. Summer had arrived, and with it, more humidity than Shaylee was accustomed to.

She looked around and smiled. She was close to the stream and cottonwood grove. She quickened her steps slightly, thirst spurring her forward. They had been on the move since just after sunrise. The day had started typically with morning sparring before sitting in the magical theory classroom for a brief lesson. After a hasty late breakfast, they headed into the forest, learning how to patrol.

Midday had come and gone now, but still, they walked, making a slow loop around the Monastery Valley. It was her group's turn for deep patrol, the furthest out, walking along the very base of the volcanoes that rung this side of the valley.

She paused at the stream, looking around one more time. A sunbeam flickered through the leaves, blinding her momentarily when a breeze swept through the treetops. The smell of mint rose around her from the mint she had walked through moments before. She knelt beside the stream to refill her waterskin and splash the refreshing water on her face. Suddenly, there was a loud crack behind her, causing her to jump and spin around, still on her knees while fumbling to reattach her waterskin to her belt. Attempting to maintain quiet and calm herself, she slowly placed a palm on the damp grassy bank waiting for the next sound. Quickly, she gathered up her bow and determined the direction the sound originated from. *Definitely walking on four legs,* she sighed with relief. *Too quiet for an ogre or troll anyway. Maybe an elk?*

She decided to follow it. With so many people living in the valley now, all the large game had left before winter, forcing the hunters to venture further and further from the valley to supplement their increasingly vegetarian diet. Movement to her left brought her to a stop.

A large animal crashed through the forest, then two, then three. Shaylee quickened her careful steps and attempted to circle in front of the large animals. She saw flashes of a brown rump streak through the dense foliage. She held off on firing the nocked arrow. *Always verify what you are shooting at,* Talon's words flowed through her head. She needed to see more of the animal before firing. She spurred herself faster, pushing her lungs and legs to their limits. Finally, the forest gave way to a small clearing. The three animals burst from the cover moments before Shaylee did.

She stopped and steadied herself, preparing to fire. Her first thought was *three elk, fire!* But she knew better than to rush her shot. Her heart was racing, and her breath was labored; after a few precious moments, she aimed at the closest animal and let her arrow fly.

She reached for the shaft to steady the shot with her magic and then looked closely at her target. The animal stopped running, turning to face her broadside. She smiled, but her smile quickly turned into a frown and then a scream of terror. The animal in front of her was not an elk. It was a member of one of their new allies, the great stags.

Hastily, she tried to change the arrow's path. The arrow wobbled, veering slightly. The razor-sharp tip nicked the stag's shoulder as it glanced off its thick hide. The stag screamed in surprise; the other two stopped running and returned to their companion.

"Oh, my. I'm so, so sorry. Are you okay?" Shaylee hurried up close to the wounded creature.

Stay away from her!! One of the other stags screamed in her mind.

Shaylee skidded to a halt, falling backward, her hands pressed against her ears.

"I'm so, so sorry," she repeated. "I thought you were an elk. I tried to stop the arrow. I'm so, so sorry," she sobbed.

The third stag ran toward her, stopped abruptly before her, and reared, thrashing his legs in the air. Shaylee curled in a ball at his feet, shielding her head with her arms.

We trusted you humans, and this is how you show your appreciation. Trying to murder my mother, he screamed in her head.

Ky, be calm, a female voice said. The wounded stag approached and nudged Shaylee's shoulder. Shaylee shrieked and tried to scoot back.

Be calm, young one. No harm will come to you; please stand, she said kindly.

Shaylee looked up, tears flowing freely down her cheeks, "I'm so sorry. Are you okay?" She managed between sobs.

It is just a scratch. Thank you for stopping your shot.

"But I shouldn't have fired at you in the first place. I thought you were an elk."

An elk! the older male exclaimed. *Does she look like an elk?*

Shaylee looked at the three stags in front of her. Now that she was not struggling to breathe, she saw the immediate differences. The stags were much bigger than the largest elk she had ever seen. Their hide was a similar shade of brown, but unlike an elk, the stags were dappled with almost glowing silver spots. They also had enormous antlers that sparkled in the sunlight. The males had two sets of massive antlers sprouting from both sides of their heads. The female had one set with brow tines extending forward before swooping back over her head.

"My impatience to release my arrow clouded my judgment. My deepest heartfelt apologies. Please forgive my error," she bowed deeply.

Rise, human. I hold no grudge against thee.

How can you say that, mother? She could have killed you.

But she did not. This is not our home territory, and she had no knowledge of our return. Assuming we were elk was a logical assumption. When was the last time you consumed meat, child? the female asked.

Shaylee's cheeks flushed, her eyes darting between the stags, uncertain how to answer.

Be not afraid; humans eat meat. It is nothing to be ashamed of.

"I'm not a human. I am an Elvenfae."

A what? the young male asked.

"An Elvenfae. My father is an elf, and my mother is a fairy."

I am sorry, but there is no such creature. All crosses that you describe die at birth, the older male said.

"I did not die."

And you are not an Elvenfae, he replied.

Shaylee jumped to her feet. She had never thought she would have to explain herself to another magical creature.

"I again apologize for my error. I will depart now."

You will do no such thing! Ky, the younger male, screamed. *You almost killed my mother.*

But she did not, did she? his mother asked him. *Shaylee, please have a safe journey. I'm sure we will see each other again soon.*

"H…how do you know my name?"

I know a great many things about you. Go, young one. You have answers to seek.

Shaylee grabbed her bow and retrieved the fallen arrow before walking numbly back to the Monastery, completely forgetting about her reason for being in the forest.

It was almost dark before the wall surrounding the Monastery was visible. Shaylee strode with her head down.

"SHAYLEE!!!" Fawn screamed and ran toward her. "Where have you been? Are you hurt? What happened?" Fawn crushed her in a fierce hug.

A grin tugged at Shaylee's lips, "I'm fine. I need to speak with my ma and pa," she said gently, shaking Fawn off.

"They're at the Monastery arranging a search party."

"Oh!" Shaylee glanced at the sky. "I didn't realize what time it was."

Fawn grabbed her hand and pulled her forward. They ran as fast as they could into the courtyard, and all eyes turned to them.

A loud, startled scream ripped through the shocked party as Rosepetal shot into the air and flew toward the two girls.

"Shaylee! I'm so happy to see you," Rosepetal barreled into her, almost knocking her over.

"I'm okay, mother. I'm sorry I made you worry. I had a run-in with a few stags and then lost track of time."

"We already heard the story from the stags. They arrived about an hour ago."

Shaylee looked away from her mother's panicked face and saw the three stags standing a short distance away; the female nodded to her.

"What did they tell you?"

"That it was all a mistake, and no one was hurt."

"Did they tell you about the rest of our conversation?"

Rosepetal gave her a puzzled look.

"We need to talk, Mother. Where's Father?"

Rosepetal looked behind her; Talon was jogging toward them.

Shaylee crossed her arms, waiting for her father to join them. Fawn started to leave, "Please stay."

"Are you sure?"

"You are family now. I want you here."

"Shaylee, what's wrong? Where have you been?" Talon asked.

"I've had a lot to think about. You already heard from the stags about my error?" Everyone nodded. "But from Mother's confused expression, they didn't tell you the rest of the conversation. They called me a human," she paused to see their reactions. Rosepetal's face went even whiter than usual; Talon's face didn't change. Shaylee turned to face her mother. "Why would they say I am a human? They say that no Elvenfae has ever been born alive. What am I? Are you really my mother?"

Rosepetal slumped to the ground, hugging her wings in tight.

"You once called me your found miracle. Where did you find me?"

"Rose, what is she talking about? Shaylee, your mother was pregnant with you. I know she was."

Shaylee looked at Talon, concern etched in his eyes, "You saw her pregnant, but did you see me being born?"

Talon swallowed loudly, "Well, no. She was getting close, and I told her to stay in the house. She was so worried about you. Because…" he trailed off.

"Because what?"

"Because like you said…" he paused again. "No Elvenfae had ever been born alive. But she felt you kicking all the time, *I*… felt you kicking. The day you were born, she left early in the morning to replenish a few herbs; when she returned late that night, she was carrying you. My wonderful baby girl."

Shaylee returned her eyes to Rosepetal, "What happened. Please tell me. I deserve to know," she knelt beside her.

"I was replenishing herbs like your father said. I was close, but I still should have been a few days off. I went into labor. It felt so wrong, so painful. I couldn't get back to you, Talon. I... I... thought I was going to die. The baby..." she broke down in tears.

Talon rushed to her side and sat next to her. Fawn stood a few steps away, not sure what to do.

After a moment, Rosepetal continued, "The baby was born alive, but as soon she opened her eyes, I knew she would never survive. She did for a few hours. Long enough for me to name her, but she refused to eat. A... af... after she passed, I couldn't move. I was numb all over. I sat there until the full moon was high overhead. I heard someone rushing through the forest. They stopped a few bushes from where I was," Rosepetal kept her eyes downcast. "The woman was in tears, sobbing and praying. She asked the gods to watch over the poor infant. Its only crime was being born. And then she left. I was about to leave, but then I heard crying. My heart felt like it was going to break in two. I slowly approached the bundle on the forest floor. The infant looked at me with big brown eyes and stopped crying. The baby was so small, so innocent, I couldn't just leave it there," she choked back a sob, "leave you there." She finally looked up at Shaylee, tears running down her cheeks. "The green in your eyes sparkled in the moonlight. You became my Shaylee. My Shaylee that I could bring home and be a mother too."

Shaylee stepped backward, her whole body shaking, "You're not my mother?" she asked quietly.

Rosepetal shot to her feet. "I am in all the ways that count. I raised you as my own. Whoever left you there didn't want you, so I rescued you," she said, reaching for Shaylee with both arms.

Shaylee retreated another couple of steps, shaking her head. "I need time to process this." She looked at Talon, who had tears glistening in his eyes.

"I had no idea," was all he said.

Shaylee nodded, too stunned for words.

Suddenly, a cacophony came from the sky as three griffins circled, screeching and growling. All those below quickly got out of the way as the griffins landed one by one. The Prioress, Leilatha Moryra, ran down the steps of the Monastery.

"What has happened?" she asked the griffins.

One of the griffins collapsed on the ground, exhausted. The other two hung their heads but remained on their feet.

We were attacked, the others were taken, but we escaped.

Shaylee and Fawn rushed up to the griffins.

"You were with Tar and Leo?" Fawn blurted.

The griffin nodded weakly.

"Are they okay?"

When we parted, they were alive.

"Please, rest a moment," the Prioress said. "Quickly, bring food and water for our brave compatriots."

The other two griffins finally lowered themselves to the ground.

We had just left the firebush grove when eight wyverns ambushed us. He nodded to a large bag one of them had dropped. *We fought them off the best that we could. Tar and Leo took out one of them, and we managed to kill two more, but there were just too many of them. Tar and Leo were both injured as they forced us to land. On the ground, a dozen ogres and fifteen trolls waited for us. We were all captured.*

How did you get away? Shaylee projected without meaning to.

All the griffins snapped their heads in her direction.

How are you projecting to us?

Shaylee's eyes widened, "I didn't mean to. I'm sorry," she said aloud.

"Shaylee, what did you ask them?" the Prioress asked.

"How they got away. How did I project to them?"

"Another time. Please continue your tale." She gestured to the griffin.

Tar and Leo were able to free the three of us before they were recaptured.

"How soon can you take us back to where you left them?" Fawn asked.

"Now, hold on, young one. This is not a time to rush into a rescue," the Prioress said.

"Why not? You were organizing a search party for Shaylee not more than thirty minutes ago. And she was just lost in the valley, not in mortal danger!" Fawn screamed.

"Calm yourself, child," she said sternly. "We need a plan before we rush in and get more people captured."

"They might not have time for that," Shaylee said passionately.

"Please let the adults handle this, children," she scolded them and returned to the griffins.

Shaylee and Fawn stared at the Prioress's back, their anger rising.

"How can she say that? I am not a child," Shaylee fumed. "I am almost fifteen."

"Come on." Fawn grabbed Shaylee's hand and pulled her away.

They walked back to their home in silence, but instead of going inside, Fawn led Shaylee to the back and sat on the ground.

They sat lost in their thoughts. First, Shaylee learned her parents weren't her parents, and now their leaders were missing.

A short time later, they were startled when one of the griffins walked around the corner of their home.

Please do not be frightened, she said to them.

"Oh, you just startled us. We're not scared. I'm glad you were able to escape," Shaylee said sadly.

The griffin bowed her head. ***My name is Starfire. I was Leo's companion on our trip.***

"Is that a saddle on you?" Shaylee asked.

A human named Ben found a diagram of a griffin saddle and made these for us.

Shaylee perked up. "A griffin saddle! Do you think it would work for a pegasus?"

The griffin swiveled her head to look at the saddle. ***I don't see why not.***

"Why have you come here?" Fawn asked, looking up at the griffiness towering above her.

I sensed your passion and desire for rescuing Tar and Leo, and I wanted to ask what else you desired.

Shaylee blurted without thinking, "To rescue all those taken, human, elf, and griffin, and to kill those wyverns, every… last… one of them."

The griffin was silent for a moment. ***I feel the truth in your words. I will help you, but I can only carry one of you. We will need to find another willing to help.***

Shaylee closed her eyes and then opened them with a smile.

"Our help will be here shortly."

Shaylee and Fawn rushed into their home to pack what they could before Rosepetal and Talon returned. Shaylee paused momentarily. *Can I still call them Ma and Pa?* she thought. Lyra swooped in through the open window.

Of course, you can. It matters not if they are not your true parents. They raised you; they are family, just like you, me, and Fawn. Families do not have to be related.

You're right, Lyra, thank you.

She scribbled down a quick note for her parents and then hurried to the back of the house again.

She rounded the corner with Fawn on her heels; Starfire was still there, but so was Ben.

"Are you going someplace?" he asked.

"Yes, we are going to rescue Tar and Leo. Are you here to stop us?" Shaylee asked, rolling her wrists in a tight circle.

Ben took a step backward and held out his hands, "Hold up. I'm not your father. Starfire asked if I had another saddle."

"Oh, um. Thanks, Starfire, and thank you, Ben, for helping her. How did she speak to you?"

"I guess I have a spark of magic," he shrugged his shoulders. "And, no problem, it's the least I can do. Actually, it's the most I can do," he chuckled. "I'm not the courageous type." He began showing them how to attach the straps he had brought.

"Why did you stay here and join The Blade?" Fawn asked him.

He shrugged, "Nothing better to do, and I don't like feeling helpless. Defending my home is different than rushing off to rescue people. Okay, now, where is the other griffin?" He glanced into the sky.

"I won't be riding a griffin." A gust of wind blasted them as a winged creature descended.

"Thank you for coming, Dreamcrest."

It is my honor to carry you into battle. Have you figured out how to stay on my back?

Ben explained the griffin saddle design to her and assisted Fawn onto Starfire's back.

"So, what do you think?" Ben asked.

Dreamcrest walked around Starfire. Starfire nodded.

I accept.

Ben quickly placed the saddle on Dreamcrest, shrinking the straps to fit her slightly smaller size, and then helped Shaylee get into position.

"Here, you might need this." He held up a large bag.

"What is it?" Shaylee asked.

"Food and medical supplies. You know, just in case."

I will carry the bag, Starfire offered.

"Thanks, Ben. I don't know how to thank you enough."

He shrugged, "Just bring our leaders back and come back yourselves. In one piece, mind you."

He stepped back as the pegasus and the griffin opened their wings and took to the sky.

CHAPTER

-12-

TWO days later, Shaylee and Fawn stared in awe at the ocean before them. Neither of them had seen the sea before, especially from the air. The blue water seemed to be alive. Waves rolled, dipped, and crested, breaking at the tops and changing colors from deep blue to white as they reached their peaks. The setting sun cast a red glow across the sky.

"How much further?" Fawn yelled to Starfire so she could be heard above the wind and waves.

We will soon stop for the night. By midday tomorrow, we will reach the place where I last saw the others, Starfire projected to Fawn and Shaylee.

This is the last place I saw the others. They had us tied up there. After Tar and Leo freed us, Leo somehow cloaked us in magic so the trolls could not find us. We watched helplessly as the others were carried away. Only after we were sure they were gone did we leave. We waited a whole day—a precious day lost while we waited like cowards.

"Don't say that; you are not a coward." Fawn ran her hand down the griffin's neck. "You came back here willingly. You are courageous." Starfire didn't look convinced but nodded. They circled the small clearing and then set down. Shaylee and Fawn quickly found the trail the ogres and trolls left.

"Should we follow them on foot?" Fawn asked.

"I don't think we could catch up to them alone. They can move much quicker than we can. Dreamcrest, are you comfortable running on the ground? Starfire?"

If we were in the open, I would have no problem. The tree canopy is too thick for my comfort, Dreamcrest shook her head.

"So, what do we do now?"

You ask for help, a new voice projected. A large stag walked into the clearing. *I saw where they took your friends. I will help you if your companions agree,* he nodded to the pegasus and griffin.

We would be honored, Starfire bowed her head.

I request the human to ride with me. We, he paused as four more stags emerged from the trees, *will track on foot. The ariels can follow from above.*

"Why do you want Shaylee with you?" Fawn asked with her eyes narrowed.

Your friend can project her thoughts. We will be able to communicate with the ariels through her.

Fawn looked at Shaylee in surprise, "You can project your thoughts to others - other than Lyra?"

"I learned that from the stag I almost killed."

Fawn smiled at her friend, shaking her head, "Can't wait to see what else you can do."

If this heartfelt moment is over, I believe you have some friends to rescue, the stag projected.

"I believe he's right," Shaylee said as she mounted the great stag's back once he knelt.

Dreamcrest and Starfire took to the air.

We will follow their trail; you keep your connection open to the pegasus so she can follow you.

"How do I keep it open?"

Just do it, don't worry about the how, Lyra told her.

Is that your answer to everything?

If it keeps working, why change?

Shaylee shrugged as she cleared her mind and centered her thoughts on Dreamcrest.

I feel your mind, Shaylee.

Good, let's go.

The stags were just as fast on the ground as the ariels were in the air and were excellent trackers. A couple of times, the trail they were following branched off, and they immediately, without hesitation, followed what appeared to be the correct one.

When the sun dipped below the western horizon, they all decided to stop for the evening. Shaylee and Fawn quickly gathered tree branches and started a small fire. All their animal companions assured them that no ogre or troll was nearby.

While they were setting up camp, Starfire departed only to return a little later with a boar clenched in her front talons.

I have returned with dinner! she announced.

The stags and Dreamcrest snorted their disgust, but Shaylee and Fawn jumped up to help prepare their dinner.

Night fell, but not the temperature. Shaylee and Fawn watched the boar haunch slowly roast over the fire while not sitting too close to the heat.

"I didn't know there could be any place hotter than Newhaven," Fawn remarked.

Shaylee nodded her agreement.

"So, how did the ogres and trolls sneak up on you?" Shaylee asked, breaking the silence.

Starfire looked up from her dinner, her beak slick with blood.

She was silent for a few heartbeats. *We saw a small troop walking through the forest. It didn't look like very many. They all smell the same, mind you. We started to attack the ones we saw, and the wyverns assaulted from above.*

"Do we need to set a watch?" Shaylee asked, looking around nervously.

We will handle that, one of the stags projected. *We do not require as much sleep as you.*

Something approaches! Dreamcrest projected suddenly. Shaylee and Fawn were on their feet, staffs at the ready.

"Hello, the camp!" a young boy called from the forest's shadows.

"Who are you? How many are with you?" Shaylee called out.

"My name is Zarren. I'm by myself. Can I come into the light, please?"

Keeping her staff before her, Fawn replied, "Yes, of course, you may approach."

Is he alone? Shaylee projected to all her allies.

Fawn snapped her head and gazed at her with her mouth open, "I heard you," she whispered.

Shaylee's eyes widened, *Okay, new ability,* she projected to her. Fawn smiled and nodded.

The young one is alone. He is a dragon, so he is much older than he appears, Starfire told them.

The young boy walked slowly toward the light; he looked to be about thirteen. His black hair was disheveled, his face bore numerous scratches, and his clothing was dirty and torn.

"Welcome," Shaylee said to him, "we were about to have dinner. Are you hungry?"

"Starving," he said with a shy smile.

"Come, sit and tell us your tale," Fawn said.

He stopped, his eyes frightful, "What do you mean, my tale?" He subtly turned his head and glanced behind him.

"How you became alone in this forest at night," Shaylee said.

His shoulders relaxed, "Oh. Yeah, I can do that."

Shaylee and Fawn shared a look but said nothing. They ate in silence, watching their visitor as he devoured his portion of the boar.

"You must have been out here for a while," Shaylee said when she finished.

"What makes you say that?"

"I haven't seen anyone eat so fast or so much before."

"Oh," he slumped, "I'm sorry."

"Don't be, it's okay. We've all been hungry before."

"So, Zarren. How did you become all alone out here?" Fawn asked.

"My family was traveling through these woods; somehow, I got separated from them. I don't know where they went."

Nice story, but now try the truth, dragon! one of the stags projected.

Zarren's eyes widened in surprise. "Y…y... you know what I am?"

I know you are a dragon in human form, yes. I can smell your true identity.

"Oh, I guess I never thought anyone could do that."

All magical creatures can tell another magical creature.

"So, what is the truth?" Shaylee asked.

He sat in silence for a few moments, "My parents were slaves to the wyverns; I was born a slave. We finally escaped, or so we thought. We ran and ran. But they found us. They sent a whole mess of ogres and trolls after us. Th-they killed my pa and captured my ma. I stayed hidden until they moved on."

All eyes were on him now.

Did the ogres have anyone with them? Starfire projected.

He nodded, "Yeah, a couple of griffins, an elf, and a human."

"How long ago did they attack your family? How far from here?" Fawn asked in a hushed voice.

"Oh, uh, um," he stammered. "A couple of days ago. I think. I'm unsure how long I've wandered or how far I've gone. I stayed hidden for a day, and then I just started walking in the same direction my father was taking us."

Shaylee nodded, "Thank you for the information. We will be continuing on in the morning."

"Where are you headed?" He asked.

"The same place you fled from. Those ogres have our friends," Fawn said. "Wait a minute. How did they capture your ma and kill your pa? You're a dragon, right? Why not just change and fly away?"

"We're trapped in our human forms," he said, holding up his wrist, a gold bracelet dangling loosely from it. "This keeps us from transforming."

"Can I see it?" Shaylee asked.

He shrugged and scooted closer to her.

She tried to unclasp it, but it wouldn't come off.

He shook his head, "Only a wyvern can take it off. My pa even tried to cut off his hand, and the knife broke before it even nicked his skin. I'm stuck in human form forever."

Shaylee laid a hand on his shoulder, "We'll figure out a way to get that off you. Don't worry."

He nodded his head with his eyes downcast.

"Do you know where your pa was taking you?" Fawn asked.

He shrugged, "Somewhere safe was all he would say. That, and he would say to my ma that he hoped The Chosen would be willing to help us."

"The Chosen?"

"Yeah, have you heard of them?"

"Our group used to be a part of them. Our leaders decided they were not following the correct path."

Zarren's eyes widened. "Wow, now two groups are fighting the wyverns?"

"Kind of," Fawn nodded. "The Chosen will help when there is an active attack or help those attacked after the fact. The Blade is gathering forces to take the fight to them."

"Oh, I would very much like to meet your leaders and join their cause."

"Those ogres captured them. We are going to rescue them," Fawn told him.

He thought for a moment, "I want to help."

"Are you sure you're up to it? You just escaped a life of slavery. We can't ensure your safety right now. If you go to Newhaven, that's where we live; you can learn how to be independent and learn useful skills," Shaylee said.

"Oh, no. I want to fight, and I want to meet your leaders. Maybe they know someone who can get this bracelet off." He nodded, his lips set in a grim line, his eyes seeming to shine in the darkness.

"Okay, we leave at sunrise; try to get some rest."

CHAPTER

-13-

SHAYLEE and Zarren each rode with a stag through the forest. Even with their enormous antlers, they could travel at speeds rivaling any horse.

They followed the trail for two full days before it finally appeared that they might be reaching the captives.

I see a camp up ahead, Dreamcrest projected.

Can you see Tar, Leo, or any of the griffins? Shaylee projected back.

No, the camp is quiet. I don't see anything moving, but there's a large cave next to a small pond.

They must be inside, Dreamcrest told Shaylee.

"Dreamcrest thinks she found their camp. Let's stop here." Shaylee relayed what Dreamcrest shared with her out loud. She still hadn't thought letting their new companion in on all their secrets was wise.

"So, what now?" Zarren asked.

"We need to make sure they are still here. I don't want to rush into a dark cave and get captured. Hopefully, they will be moving again soon. I would rather tangle with them in the open," Shaylee said.

Sound plan, Starfire projected.

The small group spread out through the forest and in the air, hoping to see movement.

When it became too dark to see, they regrouped and stayed close together in a cold camp.

The following day, they resumed watching the cave for signs of life.

"I think we missed them," Fawn said that evening as she tore off a piece of dried jerky. "They must have moved on."

"How could they have? There are no signs anywhere around here that they continued." Shaylee retorted.

"Underground," Zarren said quietly.

"Sorry, what was that?" Fawn asked.

"I said they went underground. Trolls like to use dwarf tunnels. I bet that cave is an entrance to a dwarf tunnel."

"I don't like the sound of that," Fawn whispered. "We can't follow them down there. What if there's a fork in the tunnels, and we take the wrong one?"

"We can't give up now," Shaylee said gently. "But I understand if you want to stay here or go back. I'm going in tomorrow."

"What! Really! You would risk your lives further for your leaders?" Zarren asked.

"Tarrid and Leo'venath are more than just our leaders; I consider them my friends."

Zarren pursed his lips, "I have never known a friendship like that."

Shaylee placed her hand on his arm, "You are still young, and up until a few days ago, you were a slave. Don't worry, you will find true friendship."

Shaylee turned to face their animal allies. "I can't ask any of you to venture into the cave with us. I don't know how big the tunnels remain or what we will face down there."

One of the stags stood. *This is where we leave you. We wish you great speed and courage. I know you will be successful. I will send you some help. I know a tunnel expert. He will be able to assist you.*

"Thank you for all your help. We couldn't have gotten this far without you." Shaylee bowed.

As one, all the stags stood and quickly departed.

"What about you two?" Fawn asked the pegasus and griffin.

We will travel with you, Starfire said.

"What? No, we don't know how tight it gets down there," Shaylee said.

My brother and two others were taken down there. If they fit, I will fit.

And I am smaller than Starfire. I go where you go. Dreamcrest nodded her head.

"If you two are sure," they both nodded. "Okay then. Zarren, what about you?"

Zarren was staring off into the trees.

"Zarren?"

"Oh, sorry. Lost in thought. Please call me Zar."

"Okay, Zar. Do you want to come with us into the caves?"

"Of course, I'm with you all the way."

Fawn nodded her head, a small smile on her lips.

Shaylee patted him on the back, "Let's get some rest. We will go in after the sun rises."

It was difficult to tell time in the dark cave. Shaylee was in the lead with a floating sun-orb a few feet before her. She modified the spell so that the orb only showed light behind it instead of all around. It made travel difficult but also ensured that their light didn't flood down the tunnel, giving their presence away.

After walking a constant downward slope for what felt like an hour, the tunnel opened into a large cavern. The ceiling was high overhead. Glowing pink rocks scattered across the ground made the quartz veins that snaked across the walls and top of the cavern sparkle.

"So, where is this guide we were told about?" Fawn whispered.

The ground started to rumble as if on cue, and the pink stones began to hop and jump around. The five rescuers huddled together in the center of the cavern. Three tunnels led out of the cavern, but only two looked promising.

A low growl and a scratching sound came from the third tunnel, like thousands of claws scraping across the rock floor.

"Weapons at the ready. I don't know what is coming out; be ready for anything," Shaylee said quietly.

A large creature strode out of the tunnel. Shaylee stared in awe. She had never seen the likes of it before. The beast almost filled the entire tunnel with its bulk. Its round face was covered with dense tan fur, and two impossibly small, black, beady eyes looked at them unblinking. The creature had a long, bright pink snout that wiggled back and forth as it sniffed the air in their direction.

When the creature was entirely in the cavern, Shaylee could see a thick, hard-looking, black shell covering its back like a turtle; three pairs of legs were covered in dark brown scales and ended in a mess of eight, foot-long claws on each foot.

The creature moved slowly forward, stopping a few feet from them. It opened its tiny mouth and emitted a little squeak followed by a deep purring sound.

Greetings, surface-dwellers; I guide you through my tunnels.

"Thank you. Did the stags ask you to help us?"

He squeaked again. ***Follow,*** he projected.

He lumbered slowly toward one of the other tunnels, stopped before one, and sniffed the air. He left that tunnel and shuffled over to the last tunnel. When he sniffed the air this time, he broke into a fit of sneezes. When he stopped, he turned his great head toward them. ***They went this way.***

Together, they walked into the tunnel. Shaylee cast a sun-orb in front of her.

No light, the creature hissed. ***I guide you.***

Shrugging, she eliminated the light and grabbed Fawn's hand.

Blindly, they followed their new guide as they plunged deeper into the tunnel system.

After walking for what felt like an eternity, their guide stopped.

Need rest, their guide projected. He slumped onto his belly and was soon snoring.

"Well, isn't this just great," Fawn whispered with a huff. "I guess we should get some rest, too."

"Great idea. Cold rations again. What about you two?" Shaylee asked the ariels.

We are fine for now. We can both go for a couple of days in between meals.

Shaylee smiled, "I brought a little bit of grass and a rabbit for you, but if you wish to hold off a bit, that's good too."

They sat with their backs to the cool rock wall. The cave was comfortable and had a moderate temperature, which Shaylee was thankful for. She started to drift off when Zarren's voice snapped her head back up.

"So, what's your story?" he asked.

"What do you mean?" Shaylee replied.

"You know? What made you join a resistance? And why are two young girls, a pegasus, and a griffin the only ones looking for the leaders of The Blade?"

Fawn smiled and dove into their story. She told him how a wyvern, along with an ogre and a few trolls, attacked their village, killing many elves, and how Tarrid and Leo'venath arrived just in time to stop the complete destruction. When the wyvern returned, Shaylee saved everyone by alerting them to the danger, but the village was leveled. At that moment, Shaylee and Fawn decided this was their fight, too, and did everything they could to learn how to protect themselves and fight.

Zarren sat engrossed in her retelling, hanging on every word. His facial features were hard to decipher. Shaylee couldn't tell if he was happy the wyvern got away or annoyed. Fear was definitely not on his face.

Fawn and Zarren continued to talk in hushed voices while Shaylee drifted off to sleep.

Awake!! We move.

Shaylee and Fawn jumped to their feet, spun in a circle, and looked around. Their hearts were hammering in their chests.

"Are we under attack?" Fawn asked, panicked.

No. We move. Come! their armored guide said.

Shaylee and Fawn both let out a relieved breath. They gathered their few belongings and prepared to move out. Fully awake now, they followed their plodding guide.

They continued down the tunnel and into two additional branches before their guide stopped again.

What is it? Shaylee projected.

Did not know you, Vaelum, the creature said with a purr.

What's a Vaelum?

The creature swiveled his head so one eye stared at her. *You don't know? Thought all humans knew.*

"No, I just found out I was a human and not an Elvenfae," she said out loud.

Zarren looked at her. "What's an Elvenfae?"

"Another time, maybe," she said to him. "Why did we stop?"

Your prey ahead.

Shaylee shook her hands and rolled her shoulders. "Are you ready for this?" she asked Fawn.

Fawn nodded, mirroring her actions.

I go first. Who are enemies? their guide asked.

"Any ogre or troll. The elf, the human, and the griffins are friends."

No elf, only human and two griffins.

Shaylee's heart sank. *What happened to Tar?* She wanted to scream. She closed her eyes tightly, *Not now, hold it together.*

Lyra wrapped her body around Shaylee's legs, purring. *One thing at a time,* she projected. *Rescue Leo, and then we'll find Tar.*

Thanks, Lyra.

The creature plodded forward, and a low rumble started to come from him. As they neared what looked to be the end of the tunnel, the beast began to squeak loudly like an overgrown mouse.

"Who there?" a garbled shout came from in front of the creature.

"It's nothing, only a tunnel mole," another voice said.

Up ahead, the tunnel grew larger and opened into another vast cavern.

"Hurry, push it in before we distracted," a troll snarled.

Heat rolled into the tunnel, growing increasingly uncomfortable.

When the tunnel mole emerged, a roar ripped from his throat. Up ahead, three ogres and four trolls were prodding and pushing two griffins closer to the edge of a cliff. Their wings were strapped down, but their eyes shined with fury. Shaylee and Fawn looked around, unable to spot Leo'venath at first. Finally, Shaylee locked eyes with Leo'venath; he was tied up and on the ground next to an ogre. His eyes lit up, and then he closed them tightly.

Two ogres advanced on the tunnel mole while the others tried to get one of the griffins to fall off the edge.

The tunnel mole rose on its two hind legs while holding its remaining four out in front of it, all eight claws on each leg spread out wide. The two front feet started to spin until the claws were nothing but a blur. The ogres looked at each other and charged forward. The tunnel mole roared, shaking the cavern and causing a shower of small rocks to fall on everyone's head.

The ogres answered his roar with one of their own. Both charged forward only to be knocked aside by its spinning clawed feet. One ogre screamed as it lost its footing and fell over the edge. Shaylee rushed to the precipice and looked down. Hundreds of feet below, a river of lava flowed. The ogre spun with its arms flared out, screaming as it fell. The ogre hit the lava, its screams falling silent immediately as it was engulfed in the burning liquid.

Shaylee brought her eyes back to the ledge. Dreamcrest and Starfire were airborne, flying around the cavern, trying to distract the two trolls still holding the griffins hostage. The tunnel mole kept the rest of the trolls and the remaining ogre occupied. Fawn and Zarren were at Leo'venath's side, untying him. Shaylee looked back at the griffins and trolls again. One griffin only had three feet on the ledge now. Anger exploded within her. She screamed and stretched her arms out in front of her; a purple light flared from her fingertips, hitting a troll squarely in the chest. It crumbled in on itself; the other troll lost its footing from surprise and fell over the very edge it wanted the griffins to fall from.

With her dagger in hand, Shaylee ran to the griffins; she quickly sliced the bindings holding their wings in. Both griffins roared and took flight.

Leo'venath was slowly getting to his feet, with Zarren's help and Fawn hovering in case he started to fall.

The tunnel mole fell silent, slowly advancing on the last troll. The troll backed up until his feet were mere inches from the cliff edge.

Without removing his gaze from the troll he said, **When you ready, I help you out.**

"Thank you, mighty beast," Leo'venath said. "How did you find us? Why are you even here? Who is this?" He nodded to Zarren.

"We'll answer all your questions later. Where's Tar and the last griffin?"

"You never find them," the only troll left on the ledge said. "Princess Drakaina take him to her father, King Ichakik. You die at his hands." The troll got to his feet. Shaylee was about to cast a capture spell around him, but he threw himself over the edge and into the lava raging below.

"Princess Drakaina?" Fawn asked.

Zarren nodded his head, "Firstborn to the wyvern king. Your friend is unreachable now; I'm sorry."

"Who is this?" Leo'venath asked.

"My name is Zarren; I was a slave to the wyverns before I escaped."

"Come on, Leo, let's get out of here," Shaylee took Fawn's spot, helping to hold Leo'venath up. Slowly, they followed the tunnel mole back to the surface.

"Thank you, my friend. I'm sorry I never asked your name," Shaylee said to the tunnel mole, shielding the bright sunlight from her eyes.

The tunnel mole had his eyes clamped tightly shut, ***Dirt!***

"What? Your name is Dirt?"

He squeaked. ***Stay safe, stay above ground,*** turning quickly, he ambled back into the tunnel.

Zarren and Shaylee helped Leo'venath sit with his back against a tree.

"I think we should stay here the night," Fawn said.

"So close to the tunnel?" Zarren asked.

"I don't think anything will harm us tonight, and Dirt isn't far away. I can still feel his mind," Shaylee replied.

Leo'venath looked at her, "How can you feel his mind?"

"Shaylee can project her thoughts to any magical creature, not just her familiar," Fawn told him.

"Wow, you are full of surprises."

"You don't know the half of it," she said.

"Care to explain that?"

"Not right now. I'm going to collect firewood. Can you find food, Starfire?"

Of course.

"Thank you for coming back for us, Starfire," Leo'venath said.

I had to. No thanks required, she vaulted into the sky with the other two griffins close beside her.

"When was Tar separated from you?" Fawn asked.

"We waited here in the clearing for two days before the princess arrived."

"What did she look like?"

He shook his head, "We were blindfolded. Her voice wasn't what I expected, though."

"How so?"

"She didn't have the typical wyvern speech, no slurring. She told her war party to dispose of the rest. I haven't seen Tar or Cloudfeather since. I hope they're okay."

Fawn hugged her knees to her chest, "I hope so, too."

Soon, they had a fire roaring, and several rabbits cleaned and roasting slowly.

"You found the firebush, right?" Fawn asked.

Leo'venath nodded.

"And the griffins let you collect some, no problems?"

"Not at first; we had to pass some tests. But in the end, they found us worthy. It turns out we weren't the only ones looking for the plants."

"No? Who else?"

"Two humans, an old man, a boy about Shaylee's age, and a dragon. We met them briefly but lost track of them during the trials. They needed the plants for the boy's mother. She has the wasting as well."

"The wasting?"

"That's what humans call it. It appears it was a fairly common illness among natural-born magical humans; it never affected elves before."

"I wonder why it is now," Shaylee said.

"I told them about the bluebirds with odd yellow feathers that looked like dots all over them. The old man's eyes flew open. He says two years ago, he saw strange blue and yellow birds being released from the palace."

"The palace? You mean the King of Evansshire released those birds? I wonder if it was on purpose," Fawn said in surprise.

"I would venture to say yes. After we passed the griffin's tests and filled our bags, we started to head back. That's when we were ambushed. The wyverns were flying up high in cloud cover, with the sun at their backs. We had so little time to react. It was a blur," he hung his head.

"We'll get him back, somehow," Shaylee said, trying to sound confident.

"I don't know about that," Zarren interjected.

Leo'venath lifted his head, "Why?"

"You've never met the Princess. She has a deep hatred for bipeds, and her father, the king, wants to stop The Chosen and The Blade. Do you think any of the wyverns that captured you know who you are or who you're with?"

Leo'venath started to shake his head but paused, "I have a hard time telling one wyvern from another, but one may have recognized us."

"Then I don't think your friend will live long enough to be rescued. I'm sorry."

"So, what do we do?" Fawn asked.

"I'm not giving up," Leo'venath said with grim determination.

"Maybe we should go to the Griffin Valley and get their help," Shaylee suggested.

"We can try. I don't think they will help, though," Leo'venath shrugged.

CHAPTER

-14-

WAKE *up, Keelan, wake up.* A voice slammed into his head. *It's no use, Lance; he won't wake.*

Aurora! He thought, shaking his head slightly. His head was pounding, and everything was fuzzy. *Aurora, is that you?* He thought out loud.

Oh, thank the stars, you're alive! Aurora screamed in his head.

"How do you feel? Can you see or move?" Lance asked in barely a whisper.

Keelan groaned and wiggled his extremities. His wrists and ankles were bound together. He opened his eyes, but everything was black. "I'm tied up, I can't move. Where are we? I can't see." He tried to sit up but was unable to move off his side. *Are you two okay? Are Jonal and Stormbreaker here?* He projected.

I'm here. Your other friend is still unconscious. He's right next to me, so I know he lives, Stormbreaker said.

"Aurora and I are okay. I'm tied up, blindfolded as well," Lance replied.

I am in a cage! Aurora squawked out loud.

"Enough noise, bird," a gruff voice barked.

I am not just a bird, you overgrown boar, Aurora yelled.

Keelan heard metal clanging against metal and Aurora's surprised chirp.

Are you okay? he asked her.

I'm fine. Our friendly troll guard just rattled my cage. He'll pay for that when I get out of here.

Calm yourself, Aurora. We need a plan, and until I can see where we are, we need to just hold tight.

Easy for you to say, I can see where we are.

How long was I out?

Two days!

"Bird and dragon awake, Princess. Humans still out."

"Arveth used too much, didn't she," a feminine voice said. Her voice was soft and nothing like a troll's or wyvern's.

"Arveth only know how to spew mist, not control amount," a troll said, growling in what must have been a laugh.

"They will wake soon enough."

"Princess, more griffins with riders found," a new voice said.

"Excellent. Capture them…" her voice trailed off.

Keelan shifted his weight slightly, causing his feet to scuff across the coarse ground.

"One human wake," a troll said. "Sleepy for now." Keelan felt a hand whack him on the head. Footsteps leaving was the last thing Keelan heard.

When Keelan woke again, his blindfold had slipped a little, allowing partial vision out of one eye, and his head was still pounding. He looked around and saw he was in a cave. Lance was close to him, and Aurora was in a cage hung in the middle of the cavern. Stormbreaker and Jonal were a few feet past Lance. On the other side of the room was another griffin and a person. The griffin was a large male, not Snowcap.

"Lance, are you awake?"

"Yes, glad you're awake again."

"Me too. Who are our new friends?"

"The griffin's name is Cloudfeather; the other is Tarrid. He's still unconscious," Lance told him.

Keelan gasped in a sharp breath. "Is Leo here?"

"No, they were separated from the others. A couple of the griffins escaped and went for help."

"Do you think they'll be able to find us?"

"I don't know," Lance whispered sadly.

A few hours later, Keelan, Lance, Jonal, and Tarrid were moved to a different section of the cave. Carved into the cave's walls were small crevices, each about eight feet by eight feet, with thick iron bars blocking the entrances. Dim torchlight flickered from sconces on either side of the small openings, casting long shadows and providing the only light in the damp, oppressive space.

Their bindings were cut one by one before they were thrust into the crevices.

Keelan looked around his cell. Next to the bars, he had a bucket and a musty hay mattress on the ground.

"Are you okay, Keelan?" Jonal called from his cell.

"Yes, and you?"

A deep sigh came from Jonal, "I'm alive," he chuckled dryly.

"Tar, are you okay?" Keelan asked.

"I think so. My ankle is sore and swollen, but I think it's only a sprain. How did you get caught?"

"I was about to ask you the same thing."

They were interrupted by the sound of clicking heels on the rock floor.

Keelan wasn't sure what he expected to walk into the torchlight, but what did totally caught him off guard as a human female sauntering in. Her hips swung from side to side as she walked. She wore a black, floor-length, low-cut dress that sparkled in the light as if it were covered in stardust. Her auburn red hair hung loosely over her shoulders and down her back. A few loose strands framed her face with her high cheekbones and twinkling eyes. Keelan's breath caught in his throat. *She's beautiful,* he thought.

"I'm glad to see everyone is awake now," she said with almost a purr. It was the same voice from earlier. Her ruby lips curved into a sneer, and her eyes seemed to smoke. "Bow before your Princess," she snapped.

The four men remained on their feet.

"We will see how far you bend after a little encouragement," she said, her features twisting with anger. "Arveth!!" she yelled.

Something came down the hallway. Its awkward gait had Keelan's brain running in circles as he tried to imagine what sort of creature was approaching. He could hear long claws scratching and clicking on the rough stone floor. A brown wyvern poked its head into the cavern.

"Yes, my Princess Drakaina," it slurred.

"Be a good girl and put them to sleep, but only for a little while, mind you. I can't have them starving to death before I get answers."

"Yes, as you command," Arveth hissed and opened her mouth. More of the gray mist crept toward them.

"Now, don't fight it this time. From what I hear, it hurts worse when you fight," the Princess said.

Keelan groaned as he regained consciousness yet again. Now, he found himself tied to the cave wall with his hands above his head and his feet spread wide. He pulled on the chains, but they held fast.

"So good of you to wake," the Princess said. She was sitting in front of him with some sort of creature that he had no name for. The creature was straight out of a nightmare. It looked like a wolf gone horribly wrong, with pitch-black greasy fur, red eyes, and razor-sharp fangs that were too large for its pointed muzzle. On the creature's head sat four curved horns.

The Princess reached over and absentmindedly scratched it behind its short, nubby ear. The creature sat on its haunches, its long, black, forked tongue flicking out of its mouth as it wagged a tail that looked like it belonged to a rat.

"By the look on your face, I would venture to say you've never seen a hellhound before."

"Never even heard of one," he replied, his eyes glued to the beast before him.

"Well, then. You are in for a treat. You see, hellhounds are used to make uncooperative people talk. Its breath will make you see things that, while not real, will feel all too real. The longer you are exposed to the pheromones, the worse the hallucinations will be."

"Why are you doing this?" True panic was starting to set in. "What do you want to know?" Keelan struggled against his chains again.

"Calm yourself. If you cooperate, no harm will befall you. I need information about The Chosen and the new group that fractured off them."

"I don't know anything about The Chosen. I'm from Evansshire. I only found out recently that I had magic."

The Princess frowned. "I had heard Evansshire hated magic but wasn't sure if it was true. What about your friends, then? The other magic user and the dragon?"

Keelan didn't reply.

"I see. Well, then, I guess I will start with the elf." She shifted her eyes to his right. He hadn't seen Tarrid chained to the wall a few feet from him.

Tarrid glared at the Princess.

"What's your name, friend?" she said sweetly to him.

No reply.

"My name is Princess Ashrozo, Princess of the Wyverns."

Again, no reply.

"Impossible, wyverns can't take human form," Lance yelled from his cell.

"Well, I am special. I am a wyvern-dragon cross."

"Prove it. Take your grotesque wyvern form," Lance challenged.

Ashrozo stood and marched toward him. "I have nothing to prove to you, you dragon," she said, her voice elevating into a shout. She stopped halfway to him, spun on her heels, and slowly walked back to her seat, smoothing out her dress. "I'm sorry for the interruption. I believe you were about to tell me your name. No? Well, what a pity, but at least I have something to make you talk."

The hellhound rose and padded over to Tarrid. It stood a few feet before him, staring him in the eyes. It slowly opened its mouth, and a black mist drifted toward Tarrid. He closed his eyes tightly, his face twisting and contorting in pain. The hellhound stood motionless, but it was evident it was doing something to the elf. After a few tense minutes, Tarrid screamed and then passed out, hanging limply by his wrists.

"Tsk, tsk. Such a pity. He's strong. Most elves can't withstand that much. Now, tell me his name."

Keelan clamped his mouth shut, fear crawling through his veins like ice.

"Do you want him to die over a name?"

"Tar, his name is Tarrid."

"Now, that wasn't so hard, was it? I will return. I will have the answers I seek."

She stood and departed the cavern, leaving Tar and Keelan staked to the wall.

Ashrozo hurried down the tunnel, her stomach flipping and turning. When she thought she was far enough away, she bent over, emptying her stomach. She leaned against the cave wall, her legs and arms shaking. *I don't know if I can go through with this,* she thought. An image of her father standing proud before her as she gave him the information he needed while her brother hung his head in shame for failing made her straighten her back. *I have to do this.* She steeled herself, taking in long, deep breaths. *The young human seems weaker than the elf. If the hound tortured the elf, the human should talk, but what if the human really doesn't know anything?* She shook her head, *There has to be a better way.*

Keelan and Tarrid spent an uncomfortable evening chained to the wall. *Just one evening,* Keelan hoped. With no outside view, telling time was impossible. At some point, the torches were changed out once by a smelly troll, their only way of telling the passage of time.

Keelan's arms burned from being held above his head, and the chains bit deeply into his wrists. Princess Ashrozo returned when the torches were changed again. But this time, she wasn't alone. Two human men were with her, carrying a large basket. Both had their heads down and walked with slumped shoulders.

They placed it next to the chair Ashrozo sat in the previous day.

"Leave," she snapped at them.

Both men bowed and left. Keelan noticed both wore a bracelet similar to the one on his wrist.

"Sorcerer or dragon?" Keelan asked. His voice cracked. He licked his parched lips with an equally dry tongue.

Ashrozo smiled and walked over to him. When she neared, he could smell a faint scent of roses on her. Her dress, this time, was deep purple with gold lace on the bodice.

"Does it matter?" she asked him, looking him up and down like a piece of meat.

"I would like to know," he gritted his teeth.

"They are dragons. All servants of The King, my father, are dragons. Even his wife is a dragon."

"Impossible, no dragon would marry a wyvern. She's not his wife, just another slave," Lance shouted.

"If your friend isn't nice, he's not going to eat, make him be quiet," she said to Keelan.

"Lance, I'll handle this, please," Keelan said in little more than a whisper.

Lance didn't reply, but the scowl on his face said he would be quiet for now.

"Excellent. I have brought food for you all." She clapped her hands, and a woman hurried down the tunnel.

"Yes, my lady?"

"Feed the other human and the dragon."

"Yes, my lady."

The dragon woman retrieved two small baskets from the large one. She placed one before Jonal's cell just outside the bars and walked to Lance's cell. She put the basket down, but Lance grabbed her wrist before she let go.

"Theresa?" he asked quietly.

The woman looked up and gasped, dropping the basket. "Little Lord?" Keelan thought he heard her whisper.

"What is the meaning of this? Is this how my graciousness is rewarded? Release her at once," Ashrozo demanded.

"Patience," Theresa mouthed. Lance nodded and released her hand.

"I'm sorry, I thought I knew this woman. I was wrong," he said. He reached his hand through the bars to grab his basket.

Theresa curtsied to the Princess and then ran down the tunnel.

"Now then. We will resume our discussion while your friends eat. Tar, tell me about The Chosen."

Tarrid was once again silent.

Ashrozo sighed. "You must like pain." She nodded to the hellhound. Tarrid's defenses were weaker this time, his scream coming sooner.

"Why are the followers of Iton divided?"

Tarrid attempted to resist again.

"Why are the followers of Iton divided?" she repeated.

"They don't want to attack the wyverns, only defend against them," he finally said through gritted teeth, panting heavily.

"Now, that wasn't so hard, was it?" Ashrozo clapped and smiled. "So, it's the new group attacking, not The Chosen. Intriguing. My father is going to appreciate this information. What is the new group called?"

Tarrid was silent again.

She repeated herself three times before Tarrid blacked out from the pain.

"Oh, this will never do. I do believe he will die before giving me my answers."

She stood and approached Keelan.

"I've never met a sorcerer before, or human for that matter, you know. You look just like any dragon in human form." She ran her finger down his arm, tracing the muscles in his bicep. The path of her finger sent a shiver through him. "It is curious how dragons even have a human form." She ran her finger along his jawline and traced his cheekbone from one ear to the other, brushing across his lips. A smile tugged on her lips. "But dragons never get facial hair. I can feel some growth on your upper lip. How animalistic," she chuckled.

He tried to move his head away from her touch, his head thumping against the wall.

"Now, now. I won't hurt you."

"Forgive me if I don't believe you," his breath was ragged, his feelings and emotions battling.

"As long as you answer my questions, no one has to be harmed," she said sweetly. *Such a handsome face,* she thought.

CHAPTER

-15-

ASHROZO left the prisoners behind and strode purposefully toward her chambers. The dragon-sized hallways stretched endlessly before her as she walked with her back straight and nose held high. Dragon slaves hurried past her, shoulders slumped, chins pressed tightly to their chests.

As she rounded the corner, she came to an abrupt stop. Two of her father's honor guards stood stationed outside her door, their gleaming eyes shifting toward her. *No turning back now*, she thought, squaring her shoulders and continuing down the corridor.

Neither guard moved to block her path nor spoke a word. She pushed open the heavy door and entered. The heat inside hit her instantly. The hearth blazed furiously, making the room uncomfortably warm. Her father, King Ichakik, sat on his haunches near the fire, his eyes closed.

"Where have you been?" His voice, low and menacing, carried across the room though his eyes remained shut.

"I spoke with Mother briefly this morning and then went for a walk."

"Do not lie to me!" he roared, spinning around, baring his teeth. "Your mother is currently brooding and under constant watch. I will repeat myself one last time. Where have you been?"

She forced herself to stand firm, resisting the instinct to flinch under his fiery gaze. Swallowing hard, she answered, "I've been working to help you. I had an elf and a griffin captured, and I've been interrogating the elf with the help of a hellhound. The group that fractured from The Chosen did so because The Chosen refused to wage war against us. They only respond to our actions. It's this new faction that's been fighting us. They will only retaliate against our justified actions. The new group is the one that has been fighting."

He stared at her momentarily. "And why have you kept this information from me?"

"I only just uncovered this information," Ashrozo replied quickly. "He hasn't revealed the name of the group or their location yet."

He narrowed his eyes, his forked tongue flicking in and out. "Excellent work, daughter, but next time, do not hide it from me. You may continue your questioning for now. But don't take too long. I grow weary waiting for your brother's return."

Turning abruptly, he walked out of her chamber, his folded wings brushing against a shelf as he passed. She rushed to the shelf, catching it just before its contents spilled onto the floor. A few books tumbled down, but the rest remained in place.

Pausing, she glanced at one of the books in her hand. The title read *Ember, Eldjren's Familiar.* She gazed at the image of a phoenix etched into the leather cover, accented with gold and red ink. *Where did this come from?* she wondered.

A knock on her door made her jump. Quickly, she shoved the book into the inner pocket of her skirt before answering.

"Who is bothering me?" she yelled.

"King Ichakik wants you to move the griffin and elf, my lady."

"Now? He just said I could question them further," she flung open her door.

A male dragon slave stood there wringing his hands. "I cannot guess my King's thoughts, my lady. I am to help you."

"Fine, this way." She led him to the cavern she was using for her prisoners. She knew the slave would not divulge information to her father unless asked, but to be safe, she made him wait.

"Wait here, I will have the griffin and elf brought out."

"I am supposed to get them, my lady."

"All by yourself? You cannot carry one, let alone both. Wait here!" she repeated sternly.

He bowed, then recoiled as if she had struck him. She wasn't ready for her father to know about the two humans, the dragon, and the other griffin—not yet. She hurried down the hallway.

Arveth stood guard, one of the few wyverns that seemed loyal to her.

"Arveth, please put the griffin and elf to sleep; Father wants them moved."

"Yes, my lady." She first approached the griffin, gray mist pouring out of her mouth, then approached the elf.

"What is your father going to do to them?" Keelan asked. The elf only glared, grinding his jaw.

A pang of regret stabbed her as she locked eyes with the elf. He was brave, but that was going to get him killed. If only he had spoken to her, she could have spared his life, but his fate was out of her hands now.

"He is going to question him. For your sake, elf, answer him. Either way, you will die. Answer him, and it will be quick. I only wish you had told me what I needed to know."

"Tar, speak to her. Tell her now! You can save him if he speaks to you, right?" Keelan pleaded.

She shook her head sadly. "I could have, but now he wants them. I do not control their fate."

"What are you going to do with me and my friends?"

"He hasn't asked for you… yet." She tried to sound confident but didn't think she was succeeding.

Arveth grabbed the griffin and dragged him down the tunnel. After a brief pause, she returned for the elf, her expression grim. Ashrozo followed her out of the cavern to the waiting dragon slave. Theresa stood beside him, murmuring quietly.

"What are you doing here?"

"The Queen Mother has requested your presence, my lady."

Ashrozo sighed. "Fine. I'm coming." She turned to Arveth, who looked at her with her head tilted slightly. *Can I trust her? She has always been loyal to me.* "Arveth, can you move my remaining prisoners somewhere safe? I don't trust that slave who was just here. I must continue my questioning before any of the council finds out they are here, especially Avaaz. I don't trust him."

Arveth sneered. "A despicable Left Hand for the King," she spat.

Ashrozo smiled. "I couldn't agree more."

"I will move them to where only you and I will know."

"Thank you. I will never forget your kindness."

Arveth bowed and then left to move the remaining prisoners. Ashrozo turned to Theresa and raised an eyebrow.

"She's in the brooding chamber, this way, please."

"Lead the way," she said, annoyance lacing her words.

Theresa led her deep into the castle fortress, descending several stories until they were nearly at the same level as the cells and caves where her prisoners were kept. *I really need to get back down there,* she thought. *This had better be important—what a waste of time.*

Finally, Theresa stopped before a door and bowed. "I am not allowed inside," she said, sweeping her hand toward the entrance. "Please, go on."

Ashrozo squared her shoulders and entered the chamber. The brooding chamber was as she expected—well, most of it anyway. Several nests filled with eggs were scattered around. Numerous young wyverns scurried about, playing or eating. Several ran toward her, hissing and baring their teeth. An old female wyvern hissed and growled at them.

The young wyverns skidded to a halt, looking back at their brood mother and then back to the biped walking amongst them.

"No!" The brood mother said with a blast of fire.

Satisfied she would be left alone, Ashrozo continued to the very rear of the chamber where it was slightly cooler away from the central firepit.

Her mother sat on an enormous nest, three times the size of a wyvern's. It had to be that big to accommodate the Queen Mother in dragon form.

Ashrozo rarely saw her mother as a dragon. The icy blue scales glistened in the torchlight, shimmering like frost on glass. Her silver wings, folded neatly against her sides, gleamed softly. Two long, slender silver horns twisted elegantly, curling back along her head and neck, giving her an air of regal grace.

Her silver-blue eyes lit up when she saw Ashrozo walking toward her. The tip of her tail flipped lazily back and forth beside her.

Thank you for coming, she projected.

A warmth passed through Ashrozo. She shivered at the sensation.

"Why must you invade my mind?" She tried to sound annoyed. She hated how dragon telepathy seemed so right compared to wyvern hissing.

"I'm sorry. I'm not comfortable speaking in this form," Arlayna said, stumbling over her fangs.

"Fine, do what makes you comfortable," Ashrozo replied.

Thank you, daughter.

Ashrozo suppressed a sigh as the comforting sensation flowed through her.

I wanted to see if you knew of your brother's whereabouts.

"Which brother?" she asked.

Arlayna snapped her head back. *Zarret, of course. Who else would I speak of?*

"I thought you might finally tell me about my older full dragon brother, that is all. Zarret has not checked in. Last I saw him, he met up with a couple of elven women."

The King told you about your brother? Her telepathy was barely a whisper in Ashrozo's mind, full of sadness.

Ashrozo's heart instantly sank with a sense of sorrow, but she clamped it down. *I will have no pity for the creature in front of me.* "My Father told me you had a son before coming to him. He searches for him, you know."

Arlayna bowed her head. *I pray daily that he never does.*

"Why am I here?"

A loud crack echoed through the chamber. Arlayna's eyes widened. *It is time,* she said sadly.

"Time for what?"

Arlayna stood and stepped off the nest. In the middle of the nest, a large black egg with golden striations sat. The egg pulsed, causing the golden strains to flare with each beat.

"Step aside." The brood mother rushed to witness the hatching.

The egg splintered. Ashrozo took a couple of steps closer, her heart quickening. *Would Father finally have the twins he craved?*

With one last blinding flare, the dragonette was released.

Ashrozo held her breath. *What would her new sibling look like? Would it even be alive? Would it look like a wyvern like her brother did, a human as she did, or a dragon? So many unknowns when dealing with species cross.*

A single cub lay in the middle of the egg shard; she looked like any other wyvern, except she was gold in color. She stretched her tiny wings out and flicked her tail. Ashrozo's eyes watered. She was beautiful.

"Cursed!" the brood mother screamed. She spun around and rushed out of the chamber.

Arlayna leaned down and nuzzled the tiny cub. The cub purred and then hiccupped, and a tiny ball of smoke escaped from her mouth.

"Did Zarret look like this when he was born?"

Arlayna nodded.

"What did I look like?"

Arlayna looked up at her. *I wasn't allowed to see you, as you were the first. Has your father described it?*

She nodded her head, "A disgusting pink human baby with no scales and little hair."

When I saw you, I thought you were the most beautiful thing in the world. You are still beautiful.

"Why are you crying?"

She will not be allowed to live.

"What?" Why not? Only Zar and I have survived hatching. Why would he have her killed?"

He allowed you and Zar. Unless I produce a twin, none other shall live. Also, she is seen as cursed among wyverns because she is golden. Very rare.

"None of this makes sense. He has killed all the others that you produced?"

Yes. I know, and I am so, so sorry. I wish I could get you away from here and teach you what you should know.

She stared at her mother and was about to ask her what she would teach her when the door to the chamber was thrown open.

The King scrambled in, walking with his wings as front legs.

"Let me see this cursed cub," he bellowed.

He rushed to the nest. His eyes went wide. He hissed and growled. "I grow weary of your failure." He whipped his tail around and smacked Arlayna in the face. "I must wait another three to ten years for another lone egg. You are doing this on purpose," he screamed.

"How is she doing this on purpose? That makes no sense, Father. She cannot determine when twins will be born."

"If she were a wyvern, it would have happened already, two to five eggs every other year. Damn dragons," he roared.

Ashrozo shook her head at her father's ramblings. "What will happen to my sister?" Ashrozo climbed into the nest and sat down next to the cub. The little wyvern chirped, snuggling next to her before rolling onto her back.

Ashrozo smiled as she tickled her belly; the cub cooed and started to purr. She looked up at Arlayna. Her mother had tears running down her face.

Suddenly, the cub screeched and then fell silent. She glanced down at the cub in her lap. The cub was slumped with her tongue hanging out of her mouth, the spike from the King's tail still buried deep in her chest.

"What have you done?" Ashrozo screamed. "She did nothing wrong. Why did you kill her?" Disbelief and terror raced through her body.

Ichakik bared his teeth and snapped his powerful jaws inches from her face, "Watch your tone with me, you pathetic, worthless creature."

Ashrozo's face twisted in anguish. She took a few stumbling steps backward, falling out of the nest. Everything she did was to win favor with her father. At that moment, she realized that would never happen.

"I should end your life and be done with you as well." His tail whipped back and forth as he contemplated.

He doesn't mean that, her mind raced.

Yes, he does. Back away slowly, a male voice whispered in her head.

The King growled, "Pathetic, weak creature." His tail whip gained momentum, and then he lashed out. Ashrozo threw her hands up to shield herself, knowing it would do no good.

The expected impact never came. Her father roared in pain; Ashrozo's eyes flew open. Her mother stood before her with Ichakik's tail in her great jaws. As a full dragon, she was twice his size.

"You will not harm her!" she declared, still holding his tail.

"I am King. I will do as I please," he screeched.

You will not harm my daughter, she projected.

The King roared again, "Get out of my head, dragon. She is my daughter; I will do as I please."

She is not your daughter, vile beast.

The King thrashed, trying to free himself.

Arlayna glanced over to her daughter. ***Run child. Find Theresa and Samuel; they will keep you safe. If I don't see you again, know that I love you very much.***

"What do you mean I'm not his daughter?"

No time, please go. Be safe. Find Lancet; he will protect you.

The King's roar echoed through the brood chamber, finally drawing attention. Three wyverns leaped onto Arlayna's back, their claws biting and scratching her. One of them slapped a bracelet onto her wrist. With a scream, Arlayna shifted into her human form and collapsed, weeping. Ashrozo scrambled backward, hiding behind a nest, momentarily forgotten in the chaos. The King cradled his partially severed tail with his clawed wings, his fury palpable.

"Get me a healer!!" he shouted.

Quickly, you must get out of here, the male voice urged again.

"Where are you? Who are you?"

Stay down and run to the rear of this chamber when I say so.

Ashrozo's heartbeat quickened. She wiped her brow from the sweltering heat.

Two dragon slaves entered and gathered up Arlayna, slinging her over one of their shoulders. The golden cub was left abandoned in the nest.

Run to the rear of the cavern. You will see a small hole in the wall. You must hurry. The brood mother is returning.

Heeding the strange voice, she ran to the back of the cavern, searching for the hole. She fumbled along the wall, feeling all over it; there were no torches back there.

You're almost there, just a little more.

A startled squeak escaped her as she fell into the hole.

You found it! Now, stay down and follow me. A long, fluffy orange tail disappeared down the tunnel.

Crawling on her hands and knees, she followed the strange creature into the dark hole.

Tears streamed down her face. ***What's going on?*** she thought.

I will answer what I can soon. We must keep going.

She stumbled. ***How does he hear my thoughts?*** The tunnel narrowed from all sides, squeezing in on her. She started to panic. ***I'm going to get stuck down here. Where are you taking me?***

We are almost through, just a little further.

Suddenly, the tunnel opened up. She took a deep, shaky breath as she peered into the darkness. "Where are we?" she whispered.

Welcome to my home. A small stream of fire pierced the blackness, igniting a pile of rags in a corner. The glow from the fire brightened the small cave.

Ashrozo looked around. There were numerous piles littered throughout the room. Her gaze shifted from one to another before settling on her rescuer. A small orange and gold tabby cat sat behind a pile of clothing.

"Thank you for saving me," she said hesitantly to the cat, not entirely sure if he was her savior.

You're welcome, he projected.

"H-how are you speaking to me?"

I'm a vaskakat, he said as if that answered the question. He opened his feathery wings and then snapped them closed again.

"But why did you save me?"

Arlayna asked me to help you.

Ashrozo lowered herself into a seated position, drawing her legs up to her chest and hugging them tightly. "I think he was going to kill me," she whispered, tears threatening to spill from her eyes.

He was going to kill you and then Arlayna. The vaskakat bowed his head. *He may still kill her.*

Ashrozo's breath caught in her throat. While she had never liked being around her mother, hearing that she was probably going to die was unsettling.

"Who are you?"

I am Zephyr.

"What are you doing here?"

I was born here.

"How have I never seen your kind before?"

This fortress didn't always belong to the wyverns, you know. Many years ago, this was the home to the Ragnis Dragons. Countless magical creatures once called this hallowed palace their sanctuary. Now, it's a death trap for most who dare enter.

"How have you survived?"

Zephyr stood and approached her, stopping just within reach. *My clan lived in these lands long before the wyverns took over. I'm the last one now, but I've managed well enough. He glanced around his surroundings. I have everything I need... and wyverns, well, they're terribly messy eaters. There's always food lying around,* he chuckled softly.

Ashrozo couldn't help but smile at the amusing creature before her. She glanced at the pile of clothes nearby, swung her legs around, and crawled over to it. Pulling out a couple of shirts, she held them up and asked, "And how exactly do you use these?"

Zephyr puffed out his chest. *Watch!* He sprang into the air and dove into the clothing, snuggling down deep before peeking his face out. *Very warm,* he projected.

Ashrozo couldn't help but giggle at his antics, but then the weight of her situation crashed over her. "What am I going to do?"

Stay with Zephyr. I protect you.

She looked up at the orange vaskakat, who was now purring loudly. A small smile spread across her face. "That is very kind of you. But I can't stay here."

Oh, I didn't mean here. I mean we stay together. Dragon-thingy and vaskakat companions.

"Dragon-thingy, huh?" Ashrozo straightened up and rubbed her eyes. "Do you know where Arveth took my prisoners by any chance?"

Of course, no wyvern does nothin' without Zephyr knowing.

"Good, can you take me there? I need to get them out of here." Zephyr jumped out of the clothing. *This way.*

KEELAN woke to find himself in a new cave alongside Jonal, Lance, and Stormbreaker. This one was damper and darker, but the smell was much improved.

His head throbbed, and his mouth felt beyond dry. *That mist she keeps spraying us with can't be healthy,* he thought.

He crawled over to Jonal and laid his hand on his chest. "Still breathing," he whispered.

"Keelan, are you okay?" Lance wheezed.

"Yeah, I'm fine; my head isn't, though."

"Oh good, glad it's not just mine. Where are we?"

A wyvern moved us here, Stormbreaker projected. *She asked for my assistance to help save you.*

Keelan and Lance both stared at him in disbelief.

"A wyvern is helping us?"

She said that a corrupt council member would kill us if she didn't get us all moved.

"Why didn't she tell us that? I would have walked here," Keelan rubbed his temples and stood shakily on his feet. "No bars this time, at least."

"Only looks to be one way in and one way out, though," Lance remarked.

"I think we should stay until the wyvern that helped us returns," Keelan said.

"You're not serious?" Jonal said softly.

Keelan rushed to his side. "How are you feeling?"

"Like a griffin fell on my head."

I'm fine, too, thanks for asking.

"Aurora! You're here, thank the gods. I didn't see your cage."

Aurora stood from behind Jonal and ruffled her feathers.

"Are Cloudfeather and Tar here, too?" Jonal asked.

Afraid not. The wyvern said the King found out about them and had them moved to question them himself. The Princess didn't tell him about us.

Keelan froze from exploring the cave. "Why did she do that?"

Stormbreaker didn't reply.

They're down here, a male voice projected. *Not too far.*

Yes, they're all awake.

Don't ask me why she didn't keep them under longer. I don't speak to wyverns.

Who are you speaking to? Keelan projected to the creature, having a one-way conversation.

How are you projecting to me, human? The creature screamed in Keelan's head.

"What's the matter," a hushed female voice drifted down the tunnel toward them.

One of them can project to me. I am not his familiar, he screamed.

Hissing and growling came from the tunnel. Lance and Keelan braced themselves for an attack.

A streak of orange and gold flew into the cave right at them and barreled into Keelan's chest, throwing him backward.

Who are you? The vaskakat on his chest projected, smoke coming out of his mouth.

"Hold up there! I'm not going to hurt you. I'm sorry I startled you. I forgot projecting back is not normal."

How do you do it?

"I don't know." Keelan tried to stand and brush the angry creature off of him.

The vaskakat opened his mouth, and a thin stream of fire shot out, missing the top of Keelan's head.

Keelan threw his hands up and laid back down. "Really, I don't know. I'm told I have conceptual magic. I don't know if that makes any sense or not."

Aurora came out of nowhere and tackled the vaskakat, pinning him to the ground. ***Why are you attacking us?*** she screeched.

The vaskakat growled, attacking Aurora with all four paws full of claws. Fur and feathers flew in a cloud of smoke and flames.

Zephyr, stop this madness, a new voice projected.

Drake? Is that you? Zephyr stopped and peered around the cave.

Aurora tackled Zephyr, pinning him to the ground again, before she spun to face the newcomer. ***Who are you, and what do you want?***

"What's going on around here?" Jonal asked.

Yes, it's me, you fool. Now leave the prince and his friends alone, the new voice projected to them all.

A lizard about the same size as the vaskakat entered through a hole in the wall. It walked up to Lance, sat down, spread its wings wide, and bowed deeply. ***I am honored to be in your presence again, Prince Lancet.***

Lance stared at the lizard. "How do you know who I am?"

I am your familiar. I would recognize you at any age. It is me, Drake.

Drake the Firedrake, Zephyr, chuckled as he pushed Aurora off him. ***Such a clever name, I've always said.***

The Firedrake spun and shot a stream of fire at Zephyr, forcing him to take flight.

I was named by my prince. I was and still am honored by the name.

"Hold up here. Everyone needs to slow down. There is a lot of history most of us have no privy to," Jonal said.

"Can I enter the cave? What's going on in there?" A familiar female voice asked from the tunnel.

The three men spun to face the tunnel entrance.

"You may enter, Princess," Keelan finally said with a huff. "But we are not going back with you."

"I'm not taking you back. I'm going to get you out of here."

"And we are supposed to believe you after you tortured Tar and let him and Cloudfeather be taken to your father," Lance fumed.

"I don't know how he found out about them, but he doesn't know about you five. Please, Zephyr says he can get us out of the fortress, but we must leave now."

"We aren't going anywhere without Tar and Cloudfeather," Keelan crossed his arms.

"There's no time. We must leave now." Panic laced her words.

All eyes turned to the princess, trying to stand her ground. She visibly shook and slumped her shoulders, looking thoroughly dejected. "Zephyr, can you take us to them?"

Of course, this way. And then we finish our discussion, strange human, he glared at Keelan before bounding down the tunnel.

Keelan followed behind the princess, marveling at her turnaround in behavior. The confident, cold, and calculating woman he had come to know over the past few days was gone and replaced by the husk that walked before him.

He heard Lance's quiet murmuring from the rear of their group but couldn't make out the words.

What a strange turn of events, he mused.

Hold up here, Zephyr projected.

He disappeared down another corridor, only to return a moment later.

All clear, the hellhounds and the king just left.

"Hellhounds? He used more than one at a time?" The princess sounded horrified.

He had three. Now hurry. I don't think they will be left alone for long, and then the whole fortress will be looking for them.

The princess slumped onto the ground with shaky knees.

Keelan grabbed her wrist and yanked her to her feet, "This is your fault, come on."

They rushed around the corner, following the vaskakat into another room. Tarrid was chained to the wall with his head slumped onto his chest. Cloudfeather was lying on the ground, not moving.

Keelan and Jonal rushed to Tarrid and started working on the locks, while Lance and Stormbreaker went over to Cloudfeather.

"He's already gone," Tarrid whispered. "They killed him because I wouldn't talk," he croaked, breaking into sobs.

With Tarrid's arms free, he crumbled to the ground.

Quickly put him on my back, Stormbreaker said.

They raced down the tunnels, following Zephyr without question, hiding in vacant rooms occasionally before resuming their frantic escape. Suddenly, Ashrozo stopped.

"Wait, we must go back. There is one more to save."

"Whom else did you kidnap?" Keelan asked sharply.

"Not me, my father."

"Your father, the King?" Keelan almost screamed.

"No, that's not what I meant. I need to save my mother. My father captured her years ago."

"We don't have time for that!" Lance said in a panic. "Tar needs help. We have to get out of here."

Tears streamed down Ashrozo's cheeks.

The firedrake approached. ***Don't worry, Princess, your mother is escaping as we speak.***

She stared at the firedrake, "Are you sure?"

He nodded. ***Come, we must flee.***

With a grim expression, she nodded. "Zephyr, lead us out of here."

Actually, you will have to follow me now; come, Drake took off down the corridor.

The fortress was alive with activity. Every torch was ablaze, and the sky was filled with leathery-winged wyverns.

Samuel looked around the corner. "It's clear. Come, we must hurry. We'll be outside soon, and then we can hide in the forest."

"Are you sure this is the only option we have?" Arlayna asked.

"Please, my lady, we must leave," Theresa pleaded. "We have lived within these walls for far too long."

"But this is my home."

"Not anymore, my lady. We must get you back to your husband and son," Samuel said, grabbing her arm to keep her moving.

"But what about Ash? She's not safe here anymore."

"Drake says he found her. We will rendezvous with him outside the walls."

Arlayna gathered her skirt in one hand and rushed down the hallway.

"Find them, find them, find them!" King Ichakik screamed, green acid flame spraying around his throne room. Arlayna and her insufferable daughter had escaped, along with the elf prisoner. How could this have happened? "Everyone dies—no prisoners!" he screeched.

They sprinted through the dark forest, and for Ashrozo, it felt like an eternity. Never had she run so fast for so long. Her lungs and legs burned, yet she pressed on, fear propelling her forward. The screeches of searching wyverns echoed through the night sky. Thankfully, the forest provided cover from watchful eyes, and wyverns struggled to navigate on the ground.

Only a little further, make no sounds. Everyone is doing well, Drake projected.

They stopped next to a large pine tree with boughs reaching the ground.

Everyone in here. We'll be safe inside this sheltering pine, Zephyr said as he squeezed through the branches.

Keelan and Lance held a few branches aside for everyone else to fit through. Once inside, they fell to the ground, exhausted.

"Are we safe in here?" Ashrozo asked.

If the sorcerer could please put a sound barrier up, then we will be, Drake said.

"I can't access my magic," he held up his wrist, showing the bracelet dangling there.

"Here," Ashrozo said, extending her hand toward him. "I placed these on you. I'm the only one who can take them off."

He held his wrist out to her, and her fingers brushed lightly across his hand, sending shivers up his spine. As she unclipped the bracelet, it fell to the ground with a soft thud. She looked up into his eyes, and he held her gaze momentarily before looking away.

Lance and Jonal held out their arms next. All three took deep breaths as their magic returned to them.

Keelan recalled the meeting with his mother months ago, when she had cast a sound barrier around him and Lance to keep their conversation hidden from his father. Gripping Cedric's scale tightly in one hand, he summoned light in his other hand. It bloomed slowly, growing until the small clearing under the tree was illuminated. When the light faded, everyone breathed a little easier.

"Where to next?" Jonal asked.

We will stay here until the other three arrive, we will rest, and then we will leave, Drake told them.

"Who are these other three?" Lance asked.

Footsteps outside their tree caused everyone's hearts to skip a beat.

A man pulling two women approaches, Aurora told them.

The branches were being moved. Keelan and Lance jumped to their feet, ready for a fight.

An old man peeked his head through.

Samuel, you made it, Drake projected. *Stand down. These are our friends.*

"Boys, quickly. Help me. My friends have been injured."

Keelan and Lance rushed outside with him and brought back two women.

Lance gently laid one of them down and brushed her hair away from her face. "Theresa, oh no. What happened? She's dead."

"How do you know her?" the man asked.

"What happened?" Lance asked sternly, his eyes suddenly glowing.

"We were escaping when a wyvern found us. I was able to kill it, but it wounded Theresa and Arlayna."

"Arlayna?" Ashrozo squeaked. She crawled to the other woman's side, starting to weep.

"I'm so sorry. I'm so, so sorry," she whispered.

Arlayna looked up weakly and smiled at Ashrozo, patting her hand gently.

"How do you know Theresa?" Samuel asked Lance again.

"She was my nanny long ago," Lance said without looking up.

Samuel looked down at Arlayna; her eyes were wide, and her mouth was open in surprise. "Lancet?" she whispered.

Lance looked up at the sound of his name being whispered.

Ashrozo stared at her mother. "She's dying and calling for her firstborn," she whispered softly; Keelan almost didn't hear the words.

Lance left Theresa and crawled over to the other woman.

"How do you know that name?" he asked her.

"Oh!" Arlayna cried out when she saw Lance and reached for his hands. "Oh, my dear Lancet. I never thought I would see you again." Sobs overtook her.

"Lancet? You are Lancet—firstborn heir to the Ragnis line," Ashrozo hissed out. Her eyes clouded over, and her knuckles blanched. Keelan grabbed her shoulders and pulled her backward.

"Give them a few moments," he growled in her ear.

"You don't understand."

"I don't think you do either. Now, quiet."

"Lancet, how's your father?"

"Mother, is that you?" He pulled her hands to his lips, tears running down his face. "I never thought I would see you again. Why did you never return?"

Samuel knelt beside them. "The wyverns captured us. We stayed to protect Ash."

"What do you mean stayed to protect me?"

Lance turned his eyes to Ashrozo. "What do you mean *you*? Who is this woman to you?" he asked, his voice strained with emotion.

"Lancet, please, be calm. I need to speak with you, both of you," Arlayna said softly.

He momentarily glared at the wyvern princess before gazing at his mother's pale face. "What is it, Mother?"

"So many years ago, our home was attacked by wyverns, and your sister was stolen from us. Samuel and I tried to get her back, but I could not free her. I stayed to protect her the best I could. Ash, my dear," she reached for the princess's hand. Ashrozo hesitated before grabbing it.

Keelan stared at the family reunion wide-eyed, feeling like a thief stealing their last precious moments from them.

Ashrozo knelt on the other side of Arlayna.

"Ashera, my dear Ash, this is your brother Lancet, your twin brother."

"Twin!" Ashrozo exclaimed. "I was told he was older."

"Of course, that's what we told Ichakik," Samuel spat. "If he would have known you were a quarter of the prophecy, he would have killed you instantly."

Lance and Ashera stared at each other, words forgotten.

Arlayna squeezed both of their hands, drawing their eyes back to her. "Stay together and protect each other. Find the Vaelums and fulfill the prophecy. Bring peace to our lands once again." She placed Lancet's and Ashera's hands together and squeezed again.

Her breath became labored, and then it stopped with a slight hiss, her hands going limp. She was gone.

Ashrozo recoiled from Lance and her mother, turning her eyes to Samuel. "Samuel, why did she call me Ashera?"

"That's your real name, child. Ichakik changed it to suit him."

"But I'm not a dragon. I have no dragon form," Ashrozo said in disbelief.

"You have no wyvern form either, child. Look at your wrist."

She looked at the bracelet.

"Ichakik gave that to you and told you never to take it off, right?"

She nodded.

"It might be prettier than the rest, but it is still a magic suppressor." Ashrozo grabbed hold of it, desperately trying to remove it. Samuel grabbed her hands.

"We will capture a wyvern and have them remove it. It is the only way." Ashrozo nodded, looked back at her mother and brother, and then scooted backward, placing her head on her knees.

"Give her some time, boys. She's been lied to her whole life. We will bury these two before we leave."

Lance stayed beside his mother, holding her hand and trying to memorize her features. Growing up, he always tried to recall her face but never could. Her voice calling his name and her singing were all he was able to remember.

He finally found her, only to lose her again with so few words passed between them, fate's cruel joke. He shook his head and prayed silently, *I will see that he pays for what he did to you. For what he did to our family.* He felt something between cold resolve and warmth flow through his body.

He opened his eyes, scanning the dimly lit shelter. His gaze burned with fury. Glancing down at his hands, he twisted them slowly back and forth, watching as they began to glow with a fierce silver light.

Two shallow graves were dug under the shelter pine's protection. Keelan, Tarrid, Jonal, and Stormbreaker stood back, giving the grieving family as much space as they could.

Soon, it will be time to leave this sad place, but where to? Keelan thought and accidentally projected.

Back to Griffin's Keep. You can rest there before heading back to your homes, Stormbreaker told him.

"Thank you, my friend. I fear it will take a long time to reach it." Keelan knelt beside Tarrid. "Do you think you can travel?"

"I think so. Other than the mental attacks and a sprained ankle, I am well."

"How long will the wyvern keep searching for us?" Jonal asked.

Samuel sighed, "I don't think they will ever stop."

"Then how are we to escape?" Ashrozo whispered, her voice hollow and distant.

"With the cover of darkness for as many nights as possible. I will see you reunited with your true father, Princess."

"No, that will never do," Keelan stood and started to pace back and forth.

"Calm down, boy. You are doing no one any favors getting all worked up," Jonal snapped.

Keelan stopped pacing and turned to face Jonal. "I'm not the only one worked up, old man," he smiled.

Hey, that's what I call him, Aurora projected. The three familiars were outside of their protected tree, keeping watch.

"Jonal, tell me. Are there any spells that can get all of us from here to Griffins Keep quicker?"

"No, I'm sorry. I've never heard of any transportation spells."

"Hum," Keelan resumed his pacing.

Wyvern activity was heavy all day and into the early hours of the evening. The patrols seemed to thin a bit after midnight, so that is when they continued their escape.

Each morning, Drake scouted ahead, locating shelter pines for the group to rest beneath when the sun hung high overhead.

On the fourth day, Aurora announced that she hadn't seen a single wyvern in the sky. Zephyr and Drake both confirmed her findings.

"I still think we should travel only at night for a while longer," Samuel cautioned.

"I agree. I do not want to end up back in those caves again," Jonal grumbled.

Keelan, Lance, and Tarrid nodded their agreement. The only one who stayed silent was Ashera or Ashrozo; Keelan wasn't sure which name to call her. He glanced over at her. She didn't speak unless asked a question and seemed entirely withdrawn from life. She kept up with them without complaint, but it appeared a husk of a person was walking with them. He shook his head, *Can't help her right now,* he thought.

Don't worry. Zephyr's keeping an eye on her, Aurora interrupted his thoughts.

Do you mind? he said with an internal smile, ***this is my head, you know.***

Then you should guard your thoughts better, she chuckled.

"I think Stormbreaker and I should head to Griffins Keep tomorrow. We will gather a few griffins and then come back for you," Tarrid said.

"I can fly as well, you know," Lance replied. "If it's safe for one, it should be safe for two."

I can carry one person. Can you carry the other four? Stormbreaker asked.

Lance thought for a moment, "I don't know. I carried Keelan and Jonal before. It was easy enough. I'm willing to give it a try."

Ashera bolted to her feet.

"Problem, Princess?" Tarrid asked gruffly.

She looked at him with fear in her eyes, "I don't want to ride on the back of a dragon," she said softly. Keelan detected a vein of ice in her words.

"Well, you aren't riding the griffin with me," Tarrid spat.

Ashera's face twisted in rage, "How dare you speak to me like that."

"Now, hold up, everyone. Tar, who said you were riding Stormbreaker? That's his choice."

"Who made you the leader?" Tarrid asked angrily.

Keelan stared at him for a moment before answering, *He's changed,* he thought.

If you went through what he did, you would change too, Aurora projected privately.

I agree with Keelan; I will choose who accompanies me, Stormbreaker said.

Tarrid's face fell. "Of course, forgive me. I'm not thinking straight lately." He sat heavily on the ground.

Thank you. Stormbreaker nodded. *I will attempt to carry Keelan and Ashera. Lance can try to take three. If you are feeling up to it?* He asked Lance.

"I'm willing to try. Should we fly at night?"

I think that would be best. We will take it slow. I'm not sure how far we are from my home. Once in the sky, I will have a better idea.

Samuel watched the young men interact. He was eager to learn their stories, but now was not the right time. His priority was to get Lance and Ashera safely away from the wyverns, and then he would set out to find the human twins.

Night fell, and finally, Stormbreaker had air under his wings.

Thankfully, his saddle hadn't been removed during his captivity, not that it was much help with two bipeds on his back. But compared to walking on the ground, this was the next best thing. He glanced over at Lance, his three riders not faring entirely as well without a saddle.

Is there something wrong? Keelan asked him.

No, nothing. I was just thinking. How are you two holding up? Lance replied.

We're fine right now. Getting cold, though. Keelan projected. *Another item on the long list of why being a griffin was far superior to being human,* he chuckled to himself. He turned his awareness to Stormbreaker. *We are making good time, but I don't think Lance can go much further tonight.*

I already asked Drake to find a place to rest. He's coming back now.

Lance landed heavily on the ground; a giant sigh of relief escaped his lungs. ***That was harder than I thought it would be.***

"Sorry about that, my boy," Jonal chuckled.

"I wish I could get this infernal bracelet off. Then I could fly with you," Samuel huffed.

Ash can't do it?

"No, she didn't put it on me."

But you said any wyvern could take it off you, right?

"Well, yes. That's right. But she's not a wyvern."

"She put those bracelets on us and was able to remove them. Maybe they made all of them attuned to her."

Samuel opened his mouth and then snapped it shut. "It's definitely worth a try. Princess, do you mind?" He held out his wrist.

She shrugged and tried to unclasp it. With a soft metallic click, the bracelet fell to the ground. Somehow, her face fell into an even deeper frown.

Samuel's face broke into a large smile; he stretched his back and arms and rolled his neck. "I can't tell you how good that feels," he thundered.

"How long has it been since you transformed?" Jonal asked.

"Over forty years, I don't know if I remember how." Suddenly, a gold and purple mist engulfed Samuel. Everyone closest to him scrambled out of the way. The mist grew and grew until a cloudy mountain stood before them.

When the mist cleared, a roar shook the ground, knocking pinecones from the trees. An enormous purple and gold dragon stood next to them. He shook out his body and unfolded his wings, then started to laugh.

What's so funny? Lance asked.

I actually thought I would be all gray. Let's see if I can still fly. He leaped into the air and blasted everyone below him with a gust of air.

His flight path was unsteady, but soon, he was soaring so high they lost him in the predawn light.

Lighter load tomorrow, Lance remarked. *How many more days do you think?*

We will leave earlier tomorrow and be at my home before daybreak, Stormbreaker projected.

CHAPTER

-17-

VOLCANOES encircled Griffin Valley, but it was the windswept mountain before them that captivated Shaylee the most. The rugged land jutted sharply into the sky, resembling a monstrous wave of rock and earth frozen in time. As the sun began to set, the aerials descended into the valley, only to be greeted by the thunderous roars of six griffins swooping in to intercept them.

Halt! Why have you returned?

Starfire flew forward and took charge. *After we left, we were attacked by wyverns. Three of our group and the two bipeds were captured. We found Leo and two griffins. Our leader and the leader of The Blade are still missing. We request assistance.*

Follow me, the lead griffin projected.

The griffins circled their group, leading them to a rock spire in the middle of a large lake. Shaylee stared in awe at the rock structure. The lead griffin landed on a large platform that jutted out of the structure.

Wait here!

Shaylee, Fawn, Leo'venath, and Zarren dismounted to wait; thankfully, they didn't have to wait long.

Why have you returned? A large gold griffin projected, his piercing eyes glaring into them.

Thank you for meeting with us, Chief Stormwing. The wyverns have captured some of our group. We are asking for your assistance in their rescue, Starfire said to him with her head bowed.

He stared at them silently for several uncomfortable minutes. *I will risk no more against the wyverns. My son was stolen; they have taken enough from me.*

You are just going to allow our friends to remain captive along with your own son? Shaylee projected to him.

Stormwing's head snapped back. *Who are you?* He demanded.

Shaylee Faeven, she replied, allowing her projection to reach everyone. She glanced at Leo'venath and Zarren; both looked at her with their mouths open.

How are you projecting to me?

I don't know how I do it. I just can.

Are you related to Keelan Keifman? Stormwing asked.

Shaylee's eyes widened. *I met him once two years ago. How do you know him?*

He came here looking for the cure. His mother is afflicted, Starfire clarified.

Shaylee tilted her head. *Why do you ask if I know him?*

He can also project his thoughts when he shouldn't be able to.

Where is he now? Shaylee asked.

With my son and his two companions. You may stay until you are rested. Then you must leave my valley and never return. He turned abruptly and flew off.

"What do we do now?" Zarren asked.

We shall rest and then start our search. Come, I know a place to refresh ourselves. Starfire took to the sky.

She led them to the base of a sheer-faced mountain, where a waterfall cascaded down into a steaming pool below. Water vapor rose, creating a thick mist that shrouded the surrounding forest in fog. The hot springs turned out to be exactly what they needed after their long journey. Starfire and her two griffins went hunting while Dreamcrest foraged on her own.

Fawn sat on a rock with her feet dangling in the warm water. Nearby, Leo'venath and Zarren were fully submerged in the steamy pond, their tension slowly dissolving. Fawn glanced around the misty clearing but noticed Shaylee hadn't returned yet. She had mentioned needing time to think before quietly walking off into the woods.

Shaylee walked away from the humid clearing, with Lyra jumping from bush to bush keeping pace with her. Life was changing so quickly. Two years ago, she was a young girl living a carefree life in the small village of Threndy. Now, she was traipsing across the kingdom, trying to rescue a friend. She sighed deeply, sitting down next to a berry bush.

Why has everything changed? She asked Lyra.

Life changes as we grow. Nothing you can do about it, so why worry?

There are plenty of reasons why I should be worried. What am I doing out here? If Leo and Tar could be captured when they had six griffins with them, what makes me think Fawn and I can rescue them?

We rescued Leo and two griffins, she said matter-of-factly.

By pure chance. I don't know how we are going to infiltrate a wyvern fortress to rescue Tar and Cloudfeather. She stopped and crumbled to the forest floor, tears streaming down her cheeks.

You just need help, a new voice said.

Lyra's hackles rose, and her tail puffed twice as big, a deep growl resonating in her chest. Shaylee scrambled to her feet.

"Who's there?"

Someone who can help you get your friend back.

"Show yourself!"

A small blue light flew through the canopy toward them. Shaylee took a couple of steps backward.

Be not afraid. If I wanted to hurt you, you would already be dead. The blue light flew closer.

Shaylee finally recognized what the creature was as it approached. "I've never seen a pixie before," she said.

The pixie looked like a tiny version of a fairy with light blue skin, copper hair, and emerald, green eyes. Her green and blue shimmering wings moved as fast as a hummingbird's.

"You said you could help me?"

Name's Meta. The tiny pixie bowed at the waist so deep she did a full flip in the air. *But no, I can't help you. Look at me. I'm tiny,* she started to laugh. Her laugh sounded like tiny bells ringing.

You said you could help! Lyra growled at the pixie.

Meta glared at the vaskakat. *Keep your predator away from me!* Meta shrieked.

Lyra, please, Shaylee projected. *I apologize for her behavior,* she directed her projection to the pixie.

Meta flew closer to Shaylee, stopping inches from her nose, causing Shaylee's vision to double and her head to snap back.

Oh, you are special, aren't you? My mistress said you were special. I didn't believe her, but here you are, projecting your thoughts to me. Me! She shrieked again. *A magical creature having a two-way conversation with a human.* Again, the pixie broke into melodious laughter.

I'm growing weary of this conversation. Now, tell me what you can offer me, or be gone!

Oh, mistress is going to love you! I cannot help you, but my mistress can. I'm traveling with some men. They are camped just outside this valley. They are gathering a human army to fight the wyverns. Likewise, they can help you get your friends back.

I would like to meet these men.

Oh, goody. The pixie fluttered her wings even faster. *Come, come. We shouldn't keep them waiting.*

I can't go without my friends, Shaylee replied.

Meta's lips turned into a deep scowl. *I don't know about them. Do you really need their help if you have my friends' help?*

Shaylee folded her arms. "We all go."

Meta's face brightened. *Okay, let's get your friends!*

It took a little convincing before everyone agreed to at least meet this human army. By daybreak the next morning, they were following the flighty pixie out of Griffins Valley. The pixie took off at an impossible speed, leaving them all behind.

"Is she just leaving us?" Fawn asked.

"I don't know. Let's land here and see if she returns," Shaylee said as she pointed to the ground.

Dreamcrest descended, circling the valley as she did so.

When they landed, several men walked from the cover of the trees.

"I don't see any weapons," Leo'venath said quietly.

Suddenly, Meta reappeared.

Shaylee, this is General Lucas. He has agreed to help you find your missing friends.

The one identified as the general approached and bowed slightly.

"Good morning. I am sorry to hear about your troubles. How can we help?" He sounded sincere.

"Wyverns ambushed my group and took an elf and a griffin hostage. We need to get them back," Leo'venath told him.

The general scratched his chin in thought. "I think we can help you. Come, let's talk and eat."

General Lucas led them to his camp and then excused himself.

Shaylee and Fawn stayed next to Dreamcrest while Leo'venath spoke to Starfire, walking away from the camp a bit. Zarren walked around, watching the general's men as they repaired tack and sharpened their weapons.

General Lucas glared at the pixie as she flew off. She brought four people, a cat, three griffins, and a pegasus into his camp. *Griffins and a pegasus,* he marveled. *This could be a profitable meeting if I can subdue them.*

He gestured for one of his men to follow him. "Keep everyone in line. Best behavior. The girls are not to be touched. I don't want them even looked at," he growled. "I don't know what we are going to do with them yet. I need to send a message to Sephra."

"Yes, sir. Aren't going to be easy. Most of the men haven't seen a woman in some time." He leered in the girls' direction.

"They aren't women, they're girls, can't be more than fourteen or fifteen. You tell all the men if either is harmed or touched in any way, their loins will feel my dagger."

His man snapped his eyes back to the general's scowling face. "Yes, sir. They won't be touched."

"Meta!" Lucas hollered. The pixie hastily flew to him.

"What do you want, human?" She snapped.

"Watch your tone with me, pixie!"

Meta's eyes glazed over, her pupils growing in size. "Watch your tone with me, HUMAN!" She screamed the last word.

"Fine, fine, you little demon. I need to send a message to our mistress. How do we do this?"

"You tell me the message, I deliver it, same as always."

"I've never seen you leave; how do I know you're going to her?"

"I'm magical and spectacular. That's all you need to know. What's the message?"

"Are you sure this is the girl she's been looking for?"

"Oh, yes," she nodded her head so hard she did a somersault in the air. "I was there when she was abandoned. If it weren't for a damn fairy, she would have been raised by my mistress."

"Fine, tell her we found the girl, but we need to get her away from her friends somehow. Our mistress promised me I would lose no more men, and I see that happening with those three monsters out there."

"Monsters? The griffins? I can handle them," she said, rolling her shoulders.

"Now, now. Let's not be hasty. Let's see if Sephra has any ideas." Lucas shook his head at the pixie's bravado.

"Sephra? You mean our mistress, the magnificent Mistress Warlock." Meta's face twisted in rage.

"Yes, of course. My apologies. Please send my message."

Meta smiled sweetly at him and then disappeared.

He jumped backward at her disappearance, swearing under his breath.

With a flash of light and an audible snap, Meta reappeared a few minutes later. As soon as she materialized, she was dragged to the ground by the large bag in her hands—well, large for her. General Lucas glared down at the pixie.

"What did she say?" He asked.

"Our glorious leader, the Mistress Warlock, has commanded you to give the entire party some of this." She pulled out a vial of liquid from the bag. "Make sure some of this gets on all the food tonight. A little goes a long way, she says." Meta sat on the ground with the vial between her legs. She grabbed the cork and started to wiggle it back and forth.

"What are you doing?" Lucas snatched it away from the pixie. "If you open that, you're going to end up spilling it." He held the tiny vial up and swished around the golden liquid. "What will this do? Kill them all?"

"Oh, no. Even better." She started to laugh, rolling on the ground.

"Are you going to tell me what this damn liquid does?" He snapped.

Meta stopped rolling and fluttered into the air, still laughing, shaking her whole body to remove pieces of grass. "Dear General, this liquid will make those fools do whatever you say. You'll be their best friend and fully trustworthy. You could even tell them to kill themselves, and they would say thank you as they slit their own throats."

A slow smile spread across Lucas's face as he gazed at the shimmering liquid. "This is going to be a very profitable day."

"Welcome to my camp. I hope everyone will be comfortable tonight. I apologize for being pulled away earlier—very poor manners on my part," Lucas said as he rejoined his new companions.

The four people were huddled together next to the pegasus. Slowly, they left their winged companion. "My cook is preparing something that I'm sure will be to everyone's liking. Now, let's get acquainted." Lucas smiled, revealing a row of yellow-stained teeth. "I am Lucas Erzana, though General or simply Lucas will do. You've already met my little winged friend, Meta. The rest of my men will arrive later, but their names matter little." He gestured to a ring of stones encircling a modest fire. "Please, sit and share your story." He gestured to a fire. The girls looked at each other and then over to the men. The short girl and both men nodded.

That was strange, he thought to himself. *Are they somehow communicating?* He shook his head and shrugged off the thought.

"So, what brings such a unique group together?" He asked lightheartedly.

The brunette girl spoke up, "A common enemy."

He nodded his head, scratching his chin absentmindedly. "Ah, yes. The wyverns. Troublesome though they are, are you lot really equipped to fight them?"

"We don't plan on fighting them. Only rescue our friends and be gone," she said.

"I'm sorry for your loss; truly, I am. But a rescue doesn't seem possible with so few of you."

The older girl stood up, her face flushing with apparent rage. "Meta said you could help us!" she almost screamed.

Lucas raised his hands in a placating gesture. "Please, miss, calm yourself. I'm sorry I didn't catch all your names."

She took a deep breath, regained her composure, and sat back down. "My name is Shaylee. This is Fawn, Leo, and Zar."

She omitted the winged creatures' names, he thought. *Interesting, maybe they don't have names.* "Thank you, Shaylee, and nice to meet all of you. Even though I feel your rescue attempt won't work, I am willing to help you come up with some ideas. Let's eat first, and then we will discuss all the options we can think of."

Shaylee looked at her friends, and slowly, they all nodded. Lucas narrowed his eyes at the silent exchange. *We will see how well that potion of Sephra works. I need to find out what is going on between these four.*

This stew is good, Shaylee thought to everyone. Leo'venath grunted in reply, and Zarren and Fawn nodded.

Lucas's cook even supplied a large elk for the griffins, a fat ground squirrel for Lyra, and an enormous scoop of grain covered in molasses for Dreamcrest. Soon, all of them were full and sitting around the fire contently. Shaylee hadn't felt this at peace in a long time.

"How are you feeling, Shaylee?" Lucas asked, sitting down beside her.

"I haven't been this relaxed… ever." She started to giggle.

"Glad to hear it." Lucas smiled at her.

She couldn't help but smile back. *He is such a wonderfully lovely man,* she thought.

"So, why don't you tell me all about yourself and your friends."

"Okay, what would you like to know?"

"When I first met you, it looked like you communicated with your friends without words."

She nodded her head but then paused. *I shouldn't tell him anything, but why does it feel like the right thing to do? Surely, it must be okay to tell him, but not his men; they cannot be trusted,* she thought, the words seeming to come from another. "I can speak telepathically to other magical beings," she whispered.

His eyes opened wide. "How?" he whispered back.

"It's a secret. Can you keep a secret?"

He nodded.

"Growing up, I thought I was an Elvenfae, a half-elf, half-fairy. But I recently found out that I am just a human. A sorceress, but still a human."

"How can you communicate with the others?"

"Telepathically. Fawn is an elf, Leo is a sorcerer, and Zar is a dragon locked in human form. But again, that's all a secret."

"Of course. Don't worry, I understand. When did you find out you were a sorceress?" He smiled, an eager expression on his face.

"Not long ago. I haven't come to grips with it yet." She looked over at Leo'venath, who was falling asleep sitting up. "I haven't even told Leo. He's going to be so surprised." She broke into a fit of giggles again. "Why do I feel so funny?"

"Being relaxed and feeling safe can make you feel like that. Don't worry."

She nodded her head and closed her eyes.

"So, you are a human but raised by an elf and a fairy. But who are your birth parents?"

"Oh, I have no idea. My ma, Rosepetal, she's a fairy, said someone left me in the forest right after I was born. I don't know how to feel about that. At least Ma said she was crying and praying someone would save me."

Lucas was silent for several minutes. Shaylee swayed back and forth to the sounds of the wind blowing through the treetops and the crickets serenading them.

"There is only one reason I can think of. You must have been a second-born twin."

"A twin? Why would you think that?"

"In Evansshire, twins are forbidden, and if born, both must be put to death." Shaylee's hands flew to her mouth, which was open in a silent scream. "I have heard of parents trying to save one. One will be killed, and the birth of it hidden and kept secret."

"That's horrible. How could a mother choose which one to kill?"

"I think the midwives make that choice." He shook his head with a deep. "Difficult decision for sure. But a parent makes tough choices for their family sometimes."

"I might have a twin out there somewhere! I wonder if she looks like me?"

"Your twin could be a boy," Lucas replied, causing Shaylee's eyes to widen slightly. She nodded, falling silent as she contemplated this new perspective. Lucas considered her reaction, intrigued by the implications. *Sephra knows this girl is a twin; I wonder what she thinks about it.* As a former general of Evansshire, he was well aware of the reasons twins were outlawed there. *I must figure out her motives and use that information to my advantage.* He scratched his chin thoughtfully as a lone wolf howled in the distance.

"Look what I found, General."

Lucas looked up from sharpening his dagger. The afternoon sun was high in the sky. One of his men led three horses. Lucas stood and walked over to them.

"Fine horses, well, two of them are," he said as he ran his hands down the blood bay's neck. "Where did you find them?"

"Over yonder, nestled in the trees, all content and happy all by their lonesome." His man gestured to the wind-swept mountain. "Don't you recognize this one, sir?" He pointed to the perfect sword marking on the blood bay's forehead.

Lucas traced the white mark, a smile growing on his face. "I wouldn't imagine those boys abandoning these fine animals."

"No, sir."

"Tell the boys to dig in. This is where we wait."

"Yes, sir." His man snapped to attention and then sprinted away. "Beautiful horse."

Lucas looked around the horse's neck. Shaylee and Fawn were approaching, with the vaskakat circling their heads.

"Where did they come from?" Fawn asked.

"We found them grazing by themselves. We've decided to stay here for a while until their owners return."

"That is so kind of you." Shaylee smiled at him.

"We are good Samaritans whenever we can be." He smiled back. His stomach crawled at his words. *How much longer must I keep this infernal act up? Those boys better get back here soon.*

CHAPTER

-18-

WELCOME *to Griffins Keep!* Stormbreaker projected to everyone. ***Do you remember where we rested after the fall?*** He asked Lance. ***We'll rest there. I showed you the hot springs but didn't show you what it does. Follow me.***

Lance and Samuel banked their wings and followed Stormbreaker into Griffin's Valley. Just as before, they were intercepted as they crested the mountaintops.

HALT!! The lead griffin yelled in their minds. ***Stormbreaker? Is that you?***

Yes, please tell my father I have returned. Mother will know where we are.

Six griffins circled the two dragons, trying to herd them forward.

You must follow me at once.

No, if he wants to see me, he will find me.

Stormbreaker dove underneath the lead griffin. ***Follow me, my*** friends.

The hot springs were just as Keelan remembered them. Steam rose from the warm water, and a waterfall gently cascaded down, causing a cloud of mist to hang above the water's surface.

Everyone in the water!

"I'm not up for a swim, thanks," Jonal said.

No swimming is necessary. I just want everyone to relax and sit.

Keelan slid off Stormbreaker's back and held his hands out, asking Ashera if she needed help. She nodded slightly, swinging her leg over Stormbreaker's neck and placing her hands on his shoulders. Keelan grabbed her slender waist and guided her off. Once on the ground, she backed away from his touch, her face flushed.

Keelan shook his head at her reaction and then used his magic to help Jonal off Lance's back while Tarrid jumped off Samuel's, wincing as he landed on his ankle.

Stormbreaker walked toward the water quickly, entering without hesitation. He continued walking until his entire back was submerged, and a long, deep sigh escaped his lungs. *Come on, it's worth it. Trust me.*

Keelan and Lance rushed to the water's edge, with Tarrid close behind them.

"Clothes and all?" Tarrid asked.

Keelan shrugged and plunged in. Instantly, every ache and bruise seemed to be gone. Air rushed out of his lungs, and a sense of content calm washed over him.

Tarrid shouted in pain when his ankle contacted the water before his whole body shook, and then he sighed with relief.

Sorry, I should have mentioned that severe injuries would hurt at first.

"Thanks for the warning," Tarrid said. Keelan glanced at him; he sounded upset, but the look on his face told a different story.

Jonal and Samuel entered next, equally impressed with the healing water. Ashera was the only one who hadn't entered yet. Even the three familiars splashed and floated in the water.

Come on, Princess, Stormbreaker urged.

She shook her head.

"Let her be," Tarrid snapped. "She doesn't deserve any of life's little pleasures."

Ashera's shoulders slumped, and she bowed her head, staying where she was, slowly lowering herself to the ground.

Keelan wanted to chastise Tarrid for snapping at her, but she hadn't shown them kindness thus far. Still, it didn't seem entirely her fault. He shook his head and decided to let it be.

Keelan sat next to the fire, drying his clothes. He watched Stormbreaker and Stormwing having a private conversation. Tarrid and Jonal sat together, talking quietly. Lance and Samuel were also engrossed in conversation.

Just before sunset, Stormwing left them; Stormbreaker did not look pleased.

"What's the matter?" Keelan asked him.

He's old and stuck in the past.

"Care to explain?"

I told him about our capture and captivity. I told him we needed to join The Blade to help remove the wyverns from our part of the world. But he just won't listen. He insists we're safe in our valley.

"Didn't you tell him that was where we were captured from?"

Of course, but all he says is that the watch will be doubled.

"So, what are you going to do?"

I'm joining The Blade. I have no future here as the Chief's runt.

"I will be heading back to Creekside as soon as possible. Am I able to take any firebush with me?"

Yes, he will have some here tomorrow.

"I can't thank you enough."

No thanks needed.

Samuel clapped his hands loudly, startling everyone out of their thoughts. The moon was high overhead, and the fire burned brightly. Everyone was tired, but no one was ready to sleep.

"I think further introductions are in order. I've told you about my time with the Ragnis Royal family, the resistance against the wyverns, and my time protecting Queen Arlayna and her daughter, Princess Ashera. Tar, what are your next plans?" Samuel asked.

Tarrid looked startled to be asked to speak first. "I will be returning to The Blade. I have firebush to administer and wyverns to crush," he glared at the Princess.

"And what of you, Keelan and Jonal?" Samuel asked.

"I must heal my mother. The whole purpose of this trip was to obtain firebush and get back to her as quickly as possible," Keelan replied.

Lance nodded. "That was and still is our goal."

"My Prince, you will not be joining your friend," Samuel said frankly.

"What do you mean?" Lance asked, his tone curious and concerned.

"I will be taking you and your sister directly to your father. We must get both of you in hiding. I will then be off looking for the Vaelum twins."

"I'm sorry, Samuel, but that is not what I am doing," Lance said with conviction and a regal tone.

"I will not have my charge speaking to me in such a manner."

"Your charge? Says who?" Lance stood up; his demeanor defiant.

"Your mother."

Lance's face softened. "You will take Ashera to our father. I will be staying with my friend, helping him complete his mission. I cannot abandon him in his time of need."

"I'm not leaving Lancet," Ashera blurted out.

All eyes turned to her.

"You don't get a say, Princess," Tarrid growled. "You lost that right when you became a torturer."

"That's enough, Tarrid," Keelan said, standing up. "Everyone is here by choice. Everyone gets a say. We do not dictate others' lives. What she did was wrong, but everyone deserves redemption if they can prove they've earned it."

"You can have her then," Tarrid said with open disgust.

Keelan looked down at Ashera, her large, almond-shaped, blue eyes glistening with unshed tears. *She's beautiful in the moonlight,* he thought.

Zephyr swooped into the center of the group, his hackles raised and tail fully fluffed. ***What is all this negativity surrounding my dragon? I will not tolerate such thoughts and feelings.***

Tarrid stared at the vaskakat who was stalking toward him.

"Tell me, vaska. How can you align yourself with this creature? She's not fit to be called a dragon. Dragons are noble beings, not monsters."

She's not a monster. You have no idea what she's been through. You think your mental torture was terrible. The king almost

killed her! The very being she was raised to believe was her father—the one she spent her entire life trying to impress and win favor from. She didn't deserve his cruelty! Her first encounter with you made her empty her stomach.

Tarrid eyed the Princess. She wrung her hands, eyes downcast, and rolled in on herself. He huffed and then left the fire's light.

It will be ok, Ash. I will stay with you and help you.

Ashera looked up at the vaskakat and reached her fingers toward him. As he approached her, he started to purr and curled up at her feet.

"I have a question," Lance said, breaking the awkwardness. "How does it appear that Ashera and I have familiars? I didn't think dragons had that ability."

Drake and Aurora landed on the ground next to them.

Most dragons do not, Drake said. *The Ragnis Royal family is different. But it's not the only family line that is different, mind you. I think it is time for a brief history…*

Make sure it's brief, lizard, Aurora chuckled. *You tried that earlier, but let me tell you, that was not brief.*

Drake glanced at the Phoenix before shaking out his wings. *Fine,* he grumbled. *Before the two kingdoms came into existence, there was only one. Humans and dragons coexisted, working together and supporting one another. Dragons have always possessed magic and learned long ago how to take on different forms. In those forms, they discovered the ability to interbreed, leading to the emergence of dragon hybrids. That is how humans acquired their magic. As you know, dragons age slowly, so those hybrids that bred back with dragons retained both their dragon and human forms, along with their longevity. However, those who interbred with humans lost their dragon forms and their long lives but kept their magic. Centuries passed—few generations for dragons, but many for humans—resulting in a further decline in abilities for the humans.* He turned to Jonal.

"So, if mages' and sorcerers' magic comes from dragons, does that mean having a familiar originated with us?" Lance asked.

Not exactly. The bond with a familiar helps magic remain controlled within the human. More mages tend to have familiars than sorcerers, as those further from dragon heritage need extra assistance to maintain control. While dragons don't require a familiar for this purpose, the connection calms their emotions, Drake explained.

In summary, he glanced at Aurora. *The human Royal line infused dragon magic through marriage to ensure their heirs retained significant magical power. Despite the dilution, they retained a high level of magic even after the fall of the Kingdom of Oshana.*

Keelan pondered his words. Out of those gathered, only Jonal and Lance knew he was the Vaelum heir. "Do you know anything of the prophecy?"

Drake nodded his head. *I once met Ember…*

You met Ember? Aurora asked excitedly.

Drake nodded.

He's my sire! She exclaimed, hopping up and down, her tail igniting.

What does Ember have to do with the prophecy? Keelan asked.

Ember was Eldjren's familiar. And Eldjren is the seer that foretold the twins before you ask.

"Do you know what the twins must do?" Lance asked next.

The Ragnis twins stand before you, tasked with locating the Vaelum twins. Their union is essential, and they must unite before the world is cast in red by a solar eclipse before their sixteenth name-day. In their search, they must also find the Infinite Medallion, which will guide them in their destiny.

"What's this about their sixteenth name-day? Ash and mine are long gone."

I always assumed it was the Vaelum twins' name-day being referenced.

"I've never heard that part of the prophecy before," Lance said. Jonal nodded in agreement.

Oh, yes. Eldjren wanted to keep some things secret. Ember had his own book. I read it in that one.

"Do you know where the book is?" Keelan asked eagerly.

It's in Ash's pocket.

Ashera's hand fell on her hidden pocket. "How did you know?"

I put it in your room, silly child.

Ashera slowly pulled out the book, fingering the scrolling and imprint of a phoenix.

Yup, that's him, all right; look, one wing is shorter than the other, Aurora projected, peering over Ashera's shoulder.

"May I see the book?" Jonal asked her. She shrugged and handed it to him.

Jonal scooted closer to the fire and cast a couple of sun-orbs to read by.

"Samuel, how will you find the twins?" Keelan asked.

"I'm not sure yet, but I will figure out a way," Samuel said.

He nodded shyly and turned back to the firedrake. "Why are twins needed?"

That I do not know. Something about the magical bond between them and then the solar eclipse making them even stronger.

"Well, Samuel, you are in for a bit of a surprise. I am the last of the Vaelum line."

All eyes fell on Keelan.

That's excellent news. Why didn't you tell us about it before now? Where's your twin? Drake projected, excitement evident in his words.

"My twin died at birth. I'm afraid the prophecy is going to have to wait a while."

"That's not possible. Your twin must be out there, somewhere. You have magic," Samuel said.

"That's because he has a familiar and found a natural artifact. His latent magic was able to surface because of it. It is quite remarkable," Jonal said, shaking his head as he skimmed through the small book.

No, that can't be true," Drake protested, his voice rising with disbelief. *Ember had spent countless hours discussing this prophecy with Eldjren, both convinced it was the most significant one they had encountered. Twins are two halves of the same being. When they possess magic, that magic is divided between them. If they are separated, each twin retains only a spark—a mere shadow of their true potential. When they come together, that spark ignites into their full magic. Since you were separated at birth, it's likely you encountered each other just before your powers fully awakened.*

"Many years ago, I met a woman who was born a twin. Her sister was given to another family, and they never had the chance to meet. Although she possessed magic, she was largely cut off from it for most of her life. Even after I gifted her one of my scales, she remained weaker than the most novice mages, capable only of minor feats like conjuring sun-orbs and creating sparks," Samuel reminisced,

"I don't know what else to say. My twin died. Is there anything more you can tell us about the prophecy?" Keelan asked.

They thought when a male and female twin were born to each line, that's when the magic would awaken, so to speak. Was your twin a girl? Drake asked.

"I don't know. My mother never said. She only said that my sibling died at birth."

The conversation continued for hours, but Ashera remained silent, lingering at the edges, unsure of how she would ever fit into this new world. Raised within the fortress, she had been shielded from everything outside and taught to believe she was superior to all other beings.

Now, everything she thought she knew had been shattered. Over the past forty years, she might have had up to eight siblings—each one murdered by the claws of a wyvern who had pretended to be her father. Her mother had allowed this, sacrificing her other children to save one, while the king poisoned Ashera's heart against her. Her breath hitched. *My mother is dead now. Not by his claws, but it might as well have been.*

Then, Zarret came to mind—the only sibling the king had spared. *Where is he now?* A surge of determination filled her. She had to find him, to tell him the truth of what Ichakik had done before the wyverns deceived him again.

PART 3

CHAPTER

-19-

THE rising sun bathed the sky in soft light, stirring Keelan awake. He stretched, feeling rejuvenated after his dip in the hot spring. Nearby, Stormbreaker lifted his head and nodded in greeting. One by one, the rest of the group began to stir, preparing for the journey ahead.

Where did you leave your mounts? Stormbreaker asked Keelan.

In the valley on the other side of that mountain, Keelan replied, pointing to a large, rocky, barren peak.

It's been quite a long time since you left them. Are you sure they're still there?

I hope so, he shrugged. *Jonal said he would take care of it. I hope he did. Rogue is the best horse.*

A better mount than me?

Keelan's mouth gaped open. *Uh, um, I'm not sure how to reply to that. I don't consider you a mount, at least not in the same way.*

He's just teasing you, Aurora laughed in his head.

Keelan looked over at Stormbreaker; soft laughter reached him from the griffin, *Very funny,* Keelan projected but couldn't help but smile.

The air was calm and warm, hinting at the heat yet to come. Lance and Samuel, in dragon form and carrying Tarrid and Jonal, led the way out of Griffins Valley. Stormbreaker followed, soaring into the sky with Keelan and Ashera, closely pursued by the three familiars.

Once they emerged from the valley, they directed their flight toward the spot where they had left their horses, with Jonal taking the lead. The meadow at the mountain's base was no longer the vacant space they had left behind. Several campfires smoked in the distance, and the savory aroma of cooking elk and rabbit wafted through the air. Dozens of men wandered about the clearing, creating a bustling scene. He spotted Rogue, as well as Lance's and Jonal's horses tied with a string of others. They appeared to be okay.

What's the plan? Samuel projected.

I was just trying to think of one, Keelan replied.

I say we rain fire down on them, Lance said, a plume of smoke curling out of his nostrils.

Keelan shook his head as he looked at Lance. Like Tarrid, his demeanor had changed since their captivity. *I think we should speak to them first.*

I agree, said Stormbreaker.

Keelan, Stormbreaker, and I will approach and speak to them, Aurora chimed in.

That is a sound plan, Drake agreed. *Jonal and Ash can stay hidden with Zephyr to guard them.*

Lance, Tar, and I will stay in the air and provide support if needed, Samuel said.

I don't think we need to make battle plans, do we? Keelan asked.

I see many weapons down there, boy. We need to play this cautiously and think of every possibility, Samuel told him.

They circled away from the clearing, all the men below watching them leave the area. Once out of sight, they found a place to land.

"Are you going to be okay here?" Keelan asked Jonal.

"We'll be fine, my boy. Just make sure you return to us. I don't want to walk back to Kingston," Jonal said sternly, but his eyes danced as a smile curled his lips.

Keelan glanced at Ashera. Since leaving the Wyvern Fortress, she had said little. He didn't know what to say to her but felt he should say something. She walked several steps, stopped beside a giant redwood, and sat on the ground. Keelan sighed, raking his hands through his hair.

She is beautiful, isn't she? Aurora broke into his thoughts.

Aurora!

Well, she is. Go and speak to her.

What would I say?

Ask her how she's doing. See if she needs anything.

Keelan stared at Aurora. *What are you trying to do?*

Aurora squawked loudly. *Trying to get you to speak to her. She's miserable. Her whole life has been thrown upside down. She requires a friend. Zephyr's been trying, but he's being ignored.*

Keelan nodded and started toward her. *I am drawn to her, but I don't know why,* he admitted to himself. *She definitely hasn't done anything to warrant all this.* Without speaking, he sat beside her. Ashera's eyes were glazed over as she stared at some unknown spot. Keelan cleared his throat, causing her to jump; she turned to face him, her eyes wide with fear.

"Sorry, I didn't mean to scare you," Keelan said.

"Y..you did not… scare me," she stammered.

"Oh, um. I just wanted to see how you were doing."

"Why?" She looked at him, puzzled.

Keelan opened his mouth and snapped it shut. "I just wanted to check with you. You've been quiet since we left." She opened her mouth to speak, but he held up a hand to stop her. "And you have every right to be. Your whole life has been shattered. I can't even imagine what you're going through right now. I just want you to know I'm here to listen if and when you want to talk."

Ashera stared at him for a few breaths before nodding. "Thank you, Keelan. I do appreciate that. Though I don't deserve your kindness, I do deserve the looks Tarrid gives me."

Keelan grabbed her hand. "No, you do not. While I don't condone what you did, I understand your reasoning. We'll be leaving him soon. I will come see you when I return."

"If you want," she said quietly.

Keelan smiled and patted her hand. He walked back over to the others.

"What did you say to her?" Tarrid asked sharply.

"I just wanted to make sure she was okay. Aurora, Stormbreaker, are you ready to go?"

Both of his companions nodded. Stormbreaker started to kneel to allow Keelan to mount, but Keelan held up a hand to stop him.

Stormbreaker stared at him and then tilted his head. *How are you going to mount?*

Keelan closed his eyes briefly. When he opened them, he started to float. "Whoa!" he exclaimed as his feet left the ground, and he began to tilt to one side. He threw his arms out wide until he felt balanced. "It's a lot harder to levitate yourself than someone else," he remarked. Slowly, he drifted toward Stormbreaker and then up onto his back. "That's much easier. Tar, would you like a hand up?"

Tarrid smirked and then leaped into the air, stepping lightly on Samuel's shoulder and vaulting himself into place in front of his wings. "I'm good," he said with a broad smile.

"All right, let's see what these men are doing here."

They circled above the clearing twice before slowly descending. The dragons, along with Tarrid, stayed high in the sky, and Drake took a position hidden in the trees.

Stormbreaker landed a little way from the camp. *Stay mounted,* he projected.

I plan on it, Keelan replied. He looked at the waking camp. Some men were grabbing weapons and gathering in small groups. One man stood out, walking toward them slowly.

He was finely dressed and walked with the calmness of a seasoned warrior. Keelan's gaze shifted when movement closer to the trees caught his attention. A pegasus, three griffins, two men, and two women emerged from them.

Stormbreaker's body went rigid. *What's the matter?* Keelan asked him.

That's Starfire. She was Leo's companion when they came to my valley. She welcomes us and says these men are friends.

Keelan nodded slowly. *I will make my own opinion.*

Agreed.

The apparent leader strode toward them with a large smile. "Welcome, friends," he called out loudly.

Keelan raised a hand in greeting.

The foursome, along with the pegasus and one griffin, continued walking in their direction as well. As they neared, he recognized Leo'venath.

"Leo, my friend. I am glad to see you are well. How did you escape the wyverns?" Keelan asked as they drew closer.

Leo'venath smiled. "Long story. How did you know I was captured?"

"We were captured and escaped. Tarrid is with us."

Relief washed over his face and the faces of the two women. Keelan's jaw dropped. "Shaylee," he whispered.

"Where's Tar now?" the younger woman almost shouted.

Keelan pointed up, drawing everyone's attention to the sky.

"What are those?" Shaylee asked.

"Dragons," Keelan answered her.

"Greetings," the well-dressed man said. Keelan brought his eyes forward and looked at the speaker for the first time.

"You? What are you doing here?" Keelan asked, surprised, when he recognized the man walking toward him. His eyes narrowed, his lips curled into a snarl.

"Yes, it is I, General Lucas," he said, bowing with a flourish of his hands. "So, your young dragon friend is providing cover." He chuckled softly, looking up.

"How did you survive our last encounter?" Keelan growled out the words.

"Pure luck, boy, pure luck. Don't worry. I've turned over a new leaf since then. Only the straight and narrow for me now," he said with a smirk. "I've found a new crew, and we're taking our aggression out on the wyverns. But we've been waiting for you for a few days now. I'm very glad to see you." Lucas looked up again. "Fine winged companions you have found. So many new creatures are to be found in this part of the world." The general walked closer to Shaylee and said something quietly to her.

What's going on down there? Lance projected.

Keelan is finding out who they are, Aurora answered before Keelan could.

Why didn't you tell Lance who this is? Keelan projected privately to her.

Lance is angry right now. He might attack if he knows.

Keelan redirected his attention to the man before him. "What do you mean you've been waiting for me?"

"We found three horses while we were resting from our travels. I recognized yours, such a fine animal. It would have been a shame for him to be eaten by one of those creatures." He gestured to Stormbreaker.

Stormbreaker squawked and hissed, taking a couple of steps closer. Keelan placed his hand on his neck to calm him.

The General's eyes opened wide in surprise.

"I can assure you, these creatures, as you put it, are far more civilized than you," Keelan said calmly.

General Lucas broke into a roaring laugh. "You've changed much since I last saw you. To think, this man before me almost wet his pants on our first encounter. Good for you, lad. Now, why don't you dismount your companion there and join us and share your traveling tale."

"Shaylee, it's nice to see you again," Keelan said, ignoring the general's request.

Shaylee looked up at him, her face twisting in puzzlement. "Do I know you?"

"I met you briefly in Verndale. I'm Keelan."

Recognition dawned on her face. "I thought you looked familiar. Small world, meeting you here." She smiled broadly. "Please, come join us. You can sit with us if you don't trust the General here." She gestured to her diverse companions.

"I would like that. Thank you."

Samuel, Lance, come on down. Tar, Leo is here, and he looks to be well.

"I will have my cook prepare extra. Welcome to our camp. When you are ready, I will have your horses brought over to you." General Lucas bowed his head, spun on his heels, and marched back to his men.

Keelan dismounted when Samuel and Lance landed. Tarrid jumped off Samuel's back and ran toward Leo'venath. They shook hands and gave each other a quick hug.

Samuel, could you remain on lookout? Keelan asked him privately.

I would prefer it. Samuel nodded and leaped back into the air, buffeting everyone with a gust of wind.

Lance began his transformation with a swirl of blue and black mist and smoke.

I will remain hidden as well, Drake projected from his hiding spot.

Thank you, Drake, Lance replied. Lance nodded to Keelan.

Lance looked around at the gathered group. Two young women were speaking with Tarrid and Leo'venath, both smiling brightly at Tarrid. The brunette turned her head to look over at him and Keelan. Lance's breath caught in his throat; it was Shaylee. *The Elvenfae from Threndy. She is even more beautiful in person,* he thought. Their eyes locked, a shy smile curled Lance's lips, Shaylee returned it.

"Come on, Lance," Keelan said.

By the time they made it over to Shaylee's camp, several cooked rabbits were waiting for them next to their fire.

"Oh, look!" the young elf exclaimed. "They already brought over food for us. You are in for a treat. The cook has some wonderful secret seasonings."

"Fawn, why don't you serve our guest first," Shaylee said.

She nodded, grabbing the rabbits to hand out. Tarrid and Lance each took one, sitting down next to the fire. She handed one to Keelan next. He looked at the rabbit and then tossed it in the air. Aurora swooped down and snatched it while it was still flying upward. "I'm going to see how Rogue is doing."

Lance watched his friend walk toward the band of men a short distance away and then turned his attention to the two women sitting across from him. He slowly took a bite from the rabbit in his hand. An explosion of flavor hit his taste buds. "This is amazing," he said.

Shaylee smiled. "The General's cook is the best."

"The general?"

"You didn't meet him. He walked away before you arrived. Where did you come from? I didn't see you arrive." She looked around the clearing.

A sense of calm washed over him after he took another bite of the rabbit. A lazy smile crossed his lips; he just pointed up instead of speaking.

Shaylee looked up, and a smile slid across her lips. "You're a dragon!"

He nodded.

"Oh, that's wonderful. Then you already know the general. He's been waiting for you."

"Why would he do that? I don't know any generals."

"Oh, you met him a while ago. He was not a nice man back then, but let me assure you he has changed. He may have attacked you twice in the past, but he has gone to great lengths to find you and beg your forgiveness."

Lance jumped to his feet. "Where is he?"

"He's with his men. He's the one that supplied us with breakfast," Fawn replied.

A strange sensation filled Lance; his rage at the man who had tried to kill him twice was slowly being replaced with acceptance and calm. He shook his head and started to pace around the fire. *What's going on?* he asked himself. *Drake, I think we are in danger. Well... maybe not. I feel funny.*

Calm yourself and finish that delicious rabbit you abandoned. Aurora just shared hers with me. How can a man who can cook so well be with someone who tried to kill you? Doesn't make sense to me.

Lance returned to his seat and took another bite. *You're right, Drake. I must be tired, that's all.*

Lance turned his attention back to the two girls. "So, how did you meet up with the general?"

Keelan walked purposefully toward the string of horses. He whistled as he approached and smiled when Rogues' head shot up, and he nickered in greeting. He walked up to his horse and rubbed his forehead softly, saying, "I'm glad to see you doing okay, boy. Have these men been taking good care of you?" Rogue tossed his head up and down. After a few moments, he slowly made his way back over to his companions. He saw Lance speaking with Shaylee and the young elf. Lance was telling a story to them, gesturing with his hands as he did so.

Tarrid and Leo'venath joined them at the same time as Keelan. Suddenly, from up above, Keelan heard Aurora loudly screeching. He looked up and saw her, entirely on fire, streaking through the sky toward him from the trees. ***Whatever you do, do not eat the meat!*** She screamed into everyone's head. Simultaneously, everybody covered their ears from her loud projection.

"Whatever are you talking about, bird?" Tarrid asked.

The meat is tainted, she replied.

Drake flew in from behind her and tackled her to the ground. ***Don't listen to the Phoenix. She's going crazy***, he said to everyone.

Keelan rushed up to them and removed Drake from his familiar. "Now, I want everybody to slow down and tell me what's going on," he said.

It's just like I told you. The meat has been tainted by magic; it didn't taste right. Now Drake is saying he's never been so relaxed, everything is all right in the world, and all those men over there are his new best friends. Aurora stretched her wings out wide, igniting the tips.

I've been trying to tell the silly Phoenix that now that I have a full stomach, I'm just seeing more clearly, Drake countered.

Lance stood up and walked over to his firedrake, picking him up. "I know exactly what you're talking about, Drake. Everything just seems perfect right now. I can't explain it. I think finally being free, finding my sister, and knowing we are heading home with no danger in sight puts me at ease."

Keelan looked at Aurora, shaking his head. *You're right, Aurora. There's definitely something wrong with that meat. That's a complete turnaround in his attitude,* he privately projected.

You didn't eat any? She asked him.

He shook his head. *No, I gave mine to you. I'm glad you didn't eat any.*

Oh, but I did. I took one bite and then spit it out. Phoenixes are highly sensitive to magic. That meat was certainly tainted with something evil.

So, what do we do now? It appears that everybody's been affected, Keelan said.

I don't know. Since we are too late to stop them from eating it, I'm still trying to figure out what to do next.

"Why doesn't everybody just calm down and sit around the fire? I'm going to take Aurora for a walk and see if I can calm her down," Keelan said to everyone. Leo'venath shrugged, and Lance and Shaylee nodded.

Did Stormbreaker eat anything yet? Keelan asked Aurora privately.

No, he said he wasn't hungry.

Good, let's see if we can get back to Jonal. Maybe he'll know what's going on. Samuel, can you keep an eye on everyone?

Yes, of course. What's going on? He asked.

Keelan mounted Stormbreaker, and together, they flew into the sky heading to where they left Jonal. They told Samuel everything that had transpired while in route.

CHAPTER

-20-

JONAL and Ashera sat beside each other, a small fire crackling before them. They looked up as Stormbreaker flew over the trees, stirring the leaves. Jonal waved and stood.

"How did everything go? Where are the others?" Jonal asked.

"Let's sit, and I'll tell you." Keelan recapped the morning; Jonal and Ashera listened quietly.

"Do you have any idea what could be afflicting them?"

"Hmm." Jonal scratched the stubble on his chin, deep in thought. "I've heard of potions that can sway a person to like you, but they don't last very long."

"So, he's been poisoning their food at every meal?"

"At least daily, I would guess."

Keelan's face twisted in rage as he considered what to do. He began pacing, nodding and shaking his head in thought. Finally, he stopped and turned to face Jonal. "I don't know what to do," he admitted, sitting down heavily.

Jonal approached and laid a hand on his shoulder. "Let's try to get them away from this general. Once they stop eating his food, they should be fine in a few days."

Keelan nodded.

Keelan! Samuel shouted into his mind. *Someone new has arrived.*

Who is it?

A woman just rode into camp, and she has a pixie with her, he projected with a snarl.

"What's wrong with pixies?" Keelan asked Jonal.

"Pixies are little demons. Pure evil, even though they look cute," Ashera answered instead.

What is she doing? Keelan asked Samuel.

She's speaking with the better-dressed man. Now, they're walking toward Lance.

"Okay, I'm heading back. I will have Aurora update you through Zephyr," Keelan said to Jonal.

Jonal nodded. "Be safe, my boy."

Keelan sprinted toward Stormbreaker, leaping as he neared and using his magic to levitate into the saddle. As soon as his feet were secure in the saddle slits, Stormbreaker vaulted into the sky.

Within moments, they were circling above the clearing, with all eyes on them.

The newcomer was a slender woman with jet-black hair and something blue buzzing around her head. As Stormbreaker descended, Keelan recognized her.

"Sephra, what a strange place to run into you," he said as he dismounted.

"Ah, Keelan. Such a pleasure," she said sweetly. "I was just telling the General here that Lance's father wants him back home quickly. I've been sent to fetch him."

"How's my mother doing?" Keelan asked, rushing over to her.

She scowled. "How should I know?" she replied sharply.

Keelan stopped mid-step. "I figured you might. She's staying with Douglas."

"Oh, yes, yes." She waved her hand in front of her. "There is a woman staying there. I didn't realize she was your mother. She's doing just fine. Fit as a fiddle," she replied quickly.

Keelan looked at her, his brow scrunching. "We're planning on heading back tomorrow. We'll go straight to Creekside. Thank you for checking on us." He paused briefly before asking, "How did you find us?"

Sephra's face fell. "My pixie friend has been helping General Lucas find Lance. She told me."

Keelan felt someone touch his shoulder, and it felt like lightning. He jumped forward, hearing Shaylee yelp in surprise. He spun around and looked at her; her eyes were wide with fright.

"Why did that hurt?" she asked, looking at her hand.

"I don't know." Tentatively, he reached his hand toward her. She hesitated briefly before grasping his hand. A sharp, tingling sensation passed between them. Shaylee yelped again and tried to let go, but

Keelan held her hand tight. He stepped closer to her and took her other hand in his.

Shaylee winced, looked at their joined hands, and then up into his eyes.

"Keelan, what are you doing to her?" Lance's angry voice drifted toward him.

Keelan ignored him. Suddenly, a bright light flared around them. When it diminished, Keelan and Shaylee both smiled.

"Sister!" he whispered, relief washing over him.

"Brother?" Shaylee asked just as quietly. "How do I know this?"

Keelan shook his head. "I don't know. Mother's going to be so surprised when she meets you."

"Mother? Your mother?"

"Our mother, sister. You are my twin."

Shaylee yanked her hand back. "Your mother left me to die," she whispered in shock. "My mother, Rosepetal, found me and raised me. Your mother is a monster." Her face twisted in grief, and her voice elevated.

"No, you must understand. Our mother was told you died at birth. Our father wasn't informed about you until recently," Keelan said quietly.

Lance walked over to Shaylee and placed his arm around her protectively. "Is there something wrong over here?"

"No, Lance. Shaylee and I have some things to talk about. You're not going to believe me, but—"

Sephra interrupted with a loud, menacing laugh. "Lance, Shaylee, please come over here."

They looked at her, their faces going blank. They nodded and began walking toward her.

"Hold up there. You don't have to do what she says," Keelan reached for them. His fingertips caught Lance's shoulder. Lance shrugged off his hand and then turned his head to look at him. Lance's eyes were glazed over and unblinking. Shaylee grabbed Lance's hand and led him to Sephra.

"That's right, my children. This way."

Keelan turned to face Sephra, his hands starting to glow.

"I don't think so, Keelan. I don't know how you weren't affected by my potion, but no matter. I only need two: one from each line. I thought that was going to be you and Lance. I have been tracking your every movement with the enchanted bracers I gave both of you. I must say, escaping the wyverns was not something I thought you could have done. But this"—she gestured to Lance and Shaylee, who held hands next to her with Lyra and Drake at their feet—"this is so much better. Now I have two halves of the prophecy, two who can unite. Now, all my preparations and planning will succeed." Her voice dropped three octaves. "Together, we will find the medallion, and then I, The One, will rule the world." Sephra's eyes blazed blood-red, and her hair rose all around her.

Keelan held his hands before him, about to attack, when suddenly, a blinding flash of light exploded between them.

When Keelan could see again, Lance, Shaylee, Sephra, the general, and all his men were gone.

Samuel, where is everyone?

Gone. They're all gone. Samuel roared high above them. Keelan glanced up; Samuel was spraying fire into the sky.

Samuel retrieved Jonal and Ashera while Keelan walked around the clearing, looking for signs.

Dreamcrest was beside herself. *My link to Shaylee is gone. It's simply gone.*

Aurora and Stormbreaker stood beside her, trying to calm her down. Tarrid, Leo'venath, Fawn, and the griffins wandered around, confused and disoriented, the spell now broken.

"Tell me everything that happened," Jonal yelled from Samuel's back as they landed.

Keelan assisted Jonal and Ashera to the ground and recounted the events.

"Shaylee, the Elvenfae, is really your twin sister?" Jonal asked, dumbfounded.

"The demon took my twin and your twin. What does this mean?" Ashera asked.

"Demon?" Keelan asked, puzzled.

"The sorceress, Sephra. You said the pixie was her friend, right?"

"That's what she said."

"The pixie, was her name Meta?"

Keelan nodded.

"Meta was having my father search for a human living with elves. Meta works for a demon possessing a sorceress." Ashera shivered, hugging herself tightly.

"What does a demon want with two of the prophesied twins?" Keelan asked aloud, not expecting an answer.

She called herself The One, right? Aurora projected. *There is more to the prophecy. I told your mother about it, Keelan, but I never told you the rest...* She landed in front of him, looking up at him intently. *Centuries long ago, peace and harmony ruled the land. Beast and man living hand in hand. Two mighty Kingdoms rose. Two royal families came to power: one to rule the beasts and one to rule man. Their legacies once aligned but still forever entwined. The two mighty Kingdoms will fall and lose their power. New blood would rise to rule and dictate. The kingdoms would divide, and tyranny would be unleashed on the realm. Beast and man separated by hate and fear, unity lost.*

But in secret, magic would survive. Freedom would dance, and unity would find its sacred room. Twins would be born from royal birthright in the darkness of night. The twins from the royal lines would be tested, their strength grown from strife. But the twins must unite. They must entwine their legacies to take a stand. With the help of a Phoenix, lost in the world, they will find the Infinite Medallion. Only with the medallion can they unite and save the land from tyranny while overcoming the shadow cast by The One.

Aurora hopped up and down, flaring her wings out wide. *I thought I might be the lost phoenix, the one in the prophecy. I thought I would have to wait until you had twins and help them with their quest, but now I see I am already on that quest. Keelan, you are the prophesied twin, as are you, Ashera. I am the lost phoenix. Let's go get your other halves back and find that medallion before that demon does.*

Keelan looked at Ashera, an expression of shock on her face mirroring his.

"How do we do that?" Ashera asked.

"This book," Jonal said, rummaging through his bag to find Ashera's book. "Eldjren included a cryptic map in this book. I bet it leads to the medallion."

Keelan nodded, a plan forming in his head. "Tar and Leo, thank you for your help. Can you please help Fawn get back home? This is where we part ways."

"I'm not going anywhere. Shaylee is my sister; I'm not abandoning her," Fawn cried out.

Leo'venath grabbed her shoulder, turning her slightly. "We have the firebush. We need to get it back to your mother."

Tears started to flow down Fawn's cheeks, "But I can't. Shaylee would come for me."

Tarrid walked over, "Leo, you and the griffins should head back. The Blade needs one of us there. Help Fawn's mother and tell Talon and Rosepetal what has happened. I will stay with Fawn and Dreamcrest if that's okay with you, Keelan."

Keelan nodded.

Tarrid glared at Ashera but didn't say anything to her.

"Samuel, please take Jonal and Ashera to Douglas. Jonal, please heal my mother and tell her we found my twin."

Samuel nodded his mighty head, and a plume of smoke curled out of his nose.

"I'm not leaving," Ashera said, crossing her arms.

Now, wait just a minute… Samuel started to protest.

"I agree with Ashera," Jonal said. "The twins must stay together."

I am not leaving her behind, Samuel replied.

"Please, Samuel," Keelan begged.

Ashera walked over to him and placed a hand on his snout. "Please take Jonal to my father," she paused, "my real father. Tell him about mother and me. Tell him I am fulfilling the prophecy. If he allows it, come back and find us."

Samuel stared at the dragon in human form before him, his eyes slowly blinking, *Fine, I will be back—Jonal, when you are ready.*

"What about the horses," Keelan asked. Looking at the large group of horses behind them.

I will tell Douglas about them. He'll send a few dragons to round them up and take them to his ranch.

"Here, take this book." Jonal handed it to Keelan. "Concentrate on finding the medallion. When you find it, the demon will find you. From what I deciphered from Eldjren's writings, you need to find the medallion on or before your 16th name-day, and all four of you need to be together."

"Then what?" Ashera whispered.

He shook his head. "He only said, 'Then the twins would know what to do.' I wish I had a better answer for you. Look out for each other. Aurora, I'm counting on you."

Aurora nodded. ***On my life, old man.***

He smirked. "Keelan, if you would be so kind." He gestured to Samuel's back. Keelan levitated him into place.

"Now, fly smoothly, you overgrown lizard."

A low grumble echoed out of Samuel, followed by an amused hiss as he vaulted into the sky. Jonal cried out in shock and anger.

Leo'venath bid farewell and took flight with the griffins.

Keelan glanced at the remaining members of his group as it shifted again: Tarrid, Fawn, and Ashera, along with Dreamcrest, Stormbreaker, Aurora, and Zephyr.

"We appear to be two aerials short," Tarrid said.

"Stormbreaker can carry Ash and me. Dreamcrest, can you manage Tar and Fawn?"

I'm afraid not, she shook her head, flipping her mane back and forth.

"We can wait here until Samuel comes back," Ashera offered.

"Ashrozo, is that you?" a male voice came from the trees.

Ashera spun on her heels. "Who's there? How do you know me?"

A young boy with black hair emerged from the trees.

"Zar, is that you?" she rushed toward him.

"Zar, where have you been?" Fawn asked.

Ashera stopped and spun, looking at Fawn. "How do you know him?"

"It's a long story, and most of you don't know the whole of it. Let's sit and talk," Zarret said, walking toward the fire.

Ashera followed him, gesturing for everyone to stay back. She was just about to sit next to him before she saw the look in his eyes.

"Why are you angry?" she asked him. She slowly moved to the other side of the fire and sat down.

"I think there are many lies being told."

"You're right, Zarret. I must tell you the most important lie we were both told."

"I'm listening."

"Our mother is dead."

His face fell, anger gone. "H-h-how?" he stammered.

"Your father killed her."

"What do you mean, my father? He's yours as well."

She shook her head. "Ichakik is not my father. He stole me. Mother and Samuel followed my abductor, and then they were captured and imprisoned by him."

"No, that's all a lie. Who told you this?"

"Mother did right before she died. But I have seen the true evil of your father."

"Explain." Zarret was visibly growing frustrated.

"Mother wanted to speak to me while in the brooding chamber. I was there for the hatching of her latest egg. She was absolutely beautiful, a pure gold wyvern."

"There is another who has been born a wyvern, like me," Zarret began, his voice distant. "I wonder if it will take her as long to learn to transform." His tone shifted, and he seemed to relax.

"Brother, please, there's more to the story. Father arrived and saw the hatchling. He was… very disappointed. Not just that she wasn't a twin, but that she was gold."

Zarret waved dismissively. "Ah, the prophecy—'A gold wyvern's birth will destroy the empire.' Father doesn't believe in such nonsense."

"Oh, but he does, brother. He killed our sister. Your full-blooded sister, my half."

"Enough with this 'half-sister' talk!" Zarret snapped. "Father was there at your hatching, too. He almost killed you for looking human when you were born, but since you were the first, he let you live. You've heard that story as well as I have."

"I have heard that lie as well. Your father almost killed me. If Mother hadn't bitten his tail before he impaled me with his spike, I would not be here. And then a vaskakat led me out of the fortress and saved my life. Samuel, Mother, and Teresa escaped that very night. We met up sometime later, completely by accident. Teresa died sometime in their mad dash, and Mother a short time later. Before she died, she told me of my true origins. I am a full dragon; Mother's eldest son is my full brother, not my half. He was just here; I don't know if you met him."

Zarret's face twisted in anger. "Lance," he sneered.

You better leave out the twin part, for now, Zephyr whispered into her mind.

"What are your plans now?" Zarret asked her.

"I'm going to help this group rescue him. Zarret, I want you to come with us. We have been lied to. We need to find the truth. The truth can only be believed when you see it for yourself."

Zarret softened his facial expression from a scowl to a slight frown. "Can you take off this bracelet?" He held up his wrist.

Ashera gasped in surprise. "Why do you have that on?"

"Father's idea. He wanted to ensure I couldn't slip out of human form until I returned home."

"He left you vulnerable," she whispered, "unprotected and weak."

He nodded. "I would like to be free of it."

"Only if you remove mine," she said, holding up her wrist.

"That isn't a suppression bracelet."

"I think it is. I can't remove it. I never tried until recently."

"I will remove it, but it's not what you think it is." She walked over to him and held out her wrist.

Zarret gently took her hand, turning her wrist back and forth as he examined the bracelet. His fingers traced the clasp, and with a simple motion, he unhooked it, letting the bracelet hang loosely from her wrist. Ashera sucked in a sharp breath, startled by the sudden sensation. She stared at the bracelet, her eyes widening. Slowly, she twisted her wrist, allowing it to slip off and fall to the ground. Suddenly, a piercing cry escaped her lips, and Zarret jerked backward, eyes wide in shock. Keelan and the others rushed forward, concern flashing across their faces.

Ashera held up a hand, panting. "I'm okay. That sensation was just surprising."

Keelan tilted his head to the side. "What are you talking about?"

"That bracelet has been blocking my transformation since the king of the wyverns stole me. I finally have it off. Come, brother, let me remove your bracelet."

"What do you mean, brother?" Fawn asked, confused.

"What are you all talking about?" Keelan asked.

"While my mother was in captivity with the wyverns, the king took her as his bride and forced her to produce an heir. Zarret here was born first. The King potentially killed all the others, up to eight." Ashera shook her head sadly.

"Why would he do this?" Fawn asked, utterly shocked.

"He wanted her to produce the twins of the prophecy."

Nobody tell Zar anything, Aurora projected to everybody except Zarret. ***We don't know if we can trust him yet.***

Ashera grabbed Zarret's wrist and unclasped his bracelet, letting it fall to the ground.

He inhaled sharply, eyes widening. "I didn't realize how weak this human form was," he muttered, a grin spreading across his face. "I can feel my true strength returning." He bent down, picking up the bracelet. "What a cruel thing to be imprisoned by such a simple piece of metal." Straightening up, he fixed his gaze on her. "Alright, sister. You claim to be a full dragon, locked in human form my entire life—maybe longer. So, transform. Show me your true form. What are you, really? A weak human, a wyvern, or a dragon?" His glare intensified as he rolled his shoulders, flexing his fingers, ready for whatever might come.

"I don't know if I can, brother. I don't remember ever transforming before."

Zephyr's voice echoed in her mind, calm and steady: *Ash calm your thoughts and breath.* He then projected so everyone could hear. *Good, now feel inside your core, deep inside. You should feel a flame; embrace the fire and bring it forth.*

Ashera closed her eyes, allowing Zephyr's guidance to echo through her thoughts. She searched within, expecting the familiar heat of fire. But instead, she found something else—something cold. So cold, it felt like it could burn her from the inside out. In her mind's eye, the strange flame flickered to life, its tendrils shimmering with the pale blue of frost.

She concentrated on the ice flame, seeing it clearly in her mind. She wrapped her mind around it and willed it to the surface. Feeling dizzy, she opened her eyes. She was immensely surprised to see a blue and bronze swirling mist surrounding her.

As she stared at the mist, it slowly dissipated, and the feeling of the flame slipped away. She squeezed her eyes shut and concentrated on the ice flame again, bringing it forth to give it life. Within a few heartbeats, she knew she had done it.

"This can't be true. My eyes are deceiving me!" Zarret screamed.

She opened her eyes and found herself looking down at all the bipeds. She moved her head back and forth, trying to take in her body. She was a dragon—a four-legged sapphire blue dragon with bronze spikes running down her neck and tail. She opened her wings wide and flicked her slender tail back and forth.

This is amazing! She unknowingly projected to everyone. *Zephyr, how did you know how to instruct me?*

I spoke with Samuel before he left. I knew somebody would have to help you sooner or later, and as your familiar, it was my job to do so.

"You're my familiar?" she said aloud, fumbling over her large, sharp teeth.

I already told you our lives were intertwined. Of course, I am your familiar. Who better than a vaskakat?

A phoenix, of course, Aurora projected with a laugh.

Zarret looked his sister up and down. "So, it is true. Half-sister." Zarret closed his eyes and was soon engulfed in a black and silver swirling mist.

Everyone get behind me, Ashera projected.

"What's the matter?" Keelan asked.

I am still determining what he's going to do.

Where Zarret once stood in his human form, a black wyvern with silver-rimmed scales and striking royal blue eyes now stood.

He hissed loudly. "This is what true power looks like." He opened his leathery wings wide, speaking in the typical hissing speech of the wyvern. "Come back with me now, half-sister. If Mother is dead, maybe Father will have use for you."

I am going nowhere with you, she projected to him.

He hissed loudly when her thoughts slid into his mind. "You better run and hide, sister dear, because I don't think Father will let you live very long." With a flick of his tail, he leaped into the air and took off.

Ashera hung her head in sorrow. Zarret was the one family member she could always turn to whenever she needed comfort, but now she had no one.

You will always have me, Zephyr said. She looked up at the vaskakat and peeled her lips back in a dragony smile.

How about a test flight? Zephyr asked.

Ashera tilted her head and looked into the sky. "I'm scared," she said quietly.

Keelan walked up to her and placed his hand on her shoulder. "Stormbreaker and I will be up there right next to you. There's nothing to be scared about. This is who you are."

She nodded and stretched her wings out wide again, tentatively flapping them up and down.

A few moments later, Stormbreaker and Dreamcrest instructed her on how to get into the air. She ran across the clearing with her wings stretched wide, flapping them, and then leaped into the air. She managed two flaps of her wings before she plummeted, landing hard.

Well, that didn't go well, Aurora said. *She may need a little assistance, Keelan. All creatures that fly learn when they are very tiny.*

"What do you suggest I do?"

Use your levitation to help make her a little lighter until she gets used to her wings.

"Do you want to try it again, Ash?" Keelan asked.

She stood and shook herself off, then nodded. With a look of grim determination, she took off in the other direction across the valley. When Keelan thought she had sufficient momentum, he used his magic and lifted her slightly off the ground. She beat her wings furiously, her tail hanging limp. She wobbled one way and then the other as she unsteadily rose in the air.

Hold your tail out straight. You can use your tail to help steer you, Aurora said.

Ashera concentrated. Now, she was flying in a straight line.

For the remainder of the day, Ashera flew around, learning control and how to get airborne without Keelan's help. When night finally fell, she was exhausted.

"Do you think you'll be able to carry Fawn tomorrow?" Keelan asked.

She pondered his question for a moment and then nodded her head. *I think so. She is quite small. But only if it's okay with her.*

Fawn looked up at the large dragon curled up like a cat beside the fire. She opened her mouth, but Tarrid spoke first.

"No!" He jumped to his feet. "She will not carry someone I care for. If she must be used as an animal of burden to assist us, she will carry me," he all but growled out.

Ashera's eyes grew wide, and slowly, she hid her face under her wing, tucking herself into a tight ball.

"Was that necessary?" Keelan spat. "Maybe you and Fawn should walk back to your people."

"You can't tell me to leave. Shaylee is our friend. We're coming with you to rescue her."

"Not with that attitude, you're not." Keelan threw his hands in Tarrid's direction. "Look, we have all been through difficult situations. But what is past is past. We need to move on and judge each other by our current actions. If you wish to join us, you are welcome to, but without the attitude. I wish one of the other griffins had stayed to carry one of you, but since they didn't, we have to make do with the transportation we have. Dreamcrest already said she can't carry both of you. So, either one of you stays behind, or you curb your anger and do what must be done."

I can carry Tarrid, and you can travel with Ash, Stormbreaker offered Keelan privately.

No, but thank you. I will not bow down to him.

Tarrid stared at Keelan for an uncomfortable amount of time. His jaw clenched tightly shut, and his eyes narrowed.

Finally, Fawn broke the silence. "Tar," she said softly, placing a hand on his chest and looking up at him. Slowly, he lowered his gaze to her.

"I don't know what happened to you, and I'm not ready to hear it yet, either. But we must find Shaylee. She is a quarter of the prophecy you have devoted your entire life to. Ashera, unfortunately, is another quarter. We must stick together and see this thing through. I will ride with Ashera. She won't harm me."

Tarrid was silent for a moment. Slowly, he grabbed her hand in both of his, leaving them on his chest, "How do you know that?" he whispered, closing his eyes.

Fawn looked over at Ashera. Ashera had uncoiled her head and was watching them silently. "I don't know. But I can feel her. She's scared and unsure of herself, but I can feel the kindness in her. She's here by choice. Not only that, but she could have left with her wyvern brother, but she stayed."

"I don't know what this is that I am feeling. But," Tarrid paused, "but I can't lose you."

Fawn smiled, her eyes dancing, "I want to be with you too."

Tarrid returned her smile and brought her in for a crushing hug, burying his head in her hair as he picked her up.

Keelan cleared his throat and sat back down, looking over at Ashera.

Are you going to be okay? He projected to her.

She turned her head slightly and locked eyes with him.

Eventually, probably. She sighed, releasing a cloud from her nose. She snapped her head back in surprise.

What's wrong? Keelan looked around, looking for danger.

That was cold! She replied.

You, my dear, are a water dragon, Zephyr said from his curled-up position on her back.

She snaked her head around to look at the Vaskakat. *A water dragon? I thought all dragons breathed fire.*

Most do. Zephyr nodded, uncurled himself, and stretched his front legs. *Your mother is from a rare lineage on the non-Ragnis side. Most dragons breathe fire, and some have more than one ability—*

others, like you and your mother, breathe water. You can shoot out streams of icy water. Very helpful when battling a fire-breather.

What about Lance? Is he a water dragon, too?

"No, he breathes fire. Almost got me one day," Keelan spoke aloud with a chuckle.

Tarrid and Fawn both gave him puzzled looks as they settled beside the fire again.

"Sorry, internal conversation." He rubbed the back of his neck and shook his head. "So, are we all set?"

Tarrid looked at Fawn next to him. She grabbed his hand in hers and nodded.

"I guess so," Tarrid said. Fawn bumped him with her shoulder. "Ashera. If you can carry Fawn while we travel, I would be eternally grateful."

I will guard her with my life, Ashera replied. *And for what it's worth, I'm sorry. I wish I would have found out my true origins before we met. Or,* she hung her head, *at least before I harmed you.*

"Thank you." Tarrid shifted uncomfortably and grabbed Fawn's hand with both of his.

I'm glad everything is civil around here. So, what next? Aurora projected, landing on a large rock next to the fire. She fluffed out her feathers and nudged closer to the flames until she stood in the hot embers.

They huddled together for the remainder of the evening, looking through the book Jonal had left them, trying to decipher the clues in Eldjren's map.

CHAPTER

-21-

WHEN Samuel finally landed, Jonal couldn't remember a time he'd been happier. He slid off Samuel's back slowly, savoring the stretch in his limbs after the long flight, and glanced toward the eastern horizon where the sun was just beginning to rise. The landscape was unfamiliar; having flown all night, he hadn't had the chance to see much of it before. Now, south of the Black Mountains and at the edge of the Brightbane Forest, the view was breathtaking in the soft morning light. From Keelan's descriptions, Jonal knew they weren't far from Firestorm's Ranch—or Firestrum's, as the locals called it. Samuel, stretching his wings, shook them out before transforming back in a shimmer of gold and purple mist.

"As much as I love flying again, I have to admit, it feels good to have hands and feet once more," Samuel said, flexing his fingers and stretching out his limbs. "Which way now?"

"I'm not sure. Keelan said the ranch was west of Creekside."

Together, they walked through the forest, heading further south, hoping to cross a road. A short time later, they reached it, and just by luck, the ranch was to their right. The road was lined with fencing on each side, and black and tan cows grazed peacefully in the fields.

Jonal and Samuel walked up the road slowly. Several ranch hands in the fields whistled, and one spurred his horse and raced to the house. The house's front door flew open before the ranch hand reached the green grass surrounding the two-story building. A large man strode onto the porch wearing only pants and a scowl.

"Who goes there?" he called loudly.

Jonal started to raise his hand in greeting, but Samuel grabbed his arm and lowered it.

"Let him sweat it out," he said.

The man on the porch continued to watch them approach, his scowl deepening. Jonal looked at Samuel nervously when the man returned to his house, only to return a moment later with a sword in hand.

"What are you waiting for? If that is Mr. Firestorm, he is a dragon, you know. I don't really want to see one angry."

"That's Douglas, all right. Don't worry, I have this under control," Samuel replied with a soft chuckle.

"Stop right there! Who are you, and what business do you have here?" Douglas demanded.

"Is that the way you greet an old friend?" Samuel roared.

Douglas stared at the two men walking toward him. "Samuel! Is that you?" His face split into a large smile as he raced down the steps and sprinted toward them, abandoning his sword. "Samuel, it's been a long time." He grabbed Samuel's forearms in greeting. "Where's Arlayna? Where's Ashera?" He looked around as if they would appear by uttering their names.

"Can we go inside, and I will tell you everything?" Samuel asked.

"Of course, my friend." Douglas's scowl returned, and a thin puff of smoke escaped his nostrils.

Jonal eyed him warily for a moment and then bowed. "Mr. Firestorm, I am Healer Jonal from Kingston. I hope Maya is still with us."

Douglas's expression softened. "Welcome, Healer Jonal. She is. Come, it seems there is more than one story to hear," he said grimly.

They walked to the house, and Douglas led them to Maya's room. She was sleeping soundly.

"I need to make her tea," Jonal whispered, patting the bag dangling off his shoulder.

"Of course, this way." Douglas directed them to the kitchen.

A kettle of water was already boiling on the stove. Jonal quietly pulled out a large, weathered book and began preparing the tea for Maya. Meanwhile, Samuel recounted his time with the wyverns to Douglas. The room remained still, save for the low bubbling of the kettle, as Douglas listened in silence. His expression darkened as Samuel reached the part about their escape. Suddenly, Douglas shot to his feet, his boots echoing against the floor as he began to pace back and forth. The tension in the air thickened with every step he took. Minutes passed in strained silence before he abruptly stopped and turned to Samuel, his eyes sharp.

"Where's Ashera now?" he asked, his voice tight. Without waiting for a response, he resumed pacing as though the weight of the question itself demanded action.

"She's with Keelan."

Douglas stopped again. "Where's Lance? I thought the boys would stay together."

"That's something else. Please sit down, Douglas."

Douglas's face went ashen as he sat down.

"How well did you know Sephra?" Samuel asked.

"My gemist? How do you know her?"

"Answer my question."

"If you two will excuse me, I will see to Maya," Jonal said, holding up a mug.

"Yes, yes, of course," Douglas said with a wave of his hand.

"How well did you know her?" Samuel asked again.

"I've known her for about ten years. I've not had any in-depth conversations with her, but she seemed a nice enough person. Cedric knows her better. What's all this questioning about?"

"Did you know she was a sorceress?" Samuel asked.

"No, she's a witch," Douglas replied.

Samuel shook his head. "Afraid not, my friend. It appears she is working with a demon that refers to itself as *The One*."

Douglas's eyes snapped open. "*The One?* As in the prophecy?" His voice dropped to a whisper.

Samuel nodded. "She appeared in the valley right after we arrived. She said she had been tracking Lance and Keelan by the bracers she gave them. It seems her original plan was to steal Lance and Keelan, find the Infinite Medallion, and then the demon would have the prophecy's power. Another twist in this story is that we found Keelan's twin. Her name's Shaylee. Sephra decided to take Shaylee and Lance instead."

Douglas shot to his feet. "Take them where?" he yelled.

"We don't know." Samuel hung his head. "I have failed you more times than I can count."

Douglas looked at his friend sitting at the table, a friend he hadn't seen in over forty years. Stiffly, he walked over to Samuel and placed a hand on his shoulder. "You did everything you could."

"I could have done more," Samuel said quietly.

"So, the prophecy is coming to pass," Douglas said, primarily to himself. "Keelan has a twin."

"He was born a twin," a voice from the doorway said, "but his twin died at birth."

Douglas looked up to see Maya walking with Jonal's help.

"No, Maya, she did not," Jonal said.

Maya sat in the chair next to Douglas and then looked at Jonal. "I never told you it was a girl."

"How are you feeling?" Douglas asked her.

She waved off his question. "I'll be fine. How do you know Keelan's twin was a girl?"

Douglas placed his hand on top of hers.

Samuel cleared his throat. "Keelan's twin was rescued by a fairy and raised as her daughter. Keelan met her briefly in Verndale a couple of years ago. That's when his magic fully awakened."

"Shaylee the Elvenfae?" she whispered. "Where are they?" Her eyes round with fright.

Jonal cleared his throat. "Keelan is with Lance's twin sister."

Maya looked at Douglas. "You never told me Lance was a twin."

"I didn't know if she still lived," Douglas admitted.

"Where's Shaylee?" Maya asked.

"A sorceress named Sephra stole Lance and Shaylee."

"What!?" She tried to stand but was still too weak.

"Don't worry," Jonal said, his voice steady. "We understand what the demon seeks. It's after the Infinite Medallion. It believes it only needs one twin from each bloodline. But from my readings, all four must stand atop the Wizard's Hat during the eclipse this winter. Only then will the true meaning of the prophecy be revealed."

"I've never heard that part," Douglas interrupted.

"I was able to read a book transcribed for Eldjren's familiar, Ember. It turns out Ember is Aurora's sire."

"Where's this book now?" Douglas pressed.

"I left it with Keelan. It contains clues on how to find the Wizard's Hat. I believe it's a mountain."

Maya perched at the edge of her chair, trying to piece together the conversation while glancing out the kitchen window. Her tired brain struggled to keep up with the unfolding events. "I'm sorry, did you say demon?" she asked, slumping back into her chair as exhaustion overtook her.

"Oh, um, yeah," Jonal stammered. "Sephra has been possessed by a demon that calls itself *The One*."

"*The One!*" Maya said under her breath, her body stiffening.

"Don't worry, Maya. I'll be heading to Keelan. I will help him find my son and your daughter," Douglas told her, patting her shoulder.

"My daughter," she whispered, her eyes glazing over. After a moment, she shook her head slowly. "I've dreamed about her on and off for the past fifteen years." Grabbing his hands, she gripped them tightly. "Please, find my daughter. Bring our children home."

Douglas nodded. "I will."

Douglas paused before the small house, noting that the porch could use a good sweep and the front flowers were wilted and dying. Though the house appeared deserted, the building at the rear glowed warmly from a few lanterns and the flickering light of the forge.

Douglas squared his shoulders and walked to the rear of the house. His last conversation with Elliot hadn't gone well—it had been the day Lance and Keelan left on their quest for a cure. He and his personal healer had arrived to check on Maya, unaware of the earlier discussions that had taken place that day. Just like now, Elliot had been out in his shop. Douglas and the healer had let themselves into the Keifman's house, only to find Maya attempting to pack a bag.

The door to the farrier shop stood open, allowing a late summer breeze to flow through. Douglas paused at the entrance, his hands clasped behind his back.

"Don't just stand there staring. Say what you've come to say," Elliot remarked without looking up from his work.

Douglas took a few more steps in, watching Elliot.

He was hammering out a wagon wheel and looked to be nearly finished. With a final strike of his hammer, Elliot grabbed the wheel and tossed it into a large bucket of water. A hiss and a cloud of steam erupted as his work was completed.

"Is she gone?" Elliot finally asked quietly. His words caught slightly in his throat, and he cleared it loudly before ripping off his apron.

"No. Keelan and Lance found the cure. Her healer friend from Kingston is with her now."

Elliot finally looked up at him. He had dark bags under his bloodshot eyes. "Where's Keelan?" he asked, sounding hopeful about seeing his son again.

"The boys haven't returned yet."

"Why not?" Elliot shouted. "Keelan is supposed to be taking care of his mother."

"Please, Elliot. Calm yourself. I need to tell you things, but only if you want to hear them."

"I won't be listening to any more of your lies. Go! Until my son returns, I want nothing to do with you. You stole my family from me. Turned them against me. You have bewitched them somehow. That is the only explanation." Elliot reached for his hammer, but Douglas was already gone by the time he threw it.

"How'd it go?" Maya asked, rocking slowly in Douglas's porch swing.

"About how we thought it would." He sat down next to her.

"Did he say anything?"

"He asked how you were." He paused to look at her. Maya stared daggers at him. "Okay, he asked if you were gone."

Maya sighed and shook her head. "Anything else?"

"He wanted to know if Keelan was back. When I told him he wasn't, he got angry and said Keelan was supposed to be helping you. He still cares, Maya," Douglas said gently, "he's just scared. He thinks I bewitched you and Keelan against him."

Maya patted Douglas on the knee. "When the prophecy is fulfilled, and he meets his daughter, everything will be okay again."

"I hope you're right."

King Ichakik glared at the woman walking toward him. "How dare you enter my chamber uninvited," he slurred.

She smiled, sauntering toward him. The throne room was uncomfortably warm, with four roaring fireplaces. The infernos caused a slight breeze that ruffled her blood-red, floor-length dress and moved a few strands of her jet-black hair, which had come loose from her braid. The glass ceiling of the chamber, usually revealing the sky, now displayed nothing but inky blackness; the stars above were invisible behind a thick layer of clouds. Eight chandeliers, each adorned with two dozen candles, swayed gently back and forth, casting shadows that danced with each movement. "I go where I please," she purred.

"Not in my fortress, woman!" he sneered, a tendril of smoke escaping his mouth and an arc of flame flickering between his teeth.

"Oh, my dear king. You only think this fortress belongs to you," she replied, holding out her hands. "It is the ancestral home of the Ragnis line, long before you moved in."

"But I defeated them, and now it's mine. Be gone with you. Our deal is finished. The human cannot be found. I want no more dealings with you, witch."

Sephra laughed. "You would be fortunate if I were only a witch, but alas, you have no such luck. I am not even a mere sorceress anymore. I… am… so… much… more." Her voice dropped in pitch with each word as it echoed through the vast chamber and reverberated through the king's body. She raised her arms and started to levitate while still advancing on him.

"Be gone with you. I tire of your visits, Sephra. We are finished."

"You simple fool. You've yet to see what I'm capable of," Sephra said in a deep and menacing voice. "Sephra is but a vessel to complete my work. I am The One. My coming has been prophesied. This world will be mine to rule, so very soon. But one thing this world doesn't need is you."

King Ichakik stood up and spread his wings wide. "How dare you threaten me!" he screamed.

Several wyverns rushed into the throne room at their king's roar.

"Seize the witch!" Ichakik yelled.

"I told you before, I am NOT A WITCH!" The One shouted, its voice echoing through the chamber and rattling the chandeliers. It pointed at one of the wyverns to the king's left, unleashing a bolt of energy that struck the creature squarely in the chest. With a surprised scream, the wyvern crumbled to the ground. The remaining wyverns roared in fury, launching their attacks. The One laughed, effortlessly evading their efforts. With a flourish of its hands, a gust of wind surged through the room, pushing the wyverns back a few steps.

"Bow to me and pledge your allegiance… or die!"

"I take a knee to no one!" Ichakik yelled.

"Then you shall DIE!" The One's voice bounced off the walls ominously as the room plunged into darkness. Screams filled the night, then silence.

CHAPTER

-22-

KEELAN turned a page, frustration simmering beneath his breath. The book was a labyrinth of riddles, each one more perplexing than the last.

Why did your father make this book so hard to understand? Keelan asked Aurora.

He and Eldjren were concerned about their writings falling into the wrong hands.

Well, it's in the right hands now, and it's pointless. I can't make heads or tails of any of this! He held the book up for her to see. *Look at the map! You've flown all around the kingdoms. Does any of this make sense? I don't see Griffins Keep anywhere on it, and the ocean is on the wrong side of the world. The map is labeled 'Kingdom of Iton.' That's where we are, right?*

Yes, this land was once the Kingdom of Iton, but I don't recognize anything on this map.

Where is your father? Maybe we can ask him?

Aurora hung her head. *I'm sorry, I don't know where he is. About 25 years ago, my sire left this land and flew across the Brisbin Ocean. He met my mother, and that was where I was raised. About four years ago, I was out flying by myself. I felt a surge of magic and decided to investigate. As I neared a barren island, I saw a giant glowing disk with a woman standing before it. She looked scared, so I went in for a closer look. Suddenly, both of us were sucked into the glowing disk. I found myself deep in the Sapphire Mountains, but I didn't realize that was where I was for months. The woman was gone, and I was all alone. But then I found you. Fate has brought us together.*

Keelan looked confused. *When I met you, I thought you were raised in the Sapphire Mountains. You knew all about Evansshire and the surrounding area.*

When I arrived on this side of the ocean, I found a small group of fairies who told me where I was. My sire, Ember, told me about his life here, and the fairies filled in the new stuff.

"I'm at a loss trying to figure out this book," he said to the others. "Any ideas?"

"The Prioress at the Monastery of Iton might be able to help," Tarrid replied.

"Can he be trusted?" Keelan asked.

"The Prioress is a she, but yes, she can be trusted. The Priors have dedicated their lives to seeing the prophecy fulfilled," Tarrid said.

Then why aren't we already there? Aurora screeched, flapping her wings.

Tarrid looked down. "I'm sorry. I haven't been thinking clearly lately. I will take us there tomorrow."

Fawn nudged closer to Tar, placing a hand on his knee.

The Monastery was situated in a large clearing, nestled between a dense forest to the east and a small mountain range to the west. Further west, the enormous Sapphire Mountains loomed in the distance.

Dreamcrest took the lead, guiding Stormbreaker and Ashera to the east side of the monastery grounds. As they approached, several people greeted them, including Leo'venath.

"Didn't expect to see you back here so soon," Leo'venath said. "We just arrived yesterday. The griffins made a detour to pick up some additional recruits, and I still need to fill everyone in on all the news."

Tarrid and Leo'venath clasped each other by the wrist in greeting. Tarrid then turned to a woman in a blue robe. "Prioress, let me introduce you to Stormbreaker, Keelan, and Ashera."

"It is a pleasure to meet you all," she said warmly.

"I'll be back," Fawn said as she vaulted off Ashera's back and sprinted toward the houses.

Keelan looked over at Ashera. "Would you like to transform back? It's been a while."

That it has. I've actually been scared to do so, she projected privately to him.

He tilted his head. *Why?*

What if I can't? And what if I'm naked? She looked down at the ground.

I don't think that will be an issue. Lance was always fully clothed when he transformed back into a human. Give it a try, and if you can't transform, we'll work through it.

Okay, she projected with a huff. A small cloud billowed out of her nose. She closed her eyes, and slowly, a cloud of blue and bronze mist shrouded her. After the mist dissipated, Ashera in human form stood before them, fully clothed.

"Thank you for welcoming us, Prioress," Keelan said diplomatically, bowing as Tarrid had. "I am Keelan Keifman of the Vaelum Line, and this is Ashera Lapis Firestorm."

The Prioress's eyes widened as she dropped to her knees and bowed with her forehead to the ground. "Your Majesties."

Keelan and Ashera exchanged an embarrassed look. "Please, no need for that," Keelan said quickly.

The Prioress stood gracefully with a slight bow of her head. "Please follow me. We have much to discuss."

Only once inside a large meeting room in the middle of the monastery did the Prioress finally speak again. "Leo, you should have told me you found half of the prophecy as soon as I saw you."

"A lot has happened since I've been away, and we didn't just find half," he replied.

Her eyes burned into him.

"Please, Leilatha. Let us explain," Tarrid said, taking a seat beside her.

"Ashera's brother, Lance, and I became friends over a year ago," Keelan began. "At the time, we didn't realize who we truly were. Lance was raised with knowledge of the prophecy and his bloodline, but his sister Ash was stolen when she was very young, and they didn't know if she had survived. I grew up without any awareness of the prophecy, my identity, or even the existence of magic. Just a few days ago, I met my sister for the first time…"

"Where are Lance and your sister now?" the Prioress interrupted.

"My sister Shaylee and Lance were taken by a sorceress named Sephra, who appears to be possessed by a demon calling itself The One."

Leilatha sucked in a surprised breath. "I knew there was something special about Shaylee, and I suspected she was connected to the prophecy, but I wasn't entirely certain. Does the demon know what it has in its possession?"

Everyone nodded.

That is why we are here, Aurora projected. ***My sire was Eldjren's familiar. He transcribed a book of clues on how to find the Infinite Medallion, but we have been unable to decipher it. We have only a few months to locate it before The One does.***

"Do you have this book with you?" Leilatha asked.

"Of course," Keelan said, handing her the book. "The most confusing part is the map in the back. We initially thought it was a map of the Kingdom of Iton, as it's labeled, but it doesn't match anything we know about the area."

Leilatha thumbed to the back of the book and examined the map. "Do you mind if I share this with the others? We might be able to figure it out."

"Yes, please. Share it with anyone who might help us," Ashera said.

Zephyr jumped onto the table. ***But be careful with it. It belongs to my dragon,*** he snapped.

"Yes, of course. I will guard it with my life." Leilatha smiled at the grumpy vaskakat. "I will have rooms prepared for you here in the Monastery and ensure food is brought to you immediately."

Almost a week passed before the Prioress asked them to join her in the meeting room. Talon and Rosepetal, Shaylee's adopted parents, joined them.

Keelan found it strange to be around them. They knew all about Shaylee, except for her true origins. It turned out that Talon had discovered Shaylee's origins just after she did. Rosepetal seemed uncertain about how to act around Keelan; her face was always flushed, her expression a mix of shame and anger.

During their second day at the monastery, Talon spoke to Keelan briefly. Curious about the tension, Keelan asked, "What's going on with Rosepetal?"

"She is sad that you grew up without your sister, but angry at your mother for abandoning her."

Keelan tried to explain that if their mother hadn't acted as she did, both he and his sister would have been killed. Talon understood but mentioned that it would take Rosepetal longer to come around. She just needed to see Shaylee again.

When they arrived at the meeting room, several additional Priors were present.

"Welcome. Please, everyone, take a seat," Leilatha said. "I'm sorry for my absence over the past few days, but it has been necessary. I believe everyone knows why we are here, so I will dive right in." She opened Ember's book to the map and waved her hand over it. Suddenly, an image of the map appeared on the wall before the table. She then muttered a few Elven words and swept her arms upward. The map expanded to fill the wall. Keelan jumped backward, almost causing his chair to tip over.

"Sorry," he muttered when all eyes turned to him.

Leilatha smiled. "Here is the map that Ember drew. At first, we didn't know where this was supposed to be. We scoured every map of our known world, and none matched. It was only by pure accident that we deciphered it. You see here…" She pointed to the map. "These are actually three maps of the same area overlaid upon each other. One is backward, and one is backward and upside down." With a flourish of her hands, she separated the images, as if pulling pages apart. The three images separated. Soon, only one map remained.

Keelan stood and walked to the map quickly.

A beam of light shot from Leilatha's hand. "We are here," she said, pointing to a location on the map.

Keelan nodded, "Here is Griffin's Keep. What is this place on this island?" He pointed to the upper left-hand side of the map.

"That is the Sanctuary of Iton," Tarrid told him. "That is the main headquarters for The Chosen."

Keelan continued to survey the map as he walked to the right. "And this?" He pointed at the structure in the upper middle.

"The Wyvern Fortress," Ashera said with a quiver in her voice.

Keelan nodded. "Look at this mountain over here in the Brisbin."

"What about it? It just looks like a lone volcano," Leo'venath said, walking toward it.

"Yes, but what does its shape remind you of?" Keelan's face lit up.

Everyone stared blankly at him. He sighed and then nodded. "A couple of years ago, when I went to Kingston with my ma, we saw a magician…"

"You mean a wizard?" Leo'venath asked.

Keelan shook his head. "No, according to Jonal, this man didn't have any magic. He used tricks, illusion devices, and sleight of hand to entertain. He was wearing a robe, similar to the Priors here, but on his head was the strangest hat. It was conical."

"Can you describe it better?" Leilatha asked.

He pointed to the volcano. "It looked like this. The Wizard's Hat?"

"But wizards don't wear hats like that," Leo'venath explained.

"Someone must have at some point in history. How else would it become a symbol of a magician in Evansshire? A place that shuns everything magical. It won't hurt to go take a look."

Slowly, everyone nodded. "Aurora, can you fill in Dreamcrest and Stormbreaker on our findings?" Leo'venath asked.

Already done!

We have incoming! Dreamcrest projected to everyone in the room.

All eyes went to the window. Several dragons were flying toward the Monastery.

Ashera jumped up and was at the window first. "I see Samuel!"

Keelan grabbed her hand, and they rushed outside together.

Five giant dragons stood at the base of the stairs when Keelan and Ashera exited the building.

Samuel was the first to shift into his human form. Two of the other dragons followed suit. Keelan instantly recognized Douglas and his brother Cedric. The remaining two stayed in dragon form.

"Come on, I'd like to introduce you to your father and uncle," Keelan said, gently tugging her hand.

She resisted his pull. Her eyes were frightful, and her chest rose and fell rapidly.

"I'm scared," she whispered.

"Of what?"

"What if he blames me for mother's death?"

Keelan squeezed her hand. "I don't think he will. He has always shown me nothing but kindness and has a good sense of humor. Would you like to meet him first, and then Cedric afterward?"

She looked up at Keelan, her eyes shining, tears glistening and ready to fall. Slowly, she nodded.

Hi, Mr. Firestorm, Keelan projected to him.

Douglas stopped mid-step, looking around. *Who's speaking to me?*

Keelan, sir.

Keelan? How are you projecting to me? Douglas resumed walking, Samuel and Cedric giving him a strange look.

I'm full of surprises, sir. Ashera is nervous. Please come alone. Douglas stopped and spoke to the other two. While they spoke, he led Ashera to a bench near the monastery's main door. Sitting down, they waited for Douglas.

As Douglas approached, Ashera looked at him, her lips quivering.

Douglas paused a few steps away. "It's alright," he said reassuringly, "May I sit?"

Ashera nodded. She hesitated before speaking. "I don't know what to say."

Douglas nodded understandingly. "It's a lot to take in. I imagine it's overwhelming."

"I'm afraid…" Ashera began, her voice trembling. "Do you blame me for what happened to mother?"

Douglas shook his head gently. "I don't blame you, Ash. None of this is your fault. You're not responsible for the choices others made."

Ashera's tears finally began to fall. "I just want to make things right. I want to be part of this family and make up for everything I've done and missed."

Douglas reached out, pulling her into a warm embrace. "You're already a part of this family. We're just getting to know each other, and that's okay. We'll work through this together."

Keelan stood quietly by Ashera's side, feeling a mix of relief and pride. Douglas's kindness and understanding were what he had hoped for.

After a few moments, Ashera pulled back slightly, wiping her tears away. "Thank you," she said softly. "It means a lot to hear that."

Douglas smiled. "We'll get through this. Let's take things one step at a time and focus on what's ahead. There's still much to do, and we must stick together."

Ashera nodded, feeling a bit more at ease. Keelan squeezed her shoulder, giving her an encouraging smile. "We'll figure this out together."

With that, they all stood up, ready to face whatever challenges lay ahead, united in their quest to unravel the prophecy and rescue their loved ones.

Douglas's eyes softened as he looked at Ashera, "We have the rest of our lives to get to know each other. No rush. No expectations. I'm just so happy to see you again. You look so much like your mother." He reached up and swept a few strands of her auburn hair behind her ear.

Ashera's eyes welled up. "I wish she was here."

"So do I, more than you will ever know," Douglas said quietly. "We had many good years before we were blessed with you and Lance, but it wasn't enough." He shook his head sadly, his smile fading. After a brief moment, he looked up again, a smile returning to his face. "You were able to meet Lance again; that's good."

Ashera nodded. "How much have you been told about what happened before I escaped?"

"A little bit," Douglas replied, holding up his hand to stop her. "But it was enough for now. Let's get your brother back, and then we can heal the past." He offered her his hand as he stood.

She looked at his hand, then up at his smiling face. Slowly, she reached out and took his hand.

The tears glistening in Douglas's eyes finally fell. "I'm so glad you're home."

Back in the meeting room, they showed the three newcomers what they had discovered so far.

"One thing that has been bothering me is how Sephra was able to track you and Lance?" Cedric asked.

Aurora spoke up. ***She said she enchanted their bracers***.

"She did? I don't remember her saying that," Keelan said.

Aurora replied, ***Well, a lot was going on.***

Leilatha asked, "Keelan, may I see your bracer?" She examined it, passing her hand over the sapphire with her eyes closed. "I can feel the enchantment in the sapphire."

Keelan's eyes widened with concern. "Do you think she is still tracking me? Have I endangered everyone here?"

Leilatha opened her eyes and looked at him. "If The One chose to, yes, it could still track you."

"What do you mean, if it chose to?" Ashera asked, her voice trembling.

Keelan turned his head to look at Lance's sister. Since coming to the monastery, she had started to speak more.

Leilatha explained, "I don't think it is still tracking you. From what I have learned about your encounter, I believe it will be satisfied with half of the prophesied twins for now."

Ashera's voice squeaked with fright, "For now?"

Leilatha nodded. "I started my training here when I was six. My mentor met Eldjren when she was very young. Together, we spent countless hours learning all we could about the prophecy. All four of you must be present when the eclipse graces the sky. Two will not suffice."

Ashera's face went pale, and Keelan placed a comforting hand on top of hers. To his surprise, she grabbed his hand with both of hers, seeking reassurance.

Douglas looked around and asked, "So, what do we do now?"

Keelan murmured to himself, "I wonder…" He closed his eyes and focused on the star sapphire in his bracer. In his mind, Sephra's face appeared, revealing her as the creator of the enchantment and a weak protection spell. "She barely infused any magic into this protection spell. The bracer I enchanted for Lance is much stronger."

Cedric raised an eyebrow. "Are you sure?"

Keelan nodded. "Thinking back, Sephra frowned after I made Lance's. Another sorceress I met in Kingston said she had never felt a more powerful bracer than the one I made. I can track Lance's sapphire. I didn't place a tracking spell on it, but if I'm close to it, I'll be able to sense it."

"How can you be so sure?" Leilatha leaned forward, intrigued.

"I can feel Aurora's," Keelan explained. "I always know where she is."

Douglas interjected, "Are you sure that's not just your familiar bond?"

Keelan shook his head. "Let's test it." He rummaged through his bag and pulled out a necklace with a star sapphire. He closed his fist around it and probed with his magic. "She didn't place a tracking spell on this one, good," he mumbled. His lips moved as he pictured Ashera in both her human and dragon forms, muttering her full name and wyvern name. His hand flared with a blinding white light before fading. The sapphire remained aglow.

"Ash, this is for you," Keelan said, holding out the necklace by its chain. The sapphire rocked gently.

She reached out, trembling, and took the necklace. "It's beautiful. Can you…" She turned around, lifting her auburn hair so Keelan could fasten it around her neck.

When the clasp closed, she shuddered as the protection magic flowed through her, accompanied by another flash of white light. "Thank you," she whispered, her eyes downcast.

"So, how do you propose a test?" Cedric asked.

"I suggest Douglas and Ashera take a flight," Keelan proposed. "They can find a hidden spot, and I will attempt to locate them."

Leilatha stood. "Let's take a break until this evening. We'll regroup after our meal and plan our next steps."

As the sun began to set, Keelan set out with Stormbreaker and Aurora. He quickly found Douglas and Ashera, who had taken refuge in an empty house. After transforming into their dragon forms, they soared toward the Sapphire Mountains. The journey was challenging, but Keelan's determination kept him focused. After hours of searching, he felt the faintest trace of his magic. When they flew directly above their hidden location, the magic he placed in the sapphire necklace became vividly clear in his mind. Keelan directed Stormbreaker and Aurora to descend, guiding them to the spot where Douglas and Ashera awaited.

I found you, he projected.

Great job, Keelan. Douglas's voice echoed in his mind. *I must admit, though, it is still unsettling knowing you can project your thoughts to me.* Moments later, two dragons appeared in the sky alongside Stormbreaker and Keelan.

Drake mentioned how close dragons and magical humans are. I'm surprised more can't do this.

I'm so happy Drake is with Lance, Douglas added, shaking his head. *It's been so long since I've seen him, and I'm glad he's still around.*

Sir, I-I wanted to ask you… Keelan hesitated, unsure if he wanted to know the answer.

Your mother is well. The firebush healed her. I'm sorry I didn't tell you earlier.

Keelan exhaled a breath he hadn't realized he was holding. *That's okay, sir. I'm just glad she's better.*

By the early hours of the next day, a plan was finally in place. Keelan, Ashera, and their familiars would journey to the Wizard Hat with a small support group, while Cedric, Samuel, and the other two dragons remained at the monastery to protect it and assist with training. During Tarrid and Leo'venath's absence, a large group of new allies had formed: two dozen stags, ten unicorns, fourteen griffins, and eight pegasi.

Ben was ecstatic when he saw Keelan mounted on Stormbreaker. He quickly borrowed Stormbreaker's saddle and set to work replicating it.

CHAPTER

-23-

TWO days later, they were ready to depart. Stormbreaker carried Keelan, while Dreamcrest bore Fawn, and Shadow Wing—a gray and black griffin—transported Tarrid. Aurora, Zephyr, Ashera, and Douglas completed the group. Just before daybreak, they soared into the sky, heading northeast. They estimated it would take two days to reach the coast.

When they landed, they found themselves on the backside of Griffin's Keep. The group stood along the shore, just beyond the reach of the lapping waves, peering eastward in hopes of glimpsing the island. A thick fog clung to the water's edge, shrouding their view.

"How far do you think it is?" Fawn asked, squinting into the fog.

Keelan shrugged. "The map makes it look like it's just off the coast. Let's rest for a bit and see if the fog burns off. I'd rather not fly through it."

The fog lingered, thick and unyielding, throughout the day and well into the next. When it finally began to lift, they were greeted not by a hidden island or any sign of their destination but by the endless stretch of blue water blending seamlessly into the blue sky.

"It could be anywhere out there!" Ashera's voice carried a note of frustration. Her brow furrowed as she gazed over the empty horizon.

"We can't give up, Ash," Keelan said softly, placing a reassuring hand on her shoulder. "Eldjren placed the medallion on that island. If he could find it, so can we."

She nodded and sighed, a shiver running through her. "Are you cold?" Keelan asked, removing his cloak and draping it over her shoulders.

"Thank you," she mumbled, the warmth of the cloak a small comfort. They stood in silence for a while, gazing at the ocean as the sun dipped behind the Griffin Mountains.

"Why are you so kind to me?" she asked softly, almost too quietly for Keelan to hear.

He looked at her, her gaze fixed on the ocean. After a moment of silence, he sat down on the sand. She looked down at him then. Her pale, icy blue eyes glistened as she studied him. Her auburn hair being pulled by the breeze from under his cloak. He patted the space beside him. A few breaths passed before she lowered herself beside him, pulling her knees to her chest.

"When I first saw you, I felt an instant connection," Keelan said. "I knew from that moment that we were linked in some way."

She snorted and buried her face in her hands. "I was so horrible. I'm so sorry for what I did. I—I have nightmares almost every night about those few days."

He placed a reassuring hand on her shoulder. "I don't judge you for what happened back then."

"Back then? You make it sound like it was years ago, not just weeks."

Keelan was silent for a moment. "It feels like another lifetime, almost."

"But why the kindness? Even before you knew I was Lance's twin. You stopped Tar…" She trailed off.

"It's hard to explain. I think Lance felt it, too, the moment he saw Shaylee for the first time. My heart knows we were meant to be together."

"Together? In what way?"

"That I'm not sure of, but the prophecy says the twins must unite and entwine. I don't know how entwined we have to be."

"Marriage?" She asked, her voice elevating.

"I don't know?" he admitted with a smile when she finally looked up at him. "I don't want to think that far ahead. I think we've managed the unity part—well, we will once we have Lance and Shaylee back. Then when we have the medallion, and the solar eclipse happens, we'll understand what to do."

She nodded, turning her gaze back to the water. Keelan shifted his weight in the sand, which caused him to slide a few inches away from her, so their shoulders no longer touched. Ashera started to shiver again.

"Do you want to head back to the fire?" Keelan asked.

"Not yet. This is nice," she replied, trying to keep her chattering teeth quiet.

Keelan chuckled softly and draped his arm around her shoulders, drawing her closer. She tensed momentarily before melting into his embrace, resting her head against his shoulder.

Their moment of peace was interrupted by distant roars. Keelan and Ashera jumped to their feet and rushed back to their companions. Douglas transformed into his enormous blood-red dragon form. In the distance, a large group of wyverns was approaching.

"Brace for an attack!" Tarrid shouted, his hands glowing brightly.

"Everyone stay behind me," Ashera said confidently, stepping a few paces ahead of the group.

Keelan rushed to her side. "What are you doing?"

"I am their princess. They will not harm me," she said, chin held high.

"Your father knows you fled. What if they're looking for you?"

Terror flashed in her eyes. "I didn't think about that."

"One is breaking away from the formation!" Fawn yelled over to them.

Ashera and Keelan turned to see a wyvern indeed leaving the group and heading their way.

"Come on, fall back!" Keelan urged, gently trying to pull her away.

She shook his hand off. "That's Arveth."

Keelan paused. "Are you sure? Do you know this wyvern well?"

She nodded.

"Then let's fall back until its intentions are clear."

"She won't harm me."

As the wyvern neared and began its descent, Ashera remained rooted in place, waiting.

Arveth landed gracefully and dropped into a deep bow. "Princess, I am so relieved to have finally found you," she said with a slurred voice.

"Rise, Arveth. Why have you been searching for me?" Ashera asked cautiously.

Arveth looked up but stayed on the ground. "The King has been slain, along with his entire honor guard and any other wyvern who tried to stop her."

"Stop who?" Keelan interjected.

Arveth hissed and snapped her jaws at him.

"Enough," Ashera said sharply. "You will show Keelan and everyone here respect. Answer his question."

Arveth bowed her head lower before speaking. "A sorceress calling herself The One."

"Sephra," Keelan said under his breath.

"Then why have you come?" Ashera asked, her gaze shifting from the brown wyvern before her to the others circling above.

"We are searching for Zarret. He must take the throne and lead us."

"I haven't seen him for about a week," Ashera said.

Arveth glanced at the group. "I see you have found Firestorm. I assume you know the truth now."

Ashera's eyes widened. "You know who I am?"

Arveth lowered her gaze back to the ground. "To my great shame, I was the one who stole you."

"You? How could you?"

"I was ordered to by my king. One does not question the king. But that is why I have always stayed close to you. When I took you, you were in your dragon form, so small and precious. My heart ached, fearing Ichakik might harm you. I swore I would protect you at all costs."

Ashera hesitantly took a few steps closer. "Thank you," she said softly.

"Let me see your wrist."

"The bracelet has already been removed. Zar did it before he departed."

"So, he knows?" Arveth's eyes widened in surprise. Ashera nodded. "You have access to your true form?"

Ashera closed her eyes, and a swirling mist of blue and bronze enveloped her. Arveth reared her head back, a hiss slipping from her lips. As the mist cleared, Arveth bowed deeply once more, spreading her wings wide across the sand.

"You are beautiful," Arveth whispered. The wyverns circling above roared loudly. Arveth glanced upward and roared in return. "This is where I leave you. If you see Zarret, send him home. I hope to see you again once you rid the world of that demon. Call on me if you ever need anything. I will always be your servant."

Ashera nodded.

"How will we defeat The One if the entire wyvern empire can't?" Ashera asked, her voice subdued as they sat around the fire with darkness fully setting in.

With the Infinite Medallion, of course, Zephyr replied, curled up at Ashera's feet.

So, you know how the Medallion works? Aurora inquired.

Zephyr lifted his head and yawned. *No, but that's what the prophecy says must be done.*

Keelan chuckled as the two familiars continued to bicker. "We just have to take it one step at a time."

"Do you feel Lance?" Douglas asked.

"Not yet," Keelan sighed. "I'm planning to have Aurora fly out over the ocean tomorrow to see if she can locate the island. The rest of us will stay here and rest. My main goal is to secure the Medallion first, and then we'll focus on finding Lance and Shaylee. As I see it, we have until mid-winter to find both the Medallion and them."

CHAPTER

THE courtyard below looked like it was crawling with silver beetles from King Theodoric's vantage point in the castle's highest tower. His knights, assembled from Kingston and Lower City, stood in perfect formation. Their armor was polished to a dazzling shine. Despite his elevated position, the clamor of his men grated on his nerves and made his ears ache.

"The men are ready and await your orders, Your Majesty," his general said, arriving at the top of the stairs, breathless.

"Excellent. I will not be threatened by some witch. We will show her what true power looks like," Theodoric declared, his voice icy.

"All the residents of Kingston are in the castle as ordered. What of the people of Lower City, my liege?" the general asked.

Theodoric's gaze hardened. "What about them?"

The general flinched at the king's cold tone. "What are your orders, Sire?"

"We will fortify the castle and Kingston. I want most of the men stationed in every house on Inns Row. No one is to show themselves. We will use our gate to slow them down and, if possible, stop them. If they get past, the men in Inns Row will allow them through and then flank them. None shall breach the castle," he snarled.

The general snapped a crisp salute and hurried down the steps.

"The madwoman calling herself *The One* will meet the same fate as the Vaelums of old," Theodoric mused, his eyes cold as they swept over his assembled army. "No one will take my throne from me."

As the minutes passed, Percival stood watching and waiting for his general to carry out the orders. Gradually, the soldiers began to disperse, moving into their positions with military precision. His gaze followed the columns as they departed the courtyard. Squinting, he focused on one figure: a young man in his early twenties, clad in gleaming golden armor, a blue plume adorning his helmet. The rider, mounted on a fine chestnut stallion, stood out from the others. His wife's voice echoed in Percival's mind. *As Crown Prince, he should stand apart from the rest.* She had insisted on that ridiculous armor, ignoring tradition. He clenched his jaw.

"Such a disappointment of an heir," he muttered bitterly, shaking his head. "But he's all I have."

With a frustrated sigh, Percival turned and retreated to his study. There, at his desk, he picked up the scroll from the witch. Though he had already memorized its contents, he unrolled it once more, reading the cursed words again...

My Dearest King of Evansshire,

I wish to introduce myself before you pledge your allegiance. You may call me The One. I'm sure you've heard of the prophecy that foretold my arrival. Well, the time has finally come.

I have already decimated the Wyvern Empire, but I seek peace with you. Together, we can rid ourselves of the prophesied twins. You may keep Kingston, and I will rule the rest of Oshana, with a gracious yearly tribute on your part, of course.

I will be at your gates on the eve of the next new moon. If the gates are open and your banners lowered, I will know we have struck an accord. I will then meet you in your throne room to accept the tribute owed to my greatness.

Do not disappoint me, Percival Theodoric. You will not live to regret it.

The One, Sephra Tervil

Percival crumpled the scroll into a tight ball and hurled it into the crackling fire. The parchment ignited instantly with a sharp pop, sending tendrils of black smoke hissing into the air. A sudden, piercing howl erupted from the flames, making him flinch. His eyes widened in fear as he stared into the blaze. "Damn witchcraft," he muttered under his breath. "Magic must be eradicated before my kingdom can ever know peace." His voice grew louder, more resolute. "I will not bow to her. She will never breach my defenses!" In a fit of rage, he snatched his wine glass and flung it into the fire. His smirk deepened as it shattered against the stone hearth, the red liquid sizzling among the flames.

The night of the new moon had arrived. Percival's forces were in position: half stationed along Inns Row, the standard regiment guarding the gate, and the rest spread throughout the courtyard or inside the castle. Armend, the Crown Prince, stood alongside the knights in the courtyard, ready for whatever might come.

Inside the throne room, Percival sat with his honor guard while the queen and the residents of Kingston were safely hidden within the castle's secure chambers.

The large clock in the courtyard, a recent addition, tolled nine, then ten, and finally eleven. Percival, weary from the long wait, felt himself nodding off. Just as his eyelids grew heavy, piercing screams shattered the stillness, echoing from the courtyard. His heart raced, instinct urging him to rush to the windows, but he fought the impulse. Instead, he gripped the armrests of his throne, his knuckles white with tension, and forced himself to remain seated, awaiting what came next.

The screams died away, but the ensuing silence was deafening. Percival's heart raced, and his breath came out thin and shaky. At first, he thought the chill in the room was just his imagination, but soon he could see his breath. His guards looked around nervously, their armor clanging as they shivered.

"We should get you someplace safe, my liege," one guard said.

Percival nodded, trying to stand, but his legs felt like they were frozen. "I can't move!" he nearly screamed in panic, struggling to free himself from the chair.

The guards attempted to help, but their feet were also frozen to the marble tiles. "What's happening?" one of them asked, panic evident in his voice.

Suddenly, a blast of freezing wind threw the throne room doors open. Percival shrieked at the unexpected gale, throwing his hands up to shield his crown. The room plunged into darkness as the candles and fire were extinguished.

"What manner of evil is this?" he demanded.

Soft laughter echoed from the hall beyond his chamber. A small blue light darted into the room, flitting about like a frenzied dragonfly. The laughter grew louder as the light approached.

Percival's eyes widened as the light drew closer. "What kind of creature are you? A mini fairy?" he asked, his curiosity piqued. He had expected The One herself, not a sentient insect.

"Fairy?" the creature screeched. "I am a Pixie, not some weak fairy! How dare you?"

The pixie flew toward him, stopping inches from his nose. Her blue-skinned face had eyes that were an abyss of the darkest black. He tried to recoil from the frightful creature but remained frozen in his throne.

"Meta! Enough!" a new, thunderous voice boomed through the room. The deep, unnatural tone seemed to come from all directions. The pixie backed away, her eyes shifting colors and shrinking.

A woman strolled into the throne room, her black hair forming a halo around her. She wore a blood-red, floor-length dress that rippled around her legs in the relentless wind.

"Who are you?" Percival demanded, striving to maintain his regal tone.

"Halt! No one shall pass!" one of his guards yelled.

The woman pointed at the two guards with outstretched fingers. She slowly closed each hand into a fist and forcefully thrust them downward. Percival watched in terror as his guards clutched their throats and then collapsed, their feet still frozen to the tiles.

"Now, we can talk. Ruler to ex-ruler, in peace," the woman said in an unnaturally deep voice.

"Who are you?" Percival repeated.

"Why, I'm The One, of course. I didn't think introductions were necessary. Now, remove yourself from my throne." She flicked a hand at him.

Percival felt himself lifted from his seat and then strangely compelled to descend the dais steps and stand before her.

She smiled sweetly, her voice sounding more like a woman's now. "That's better." Striding past him, she approached his throne. "I do believe this room looks better in summer. I detest winter." She clapped her hands loudly. Suddenly, the wind was gone, the candles and fire were lit once more, and the room was warm like an early summer day. "Aww, that's better," The One said in a feminine voice.

Percival turned around to face the usurper on his throne. "How dare you sit on my throne," he thundered.

"Watch your tone with me," her deep voice returned. "I gave you a choice. You gave your answer. I do not negotiate, but…" She paused. "If you surrender now, I will spare everyone hiding within these walls."

"What about me?" he asked, his voice faltering.

"What about you?"

"Will I be spared?"

"No! But your death will be swift."

Percival's frown deepened into a scowl. "Then I do not surrender."

The One stared at him for a long moment. "Such a selfish man. One who does not deserve the loyalty of his men. They fought bravely. Foolishly, but bravely. Bring them in!" she commanded.

Four rough-looking men entered, pushing a young man clad in blood-stained gold armor. Percival's eyes clouded. His son was still alive, for now.

"Will you surrender to save his life? Or perhaps hers?" The One gestured behind Armend, and Queen Rosa was led forward as well.

"I will not surrender," he said coldly.

Queen Rosa was pushed closer. "One last opportunity," The One said.

Percival pressed his lips together, refusing to speak.

"Such a pity," The One said and then nodded. "General, if you would be so kind."

The well-dressed man standing behind the queen reached around her and, with a quick motion, slit her throat. Rosa's eyes widened in shock, a soft moan escaped her lips as she collapsed. Armend screamed, struggling against his captors. Percival maintained his regal composure, though his heart ached at the death of his wife of twenty-five years. Their marriage had been one of power, nothing more, but he would be lying if he said he wouldn't miss her companionship.

"What say you now?" The One asked as she sauntered to stand next to Armend.

Percival's lips twisted into a sneer. "Thank you for freeing me from a failed marriage."

"Father, how could you?" Armend asked, shocked.

The One sighed loudly and tsked. "And what of your son? Do you not want him to continue breathing?" she asked.

"I will not surrender," Percival sneered.

The One paced slowly around Armend, her cold gaze locked on Percival. "Such a pity," she murmured, shaking her head in mock sorrow before a cruel grin twisted her lips. She moved back behind Armend, her voice dropping into a soft, dangerous whisper. "Don't worry, young man. This will only hurt for a moment. And then… you'll be reunited with your mother in Ombrasia for all eternity."

"Wait!" Armend cried, panic lacing his voice. "Please, Father! Surrender, take her offer. I… I don't want to die," he whimpered, his desperation raw and palpable.

Percival stared at his son. "So weak. Such a disappointment," he muttered.

Sephra tilted her head, surveying the spineless figures before her. Without another word, she placed her hand on Armend's head. Armend screamed in horror and pain, his face contorting with anguish. A slight grin played across Sephra's face as Percival struggled to keep his eyes open, forcing himself to watch his son's torment. Only when the former king closed his eyes did she finally release Armend, allowing him to die.

"Take him to the courtyard. He will not be given such an easy death," she said sweetly. As Percival was led past her, she patted him on the cheek. "See you soon."

CHAPTER

-25-

AURORA glided effortlessly on the thermal currents, the vast ocean stretching endlessly below her. The sky above was a canvas of pale blue, dotted with fluffy white clouds, while the deep blue waters below shimmered with the rhythm of gentle waves. The sun, concealed behind passing clouds, occasionally peeked out, casting a dazzling reflection across the ocean's surface like flashes of molten gold.

Three days of searching and still nothing, she projected to Keelan.

Can you fly further north? But if you're tired, you can come back.

She chuckled to herself. She could hear and feel his worry through their bond. ***I'm fine. I am turning to fly north.***

An hour later, just when she was about to give up for the day, she thought she saw something in the distance a little further out.

What's the matter? Keelan's frantic words flew into her mind.

I think I see something.

What is it? He almost screamed at her.

Calm yourself, Keelan. I don't know yet.

She banked her wings and slowly changed course, heading toward the speck on the horizon. As she got closer, she let out a relieved breath.

I found the island. Looks just like the picture on the map. I'm going in for a closer look.

Wait! Keelan projected. ***Come back here. Let's converse with Douglas and come up with a plan before we just show up on the island. We don't know what awaits us there.***

If you insist. Returning now.

She slowly turned to return to the beach but found her gaze returning to the island. She narrowed her eyes and flared her tail. Abruptly, she banked her wings and flew closer to the island, increasing her altitude slightly. Keelan had told her to come straight back but her curious nature wouldn't allow her to leave just yet.

She scanned the area. Nothing moved on the ground or in the air. After circling the mountain twice, she finally headed back to the beach and her awaiting friends.

Three hours later, Aurora finally returned. Keelan, lost in his pacing, stumbled over the trench he had worn into the sand, nearly falling but catching himself just in time. The two girls behind him erupted in laughter. He shot them a mock glare, attempting to keep a straight face, but failed miserably. His cheeks flushed as his eyes met Ashera's, who was smiling sweetly at him.

"It's that far out?" Tar asked after Aurora landed. "Keelan said you were returning three hours ago."

Aurora nodded. ***I came straight back.*** Her tail feathers flared slightly, and she dropped her eyes to the ground.

"We should leave at first light then," Douglas said. "I will approach the island first and make sure it's safe."

Did you see any ariels? Dreamcrest asked.

Aurora shook her head. ***Didn't detect any magic either.***

"You can detect magic?" Fawn asked, standing and walking closer to Aurora.

Aurora nodded. ***If magic is being used actively, I can sense it. My sire said he worked so hard for years that he could detect human magic up to a week after the spell was cast. And no magical creature could hide from him, human or animal.***

"Then it's decided. We leave at first light." Keelan glanced at his team and smiled. His smile was a mask, though; he was worried beyond belief. Would they be able to find the medallion and save Lance and Shaylee? If The One could kill the king of the Wyverns and his entire honor guard, what hope would a bunch of youths have in defeating her?

Without a word, Keelan turned toward the ocean, his gaze fixed on the distant horizon where Aurora had just flown from. Somewhere out there, a Seer from long ago had hidden a medallion—a relic he was destined to find. The entire ordeal felt impossibly far-fetched. Keelan sank to his knees, bowing his head. How had his life come to this? Just two years ago, magic had been nothing more than a fairy tale, and creatures like dragons and phoenixes were the stuff of myths meant to entertain or frighten children. Now, here he was, on a mystical quest, wielding magic himself and counting a dragon and a phoenix as his closest friends. It was all too much.

Soft footsteps walking through the loose sand broke his train of thought, though he didn't turn around to see who was coming. Without a word, Ashera sat beside him, staring into the sea. They sat together silently until the sun started to sink below the mountains circling Griffins Keep.

"Do you think we will succeed?" Ashera asked in a quiet voice.

"We have to."

She sighed. "But do you think we will?"

Keelan placed his arm over her shoulders and leaned her toward him. "I hope so."

There it is! The Wizard's Hat, Aurora projected.

Everyone stay up high. I will circle down for a closer look, Douglas projected to everyone.

The mountain was just like Keelan envisioned it would be. A barren mountain jutting from the ocean, its tip lost in the clouds. No vegetation was in sight, and there didn't even appear to be any places to land.

Douglas circled the enormous mountain before returning. *I see no signs of life,* he told them.

Do you see a place to land? Keelan projected for all to hear.

Douglas expelled a cloud of smoke and ash. *I didn't see any places to land.*

Um, Aurora projected into all their minds.

What is it? Keelan projected back.

There is one place on the back side of the mountain. It will be tricky, though; it's only big enough for humans.

"How do you know?" Keelan said aloud.

Aurora dropped her shoulders and dipped slightly in the sky.

"Aurora!" Keelan said sharply. "I thought you came straight back."

Well, I was going too. But I was here and all. It didn't hurt, and I found out where we needed to go. So, all in all, I did well, right? she asked hopefully.

Keelan frowned at her, but Douglas's voice cut in before he could respond.

You did good, Aurora. I didn't see an opening, glad you did, Douglas said.

"Where is it?" Tar asked, yelling above the wind. He strained his neck, trying to find the opening.

Near the top around back. It must be shielded in an illusion if a dragon couldn't see it, Aurora replied.

How are we going to get up there in human form? Ashera projected to them.

You will have to change in the air and land as a human. Douglas hissed out a sigh when he saw Ashera's expression. *I'm so sorry your mother and I were not able to raise you. This is a trick she excelled at. When you were taken, she leaped out of the window of our home and transformed without missing a beat. I will go first so you can see it done.*

Ashera nodded slowly.

How will the bipeds get off our backs? Dreamcrest projected.

Don't worry, I'll handle that. Douglas will go first, and then I will, Keelan projected.

Douglas led them around to the backside of the 'Hat.' Keelan marveled at how much this mountain reminded him of the magician's hat he had seen a few years ago. *This formation definitely inspired the hat. I wonder if Eldjren had the first one?* He thought to himself.

Douglas flew close to the mountainside. *I don't see the ledge. Can you land on it, Aurora?*

Of course, she replied. She zipped past him and landed on what appeared to be nothing but air. She hopped around and appeared to be tracing the edge.

"If we can't see the platform, how will we stay on it," Fawn asked, panic spiking her voice.

Aurora, please trace the ledge again, Keelan said to her. He concentrated on her movement and imagined her footprints glowing bright red. She squawked and took flight for a moment when she saw her glowing prints. She quickly recovered and soon the platform was covered with glowing red spots.

Douglas positioned himself above the platform that looked impossibly small compared to his bulking size. Douglas's form started to shimmer as he was shrouded in a red and gold mist. Within mere moments, a man Keelan knew well was falling through the air, landing somewhat shakily on the now much larger platform. He waved and then ducked inside the cave entrance.

My turn. Keelan tried to swallow, but his throat instantly parched. *Get as close as you can, Stormbreaker.*

Are you sure about this? The griffin asked. Stormbreaker angled himself so he was close to the mountain without hitting his wings on the sharp rocks.

No! Keelan answered as he vaulted off the griffin's back. He found himself moving forward briefly before gravity claimed him and started pulling him down and away from the platform and Douglas's outstretched arm. Quickly, Keelan tried to calm his racing heart and thoughts in order to find his magic. Every fiber of his being was screaming at him, *You're going to die!!!* Finding his center took way too long. He craned his neck as he fell past the ledge. He felt hopeless, lost in a sea of fear.

Keelan!! Ashera screamed in his head.

His thoughts centered on her, his focus snapped to the present, and his magic roared to life. He concentrated on wrapping himself in a cushioned bubble of air and then lifted the bubble. Keelan kept his eyes up, refusing to look down. Finally, the ledge came into view, and Douglas grabbed his arm, pulling him to safety.

"Keelan, my boy. Don't scare an old man like that," Douglas said in a tight voice.

Aurora flew out of the cave and barreled into him. *I wouldn't have gone inside if I knew you were going to try to kill yourself.*

Keelan pushed the smoldering bird off him with a nod and a chuckle. "Sorry. I've never tried carrying myself so far." He jumped suddenly and started to brush his pants; Aurora's flaming feathers had singed his thigh.

Keelan sat down, took a few deep breaths, and then met Ashera's eyes. *I didn't know dragons could cry,* he thought.

Okay, Tar, you're next. Shadow Wing, fly as close to the platform as you can. Tar, you will then leap for it. I will grab you with my magic and levitate you to the ledge.

Tar gave him a look but stayed silent.

He was able to get Tar safely to the platform without an issue.

Okay, Fawn. You're next. You have to fly really close, Dreamcrest.

Dreamcrest nickered and nodded her head as she flew closer to the mountain. *Are you okay doing this, Fawn?* she asked her rider.

"If Tar can do it, so can I," Fawn yelled into the wind. She unbuckled herself and leaped for the ledge and Tar's outstretched arm.

Keelan caught her weight easily as she glided toward the mountain. He smiled. "You did most of that on your own."

She beamed up at him. "I had to try."

Keelan nodded and focused on Ashera next.

You have to get close and then transform. Keelan will catch you, Douglas projected to Ashera.

I'm scared, she projected privately back to him.

It'll be okay. Keelan won't let you fall. I've seen the way he looks at you.

Ashera's mouth flopped open. *Looks at me, how?*

Douglas smiled at his daughter. *You two are destined for each other. Don't tell me you can't feel it. Come, this isn't the time for this conversation or reflection. Just look at Keelan and me. Nothing else matters right now. Look at us and transform.*

Ashera closed her eyes for a few heartbeats and flew closer to the mountain. *You'd better catch me,* she projected to Keelan.

Always, was his reply.

Ashera tried to steady her heartbeat, but staring into Keelan's eyes made it difficult. Slowly, a mist of blue and bronze engulfed her. She closed her eyes tightly and expected to feel herself falling, but she wasn't. Hesitantly, she opened them; she was drifting toward Keelan and the others. Keelan's eyes were locked onto her. When she was within reach, he held out his hand and gently grabbed hers, pulling her toward him. She wrapped her arms around Keelan when both feet were firmly on the ground. His body stiffened and then relaxed as he reached around her, hugging her back.

"Are you okay?" he asked in a quiet voice.

She nodded, not trusting her voice.

Alright, lovebirds, Aurora teased. *If you two are finished, we have a medallion to find.*

CHAPTER

-26-

SHAYLEE sat next to the fireplace, staring into the crackling flames. The logs popped and snapped as water trapped inside the bark was released by the heat, causing her to jump involuntarily. The flames flickered shadows across the room.

Her mind felt cloudy and fuzzy, and she struggled to focus on her thoughts. *How long had it been since I saw Fawn last? A week, two weeks?* She shook her head slowly, trying to clear the fog. *Why did she leave her anyway?* These questions started coming to her in the evenings but left her just as quickly—for some reason. Tonight, she was determined to get them answered. Her days were spent sitting in this room with Lyra. Food was brought to them, and they were told they could not leave because it was unsafe… from what she was never told. They were led to the main dining hall in the evenings, where she would see Lance, Drake, and Sephra. Sephra was very strict and insisted they not speak until after eating.

The problem was that Shaylee always forgot what she wanted to ask Sephra after eating. Tonight, she was not going to fail.

Her gaze left the fire and settled on the table beside her, where her lunch lay untouched.

You should have eaten your lunch. I can hear your stomach growling from over here, Lyra complained from her curled-up position on her bed.

"I told you, breakfast tasted funny this morning. I don't know how you ate those eggs."

Even rotten eggs taste good. She yawned and stretched her front legs out.

"Is your head feeling clearer?" Shaylee asked her.

A little, much like yesterday.

"Mine is much clearer than yesterday."

A knock on her door startled her. "Come in."

"Mistress Sephra is ready for you, miss," a meek voice said from behind the door.

Shaylee stood, smoothing out her dress. "Coming."

"Good evening, Shaylee. Good evening, Lance," Sephra greeted them.

Shaylee looked over at Lance and nodded. They only saw each other at dinner.

Lance fixed his eyes on her. *Have you eaten today?* He projected to her privately.

No, you? She replied privately.

Nothing yet. I'm feeling better, other than hungry.

I don't know if we can skip out on dinner, Shaylee replied.

Lance and Shaylee walked slowly to the large table, keeping their conversation private.

I've been thinking about that. Just try to eat very little. Drake is certain there is something in the food. Our bodies are getting used to it. If Sephra suspects anything, she will increase it, Lance told her.

Are you sure she's the one doing this to us? Shaylee asked him.

It has to be her.

Shaylee and Lance sat on either side of Sephra at a long table made to seat at least twenty. They hoped their private conversation would remain hidden in their minds from her.

A bell rang, food was brought in, and dinner began. Shaylee and Lance picked at their food, but if Sephra noticed, she said nothing.

Three large chandeliers swayed slightly above the table, the only light in the massive dining hall, except for the fireplace set off to one end. The chandelier candles flickered, casting shadows on the walls.

Dinner progressed as it usually did—eating without speaking. After their plates were cleared, they retired to the three chairs in front of the fire with small glasses of Ice Wine.

Sephra swirled her brilliant blue wine, her eyes darting between her two guests. Shaylee watched the liquid sparkle in the firelight, her wine untouched.

"Shaylee, dear. Are you not feeling well?" Sephra asked.

Shaylee blinked a few times before answering. "Just tired and not very hungry, ma'am," she said.

"And you, Lance?" Sephra asked him.

"I am well, my lady." He inclined his head slightly.

"You didn't eat much either."

"Just feeling sluggish. We have been here with nothing to do for some time. I'm used to a rigorous schedule, my lady."

Sephra nodded and pursed her lips. "We will be leaving soon. So, both of you need to eat and maintain your strength."

Shaylee perked up, scooting close to the front of her chair. "Going where?"

"You will see soon enough. You don't have to worry about the where. Just be ready to leave when I say so."

They both nodded.

"You should both return to your rooms. I will be gone for a few days. Be ready when I return." She stood and left them sitting by the fire.

Lance and Shaylee stared after her and then shared a look. She never left them alone—together.

Is it safe to speak? Shaylee projected to Lance.

He shifted his eyes to the fire and lifted his glass to his lips. *I don't think so. I think she's testing us. Sit calmly and then depart for your room in a few moments,* he replied.

Shaylee sighed, closed her eyes, and then took a small sip of her wine. *Why are we here? Why did we come here?* She asked, mostly to herself.

I'm not sure. I don't think I would have left Keelan or my sister willingly. We had just found her.

Shaylee's body stiffened. *Your sister?*

My twin sister.

Twin? How funny that you are a twin, and so am I.

Lance stole a glance at her. *I forgot. You didn't hear our full story. But now is not the time. After Sephra leaves, I will try to come see you. You better go now.*

"Goodnight, Lance," Shaylee said out loud with a small smile. She stood and left the room.

Lance followed her with his eyes until she moved behind him. He stayed in front of the fire, sipping his wine. His mind was getting fuzzy again. He shook his head at the glass of wine before placing it beside him. After a few minutes, his attendant fetched him and walked him back to his room.

Is it clear? Drake asked Lance, sticking his nose through the hole before him.

Yes, I am alone, Lance replied.

Drake squeezed his head through the hole and then wiggled his body through.

Lance chuckled at the sight. "How do you fit through such a tight place?" he asked his familiar.

Talent, Drake told him, shaking his whole body from nose to tail, his wings flicking out wide.

Lance chuckled again. "Has Sephra left?"

Drake nodded. *She took several Wyverns with her and enough food for several days.*

Lance nodded. "Good. You do know where Shaylee's room is, right?"

Drake nodded again.

"Okay, let's go."

Lance went to his door. Unlocked, like always. He opened it slightly and then peered into the hallway—empty. Drake led him down the hallway and around a couple of turns.

This is her room. Drake stopped at a door that looked like every other door.

Lance knocked on the door. A quiet voice on the other side told him to enter. He opened the door and walked in, quickly shutting the door behind him.

Her room was laid out similarly to his. Near the door was a large four-poster bed with a wardrobe. Next to the fireplace sat a small couch and armchair. Several flowerpots were scattered throughout the room, empty, just like in his room.

"Lance!" Shaylee stood and rushed over to him, grabbing his hands. "So, it's true. She left?"

He beamed at her. "Drake watched her leave, and…" He dropped one of her hands and swung a bag off his shoulder. "Drake found us some food that he is certain has not been fouled."

Her face lit up even more. "I am so hungry."

Still holding her hand, he led her to the fire. He opened the bag and took out two apples. He handed one to her and tossed one to Drake. He knelt next to the fire and rummaged through the pack, pulling out a ham, a loaf of bread, and a small fish.

Do I smell fish? Lyra lifted her head, sniffing the air.

"All for you, Lyra." Lance placed the fish on the ground and the ham close to the fire to heat it. He then took an apple for himself and sat next to Shaylee.

"What are we going to do?" she asked him.

Lance pondered the question. "We are going to escape. I don't know why Sephra brought us here, but I know I don't want to stick around to find out why."

"You know her, don't you?" she asked, still looking into the fire.

He nodded. "She has been my family's guest for the past five years. We thought she was a witch, nothing more. She was always quiet and kept to herself mostly."

Lance took a bite of his apple, closing his eyes and letting the sweet juice dribble down his chin. He stole a glance at Shaylee out of the corner of his eye. She closed her eyes, taking small bites of her apple, a grin curling her lips.

"You said you would tell me your story after Sephra left."

Lance sighed, drawing her gaze to him. "What happened when you touched Keelan?"

She flinched and returned her gaze to the fire. "It was like I was struck by lightning. But then I knew, I... somehow just knew he was my brother. I don't know how to explain it. It was like looking at someone I'd known all along but hadn't seen in years. Do..." She paused.

Lance watched her silently to see if she would continue speaking.

"Do you know why I was abandoned?" she asked softly.

Lance grabbed both of her hands and turned her to look at him. "Maya, that's your mother's name..."

Shaylee nodded.

"She told Keelan he had a twin after she came down with the Wasting. She said that the midwives took the secondborn away. She was told you died. They hid your birth from everyone, including your father. He learned about you at the same time as Keelan."

"But why?"

"Why what?" he asked.

"Why did they hide me?"

Lance studied her for a minute. Her head was down, and her eyes were closed. He ran his thumbs across the soft skin on the back of her hands. "In Evansshire, twins are forbidden. Do you know of the Twins Prophecy?"

She nodded, still looking down.

"The King wants to make sure the prophecy doesn't happen, so by killing all twins born, he hopes to kill the prophecy."

"So, both of us were supposed to be killed?" she asked, her breath catching in her throat as she swallowed down a sob.

"Yes."

Shaylee nodded again and fell into silence. Lance watched her closely. Her head was still bowed, and her shoulders were hunched. After a moment, she gently squeezed his hands.

"Why did she risk it? Why did she defy the King's law?"

Lance lifted her chin with two fingers. Tears ran down her cheeks. She opened her glistening eyes, pain etched in her pupils.

"Maya knew she was the last of the Vaelum line." Shaylee's eyes opened wide. "If both of you died, the prophecy would have died with you. She saved the firstborn because her husband had already seen him. She cast you aside to save the future," he said gently.

Shaylee squeezed her eyes shut again, pushing a fresh stream of tears down her flushed cheeks.

"Who saved you?" Lance asked after the new tears stopped falling.

A smile curled the corners of her lips. "Rosepetal. My ma. She gave birth to an elvenfae, but like all those before her, she died shortly after birth. My ma was heartbroken and stayed by the grave for hours, stricken with grief. She heard someone approaching and saw them lay a bundle on the forest floor and prayed to the gods for someone to save the infant. So… she did. She took me home and told my father, Talon, I was his child. I… I haven't known the truth for very long."

"Keelan told me about meeting you a couple of years ago. Your ma is a fairy, correct?"

She nodded.

"Does Talon, your father, know the truth yet?"

"He learned right before I left to rescue Tar and Leo. I haven't spoken to him since."

The fire crackled and popped, filling the silence that stretched between them.

"Is that why Sephra took me? Because I am one twin from the prophecy?" Shaylee inquired.

Lance nodded and stood. He retrieved the ham and sliced off a few thick pieces with a small knife on his belt. He then broke off a couple of pieces of bread and placed the ham slices in between. He handed one to Shaylee and sat back down. After a few bites, he spoke again.

"The prophecy speaks of twins, one from each royal bloodline. You and Keelan are from the Vaelum line; Ashera, my sister, and I are from the Ragnis line."

Shaylee spun to face him, almost dropping her dinner. "You're Ragnis?"

He nodded, taking another bite.

"When I first saw you, I was instantly drawn to you. I didn't understand why. It was almost like my connection with Keelan, but… different."

"I first saw you when Keelan, Jonal, and I had traveled through Threndy."

She gave him a puzzled look.

He chuckled. "This was after you left. Jonal and Keelan were able to tap into the village's history and replay an image of the wyvern attack. I saw you then. Keelan recognized you instantly, and I was immediately drawn to you. You were…" Lance paused for a moment, swallowing the lump in his throat. "You are beautiful." Lance kept his eyes locked on hers.

Her face reddened, and she dropped her gaze.

"Drake is looking for an escape route right now. I'll get you out of here."

Shaylee looked around the room for the firedrake.

"He left a bit ago. As soon as I know we can get out of here, I will come for you. I'm hoping he finds something tonight."

"I hope so, too."

I should have gone with him. I am better at stealth than he is, Lyra projected to them, licking her lips and stretching her front legs and wings.

"One is easier to hide than two," Lance told her.

"I will be ready," Shaylee said bravely with a nod.

It took Drake longer than they thought to find a way out of Sephra's fortress. Most of the doors were magically barred shut. He had discovered that Sephra only had four servants to care for them, and the three wyverns who left with her were all she had. Just after midnight on the third day, Drake announced he had found a way out.

Hand-in-hand, Lance and Shaylee raced down the deserted corridor, following Drake and Lyra. Drake took them to a central spiral staircase that led up to the roof. They tackled the stairs two at a time for the first twenty or thirty steps before slowing slightly to conserve their strength.

"Do you know where we are?" Shaylee asked Lance, her breath labored from the sprint.

"Drake thinks we are in the Sanctuary of Iton."

Shaylee's steps faltered, causing her to stumble a couple of times before she caught herself. "What happened to the Order of the Chosen? And, and the High Shepherd?" Panic rose in her chest.

Lance shrugged. "No time to think about that. Come on. We don't know how long Sephra will be gone." Lance reached for her hand to steady her.

She nodded and picked up the pace, passing him up the stairs. The staircase started to narrow the further they went until they had to climb in single file.

Not far now. You're almost to the top, Drake projected to them.

Hurry up, you two. Drake and I have been waiting forever, Lyra said, trying to break the tension.

At the top of the stairs, they found Drake and Lyra standing in front of a tall, narrow oak door with simple iron hinges.

Lance grabbed the handle—locked. He hopped down several steps and raced back up, lowering his shoulder into the door. The door shook at the impact but didn't give way.

"Stand back," Shaylee told him.

Lance's eyes widened as her hands began to glow with magic. Instinctively, he retreated a few steps, positioning himself behind her. A golden orb formed between her palms, the light intensifying as she rolled her hands together, shaping the magic. The orb swelled, expanding until it was nearly a foot in diameter. It was a complex spell, one she had never been taught but had encountered before—the dreaded *Circle of Torchictum.* Her stance widened, feet planted firmly against the ground as she summoned her strength. With a soft grunt, she hurled the spell toward the door. The golden ball streaked through the air and slammed into the wooden barrier with immense force, shattering and splintering the door into a million pieces

A cold fall wind rushed in, pelting them with freezing rain droplets. A scent of snow hung in the air. Bowing their heads against the biting wind, they ran onto the roof.

"What now?" Shaylee asked, her voice tinged with anxiety as she looked around frantically. Her heart pounded in her chest, the sound echoing in her ears. The night was pitch black—no moon or stars to offer any light. Above them, a thick layer of dark, ominous clouds loomed, hanging just above their heads.

Lance walked into the middle of the roof. Shaylee started to follow him.

"Stand back," he said, waving his arms at her.

Shaylee, confused but obedient, followed the instructions. "What's going on? Do you see something?" she shouted, struggling to make her voice heard over the fierce wind.

Lance smiled in response. A heartbeat later, a swirling mist of blue and silver began to form around him. It thickened with astonishing speed, engulfing him completely. Shaylee let out a startled shriek and stumbled backward, nearly falling onto her backside.

"What's happening?" she cried, raising her hands to shield her face from the unknown foe. Her hands glowed with purple light as she prepared to cast a capture spell at whatever was attacking Lance. "Lance!!" she screamed, the dread of losing him so soon after finding him lancing her heart.

Suddenly, a giant blue dragon stood where Lance had been a moment before.

Shaylee's eyes bulged with understanding and wonder. "You truly are a dragon," she whispered. She released her spell and slowly walked toward him with a hand outstretched. Lance lowered his head. She continued toward him until she was less than a foot from his enormous head. She looked up at him standing above her, easily three times larger than any horse and twice the size of a griffin. She hesitated briefly before placing her hand on his nose. His nostrils flared as he inhaled deeply, and his eyes fluttered closed.

I've always dreamed of meeting a dragon someday, she projected to him. *And now I find myself drawn to one. In a way, I can't even begin to understand.*

A roar snapped them out of the moment they were sharing.

Quickly, hop on my back, Lance projected. *Drake, Lyra, to me.*

Two wyverns appeared above them, snarling and tossing their heads.

Shaylee jumped while levitating herself up onto Lance's broad back. Once seated in front of his wings, Lance snapped his wings out and readied himself to take flight. Drake and Lyra already in the air beside him.

"Where do you think you two are going?" a deep, menacing voice boomed from the darkness. Sephra and the last wyvern appeared. Sephra stood on the wyvern's back with her arms held out wide. Her raven-black hair stood on end like a halo around her.

"I am not done with you yet," she told them, her deep voice shaking the rooftop.

"We are not your pawns," Shaylee yelled.

Sephra laughed. "You're right. This is no game. The world is mine for the taking. I know where we need to go. And the two of you will retrieve the item I need. With the Infinite Medallion, I, The One, along with my vassal, Warlock Sephra, will be the supreme Overlord, and all will bow to me.

"Iton and Oshan imprisoned me eons ago, which is why I am starting with their beloved country. But the others… the other gods," The One's face twisted in a sneer. "Did nothing. Not even my patron, Grielan, stepped in to help me. They stood on the wayside as I was stripped of my powers and thrust aside like I wasn't one of them. Wasn't their better! I'll show them. I am the Herald of Death! I will show them what I am capable of!" Sephra threw her head back and roared as lightning careened out of her hands and shot into the sky, illuminating the clouds. "Capture them, but they must remain alive," she commanded the wyverns.

The first two wyverns roared, spewing fire into the sky. Shaylee clung to Lance's spines, gripping tightly with her knees, as Lance responded to their fiery display with a roar of his own. He launched into the sky, razor-sharp talons outstretched. With a powerful collision, he struck the first wyvern, sending it spiraling out of control with a broken wing. Without pausing, Lance swung his head around, sinking his teeth into the other wyvern's tail. His fangs pierced through its tough, scaly hide, and the wyvern screeched in pain and fury.

From her flying perch, Sephra watched as the young dragon took on two seasoned, fully-grown wyverns—and bested them both. "It's a wonder your kind managed to defeat the dragons," she muttered.

"Strength of superior numbers, mistress," the wyvern below her slurred.

She sneered at the beast for speaking out of turn but returned her attention to the aerial battle. Lance's larger size gave him the advantage during a one-on-one fight.

"Enough!" The One's voice ripped out of Sephra. A blast of magic shot from her and hit Lance in the head. Lance was knocked unconscious and started to plummet. Shaylee screamed as she clung to the unconscious dragon. Sephra cast another spell, catching them both and gently lowering them to the ground. Shaylee leaped off Lance's back and rushed to his head, cradling it in her hands.

"Lance, wake up. We have to flee. Lance?" Shaylee pleaded.

Slowly, Lance's eyes opened, and then he transformed back into his human form. He grabbed Shaylee's hand in his, "I'm okay. Let's finish this." His eyes started to glow. Shaylee sucked in a surprised breath as Lance's free hand began to glow with magic. She could instantly tell the spell he was preparing and matched it with her magic.

"I knew the rumors were true," Sephra said, her voice steady as she remained astride her wyvern. Her eyes, once burning with unnatural fire, now appeared more human, and her features softened. "Human magic did come from dragons."

Suddenly, Sephra's head snapped back, and her eyes blazed again as the demon inside her regained control. "But, unluckily for you," the One boomed, "I have enhanced Sephra's magic with that of the gods!"

Lance and Shaylee cast their spells simultaneously, aiming at Sephra. Smiles bloomed on their faces as Sephra screamed in rage, the force of their spells blasting into her and pushing her backward.

The wyvern roared in agony, its mind shattered by the magic, its massive body going limp before plummeting into the dark abyss below.

Sephra, however, remained hovering in the air, sustained by her own magic. A shimmering shield encased her, though it was slowly buckling under the relentless assault.

"I cannot... Two adolescents will **not** defeat me!" she screamed, her voice laced with fury. A surge of magic crashed into Lance and Shaylee, wave after wave, forcing them to lower their hands to shield themselves. The spell hammered relentlessly, driving them to their knees, arms raised in defense. The sapphire in Lance's bracer blazed like the sun, but it wasn't enough.

Sephra descended slowly onto the rooftop, striding toward them with cold determination. "That's more like it. I thought we could be friends, treat you as allies..." she said, now standing over them.

With a swift motion, she clasped a bracelet onto each of their wrists. "But then you stopped eating and started thinking for yourselves. No matter. You're still useful—shackled and treated like slaves."

She grabbed Lance's other wrist and unbuckled the bracer. "You don't need this anymore. It's fortunate I made it for you; otherwise, removing it would've been impossible." She studied the bracer briefly before slipping it into her waist pouch. "Now, sleep."

A mist engulfed them, and the last thing Shaylee saw before her eyes closed was a green fog seeping from Sephra's very being.

CHAPTER

-27-

THE dark cave seemed to press in all around them, even with Aurora leading the way. Her wings and tail smoldered slightly, giving them just enough light to see.

The cave entrance was small but opened into a large passageway, ending in a dead end.

"I expected a little more than this," Tarrid said, looking around the chamber they found themselves in.

The space was octagon-shaped with flat walls. The walls and floor were polished and smooth. Keelan ran his hands along a smooth surface. "There must be a door in here."

Fawn, Tarrid, Douglas, and Ashera followed his lead and started checking the walls for seams.

"I don't feel anything," Fawn remarked. Grunts and sighs of agreement echoed through the cavern.

I found something, Aurora projected, staring at the floor.

"What is it?" Keelan asked, rushing to her side.

Here, she pointed to a few holes in the floor.

"What are we looking at?" Douglas asked.

She looked up at him and clicked her beak. ***Holes,*** she said, as if it were obvious.

Tarrid groaned. "How about a little more information? Do you know what the holes are for?"

Still looking up at the bipeds, who were looking down at her, she flexed a taloned foot and then slid her claws into the holes. They were a perfect fit. A soft chime was heard moments before the wall in front of them disappeared.

A weak light illuminated the new passageway before them.

Keelan took the lead, finding a stone staircase that wound its way down deep inside the mountain. "I guess we go down," Keelan said.

Aurora rushed past him and ignited her feathers once more.

As they walked, the air grew hot and thick. An overpowering smell of sulfur attacked their noses and throats.

This is not an extinct volcano, Aurora warned them. ***I can smell lava.***

"Great," Tarrid grumbled, coughing and trying to secure a scarf around Fawn and his mouth.

"Do you think Sephra has already taken the medallion?" Fawn asked. "Do you think Shaylee and Lance have already been here?"

"I don't know," Keelan answered. "I hope not."

As they neared the bottom, the heat was almost unbearable for everyone except Aurora, Zephyr, and Douglas. As fire breathers, they could withstand the heat.

Ashera, walking just ahead of Douglas, began to slow, her steps becoming heavy and sluggish.

"Are you alright, Ash?" Douglas asked, a note of concern in his voice.

She nodded, then shook her head. "I… I don't know," she stammered, stumbling forward and bumping into Tarrid.

Tarrid spun around. "Hey, watch it!" He said with annoyance. His features quickly changed when he looked into her eyes. "Are you okay?" he asked with concern.

Ashera's eyes rolled, and her face turned as white as a sheet.

Catch her, she's falling! Zephyr cried, flying to her side.

Tarrid and Douglas caught each of her arms and carefully lowered her to the stone floor. Keelan and Fawn, who were further down the stairway, rushed back up.

"What's wrong?" Keelan asked, kneeling beside Ashera.

"I'm not sure," Douglas said, touching her forehead. "She started to slow and then fainted."

She's a water dragon. This heat is too much for her, Zephyr told them.

Everyone turned their eyes to him.

What? I thought that would be obvious. He shook his head with a slight growl.

"I just assumed she would be a fire-breather like Lance. Their mother was a water dragon," Douglas said, shaking his head. "I will carry her back to the cave entrance."

Keelan placed a hand on Douglas's arm to stop him. "She has to come with us. Whatever is down here requires at least two of the twins to find."

"How do you know you can't get it yourself?"

"Because Sephra had always planned on kidnapping two. Originally, it was Lance and me. I don't think one can do it alone."

Douglas paused before sighing. "Fine, I will carry her down with us."

Keelan nodded and gave him a tight smile.

A few minutes later, they found themselves at the bottom level. A river of lava flowed slowly through the expanse they were led to. Waves of heat radiated off the lava, making it difficult to breathe.

Stay here and relax. Zephyr and I will explore, Aurora projected.

Douglas gently lowered Ashera onto the bottom step. He removed a scarf from around his neck and wiped her forehead. Her eyes fluttered open, and a soft groan escaped her lips. "Sit and relax," Douglas told her.

It didn't take long for Aurora and Zephyr to circle around the cavern. **We found a small cave on the other side of the lava river,** Zephyr informed them, **but there's no way across except by flying.**

Keelan walked over to the lava river. "Where is this cave?" he asked.

Aurora retook flight, flew over the river, and landed before a small crack in the cavern's wall.

"I think I can get Ashera and myself across," Keelan called back to the others.

Douglas walked over and stood next to Keelan. "I don't like the idea of the two of you going over there by yourselves."

They won't be alone, Zephyr said, landing beside them. He puffed out his chest and wagged his tail back and forth.

Douglas smiled down at the vaskakat. "Protect them well, oh brave familiar," he said with a chuckle, then nodded to Keelan.

A loud purr echoed out of the familiar as he leaped into the air and circled their heads.

Keelan returned to Ashera's side and knelt beside her. Gently, he placed his hands on either side of her head and flinched. Her sweaty skin felt like it was laced with lightning.

"Don't worry, that sensation we are feeling is normal. When dragons are distressed, our magic surfaces," Douglas told him, patting Keelan on the shoulder.

Keelan nodded and then recalled how he had once healed his horse, Rogue. Closing his eyes, he focused, seeking the core of her magic. When he found it, he gasped softly, startled by the icy sensation. It was unlike anything he had felt before. Carefully, he grasped hold of the frigid tendrils of her magic and coaxed them into her extremities, willing them to spread coolness through her body. Ashera's eyes flew open at the feeling.

"Are you up for a little flight?" he asked, then chuckled at her startled expression. "Don't worry. I'll handle the flying this time." He offered his hand to her.

Ashera looked at his hand and then up to his eyes. She slowly placed her hand in his, and a small smile spread across her face. "Where are we flying to?" she asked, once standing.

Keelan pointed to the other side of the lava river. "There is a small cave over there. Aurora and Zephyr think that's where we need to go."

"A cave inside a cave?" she giggled. "You can get everyone across that?" She gestured to the river and started to walk toward it.

Keelan shook his head. "No, you and I are the only ones going over."

Her steps faltered. "Is that wise?"

Keelan glanced to his right, expecting her to be beside him—but she wasn't. He stopped, turning around. "Aurora and Zephyr will be with us," he reassured her, taking a few steps back toward her. He gently grabbed her hands, meeting her gaze. "Eldjren hid the Medallion with the intent that we would find it when the time was right. I don't believe he would set traps we couldn't overcome. That wouldn't be logical. The only obstacle I can think of is that it's just the two of us here… and it's not yet winter."

"Winter? Why does that matter?" she asked.

Aurora landed beside them. *With the help of a Phoenix, lost in the world, they will find the Infinite Medallion. In winter's tight embrace, an eclipse will paint the sky red before their sixteenth year. The two sets of twins will be bathed in crimson light, their lives entwined by fate's design, and their futures will be revealed in this divine moment,* she recited, her voice carrying the weight of prophecy.

Ashera grimaced. "Then shouldn't we wait for winter and take this time to find Lance and Shaylee?"

Keelan shook his head, raking his hands through his hair. "I hate this prophecy," he grumbled. "Why couldn't Eldjren just say, 'Do this at this time, and this will happen'? Why does it always have to be a riddle?"

That is not how prophecies work, Aurora told him.

"When I spoke to Jonal about what we were to do, he felt pretty certain that the medallion could be found at any time. But we must wait until the eclipse this winter to find out more. We are here now, hoping to find it before Sephra."

She briefly thought in silence before nodding. "So, how are you going to get us across?"

Keelan closed his eyes briefly and then raised his hand toward her. With a startled squeak, Ashera was slowly lifted off the ground. Aurora hopped closer to Keelan and touched his leg with one of her wings.

Zephyr flew up next to Ashera. She smiled at her familiar, her features softening as they looked at each other. After Ashera was back on the ground on the other side of the river, Keelan concentrated on himself.

Are you certain you can do this? Aurora asked him.

I've levitated myself before, he replied.

Yes, but only up onto a dragon or griffin's back. Never cross a lava flow.

He looked at her for a moment. *It'll be fine. Now, let me concentrate.* He emptied his mind and thought about what he wanted to do. Slowly, he elevated off the ground and started to float toward the river. The lava swirled and flowed below his feet. He glanced down, watching the churning liquid, his eyes transfixed and glazing over as the swirling orange molten rock mesmerized him.

Concentrate on Ash, Keelan, Aurora said to him.

Keelan's eyes didn't budge, and he sank closer to the raging heat.

Keelan, snap out of it! Aurora's panicked voice cut through his head.

Suddenly, like a rushing river breaking free from a dam, sounds came crashing into Keelan's ears. Ashera was screaming at him to rise. Keelan shook his head, his eyes clearing, and gasped when he saw how close he was to the lava. Without losing his grip on his magic, he raised himself and hurried to the far bank. Douglas and Fawn's voices drifted to his ears, but his thundering heartbeat blocked most of the sound.

When he was above solid ground again, he collapsed to the ground. Ashera rushed to his side. "Are you okay?"

Sweat coated his forehead and trickled down his cheeks and nose; he sucked in a couple of shaky breaths. "I think so," he finally choked out. "I'm not sure what happened. It's like there was a draft pulling me down."

"Good," Ashera said with a nod and a relieved sigh, then slapped his shoulder hard.

Keelan shied away in surprise. "Hey! What was that for?" he asked, rubbing his shoulder, more from surprise the slap caused than actual pain.

"For scaring me."

"I'm sorry." He smiled slightly.

She sighed and hung her head. "I don't know what I would have done if you…" She trailed off, shaking her head.

Keelan didn't catch the rest of her words. He focused on steadying his breath before standing. He glanced across the river and waved at the others. "Okay, Ash. Shall we?" he asked, gesturing to the cave entrance.

They approached the narrow fissure in the cavern wall. It was tall enough for them to walk through without hunching but just wide enough, causing them to enter sideways. Keelan extended his hand, summoning a sun-orb. He glanced back at Ashera, who nodded and gave him a tight-lipped smile. Taking a deep breath, he led the way into the crack.

Walking was slow-going. The ground was uneven, and the wall was jagged and sharp. Ashera moaned as she walked behind him, but she did not falter.

Aurora, are you following? Keelan projected.

Of course, but I am walking. I can't fly through this crack. So, do you see the end coming?

Not yet.

Excuse me, Zephyr said as he pushed past Keelan's legs. *I will find out how long this tunnel is.*

"Be careful, Zephyr," Ashera whispered.

"I don't think we have to whisper in here," Keelan told her.

"Probably not, but it just feels too tight a space for loud words."

You are almost out, and you will never believe what you are about to see, Zephyr projected.

The end of the tunnel could be seen ahead. The chamber they were about to enter was glowing soft blue.

Zephyr? What's causing that light? Keelan asked.

The vaskakat didn't answer.

"Zephyr?" Ashera called out.

"Come on, let's see what's going on." Keelan grabbed Ashera's hand and pulled her quickly through the tunnel.

Keelan doused his light as they entered the next chamber.

"Oh, wow!" Ashera exclaimed.

The chamber spanned about twenty feet in diameter, its shape nearly circular, though the ceiling was lost to darkness above. The smooth walls shimmered like glass in the pale blue light, which seemed to emanate from a small pond at the center. From somewhere high above, a thin waterfall descended gracefully, streaming into the pond without a splash or ripple, leaving the crystal-clear water undisturbed.

"What is this place?" Ashera asked, spinning in a circle.

"I have no idea. Do you hear that?" Keelan asked.

Ashera paused and tilted her head. "Hear what?"

"Exactly. The water is falling in complete silence." Keelan stepped closer to the pond, his eyes narrowing as he peered into its depths.

"How deep is the water?" Ashera asked.

Keelan looked up. "I'm not sure. Maybe an inch or two."

"What's making the light?" she asked as she approached and looked down. "It looks like the rocks are glowing." She reached down, intent on picking up one of the glowing rocks, but shrieked and pulled her hand back abruptly. "How is that water so hot?"

"Are you okay?" Keelan grabbed her hand to inspect it.

"I think so."

Keelan squinted up, trying to pierce the darkness and locate the source of the scalding water. "Aurora?"

I'm on it, she replied, taking flight and vanishing into the inky blackness above.

While they waited, Keelan and Ashera cautiously explored the small chamber. Keelan traced his fingers along the smooth, glass-like walls, feeling for any seams or imperfections in the unnatural surface. He kept one eye on the floor as well, wary of more holes the size of phoenix talons.

Find anything yet, Aurora? He projected. Silence. No response. Keelan's heart began to race as his eyes flicked nervously toward the suffocating darkness above. "Aurora!" he called out, his voice cracking under the weight of panic tightening around his throat.

"What's the matter?" Ashera mirrored his anxiety.

"Aurora isn't answering me."

I'll go find the flighty bird, Zephyr said, his purr rumbling through his chest.

"I don't think that's a good idea, Zephyr," Ashera told him. "We don't know if she's in danger or just too far away to hear."

Keelan shook his head. "No, we have a long range. Something's wrong. Zephyr, go ahead and see what you can find, but keep your link to Ashera open."

The familiar nodded and leaped into the air, vanishing into the darkness.

I am following the water. It maintains its glow for about thirty feet, and then the cave falls into darkness, Zephyr projected. *Without my superb night vision, I'd be as blind as a bat in daylight,* he boasted. *I don't see the phoenix yet. I'll fly higher.*

He continued to narrate his progress.

I found the source of the water. It's coming out of the ceiling itself.

The ceiling? Keelan asked. *Aurora must be there. Do you see her?*

Oh, wait. The water isn't coming from the ceiling; it's just an outcropping. The cave continues. I see a faint light up above. I'm going higher.

Keelan's heart raced. Was the light Aurora? Why wasn't she responding? *What do you see?* He asked.

The light is most definitely Aurora. Hang on a moment.

Zephyr fell silent. *Keelan! You and Ash need to get up here.*

What's wrong? Ashera's projection was almost a shout in their minds.

She is frozen in place, hanging in midair. The medallion is in front of her.

Keelan glanced up and then over at Ashera. "I think I can get us both up there. Unless you can change yourself into a tiny dragon."

"A tiny dragon?" She looked at him, puzzled. "Is that possible?"

"I'm not sure how small you could go, but Lance once shrank himself to the size of a griffin."

"Did he say how he did it?" she asked.

"He said he was once that size and just thought about being that size again."

She nodded, "I'll try." She closed her eyes, and slowly, a blue and bronze mist surrounded her. Soon, a dragon no bigger than a horse crowded beside Keelan.

He mildly shook his head and stiffened his lips.

What's the matter? She projected.

"I think you are still too big."

She stretched her wings out, saw that the tips almost hit the cave walls, and nodded. Mist shrouded her again. When it cleared, she was the size of a pony.

Keelan smiled.

What? She stretched her wings out again. *I think I'm small enough now,* she complained.

"I think so, too. I was just thinking you make a cute pint-sized dragon."

A puff of ice breath bloomed out of her nostrils, and she flicked her tail. *Watch it. I'm still big enough to eat you,* she teased.

Keelan chuckled and levitated himself into the unknown, with Ashera following a moment later.

Within moments, they came to the spot Zephyr mentioned, where the light from the pond below had failed to penetrate. Keelan felt a surge of panic as he wondered if he could produce a sun-orb while holding his levitation. He hesitated slightly, making sure Ashera was directly underneath him before trying. He smiled broadly when his light materialized without losing altitude. The water source was visible moments later. The water looked like it was flowing from the rock, but he soon saw the truth. The outcropping allowed a small river of near-boiling water to flow above the expanse before it trickled over the edge and fell into the pool below.

Keelan and Ashera continued up and around the outcropping. Aurora's familiar red glow could be seen above. Zephyr flew back down when he noticed Keelan's light.

My dragon! I didn't know you could make yourself so small, Zephyr said in surprise, flying a quick circle around her.

I didn't know I could either, she remarked.

"Aurora, can you hear me?" Keelan asked as he hovered beside her. She was frozen in midair, her wings outstretched like she was in mid-flap, and one foot reached toward the medallion; her talons opened wide. Keelan's eyes left her, and then he focused on what she was staring at.

Is she okay? Ashera asked, coming close.

Keelan didn't answer – his eyes were transfixed on the medallion in front of Aurora. It was beautiful. The medallion was a mix of three metals – gold, silver, and bronze all twisted together. The gold and silver braids were twisted into two infinity symbols offset against each other; the gold one was orientated north and south, and the silver one pointed east and west. The bronze braid wove between the infinity symbols, binding the design together.

"The Infinite Medallion," Keelan said.

"It's beautiful," Ashera said, flying beside him. "What's holding it up?"

The medallion seemed to be floating. Four chains were attached to it, two on each infinity symbol, but all four chains hung limply.

"I'm not sure," Keelan replied, turning his attention back to Aurora. He gently grabbed her and turned her to face him. Aurora gasped and shook her head.

Keelan! How long have you been here? She asked in surprise.

"Only a moment. What happened?" he asked her.

I found the medallion and was going to grab it, but then everything went dark. She shook her head, *No, not dark. Everything went white, and then there was nothing. I was frozen. Even my thoughts were still. How long was I out?*

"Not long. Zephyr flew up here to check on you when we lost contact, and then we followed." He looked down at Ashera.

Aurora followed his gaze. She squawked in surprise. *Ash? How are you so small?*

A question for another time, Ashera responded.

How do you suggest we obtain the medallion? Aurora asked.

Keelan sighed, looking back at it. "I'm not sure. I wonder if I will be frozen for trying to grab it."

Go ahead and try. We know how to break the trance now, Ashera proposed.

Keelan shrugged and glided closer to the object. Slowly, he reached his hand toward it and then stopped.

What's the matter, Keelan? Why did you stop? Zephyr asked.

Keelan didn't respond.

He's frozen, Aurora projected with an irritated chirp. She flew between Keelan and the medallion to break his line of sight.

Keelan shook his head and started falling; his magic had stopped. A startled cry escaped him as he plummeted.

Stop yourself, Keelan! Aurora's panicked squawk echoed in the cavern.

Keelan's heart raced as he struggled to calm himself and gather his magic. He had never attempted to use magic while under sudden duress. When he was falling outside of the mountain, his magic was active before his leap; this was an entirely different sensation, and fear was smothering his thoughts.

"Keelan!!" Ashera screamed aloud, and then Keelan stopped falling. Ashera's eyes widened.

"Who stopped me?" Keelan asked, looking around. His breath was labored, and his heart thundered in his chest.

I think I did, Ashera projected.

Keelan looked up at her. Her front feet were glowing, and her eyes were shining brightly.

Keelan nodded and then closed his eyes to calm and center himself. When he reopened them, he nodded to her. "I'm okay now. You can release me."

Ashera somehow did as he requested. She looked at her front paws, flexing her claws open and closed slowly. *How did I do that? Dragons don't have magic.* She looked at Keelan, her eyes wide and mouth open. She was panting, and icy vapor was wafting up around her.

"Let's get the medallion, and then we'll explore this new development."

She nodded and shook out her paws. *What do you suggest we do?*

"Let's try to grab it together," Keelan proposed.

Are you sure about that? I don't know if I can save you again.

Keelan nodded, glancing around the cramped cavern. "It's tight up here," he said. "I think the two of us can manage to grab it together, but all four of us wouldn't fit—even if Lance were your size." He shifted his weight, eyeing the medallion carefully. "Here's the plan: I'll grab hold of one of your legs with one arm. We'll both reach for the medallion at the same time."

I can't grab hold of it with claws, she explained.

"You might not have to. Let's see what happens if we both touch it simultaneously."

She nodded, and they flew back to the medallion. When they were in position, hovering side by side with Keelan holding onto one of her legs, they nodded to each other and reached toward the medallion. With one finger and one claw, they touched it at the same time. A bright flash of light filled the cave, blinding them both, and time seemed to slow. When they regained their sight, the medallion was gone.

Where is it? Ashera gasped.

"I don't see it," Keelan looked around frantically. The medallion was gone.

CHAPTER

-28-

SHAYLEE groaned as she slowly blinked her eyes open, only to squeeze them shut against the blinding glare of the sun overhead. A fierce wind whipped around her, cutting through the haze clouding her mind. Instinctively, she reached out with her magic to assess her surroundings, but her magic didn't respond. Using her other senses, she assessed that she was lying on her side, feeling something warm, hard, and uneven beneath her. She flexed her fingers, attempting to sit up, but her hands were bound tightly behind her back, and her ankles were tied together. Searing pain shot up her arms, her shoulders burning from the unnatural strain. She shook her head, trying to dispel the fog clouding her mind, but all she could hear was a loud, disorienting ringing.

Squinting, she prayed her senses were deceiving her. As her vision cleared, clouds rushed by, their shapes a blur in the fierce wind. Her eyes snapped open wide, and tears spilled, streaming across her cheeks before being ripped away by the gusts. Dark brown, leathery wings rose and fell rhythmically, jolting her body violently with each stroke. As her mind sharpened, the reality of her situation hit her—she was bound tightly, like a sack of potatoes, strapped to the back of a wyvern.

Lance caught her eye and nodded to her. He was in a similar predicament on the back of another wyvern.

Are you okay? He mouthed.

She nodded slowly. *I think so,* she projected, but then a piercing scream escaped her lips. A pain like a searing knife sliced through her head, hitting her with such intensity that she squeezed her eyes shut, shaking violently as it coursed through her. When the agony finally subsided, she dared to look over at Lance again.

Don't project, he mouthed. Numbly, she nodded her head with an eye roll.

After a few moments of breathing deeply, she mouthed to Lance, *Where are Lyra and Drake?*

Lance turned his gaze to a third wyvern. This one had Sephra riding it. Strapped to the wyvern behind her was a large sack.

In that bag, I think, he mouthed.

She nodded and then tried to relax as much as possible. Her arms and legs were cramping from the tight bindings holding her in place.

The hours crawled by, and soon, Shaylee drifted to sleep to the even rhythm of the wyverns' wings. A thud vibrated through her body, startling her awake as the wyvern landed roughly. Sephra was already dismounted and walking toward the other two wyverns.

"Time for us to begin," Sephra said with a saccharine smile that made Shaylee's stomach turn.

"Where are we?" Lance asked dryly.

"We are close to my medallion. There are two ways to obtain it. The easiest will be for the two of you to enter the Wizard's Hat and grab it simultaneously," she explained.

"What's the other way?" Shaylee asked.

Sephra ignored her question and started to untie Lance, then pulled him unceremoniously to the ground. He landed with a huff and a loud groan.

Shaylee glanced around. They were on a beach with pure white sand that sparkled in the bright sunlight. Sea birds cawed and squawked loudly, circling above their heads. They appear to be on a small baron, sandy island far out at sea. Waves slapped against the white sand with an even rhythmic motion. In the distance was a mountain with a crooked, spindly top. Sephra untied Shaylee next, gently assisting her to the ground.

"If you behave, I'll let you stay awake for the next leg of our journey. We'll be taking one wyvern, and I'll give you a few moments to stretch your legs," she said, spinning on her heels and sauntering over to her wyvern.

With some effort, Lance managed to get to his feet, aided by Shaylee. She had turned her back to him, grasped his shirt by the collar, and pulled upward as much as possible. Once he was standing, he leaned slightly into her, seeking support.

"Thanks," he muttered softly.

"What are we going to do?" Shaylee asked, her eyes never leaving Sephra.

"I'm not sure. I was hoping Keelan and my sister would be able to find us. But a rescue seems out of the question now." He hung his head.

"We will just have to figure out how to keep the medallion away from her," Shaylee stated with more confidence than she felt.

Lance bumped her shoulder gently. "I wish I was as confident as you sound."

"Me too." She chuckled dryly.

Lance nodded, his lips twisting into a slight grin, "We will do what we can."

The mountain looming in the distance grew in size as they approached it. The wyvern underneath them labored under their combined weight. The mountain looked nothing like any hat Shaylee had ever seen, but to her knowledge, she had never met anyone who claimed to be a wizard.

As the mountain came into focus, Shaylee saw a couple of large birds flying around the peak and nowhere for them to land.

Sephra's angry voice drifted on the wind back to her, but the words were foreign.

"What did she say?" Shaylee said into Lance's ear. Lance leaned backward slightly and turned his head so she could hear his words.

"I don't know the language, but she's not happy. Look!" He nodded toward the giant birds that were actually not birds. Two griffins and a pegasus were flying around the mountain peak.

"Dreamcrest!" Shaylee said in surprise.

"I see Stormbreaker, too," Lance said. "Keelan and Ashera are here."

Sephra turned her head and glared at them. "Change of plans," she sneered.

The wyvern banked its wings, pumping them faster as it left the Wizard's Hat behind. They flew further north toward a ruined structure perched on a rocky outcropping jutting into the surf. Waves crashed against the black and white rocks, spraying water onto the remnants of an ancient lighthouse. A massive, crumbling stone wall surrounded the remnants of the structure, its weathered surface bearing the scars of relentless water erosion. Behind intricately designed black iron gates that creaked on rusty hinges in the wind lay the entrance to a small courtyard. The wyvern circled the lighthouse twice before descending onto the sandy beach. Sephra vaulted off the wyvern's back, landing hard on the soft sand. The two wyverns they had left behind approached, their wings adapted as front legs, moving gracefully despite their size.

Sephra gestured for one of the creatures to approach. With a curt nod, it lumbered toward her. She unslung the bag from its back and dumped out the two familiars. Shaylee instinctively rushed forward to help Lyra, but Sephra shot her a warning look that froze her in place. With a flick of her wrist, two bracelets shot from her pocket and snapped around Lyra's and Drake's necks. Both familiars crumpled to the ground as if the bracelets were anchoring them in place.

"Follow me," she commanded.

Lance, Shaylee, Lyra, Drake, and the wyvern followed Sephra as she walked gracefully toward the lighthouse. She paused in front of the once-grand gate, pushing it open with a creak. The stone pillars flanking the entrance were worn, with large chunks missing. As they stepped into the overgrown courtyard, Sephra spun to face her small party. The lighthouse loomed dark and forlorn, ivy and vines creeping up its sides like nature reclaiming its territory.

"This decrepit structure," she began, her voice echoing with a mixture of reverence and disdain, "once served two purposes and is all that remains of a great seaport. This lighthouse was a beacon, warning ships of the treacherous waters and coral reefs nearby, and it stood as a tribute to Grielan, the God of the Afterlife. Worshipers believed that bringing their loved ones here after death would hasten their entry into Ombrasia. Such simple fools," she tsked, shaking her head. "Even if their beliefs were unfounded, this place holds great power."

Sephra swirled her arms in a wide circle, uttering words in an ancient tongue. Suddenly, the wyvern's head snapped back, and a bloodcurdling scream ripped from its throat. Lance and Shaylee jumped back a few steps, hearts racing. The wyvern lifted off the sand, spinning in a tight circle as its screams echoed through the air. The sound continued for what felt like an eternity until a sickening crunch abruptly silenced its howling. The wyvern spun once more, its limbs, wings, and head hanging limply, and then, in an instant, the lifeless creature erupted into a blazing inferno.

Shaylee and Lance stumbled back further, shielding their faces from the searing heat. The smell was nauseating; Shaylee covered her nose with her hand, fighting the bile rising in her throat.

Sephra continued her incantation, her arms raised high as the flaming carcass settled onto the ground. "Approach, Prince Lancet Lapis Firestorm, approach, Princess Shaylee Vaelum Keifman," she intoned, her voice deep and resonant, embodying the essence of The One. Just then, a gale-force wind slammed into them as a massive storm cloud rolled in, plunging the day into near darkness. Thunder rumbled beneath their feet, and jagged flashes of lightning sliced across the sky, illuminating the chaos that unfolded around them.

Shaylee looked over at Lance, "Princess?" she asked quietly.

He nodded.

"I said approach!" The One yelled as another boom of thunder accentuated her words.

Lance and Shaylee's legs started to move without their consent. They shuffled forward until they were standing on either side of Sephra.

She grabbed their hands and raised them above her head. Slowly, she drew their hands toward each other until Lance and Shaylee's hands clasped together inside hers. Lyra and Drake jerked into the air with startled squeaks. They drifted toward Shaylee and Lance, and they were forcefully moved to rest on Shaylee's and Lance's shoulders.

"With the bloodlines united, the medallion shall be theirs," Sephra said, her voice slowly rising. "Reunited at last, infinite power for them to behold. The Medallion within reach but unattainable. The heirs command the Medallion to come to them. Show us the medallion!" A white glowing circle appeared above the smoldering carcass. Sephra slashed her hand across her body like she was welding a sword. An angry red gash appeared across the dead wyvern's abdomen. A thin stream of blood spiraled out of the wound and flowed into the glowing circle.

The circle's center started to wave as the infusion of blood mixed with the magic, and a hazy image could be seen inside. It was like looking in a rippling pool of blood. Slowly, the image cleared and came into focus. Keelan and Ashera in dragon form were in a dark cavern. They were both reaching toward a golden object in front of them with their eyes tightly shut.

"At the same time, you must reach through the portal and take the medallion before they do."

Lance shook his head.

"If you refuse, you will watch them die," The One snarled.

Lance looked at Shaylee and nodded. She nodded back with a grim expression. Together, they reached their hands through the portal and took the medallion. When they pulled their hands out, the portal flashed bright white. With a loud snap, the portal winked out.

Holding the medallion together, they stared in awe. The medallion was not solid gold. It was a mix of three medals—gold, silver, and bronze—all twisted together. The gold and silver braids were twisted into two infinity symbols offset against each other. A bronze braid wove between the infinity symbols, tying the design together. Shaylee jumped and removed her hand when Sephra started to laugh in a deep and throaty voice.

"Excellent, now hand it over," Sephra held out her hand. Lance hesitated and then clutched the medallion to his chest. "The medallion is worthless to you and me until the eclipse. I will hold it until then. Don't worry. All four of you are safe for now."

Still, Lance refused to give it to her.

Sephra's eyes glazed over, and her features twisted in rage. "You must be alive but don't need all four limbs. It would be a shame for her to lose an arm so needlessly." She reached over and grabbed Shaylee's arm, wrenching it toward her.

Shaylee gasped, her face contorted in pain as her wide eyes locked onto Lance. "Just give it to her," she whispered, her voice trembling with fear. "We'll find a way to get it back later."

Lance's gaze shifted between her and the medallion in his hand, his jaw clenched in frustration. His fingers curled tightly around the ancient artifact before he finally snarled, "This isn't over, demon." With a flick of his wrist, he tossed the medallion toward Sephra.

Sephra caught the medallion, her lips curling into a sinister smile. She held it up to the sunlight, its three metals glinting brightly. She roughly pushed Shaylee into Lance, almost knocking him backward as he caught her. "We will meet again." Sephra raised her free hand, and a green mist poured from her fingers. Lance and Shaylee turned to flee but found their feet frozen in place. Her maniacal laugh was the last thing they heard as they were rendered unconscious.

Keelan, Ashera, Aurora, and Zephyr searched the cavern floor and boiling pond for signs of the medallion, but it was gone.

Sephra must have figured out a way to steal the medallion, Zephyr said, emerging from the pond. He shook himself, sending scorching water droplets into the air.

Ashera shied away from the hot spray. ***But how?*** She projected.

"She must have forced Lance and Shaylee to help her," Keelan said, still walking around the small cavern.

Would they? Ashera asked.

He shrugged. "You didn't see how they were acting when she abducted them. They were looking at her like she was their mother." He stopped beside her and raked his hands through his hair. "Let's return to the others and determine our next step."

In silence, they all headed back to the main cavern.

Aurora waddled beside Keelan. He glanced down at her and smiled. ***Do you think Lance and Shaylee are okay?*** He asked her.

Sephra needs all four of you when the eclipse reddens the sky. I don't think any harm will come to them until she unlocks the medallion's power.

The end of the tunnel became visible before they reached it. Orange light filtered into the dark tunnel, making the cavern before them appear to be on fire. The light from the molten lava cast an eerie glow, illuminating the larger cavern. As soon as they entered the main cave, Tarrid, Fawn, and Douglas stood and approached the lava river.

Douglas's face fell when he took in their grim expressions, but Fawn smiled brightly. "Did you find it?" she asked.

Keelan held up his hand, asking her to wait until they got closer.

Douglas's frown deepened when he looked at Ashera still in her miniaturized dragon form. "How are you so small, Ashera?" Douglas asked.

When I transformed, I just willed myself to be smaller. It worked! You didn't know we could do this? Ashera asked him the question privately.

Never had a reason to try, he projected to her.

Ashera nodded and then closed her eyes. A mist of swirling blue and bronze surrounded her. When the mist cleared, she stood before them in human form. When she nodded to Keelan, they reached out to each other with their magic and began levitating across the river. Keelan moved Ashera, and Ashera moved Keelan.

"Let's go nice and slow. Feel my magic and do as I do," Keelan instructed her.

"Keelan! How are you moving both of you?" Tarrid asked, surprise brightening his face.

"I'm not. Ash is levitating me, and I am levitating her."

"That's not possible. Dragons don't have magic like that," Douglas said.

"We have much to discuss, Father," Ashera said with a smile. "But later." He nodded and reached out his hand to help her back to the ground.

"So, what happened?" Tarrid asked.

"I'll recap while we get out of here. Come on." Keelan led the way back up the stone stairway, telling the others what they had found and lost.

At the top of the Wizard Hat, Dreamcrest and the two griffins were still flying in lazy circles and soaring in the air currents. Douglas leaped off the small rock ledge, changing into his dragon form before his human body succumbed to gravity. Ashera followed close behind him, along with the two familiars. Dreamcrest flew as close as she dared while Keelan helped levitate Fawn onto the pegasus's back. Once Tarrid and Keelan boarded their griffins, they started their return flight to the beach.

While you were inside a wyvern flew close to the hat. When it saw us it flew away. It appeared it was carrying riders, Dreamcrest projected.

Aurora. Zephyr. Can you two fly up and down the beach? Keelan projected for all to hear. *Sephra must be around here somewhere.*

Lance and Shaylee, too! Ashera chimed in.

Why do you think they're close? Douglas projected.

Just a hunch, Keelan replied. *Just before we reached for the medallion, I thought I felt the sapphire in Lance's bracer.*

Do you feel it now? Douglas asked.

Keelan shook his head.

I'll go north, Zephyr, go south! Aurora squawked.

Zephyr nodded and then banked his wings to head to the south. Aurora ignited her wingtips and spun in the air before heading north.

Show off, Zephyr grumbled.

"Those two bicker too much," Tarrid commented with a chuckle.

"I think they do it with affection," Fawn told him.

He smiled at her and winked. Fawn's cheeks flared.

Keelan watched the interaction between the two and then stole a glance at Ashera flying next to her father. Her sapphire scales glinted in the sunlight as she soared gracefully on the air currents. Her father's fiery red scales seemed dull in comparison.

I found something! Come quickly!

Aurora's panicked projection jolted Keelan from his thoughts. In unison, all the ariels banked their wings northward.

The air grew colder with each passing mile, the chill intensifying as they headed farther north. Keelan felt the strange contrast of the warm sun against the cool, biting wind, sending an odd sensation through his body. His mind raced, turning over the events of the day. He shook his head, forcing himself to refocus.

Over here! Aurora shouted into his head. ***Hurry!***

Stormbreaker pumped his wings harder, increasing his speed. Up ahead, an ancient stone structure came into view. Aurora, fully ablaze, hovered above it. Stormbreaker arrived before the other ariels and began circling the weathered lighthouse.

What do you see? Keelan projected to Aurora.

Look down! It's Lance and Shaylee!

Keelan looked down as instructed and saw two bodies sprawled on the sand. Without thinking, he vaulted off Stormbreaker's back. A surge of panic struck him when he realized how high he was. He cried out as his arms flailed involuntarily.

Calm yourself and get control of your magic, Aurora chided him.

Keelan closed his eyes tight and willed his arms to stop moving.

I have you, Ashera, projected.

Keelan felt his downward momentum slow. He opened his eyes and saw Ashera flying just above him, her front paws aglow.

Thanks, he replied privately to her.

You aren't very smart sometimes, are you?

Keelan opened his mouth to reply but saw her lips peel back into a dragon grin. He shook his head and took several deep breaths. ***Can you lower me a bit faster?*** He asked her.

Sure.

He sprinted toward the stone structure after his feet hit the soft sand. Though he had hoped to land inside the courtyard, Ashera placed him farther away. He stumbled through the loose sand, then leaped, tripping over the black and white rocks surrounding the lighthouse. Undeterred, he dashed through the open gate, briefly pausing to marvel at the crumbling stone edifice.

I would have loved to see this building when it was still in use, he remarked, moving forward. He slid to his knees beside Lance and Shaylee, quickly placing a hand on Lance's chest and his ear near Shaylee's mouth. He exhaled in relief. "They're okay, just unconscious."

Ashera ran into the courtyard, followed closely by Douglas, Tarrid, and Fawn. She let out a sigh of relief. "They should wake soon," she assured Keelan.

"How do you know? And how long will they be out?" Fawn asked, kneeling beside Shaylee and placing a hand on her forehead.

Ashera shook her head. "I can still smell the sleep mist, but I'm not sure how much was used."

"Keelan, grab Shaylee. I'll get Lance," Douglas said, bending down to lift his son. "Let's move them closer to the beach."

"There's a grove of trees not far from here. I say we make camp and rest here," Fawn said.

Douglas nodded, "Good idea. We need to regroup and figure out our next move."

Keelan carefully lifted Shaylee into his arms, cradling her as they made their way to the grove. Ashera led the group while the others followed closely behind. They soon found a sheltered spot beneath the trees and began setting up camp.

Keelan gently laid Shaylee on a bed of soft leaves and sat beside her, watching her sleep peacefully. He glanced over at Lance, who was being tended to by Fawn and Douglas. Despite the day's chaos, Keelan felt a spark of hope. They had found both Lance and Shaylee, and together, they would stop Sephra and recover the medallion.

"I'll go out further and see if I can find anything to eat," Tarrid said, unslinging his bow from his back.

"I'll join you," Keelan told him.

Somberly, they sat around the roaring fire, listening to the waves crash in the distance. Three rabbits sizzled above the flames, causing the fire to crackle when fat seeped and dripped into the flames.

Soon, the group settled in for the night as the sun sank below the horizon, casting long, quiet shadows over the beach. The road ahead promised difficulty, but for now, they were together—and that was enough.

Moments later, Lance started to groan. Keelan jumped up and went to his side.

"Careful, son. Take it easy," Douglas said, reaching Lance before Keelan.

"Dad? How are you here?" Lance asked, his voice scratchy and dry.

Douglas helped Lance sit up and handed him a waterskin. "Samuel told me what happened. He and Cedric are at the Monastery of Iton with Leo'venath, helping train their fighters."

Lance nodded weakly. "I hate that mist," he grumbled.

Soon, with Keelan's assistance, Shaylee sat up and gratefully accepted the waterskin from him. Once Drake and Lyra regained consciousness, the group gathered around the fire, sharing portions of the cooked rabbits.

"Do you two feel up to telling us what happened?" Keelan asked.

Lance and Shaylee exchanged a glance before Lance cleared his throat. "Sephra was tainting our food with something. It made us trust her completely, without question. She led us to the Sanctuary of Iton. I think… that's her stronghold."

"The Sanctuary?" Tarrid asked, his eyes wide. "What happened to The Order?"

Lance shook his head. "I don't know. When we were there, I only saw a few servants and five wyverns. I managed to kill one and break another's wing."

Fawn's voice faltered as she turned to Tarrid. "What does this mean, Tar? Is The Order gone? All those people who left the monastery… are they… are they…?"

Tarrid placed a hand on top of hers and squeezed. "I don't know. Hopefully, Iton was watching over them." Tarrid hung his head and then pulled Fawn into a hug. She melted into him, silently crying.

"What happened after she brought you here?" Douglas asked.

"We flew out over the sea within sight of a strange mountain…"

"The Wizard's Hat," Ashera said.

"I've never seen a hat like that," Lance said.

"I have, a couple of years ago in Kingston. You remember that magician I told you about?" Keelan asked.

Lance nodded. "Well. When we got close to the mountain, Sephra saw Stormbreaker and Dreamcrest circling it. That's when she brought us here. She performed a spell." He gestured back to the lighthouse, "And sacrificed a wyvern."

"A blood spell," Douglas whispered.

Lance nodded. "She opened a portal," he said.

"We saw you and Ashera reaching for the medallion," Shaylee told them.

"We had no choice but to take it," Lance added. "Sephra was using her power to compel us. When we reached through the portal, she forced us to give it to her."

"Is there any chance you could remember how she cast the spell?" Keelan asked.

Lance shook his head. "It all happened so fast, and she spoke some ancient language. But I do remember the shape she traced in the air."

"We need to figure out what that shape was," Douglas said. "It might give us a clue on how to counteract her magic."

"We should get some rest for now," Fawn suggested. "We've all been through a lot today."

The fire crackled softly as the stars twinkled above. Ashera and Keelan took the first watch, but no one else felt like sleeping just yet. Keelan scanned the horizon for any signs of danger.

"Do you think we'll be able to stop her?" Ashera asked quietly.

"We have to," Keelan replied. "For all our sakes."

"That's what that bright light was—time seemed to slow. We were blinded, and then the medallion was just gone," Ashera said.

Lance and Shaylee nodded.

"We reached for it together, but just as we grasped it, the portal winked out," Lance said, his head hanging low. "It was in my hands, yet I was powerless to stop her from taking it."

"So, what next? Is the prophecy dead?" Fawn asked. Shaylee grabbed her hand.

No, the medallion isn't unlocked until the eclipse sometime this winter. She will still need all of you together, Drake projected.

"So, if we all stay apart until after the eclipse, the medallion will never be unlocked, right?" Shaylee asked, her eyes sparkling with excitement. "We can stop her just by not doing anything."

I don't think it will work that way, Aurora squawked. *My sire was confident that you four would be together no matter what.*

Keelan hung his head, raking his hands through his hair. "Even without the power of the medallion, Sephra, or I guess it's truly The One that is controlling her," he paused, looking up. "Even without the medallion, that demon must be stopped."

"We should wait until after the eclipse. I'm not saying we don't try to stop that monster; just wait a while," Shaylee pleaded.

"I don't think Sephra will allow us to stay apart. I'm sure she will do everything she can to get us together," Lance said. "She threatened us to give her the medallion, saying we must be alive, but we didn't need all our limbs. She will do what she must. It would be best to stay together but build an army around us."

The group quieted into silent reflection and thought. As the sun set behind the western horizon, they finally decided to head back to the monastery in the morning and regroup to make their next move.

The next morning, they set out early, making their way back to the Monastery of Iton. The journey was somber, but determination fueled their steps.

CHAPTER

-29-

THE sun was starting to set when they began their descent into the monastery courtyard. The sky was awash with reds and oranges, and the clouds appeared on fire in the last rays of sunlight.

The courtyard and training grounds were bustling with activity. Numerous ariels were flying in scattered formations or on the ground, looking like they were getting ready to take to the sky. Griffins and pegasi in what looked like full armor carried riders engaged in mock fights. The ones on the ground looked on, waiting their turn. Keelan saw a large bronze dragon flying above the fighters, roaring and nodding his massive head.

Is that Cedric? Keelan projected to Lance.

Yes, he replied.

This all looks highly organized, Keelan marveled. Besides the ariels in the courtyard and in the sky, he saw unicorns and great stags in the large meadow outside the monastery walls performing maneuvers with riders of their own and a large group of archers.

They circled the courtyard twice before landing in the middle of the ariel formation. All faces turned to stare at them.

Douglas transformed while still several feet above the ground, his red and gold mist obscuring his drop to the ground. Ashera waited until she landed before transforming. Cedric landed a moment later.

"Glad to see your safe return," Cedric said, shaking Douglas's hand.

"Did you find anything?" Samuel asked as he approached, his eyes scanning the group.

"Not exactly," Keelan replied. "But we know more now. Sephra has the medallion, but it won't be unlocked until the eclipse. We need to prepare and gather our strength."

Cedric nodded. "Then let's not waste any time. We need to rally our allies and train harder than ever."

"We have a new development. Can you gather all those that need to hear it?" Douglas said grimly.

Cedric's lips thinned. He nodded and jogged over to the monastery.

"Come, let us rest a while until everyone is assembled," Tarrid said as he waved to someone standing next to a griffin getting fitted for a saddle.

The man smiled as he walked over to them. "Welcome back. So glad to see you safe and sound, Shaylee."

"Thanks, Ben," Shaylee replied.

"Ben, can you make sure Dreamcrest and Stormbreaker are comfortable?" Tarrid asked him.

"Yes, of course." Ben bowed to the ariels, "If you will follow me." He flourished his hand out to the side.

If you need me, I will be ready, Stormbreaker projected to Keelan.

Thank you, my friend. Keelan patted him on the shoulder before following the others to houses just beyond the monastery.

They slowly walked down the main path between the houses, each a mirror image of the next. The community was brimming with people, young and old. Only the very young seemed to have nothing to do.

Tarrid stopped in front of one of the houses. "This is my place. Everyone is welcome to relax here. I'm sure the Prioress won't keep us waiting long." Tarrid opened the door and led them inside.

"I'm going to go see my… my parents," Shaylee said with a forlorn look. "I won't be long."

Fawn grabbed her hand, and together, they rushed off.

Inside Tarrid's house, the group settled into the cozy, rustic living room. Keelan sat near the hearth, where a gentle fire flickered, casting warm light on the stone walls. The atmosphere was tense but filled with a sense of camaraderie.

Tarrid disappeared into another room, returning moments later with a tray of drinks and snacks. "Help yourselves," he said, setting the tray on a wooden table.

Keelan took a drink and sipped it thoughtfully. "Do you think the others will be able to mobilize quickly?" he asked.

Tarrid nodded. "We've been preparing for this moment for a long time. The Prioress will make sure everyone is ready."

Douglas leaned back in his chair, his expression serious. "We need to be ready for anything. Sephra will come after us with everything she has."

"We're stronger together," Ashera said, her eyes meeting Keelan's. "We'll face whatever comes."

A knock at the door interrupted their conversation. Tarrid stood and opened it, revealing the Prioress accompanied by Cedric and several other leaders from the monastery.

"Let's discuss the new developments," the Prioress said, her voice calm but commanding. "We need to be prepared for the coming battle."

As they gathered close together in the small room, Keelan felt a renewed sense of purpose. They were united, and together, they would face the darkness that threatened their world.

"So many have come in such a short time," Shaylee remarked as they walked.

Fawn nodded, "So many more than when I was here last even."

"SHAYLEE!" Someone yelled from the garden. Shaylee knew that voice. She smiled as she turned around and saw Rosepetal flying toward her, Talon running close behind.

Rosepetal barreled into Shaylee, wrapping her in a tight embrace. When Talon reached them, he wrapped both of them up in his arms.

Shaylee smiled, her eyes glistening with tears.

"I'm so happy you're home," Rosepetal said, tears running down her cheeks.

"I'm sorry I left without saying anything."

Fawn stood off watching the reunion. "I'll be back," she said, nodding to the medical houses.

Shaylee nodded, but Talon stopped her.

"Your mother is no longer in there. She is all better. I'll show you to your house," he said with a large smile.

Fawn's face fell, and then a smile spread across her face. "The cure worked?"

Talon nodded as he took her hand and led her to a house a few doors down.

Rosepetal held on to Shaylee for a few more minutes before leaning back and brushing her hand across Shaylee's cheek.

"What happened to you?"

Shaylee reached up and grabbed Rosepetal's hand, "I want to tell both of you at the same time. Come on. Let's go see Fawn's ma, and then you will hear everything."

Tarrid's house was a little too cozy, so it was decided that the monastery was the best place to conduct the meeting. As soon as everyone sat around the large table in the monastery's main hall, Prioress Leilatha Moryra officially welcomed them.

"I am so pleased to see everyone safe and healthy," the Prioress said. "I have been told that there has been a development, though."

Douglas stood, followed closely by Keelan. They looked at each other, a small grin curling on Douglas's lips. "Keelan, if you will do the honors." He bowed his head and took his seat.

"Thank you, Mr. Firestorm." Keelan turned his eyes to the others. "I see some I have met briefly and others I have yet to meet. I think introductions are in order first. My name is Keelan Keifman…"

Aurora jumped onto the table before him and spread her wings wide. *And I am Aurora, his familiar,* she projected and squawked loudly.

Keelan chuckled, gently pushing Aurora aside. "Yes, Aurora, I was getting to you." Aurora fanned her tail and bowed her head to him. "Shaylee…" He pointed to her. "I'm sure most, if not all of you, already know her. But what many of you might not know is that she is my twin sister. We are the prophesied twins from the Vaelum line." Surprised gasps echoed through the hall. "Now, I want to introduce you to the Ragnis twins, Lancet and Ashera, along with their familiars, Drake and Zephyr." Lance and Ashera stood, their familiars mimicking Aurora by jumping onto the table.

Keelan continued, "We've discovered that Sephra is under the control of a powerful demon known as The One. This demon needs all four of us—Shaylee, Lance, Ashera, and myself—along with the medallion, to unlock its power during the upcoming eclipse. This means we must stay together and prepare for the inevitable confrontation."

Cedric nodded. "We've been preparing for this. The monastery is ready to stand with you."

Leilatha Moryra spoke up, her voice steady and commanding, "We will do everything in our power to protect you and stop The One. The monastery has never faced a threat like this, but we are stronger together. Our priority is ensuring the twins' safety and strengthening our defenses. We need to gather our allies and train harder than ever."

Tarrid added, "We should use the time we have wisely. Train, gather allies, and strengthen our defenses. The eclipse is coming, but we can be ready."

"This isn't just our fight—it's a fight for all the lands," Douglas added.

Fawn looked at Shaylee, then back at the group. "We've already started forming an army, but we'll need more. We must spread the word and rally everyone willing to fight against this darkness."

Douglas nodded in agreement. "We have to unite the kingdoms and stand as one."

Keelan felt a surge of determination. "We will stop Sephra and The One. Together, we will protect our world."

Excited murmurs erupted, and several people stood and bowed deeply.

Leilatha stood and held her hands out to quiet the gathered group. "I know I speak for everyone here and throughout the land. We are blessed to be in your presence and so happy that we are witnessing the beginning of the end of tyranny. I assume you found the medallion. May I see it?" Her eyes sparkled in anticipation.

Keelan bowed his head. Everyone sat, their excitement subdued. "We found the Wizard's Hat and the medallion. But I'm sorry to say, The One, Sephra, performed a blood spell, opened a portal, and had Lance and Shaylee grab it just before Ashera and I could."

All eyes swiveled to Lance and Shaylee.

"What happened next?" Talon pressed.

Lance stood and cleared his throat, "I tried to defy Sephra, but she threatened to delimb Shaylee unless I gave her the medallion." Rosepetal's gasps echoed through the room.

"From what we understand, Sephra will need to have all four of us together this winter in order to unlock the medallion's power."

"Then you four need to split up and stay in hiding until spring," Rosepetal blurted.

Leilatha shook her head. "No, unfortunately, from what we have researched, the medallion will only unlock for the twins. I think the demon will wait until you have unlocked it, but I fear what she will do next."

SHE WILL KILL THE TWINS, Aurora yelled into everyone's mind.

"Aurora!" Keelan raised his voice. Everyone in the room was holding their heads.

Sorry, she said, bowing her head.

"Why do you think she will kill us?" Shaylee asked.

It was something that Eldjren feared even more than the twins not being born. Ember, my sire, said that if someone else were to kill the twins right after the medallion's powers were unlocked, they could take the power for themselves, Aurora explained.

"What kind of power are we talking about?" Tarrid asked, standing and starting to pace around the room.

Aurora shrugged her wings. ***No one knows for sure.***

Rosepetal flew out of her seat, hovering in the air. "All the more reason for the twins to stay apart. Let her have the worthless medallion she possesses. You four go into hiding and stay apart forever. You will all be safe, and she will never gain the power she desires."

Unfortunately, I do not think that will work, Drake replied. ***Eldjren was quite certain that if the solar eclipse happened without the twins all being together with the medallion, the sky would bleed and rain fire upon the ground. The whole world will be destroyed.***

The room fell into silence.

"Does anyone know what happened to the Sanctuary?" Shaylee asked, breaking the silence.

Leo'venath cleared his throat, "A few people arrived a few days ago. Wyverns and a sorcerer attacked the sanctuary. From what they said, it was over quickly. Few made it out alive."

"That was Sephra," Lance said. "After she took Shaylee and me, she took us to the Sanctuary. There were only a couple of servants that we ever saw."

"Is she back there now?" Talon asked.

"We don't know. She knocked us out before she left," Lance said.

"Why didn't she keep you with her?" Leo'venath asked.

Lance shrugged. "She said that we would meet again. We are destined to be together during the solar eclipse sometime this winter. She, or at least the demon inside her, is patient. It mentioned that Iton and Oshan stripped it of its power and cast it aside. It sounds like The One is out for revenge."

Oh, that is just great, Aurora scoffed.

"So, what do we do?" Ashera asked.

The group discussed strategy, training schedules, and the logistics of rallying more allies. As the night wore on, the weight of their mission hung heavily in the air, but a sense of hope lingered as well. They were united and prepared to face whatever darkness came their way together.

It was well after midnight when they finally agreed to retire for the evening. Leo'venath showed Keelan and the Firestorm family to their houses and bid them a good night.

A loud knock on the door jarred Keelan awake. Rubbing the sleep out of his eyes, he opened the door to find Cedric wearing full armor. Keelan's eyes widened, "Are we under attack?" he asked, panic lacing his words.

Cedric shook his head. "No, come outside and greet your army."

"My army?" Keelan asked. Leo, Tarrid, Lance, Ashera, and Douglas stood behind Cedric. A short distance away, Talon was bringing Shaylee and Fawn.

"Those gathered here have agreed to help you battle this new threat. With the wyverns defeated by her, The Blade has only one purpose now. To see the prophesied twins reclaim their thrones," Leo'venath said.

The four teens glanced at each other and then nodded. "Let's go greet our army then," Lance said.

Out in the courtyard, all eyes swiveled to watch the small procession walking toward the monastery. Tarrid gestured for the royals to step to the front of the group. Standing in between them, he raised his hands and augmented his voice.

"May I have your attention, please? Blade assemble!" he boomed.

Everyone began rushing around in what seemed like chaos to Keelan, but soon, they formed neat lines and rows. The unicorns and great stags stood at attention beside their riders, while all the ariels landed, their riders remaining mounted. The two dragons that had arrived with Douglas and Cedric were the last to land. A hush fell over the crowd when their wings folded tightly to their sides.

"I am blessed to see how well you all did that." Tarrid smiled and then nodded to Leo'venath.

"Good day, warriors of the Blade. Please welcome back our leader, Shield Tarrid," Leo'venath announced loudly. "And I would like to introduce you to the ones we have been seeking: the twins from the Vaelum and Ragnis lines."

Cheers and roars erupted, filling the courtyard with a cacophony. Leo'venath smiled and held his hands up to calm the group. When calm resumed, he turned to the four standing behind him, "How do you want to be introduced? Kings and Queens or Princes and Princesses?"

Keelan and Lance both shrugged. Ashera's face blanched, but Shaylee squared her shoulders and grinned. "I think princes and princesses would be appropriate until our official crowning."

Leo'venath nodded and returned to the assembly, "Prince Keelan and Princess Shaylee of the Vaelum line, and Prince Lancet and Princess Ashera of the Ragnis line."

The crowd erupted again. The four royals stepped closer to the steps, held hands, and raised them above their heads.

"Thank you all!" Keelan said, augmenting his voice. "I am thrilled beyond belief that so many are willing to come to our aid. As you all may know, the wyvern king has been slain, and the remaining wyverns have scattered in search of their prince. While it is an old saying that the enemy of my enemy is my friend, this is not the case here. The One, a fallen demon, has possessed a sorceress named Sephra. It was this demon who defeated the wyverns, and it was this same demon who attacked The Sanctuary of Iton and is bent on destroying our chances of uniting the realm and fulfilling the prophecy." He paused as the crowd murmured amongst themselves. "With your help, we can defeat this demon!" Keelan raised his voice to cut through the noise. The assembly slowly quieted once more. "But first, we must rid Evansshire of King Theodoric and end his suppression of magic and killing spree of infant twins."

The assembly cheered and roared in agreement.

Over the next few days, the monastery buzzed with activity. Warriors trained rigorously, and messengers were sent to nearby villages requesting reinforcements. The air was thick with anticipation and the resolve to stop Sephra and The One.

One evening, as they gathered in the monastery's grand hall, Keelan addressed the group. "We know Sephra will come for us. We must be ready for anything. This isn't just about the medallion; it's about stopping a great evil from consuming our world."

Shaylee stood up, her eyes blazing with determination. "We will fight with everything we have. Together, we can defeat her."

Cheers and affirmations echoed through the hall, strengthening their bonds and solidifying their resolve. They were ready to face whatever came their way.

As the days passed and the eclipse drew nearer, the group trained tirelessly. They knew the battle ahead would be their greatest challenge, but they were prepared to fight for their world—and for each other. Though the prophecy remained uncertain, their unity and determination were unwavering.

In the quiet moments, Keelan often looked at Ashera, drawing strength from her presence. Together, they were ready to face the darkness and reclaim the light for their world.

-EPILOGUE-

"DRAGONS, incoming!!" Someone on the monastery's roof shouted, drawing all eyes to him. He pointed to the south.

Douglas and Cedric transformed and took to the sky. Lance and Ashera transformed as well but remained on the ground.

Keelan looked around for Stormbreaker. They locked eyes.

I am ready if you need to take flight, Stormbreaker offered.

Thank you, my friend, Keelan replied.

Aurora took to the air and sped off toward the dragons but soon returned. ***Keelan, Jonal is riding one of Douglas's dragons. He has grave news.***

Keelan's lips thinned into a tight line as he descended the stairs two at a time. The training freedom fighters parted, making a path for him as he headed toward the main gates.

The three new dragons landed just outside the gates.

After Jonal clumsily slid off his dragon, the trio transformed, enveloping the area in a vibrant mist that completely shrouded him.

"Jonal, I'm so happy to see you," Keelan said when he saw him again. "How's my mother?"

Jonal approached him and gripped his outstretched hand in greeting. "She is fine now. Completely healed, I am happy to say. But I came with terrible news." Jonal's face was white, and his gray hair was a mess from his flight.

"What is it?" Shaylee asked, walking up to them.

"Ah, you must be Shaylee," Jonal said with a tired smile. "You look so much like your mother did at your age."

Shaylee's cheeks reddened, and she dropped her gaze.

"Your news, Jonal?" Keelan pressed.

"Theodoric is dead!"

"Dead? How?" Keelan asked.

"Kingston was attacked. A modest-sized army breached the main gates and then swept through Kingston. Their leader was a woman…"

Sephra, The One, Lance, interrupted.

Jonal glanced at the dragon towering above them and nodded. "Yes, that's her. After Maya regained her strength, I rode to Kingston to check on things there. Lower City seemed fine at first, but most of the population had fled. The gates to Kingston were smashed to kindling, and evidence of battle marred the streets leading up to the castle. The castle itself looked untouched, but the few people left told me that the King, Queen, and Prince Armend are dead. Someone calling himself General Lucas is in charge now, while Warlock Sephra, known as The One, has left to finish uniting her kingdom."

Keelan raked his hands through his hair, letting out a loud sigh. "Sephra has defeated both of our enemies, but now she's established herself as our primary foe. At least she made it a little easier for us to see who we're really up against."

"What are you talking about?" Jonal asked, his eyes widening.

Sephra defeated the wyverns and took The Sanctuary of Iton as her own, Ashera said.

"Ashera? Glad to see you've found yourself," Jonal said with a nod. "So, Keelan, my boy. What are your plans?" he asked, looking behind the royals at the gathered mass of people and magical creatures.

"We will gather all who are willing to help us and prepare for the upcoming war. We have until winter. Let's begin," Keelan replied, straightening his back as he turned to face their army.

This is what you were born to do, Keelan, Aurora projected privately to him.

Yes, it is, he agreed, his heart heavy with the gravity of their mission. *I just hope we are strong enough.*

TO BE CONTINUED...

PROPHECY FORETOLD

Forgotten Kingdoms lost to tyranny, the realm of beasts, and the realm of magic fade away. The birth of twins in the darkness of night, upon uniting, the fates of the Royal Lines shall intertwine. In winter's tight embrace, an eclipse will paint the sky red before their sixteenth year. The two sets of twins will be bathed in red light, their lives entwined by fate's design, their futures revealed in this divine.

Infinity embraced; royal birthrights restored.

Centuries long ago, peace and harmony ruled the land. Beast and man living hand in hand. Two mighty Kingdoms rose. Two Royal families came to power, one to rule the beasts, one to rule man. Their legacies once aligned, but still forever entwined. The two mighty Kingdoms will fall and lose their power. New blood would rise to rule and dictate. The kingdoms would divide, and tyranny would be unleased on the realm. Beast and man separated by hate and fear, unity lost.

But in secret, magic would survive. Freedom would dance, and unity would find its sacred room. Twins would be born from royal birthright in the darkness of night. The twins from the royal lines would be tested, their strength grown from strife. But the twins must unite, they must entwine their legacies to take a stand.

With the help of a Phoenix, lost in the world, they will find the Infinite Medallion. In winter's tight embrace, an eclipse will paint the sky red before their sixteenth year. The two sets of twins will be bathed in red light, their lives entwined by fate's design, their futures will be revealed in this divine. Only with the medallion can they unite and save the land from tyranny while overcoming the shadow cast by The One.